FIRES OF PASSION

When Hunter's lips touched hers, Alexandra nearly recoiled. She was not an innocent to a man's kisses, but no one had ever affected her like this. As their mouths met, a physical energy arced between them. Alexandra lifted her arms to rest on his massive shoulders and leaned into him, wanting to taste him.

His kiss was gentle, but probing. It was gentlemanly, yet immensely sensual at the same time.

"I shouldn't be doing this," he whispered against her lips.

He was kissing her cheek now, the tip of her nose, the length of her neck. Shivers of pleasure reverberated through her body.

"No, no you shouldn't. *I* shouldn't," she somehow managed.

"But it's been coming to this, hasn't it, Alex?"

"Yes, yes," she answered, returning his kisses. "It doesn't make any sense, but—"

"Of course it makes sense." He brushed his fingertips across her breasts and she felt her nipples pucker beneath the soft leather. "It makes sense because we're two people in need. In need of each other."

Alexandra bit down on her lower lip. How could a savage man in a savage country be so gentle? "There'll be no regrets," she whispered.

"For the first time in a very long time, I want to make love," he said, nuzzling her neck. "I want to make love with you, Alex."

Alexandra smiled. Tonight was a night to hold back nothing . . .

COLLEEN FAULKNER

FLAMES OF LOVE

ZEBRA BOOKS
KENSINGTON PUBLISHING CORP.

For Sherri,
who kept the young hounds at bay
so I could work.

Prologue

Jon gave a drunken chuckle, shaking his head. "I can't believe you're doing this. I can't believe *I'm* doing this. We're on a futtering ship to the American Colonies, Geoffry!"

Geoffry Rordan, the Viscount Ashton, leaned on the ship's railing for support and took another swig from the flask he held tightly in his hand. By the light of the full hunter's moon, he could see the outline of the dock as the ship slowly sailed out of its anchorage. "Come on! Where's your sense of adventure? I always wanted to see the colonies. You know that." His elbow brushed against his companion's and he steadied himself. "Every man should see them, and that includes you." He hiccupped. "Father said so himself."

Jon snatched the flask from Geoffry's hand and took a long pull. "But, Christ, I don't think this is what he had in mind. Right now he's up at that

7

house on the hill toasting to your betrothal with the Earl of Monthrop and wondering where the blast you are, prodigal son."

"He'll understand when he reads the letter I left him."

Jon pushed the flask back into Geoffry's hand. "Understand, hell—he's going to be furious!"

"I'm not ready to be weighted down with a wife, a gaggle of children and my father's duties." Geoffry shook his head insistently. "Not yet. I've got too many things left to do, too many things to see."

"Too many young ladies to tumble?"

Geoffry snatched off his periwig and ran his fingers through his short-cropped auburn hair. "I'm afraid that's always been *your* department." He sighed, swinging his wig on the end of his index finger. "No, I just want to see the Chesapeake Bay, smell those great pine forests, hear the Shawnee chant their songs."

"And what of the chit?" Jon turned around and leaned against the rail, crossing his arms over his chest. "Seems to me she's getting the short end of the staff. She's still up there at the house thinking her betrothed is a little late. What's going to happen to her when you don't show up?"

Geoffry shrugged his broad shoulders, still spinning his wig on his finger. "What could possibly happen to her? No doubt her father will sell her to the next earl's son who comes along." He took a long deep breath of the salty air and sighed, his betrothed easily forgotten. "Ah, freedom. Smell it, Jon?" He let out a whoop of pleasure and sailed his powdered periwig over the ship's side and into the Thames below.

Chapter One

*Somewhere west of the Chesapeake Bay
September, 1722*

Alexandra closed her eyes as her head drooped. The leather bindings at her wrists and ankles cut into her bruised flesh. She winced each time she shifted her weight to relieve the pins and needles in her bare, swollen feet. Through the tattered remnants of her brocade gown she felt the rough bark of the pine tree against her back.

She swore a foul oath beneath her breath.

How long had she been tied to this tree in the wilderness? Two days, or was it three? She wasn't certain. In the last weeks time had lost all meaning.

Now there was only alive or dead. And she was still alive . . . that was all that mattered to Lady Alexandra Lambert, the Earl of Monthrop's daughter.

Lady Alexandra . . . hah! What good was her father's title and fortune now? So far from London, so far from civilization . . .

"They don't even know I'm here," she whispered hoarsely. "No one knows I'm alive." She licked her dry, cracked lips.

She was so thirsty that she could think of nothing else. When the sun rose high in the sky her captor would bring her water. The maggot-brained red whoreson always did. But she'd been awake for hours and the pale autumn sun had barely moved in the sky.

Alexandra set her jaw and opened her eyes just a crack. She could see the crude log cabin nestled among the red-leafed oaks and white pines. Nothing stirred. Even the red calico headband dangling from the shattered doorframe hung limp in the still morning air.

She twisted her hands bound behind her back for the one-hundredth time in hopes the bonds had miraculously loosened during the night. They hadn't.

She strained to detect any sign of movement around the hovel. No doubt the red savages were still sleeping off their drunk. Last night they had drunk rot-gut whiskey and danced and howled like blood-crazed demons until nearly dawn.

Alexandra let her eyelids drift shut again. How long was that stinking half-breed going to leave her tied to this tree? If Two Crows was going to sell her like he'd said, why hadn't he done so? Just another way to torment her, she supposed. That was the way it had been since he'd kidnapped her nearly a month ago.

Memories of her capture drifted through her

head. It had been a delightful day the last week in August that her Uncle Charles had offered to take her and her cousin Susan up the river to see Kristen Landon's new baby. The sunshine had been warm, the breeze off the shore cool and refreshing. She remembered how clear and blue the moving water of the river had been. She remembered the sound of a single songbird, its voice trilling sweetly.

Then the water had turned red . . . red with the blood of Uncle Charles and Susan. The songbird's voice had been silenced by the sound of screaming.

Alexandra opened her eyes. She wasn't going to think about it, not now, because if she did she'd go stark raving mad. *What matters is that I'm alive,* she thought with determination. *I survived the attack and I'll survive to escape.*

The cabin door suddenly swung open on its leather hinges and Alexandra closed her eyes, slumping her head to feign sleep. She wanted to draw no attention to herself. Though she was the property of Two Crows, there were at least five other renegade redskins here just like him. After what she'd seen that morning on Uncle Charles's boat, she knew full well she'd not survive a gang rape.

Two Crows had brought her here to sell her. Apparently a deal had already been struck. Her new owner would be coming any day now, someone Two Crows referred to as Cap-i-tan.

The sound of soft footsteps came nearer and she fought the desire to flinch. She could smell the sour sweat of a man's skin and knew it was Two Crows.

He chattered something in his native language, then grunted when she made no response. "A rabbit that hides in the grass, no?" He chuckled as he brushed her cheek with his filthy hand.

Alexandra's eyes snapped open. "Touch me again, heathen, and I'll bite your finger off!"

Two Crows flashed broken black teeth, but took half a step back. Self-consciously, he brushed his fingertips across his blood-encrusted ear.

Alexandra smiled to herself. *Didn't think I'd bite your ear off did you? So I didn't bite it off, but I took a good chunk, didn't I?* She stared at him in bold challenge.

The half-breed wiped his runny nose with the back of his hand and then rubbed his hand on his leather leggings. "This man has no time to teach a white-face woman her place, but the next man," —he shook a finger—"the cap-i-tan will." He laughed at some private joke. "He is known for his way with the women."

"Yes, yes, you've been telling me about this man who's bought me for two days, but I don't see him. I don't see any of the muskets he promised either. Mayhap he's not coming."

The eyes of Two Crows narrowed dangerously. "He comes."

Alexandra knew she was pushing her luck with Two Crows. The man held her life in the palm of his filthy hand. "Free me and I'll pay you double what he's promised," she said carefully. "Free me and I'll get you your muskets. Christ's Bones! I'll get you a gunsmithy to make all the muskets you can carry on your back."

"I have already made the deal!" he barked.

"Afraid to make a better deal?"

Two Crows lashed out with his hand, striking her hard across the mouth. Alexandra winced, but she didn't cry out. To show weakness might mean her death. Two Crows admired her strength; that was what had kept her alive this long. She could feel a trickle of blood run from the corner of her mouth.

She closed her eyes, trying to gain control of the moment. *Take care,* a voice inside her warned. *Push him too far and he'll kill you.*

"Speak again," Two Crows spit angrily, "and you will shed more than a drop of blood. Speak again and—"

A sound in the pine woods made the Indian turn away from her in midsentence. Alexandra heard hoofbeats, slow and methodical. Someone was coming.

A moment later two men and a mule appeared through the dense pines. A white man led the way. He was dressed in Indian leggings and a quilled vest, and he had long auburn hair and a wild red beard. Behind him walked an Indian wearing a cocked hat and a red ribbon in his black queue.

Is this who Two Crows had sold me to? Is this the cap-i-tan he spoke of, she wondered. *A white man? Surely no white would deal in the buying and selling of human flesh. No decent white man . . .*

Two Crows strutted up to the travelers who had

stopped near the cabin. The one with the red beard raised a broad hand in a gesture that Alexandra assumed was some sort of peace sign. A tall man with brawny shoulders, he seemed unhindered by the heavy pack he carried on his back.

"Why do you come, Redbeard?" Two Crows demanded.

The redbeard lowered his pack slowly to the ground. "I come to trade." His voice was strong and confident. This sounded like a man who feared no one.

From a distance, Alexandra could see his piercing hazel eyes as his gaze strayed to her, then back to Two Crows. She watched the redbeard as he studied Two Crows from beneath the cover of his long scraggly hair. "And to ask a few questions."

Two Crows grunted. "Trade, yes. Questions?" He sliced the air with his palm. "No questions."

So this isn't the man, Alexandra thought, her heart sinking. He hasn't come to buy me. I'm not to be saved. She looked down at the ground, moisture gathering in the corners of her eyes. She hadn't cried, not a single tear since the morning she'd been captured, but suddenly all seemed lost. He was a scroungy trapper, a man no better than Two Crows no doubt. Why else would he be dealing with men like these?

But then she lifted her gaze.

So what if he's not the man who was supposed to buy me. How do I know who he is or what he's doing here? He's the first white man I've seen in nearly a month. Surely he'll help me. She bit down on her lower lip. Did she chance calling out to him? What would Two Crows do? Strike her? He'd done that already. Kill her? She was willing to take the chance. "Sir, please—"

Two Crows whipped around. "Silence!" he bellowed.

"You've got to help me," she pleaded. Her words tumbled out faster. "This Indian's kidnapped me! He killed my—"

Two Crows whipped his hand to his belt, and before Alexandra realized what was happening, she saw the knife flying end over end toward her. She closed her eyes, waiting for the cold bite of the steel; the pain of death.

The knife struck the tree inches from her neck, making a strange thump, then vibrating in the wood. Alexandra moved her head ever so slightly. The knife had pinned a tangled clump of her dark hair to the wood. She let out a shuddering breath of relief.

"Speak again!" Two Crows dared viciously. "Next time my blade will strike home!"

Hunter glanced at the bedraggled white woman tied to the tree. *Damnation, but the chit has guts,* he thought. His deliberately uninterested gaze wandered back to the half-breed Iroquois who stank of bear grease. "I've sugar. Tobacco. Some cloth. I'm looking for otter pelts. Prime."

The half-breed nodded, turning his attention from the woman back to Hunter. "The otter have been plentiful this season. Have you whiskey?"

"Some." He watched the woman tied to the tree out of the corner of his eye. She was staring at him with round, dark eyes. God in heaven, how long have they had her? he wondered. Not long, else she'd not be alive. He knew what kind of men frequented trading posts like this one. Men outside the law, all laws, both red and white.

Hunter gestured toward the woman. "The female. What's your price for her?"

"Two Crows will not sell the woman. She has already been sold."

Hunter tightened his grip on the musket he held comfortably in one hand. He cast a sideways glance at his companion, Jon. There would be no timely assistance there. His friend was busying himself slapping flies off their mule's rear end. "How much? I'll pay more." Hunter's gaze met that of Two Crows's. "I've a taste for a round-eyed wench. It's been a long time."

Two Crows shook his head emphatically. "No. I do not sell the woman. She is trouble. Too much trouble for you, Redbeard. You want a woman. This man will find you one. What is it you like? Yellow hair? Big breasts?"

"I like this one here."

"Then leave this place before this man grows angry." The half-breed folded his arms across his chest. "I tell you she is not for sale."

In one fluid motion Hunter swung his musket through the air, bringing the muzzle up directly between the legs of the Iroquois. "I said I'll take this one," Hunter mouthed through clenched teeth. "Name a price or I take her without payment."

Two Crows choked. "You cannot—"

Hunter cocked the musket with an ominous click, lifting the barrel just high enough to make Two Crows physically uncomfortable. "Unless you wish to lose your balls, *He-Who-Stinks*, I suggest you cut your losses and take what is offered!" He kicked the bulky sack resting on the ground.

"I fear you make a mistake," Two Crows murmured, his fingers curled around the barrel in fear. "The cap-i-tan whose woman you steal will be greatly angered. He will track you, take the woman, and kill you."

Hunter offered the barest of a smile beneath the tangles of his red beard. "I'll take that chance. Jon!"

Jon came up behind Hunter. "God's teeth, what is it, Hunter?" He cast a sideways glance at the half-breed, unable to conceal his amusement.

"Cut her loose. Now."

Jon strolled past Two Crows, giving him a wink.

Two Crows attempted to move but Hunter lifted the barrel.

"Take care, Two Crows," Hunter warned, wild-eyed. "Jiggle the musket and the blasted thing might go off. Then you'll be peeling your balls off that cabin door." He lifted an eyebrow in challenge, a silly smile on his lips.

"The woman matters not to me," Two Crows grunted. "I only tell you this in warning." He shrugged carefully. "She's been nothing but trouble. Take her. Use her. But watch your back. I tell the truth when I speak of the cap-i-tan. He is not a man to anger.''

Jon reached the woman captive and with two clean slices of his knife, he freed her.

The woman took a step forward and swayed. Jon reached out to give her support but she pushed his hand aside. ''I'll be quite all right,'' she murmured, finding her balance.

''Let's go,'' Hunter called.

Jon leaned toward her and spoke quietly. ''Can you walk on your own? I'd guess Hunter wants us out of here before the rest of the savages come out of that cabin.''

She took a deep breath, eyeing him uneasily. ''They're all sleeping off a drunk. We'll be safe enough.'' Confident she had her balance, she walked quickly toward the mule. As she passed Two Crows, she glared at him. ''Rot in hell,'' she called over her shoulder as she disappeared into the pine forest behind Jon.

Hunter slowly backed off, still keeping his musket aimed at the groin of Two Crows. ''I don't have to warn you not to follow us, do I?'' He went on without waiting for an answer. ''Because if you do follow us, I won't just shoot you. I'll have a little fun with you first. And when you finally are dead, I'll eat your liver!''

Two Crows took a startled step back, throwing up his hands in a sign to ward off evil spirits.

Hunter chuckled as he backed into the cover of the forest and then turned and ran down the game path.

He caught up with Jon and the woman a quarter of a mile through the woods. Before he could open his mouth to inquire as to her well-being she spun around on her heels to face him, tapping a filthy bare foot. "Took you long enough to cut me down," she snapped.

Hunter stopped in midstride, completely taken back. His ire rose immediately, tightening in his chest. Hadn't he just risked his life to save this jade? "What was that?"

"I said you took long enough." She brushed back a lock of tangled hair to show off the curve of her jawline.

The woman was young, and quite attractive with her dark hair, dark eyes, . . . or, she would have been attractive had it not been for the scowl on her face.

"I thought for a minute you were going to trade your stinking skins with the red son of a bitch and then walk off leaving me still tied to that tree!"

Jon threw back his head letting out a howl of laughter.

Hunter just stood there for a moment staring at the ungrateful woman. Christ's bones! She chattered like a magpie. Hunter hated useless chatter. Useless chatter was just one of the things that had driven him from London. Useless chatter and snippy women . . . He leaned on his musket. "Have you a name?"

She dropped one hand to her hip. "Of course I have a name! Everyone has a name, don't they? But I beg to ask what your name is. After all—"

"Hunter."

"Hunter? What kind of name is that?"

"It is the name given to me by the Shawnee.

Now if you would be so kind," he went on impatiently, "who the hell are you and what are you doing tied to a tree at a trading post fifty miles from the bay?"

"What? You think I came here on my own? You think I got up one morning, leaped out of my feather tick, drank my tea, and then said to myself, *I think I'll walk out to that Indian trading post and let some filthy, stinking redskin tie me to a tree and sell me to the first man that comes along?* Are you addlepated? I was kidnapped, for holy God's sake!"

"And your name, kidnapped one?"

She hesitated for just an instant—"I'm Alexandra. That's all you need know."

Hunter brushed by her, grabbing the mule's lead line from Jon's hand. "Well, Alexandra, either shut your ungrateful mouth and come along, or I'll be the one tying you to a blasted tree!"

Chapter Two

Alexandra concentrated on placing one foot in front of the other. She had to keep up or *he'd* leave her behind. And she had to keep quiet, or else *he'd* tie her to a tree to be certain Two Crows found her. Or at least that was what *he* said.

Alexandra wrapped her arms around her waist for warmth. The sun had risen high in the September sky and now was beginning to sink below the treetops in a blaze of orange light. It had grown cool and damp in the forest as night set in . . . and still they walked.

Alexandra lifted her gaze until it settled on the broad back of the redheaded trapper. The son of a misbegotten whore! If he knew who she was, he'd not treat her like this. Of course if he knew who she was, he might try to hold her for ransom. Men like him would go to any lengths to extort money from a nobleman like her father. But Alexandra was too clever for his sort. She'd known better than to give him her name or her true identity. It was best to let him think her a lady's maid, or some yeoman's daughter, she had reasoned.

But whether she was a chamberpot maid or the Queen of England, she was still a female and no woman deserved to be treated the way this man Hunter was treating her. He had ignored her pleas of exhaustion, thirst, and hunger. He'd insisted they must keep moving, and when she'd protested, he'd rudely informed her that if she didn't keep her mouth shut, he'd shut it for her.

At least Hunter's Indian companion, Jon, had given her a drink of honey-water from a skin, and a pair of moccasins for her bare feet. He'd been kind. He'd asked her how long Two Crows had held her captive and whether or not she was injured. But he'd also made it clear that the redheaded trapper was in charge and if he said they had to keep walking, walk they would.

Alexandra blinked several times to clear the cobwebs in her mind. She was so tired she couldn't think. And she was just a little bit afraid. Had she been rescued from lawless savages by a man just as dangerous? Could she trust this madman, Hunter, to see her back safely to Annapolis? Or had she made a mistake in coming with him?

She nearly laughed out loud. What other choice had there been? She could have come with these two or been sold to some soldier who apparently bought white women from Two Crows on a regular basis.

"Not much farther and we'll stop for the night," Jon called over his shoulder. He walked beside the mule, patting it. "There's a small stream up ahead. You can bathe if you like."

Alexandra glanced up. "Bathe?" She pushed back a chunk of tangled, dirty hair. "If you two gentlemen think I'm going to strip my clothes off for you, you're crazier than a pair of bedlamites! Just because you gave me a little assistance back there does not entitle you to my virtue."

Jon cracked a smile. "It's good to see the savages didn't break your spirit." There was a tone of wry amusement in his voice. "A lesser woman would surely have faltered in such circumstances. But let me assure you, we have no intention on your *virtue*." He lifted a dark eyebrow suggestively. "Unless, of course, you offer."

Choosing to ignore his indecency, she lengthened her stride to catch up with him. Having someone to talk to would make the time go quicker, even if that someone was just another redskin. "Savages? You call them savages? No offense intended, but aren't you a redskin?"

Jon came to a halt, turning to face her.

Hunter walked on, leading the mule, ignoring Jon and Alexandra.

Jon lifted a red suntanned arm to study it and then glanced up at her as if in shock. "Egad! Fancy that!" he cried dramatically. "I am a redskin!"

She couldn't resist a chuckle at his antics.

He shook his head, looking up at her. "And all these years I thought myself to be an English gentleman!" He hollered in Hunter's direction, swinging his fist. "God's teeth, why the hell didn't you tell me I was an Indian, Hunter?"

When his companion kept walking, Jon turned

back to her.

She stared at him for a long moment. "Well, you do appear to be a savage, but I must have to admit, you don't sound like one." She studied him speculatively. "You're obviously educated. How is it that—"

"Don't let me interrupt your pleasant conversation," Hunter called back to them. "But let me remind you, Jon, your scalp will lift just as easily as mine."

Jon frowned, but turned back onto the path and started walking. "The Hunter of the Shawnee calls."

Alexandra hurried to catch up. "Lifting scalps? What's he talking about?" She threw a glance over her shoulder. The shadows of the forest were lengthening now. Light and dark played in the treetops and the ground, reshaping familiar objects into eerie forms. "Is Two Crows following us? Did Hunter see something?"

Jon took her arm. "Hunter is forever suspicious. He sees specters at every turn. We're safe enough. We just want to put as much distance between us and the trading post as possible before dark. It's just a precaution."

Alexandra nodded and then was quiet for a moment as she walked beside Jon on the narrow game path. She watched the mule clop along behind the scraggly-haired trapper. Hunter's hair was the most amazing red color; the last rays of sunlight played off it, reflecting soft hues from a dark brown to a strawberry blond. A head full of hair like that would be the envy of any woman or wigmaker in London . . . or at least it would be if he'd run a comb through it in the last fortnight. She thought about a man she had been told was a redhead. Of course she'd never seen him without his wig. That was a long time ago . . .

Alexandra nodded in Hunter's direction. "Is he always so contrary?"

Jon glanced up at Hunter a good ten feet ahead of them. "Sometimes he's worse."

Alexandra fell into silence again. She wanted to ask Jon more about this Hunter. She wanted to know more about them both. Obviously they were educated Englishmen. What were they doing out here in the middle of the wilderness? But she kept her thoughts private. She told herself she wanted to know more about Hunter to ascertain whether or not she should fear him, but the truth was, somewhere deep inside she was curious about him—a curiosity that nearly lent itself to fascination.

It was well after dark by the time they reached the stream and stopped for the night. Hunter unloaded the packs from the mule and hobbled him in a small patch of grass down by the streambed.

The moment the two men came to a halt, Alexandra sank to her knees by the stream and drank her fill of the cool water. Then she splashed her face and arms, knowing she must look as dreadful as she felt. As she stared out at the dark pool of water in the center of the stream she briefly considered that bath Jon had suggested. It had been a month since she'd bathed and she knew she stank like a London sewer, but she also knew she'd be taking a foolish chance to bathe in the presence of these men, even in her shift. She'd be asking for trouble and she'd already had quite enough of that to last her a lifetime.

Feeling a little better, she rose and walked to the small clearing where the men were settling in. Hunter was digging through the lumpy sacks on the ground. Jon had piled twigs and dried grass together and was now striking steel on flint to light a fire.

"Do you think that's wise?" she asked, pointing at the first flickering flames.

"To keep warm?" Hunter asked sarcastically.

"No." She frowned. "To light a fire drawing attention to ourselves. If there's a chance Two Crows might be following us, we don't want to give ourselves away. The light and smoke from this fire will be a beacon." She dropped a hand to her hip suspiciously. "Are you trying to let him know where I am?"

Hunter drew a bow and a quiver of arrows from a sack on the ground. "If Two Crows is coming after you, fire or no, he'll find you. Christ, woman, there's no need for a fire to light his way, he could hear you as far as the Eastern Shore!"

Alexandra opened her mouth to retort, then clamped it shut. Maybe she did talk a little too much or a little too loudly, but she was nervous and she always talked when she was nervous.

Hunter turned away. "I'm going to see if I can stir up some fresh game. I'll be back shortly." Then, as if as an afterthought, he reached into a pack on the ground and tossed an object directly at Alexandra. "I know you must be hungry," he grunted. "This will keep you until something is cooked."

She caught it in a reflex action and sank down in a patch of grass in front of the fire. It was a small leather sack of dried meat. She broke off a big chunk and stuffed it into her mouth. It was chewy and the smell was pungent, but after days of no food, nothing could have tasted better.

Alexandra looked up to thank Hunter, but he was gone. He'd disappeared into the brush without making a sound.

Not ten minutes later Hunter appeared again, stepping into the grassy clearing as silently as he had left it. He tossed a dead rabbit at her feet and then a knife. She flinched as the weapon sank into the soft earth between her two feet. The knife had a long, sharp, pointed blade and a handle of carved wood with a leather strap and a feather dangling from it.

"Fresh meat," he said. "Clean it and cook it." He started to turn away and then turned back. "You *can* skin and clean a rabbit, can't you?"

Alexandra swallowed the bile rising in her throat. Of course she'd never cleaned a rabbit. She didn't even care for rabbit, but the way he looked at her—as if she was an imbecile—made her furious. She jerked the knife up out of the dirt. "Fried or fricasseed?"

By the light of the campfire Alexandra could have sworn she saw the flicker of a smile behind the matted red beard. But then it was gone. Then there was only the cold, hard stare of a hungry, impatient man again. "Just don't burn it on the outside and leave it bloody on the inside, all right?"

She watched him strut away, then turned her attention back to the rabbit lying between her feet. She took a deep breath, then reached out to pick up the lifeless animal. It was still warm to the touch. *Meat*, she told herself. *It's meat, Alexandra. The only way you'll gain back your strength is to eat fresh, red meat.*

Tightening her grip on the knife, she rose and walked a few feet to where she'd seen a small, flat rock earlier. She knelt and rolled the rabbit onto its back. She didn't have the faintest idea where to start.

She looked over her shoulder, thinking perhaps Jon could give her a hand, but he was nowhere to be seen. Only Hunter was there, leaning over the campfire to warm his broad hands. He looked at her, but she quickly looked away.

Be damned if she'd admit to him that she didn't know what she was doing! Alexandra took a deep breath and lifted the knife. He wanted rabbit for supper, he would get it!

Fifteen minutes later, Jon burst into laughter as Alexandra held up the rabbit carcass. Tears stung her eyes as she looked at it. She'd managed to get most of the hide off but there was fuzzy, grey fur stuck all over the pink bloody flesh—or what was left of it. She'd had a hard time separating the skin from the meat so that she taken off too much of the meat in places, not enough hide in other places.

Here in the better light she could see that there really wasn't much left of the rabbit to cook.

"What in God's name is that?" Jon asked, still laughing.

"Rabbit," she choked. She was embarrassed by the tears that suddenly threatened to spill onto her cheeks.

"That's a rabbit?"

She picked at the pieces of fur stuck to the warm meat. She felt like a fool. How could she cry over a stupid dead rabbit when she hadn't even cried over the slaughter of her uncle and cousin. "There . . . there's really more here than it appears. I—"

Hunter walked up and gently took the bloody carcass from her. "Not a problem," he murmured. "We'll just clean it up."

She could hear Jon still laughing, but Hunter's voice sounded almost tender.

She followed him to the stream where he got down on his hands and knees and began to rinse the rabbit in the slow-flowing water. Alexandra just stood there trying to rub the blood and grey fur from her hands. The rabbit blood suddenly reminded her of the blood spilled on the deck of the boat the day she'd been captured. Cousin Susan's blood. She rubbed her hands harder, her movements becoming frenzied.

Before she realized it, Hunter had her wrists and he was pulling her down on her knees.

"So much blood," she murmured under her breath. "I never saw so much blood."

He thrust her hands into the water and began to scrub them with sand he dug off the bottom.

"Shhhh . . . it's all right, sweeting," he whispered. "It's all right. You're safe now. We'll just get you cleaned up."

She looked up into his face obscured by the tangled hair and wild red beard. Somewhere hidden in the hair she saw a compassionate face.

"It's all right," he repeated. "You're safe. Now let's go back to the campfire and cook this."

She looked down at the clean rabbit carcass lying in the grass. Slowly she gained control of herself. Thoughts of the blood and her capture slipped away. "I'm sorry I didn't do a better job."

He stood, pulling her up with him. His rough grasp somehow seemed comforting.

"Jon can be an ass sometimes," he said, his voice barely above a whisper. "You should have said you didn't know how to clean a rabbit. I'd have shown you."

She nodded her head and then tore her gaze from his. There was something so unsettling about him. Something almost familiar. "Thank you," she whispered. Embarrassed by her own soft tone in her voice, she pulled her hands from his and walked away.

Hunter skewered the rabbit carcass and cooked it over the open campfire. That and some dried berries from a leather sack made supper.

Once the meager meal was over both men rolled out hide mats and stretched out on them only a few feet away from her. Alexandra sat down on her own mat and watched as Jon filled a clay pipe with tobacco and lit it. He lay back, relaxing as he crossed his feet, covered—not with knee-high moccasins like Hunter's but—with polished calfskin boots.

Her gaze shifted to Hunter. He lay back, resting his head on his arm, but he was no means relaxed. Beside him on the hide mat rested his musket, loaded and ready to fire. The fingers of one of his hands brushed the wooden stock almost in a caress.

"Expecting trouble?" she asked.

For a moment she didn't think he'd heard her— that, or he had no intention of answering. But then slowly he turned his head toward her. "Always expect trouble. It might well keep you alive." His voice was not unkind, but he turned away from her again, obviously ending the conversation.

Alexandra glanced at Jon, thinking to strike up a conversation with him, but his eyes were closed. Besides, she was still mad at him over the rabbit. He shouldn't have laughed like that. It was mean.

With a sigh, she lay back on her hide mat. Here was the perfect example of why she didn't like men. They made no sense to her. They seemed to serve little purpose in life other than to control the women around them.

She let her eyes drift shut as she thought of her two betrothals. Good God, what disasters! The first had been six years ago. Her father had made arrangements for her to be betrothed to Geoffry Rordan, the Viscount Ashton. She'd seen him once across a dance floor, but he'd seemed a perfect specimen of a man at the time. Alexandra had only been fifteen and had fallen immediately in love with Geoffry who was ten years her senior.

She hadn't even known his name then, but she remembered watching him from behind a stair banister as he whirled a young woman across the dance floor. She was so beautiful with her yellow-blond hair piled high in a tor. And she was laughing, laughing with him. Heavens, but Alexandra had been jealous.

A year later, when Alexandra's father announced the alliance between her family and Geoffry's, she'd been ecstatic! She'd paid no heed to the gossips that warned her Geoffry Rordan was too wild and spoiled a gentleman to make a decent husband. She paid no heed to the whispering behind her back saying how surprised everyone was that the Earl of Monthrop had finally found someone to take his eldest daughter off his hands. Her disposition, they all said, made her too sharp-tongued for any man to want her as a wife.

The wedding was set for six months later and preparations were begun despite the fact that the prospective bridegroom had not yet returned from France.

But then Geoffry didn't return. Weeks, then months passed and still he didn't appear. Alexandra should have known then that something was amiss. But she was young and in love with a man she'd never even spoken with. Finally he returned from France and a betrothal party was held in the couple's honor. It was there that Alexandra would finally be introduced to Geoffry.

He never showed up at the party . . .

Alexandra felt her face grow red with embarrassment as she recalled that night. He'd broken her heart. All evening long she sat in her bedchamber waiting for his arrival . . . waiting for him to slip her hand into his and kiss her on the cheek. How mortified she'd been when she finally realized he wasn't coming.

Later, guests said they'd seen him that night. One minute he was there, the next he was gone. Later the gossips would say it was her disposition that had scared him off. After all, why would a handsome, titled man like Geoffry want to marry a shrew?

He left his father a brief note saying he'd gone to the American Colonies and to please extend his apologies to his betrothed. No one heard from him again.

Alexandra's father had felt insulted, insisting he could find his daughter a more suitable match. Alexandra's pain and embarrassment had turned to fury. How dare Geoffry walk out on her like that!

After word got around that the viscount had run as far as the colonies to escape marriage to the Earl of Monthrop's daughter, the earl found that no one suitable seemed to be interested in his comely, but headstrong daughter. Because of the vicious talk, the only takers he could find were elderly, toothless gentlemen and obvious fortune-seekers. Rumors concerning the Lady Alexandra had spread like a fire on Cheapside. Some said that she had a mental disorder that caused her to rant and rave and drool at the mouth; others said she had an illegitimate child by a gamekeeper's son. No matter how hard the family tried to prove that there was nothing truly wrong with Alexandra other than willfulness, the earl could find no takers.

Then, finally, an old friend of Alexandra's father, the Earl of Grant had declared that his son was in need of a wife. This time Alexandra insisted upon meeting the gentleman in question. She smiled to herself at the faded memories. Roland had been delightful—her own age, intelligent and still possessing his own teeth. They had taken an immediate liking to each other and there had been a whirlwind courtship. Roland had not found her to be shrewish; he'd actually admired her outspokenness. At last, Alexandra thought she had found a husband and been able to escape the fate Geoffry Rordan had left her to.

Alexandra bit down on her lower lip. But then she discovered the truth about Roland and she had allowed him quietly to end the relationship. She opened her eyes to chase away the memories, the disappointment that still lay heavily in her chest. There was no use going over all this now, no use thinking about Geoffry or Roland.

For the next three years the Earl of Monthrop tried to find another husband for his daughter, but after two respectable men had found her unacceptable, others shied away. Every gentleman in London seemed to know something of Lady Alexandra's reputation. That was when Alexandra's father, in desperation, decided to send her to the American Colonies. Surely her reputation would not have reached the Maryland Colony! Two months after she arrived at her uncle's, near

Annapolis, Two Crows kidnapped her.

Alexandra stared up into the treetops above. She groaned. Damn men! Damn them all! But especially damn Geoffry Rordan for having gotten her in this mess to begin with. If only he'd married her as he'd agreed. If only he'd not slunk away like a coward.

Alexandra glanced over at Hunter and Jon. Both rested with their eyes closed. She was tired too, but first she had to see to necessity. She got up and quietly slipped into the brush. Unafraid of the dark she walked deeper into the woods. An owl hooted somewhere overhead.

Where are you, Geoffry Rordan? she thought bitterly. *Are you somewhere here in the Colonies still, married to a blond twit? Or did the Indians scalp you? I can only hope . . .*

Just as Alexandra went to lift her skirts, she heard a twig snap. Before she could spin around, a filthy hand clamped down on her mouth. Two Crows! She knew it was him before she saw his face.

She tried to scream, but she couldn't. Instead she bit down hard on his hand. He grunted and let go. Alexandra bolted.

"Let her go!" a voice came out of the darkness. Hunter's voice . . .

Alexandra turned to see Two Crows by the light of the moon pull his knife from his belt.

"I wouldn't do that if I were you," Hunter warned in a frighteningly even voice.

Alexandra couldn't see Hunter, but she knew he could only be a few feet away.

Two Crows drew back the hand he held the knife in. Alexandra opened her mouth to scream, but no sound came out.

Musket fire broke the silence of the forest. A streak of light leapt out of the darkness and the smoke of gunpowder filled the night air.

Two Crows screamed as the knife fell from his hand under the impact of the musket ball.

Alexandra grimaced in horror, but she didn't turn away. Two Crows went down on his knees clutching his hand as he moaned, rocking back and forth.

Hunter stepped out of the brush, the musket in his hand still smoking. "Are you all right?" he asked Alexandra.

She turned to him, dropping one hand to her hip. Her heart was beating so hard in her chest that it pounded in her ears, but she recovered quickly. "What the hell were you doing following me out here?" she demanded. "Are you some kind of deviant or something?"

Chapter Three

Hunter blinked in disbelief. "Madame?"

"Have you lost the ability to hear, to respond, or both?" She pointed her finger like a taskmaster. "I asked you why you followed me into the woods when you knew full well I'd come to tend to personal needs."

If the chit had not been so serious, Hunter would have laughed. "I damned well saved your life, you ungrateful jade, and you chastise me!"

"That doesn't answer my question."

She tapped her bare foot impatiently, painting a particularly odd picture against the moonlit sky. Here was a woman who came within an ambsace of death and she was concerned with propriety!

"I want to know why you followed me," Alexandra insisted.

Hunter's dark eyes narrowed. "I should think this conversation would be better left until later." He nodded in the direction of Two Crows. "Right now I'd best deal with the savage that nearly slit your gullet."

"You truly see yourself as some sort of knight in armor, don't you?" She took a step toward Hunter. "Well, let me assure you, sir, that I could have handled the situation myself."

"I'm curious." He raised a dark eyebrow. "Just how is it that you *handle* a knife in your stomach?"

"He'd not have hurt me. Not after he'd kept me alive all these weeks. He was just trying to take back what he still considers his, or at least this cap-i-tan's."

She had a point, but Hunter refused to give in. "Do you always prattle on like this?"

"Only when I'm right."

Hunter lifted his gaze heavenward in exasperation and turned his attention back to Two Crows.

The renegade half-breed was still on his knees, but now he was searching frantically for something in the dry leaves that covered the ground. *"Osnosa! Osnosa!"* he cried frantically.

"You should not have followed us, Two Crows," Hunter said gruffly. "Take yourself north, go to your people. You do not belong here among the Shawnee."

"Osnosa!" Two Crows wailed, lifting up his bloody, mangled hand for Hunter to see. The musket ball had sliced through his flesh, knocking the knife from his hand and taking two fingers above the first knuckle with it. *"Osnosa!"*

Hunter hesitated for a moment, then leaned his musket against a tree trunk and squatted in the leaves across from Two Crows. With his knife on his belt and the Indian in such a state, he figured he was relatively safe. "Here. Here's your finger." He offered the bloody appendage and reached into the leaves again. "And here's the other. Now go." He pointed northward. "And do not let our paths cross again, else I will kill you."

Two Crows rose, his fingers clutched in his good hand, the injured hand tucked under his armpit. "You have shamed this man." His voice was bitter, his words laced with pain.

"You shame yourself by not knowing your adversaries better. I paid you for the white woman and now she is mine. You cannot take her back."

"She was not mine to sell!" he protested. "I took whiskey for her. Muskets. The cap-i-tan will be very angry."

"Don't tell me this is the first time you have ever sold the same goods twice, else I would have to call you a liar. Now take yourself from here before I grow angry and take back your fingers to hang on my belt!"

Two Crows stumbled backward, clutching his fingers tightly. "I have warned you, Redbeard. The cap-i-tan, he will come for you."

"My name is Hunter, the Hunter of the Shawnee. Tell your cap-i-tan that, so that he may find me!" Hunter called as the half-breed backed off into the brush.

Hunter picked up his musket and waited for the sounds of the fleeing half-breed to diminish before he turned back to the woman. When his gaze met hers, he could see that she was trembling from head to foot.

"His fingers," she mumbled. "You blew off his fingers."

"Aye." Hunter glanced up into her dark eyes, amazed that she could change moods so quickly. A moment ago she had been belligerent and as cool as a rock jutting from a freshwater spring. Now she was just a frightened woman, an alluring woman. He took the awkward moment to reload his musket. The darkness mattered little. He loaded by feel, not by sight. "Aye, I did take off his fingers. I should have taken off his head, but I've always been too damned soft-hearted with the Indians. Jon's always telling me so."

"His . . . his fingers."

Hunter watched her lower lip tremble. Christ, what was it about this wench that made him want to sweep her into his arms and kiss the frown from her lips? What was it about her that made him forget his beloved wife . . . and his mission?

He was on the trail of Laughing Rain's killer. He was still in mourning. It was a dishonor to her memory to look at Alexandra the way he had just looked at her. He looked away.

"His fingers," she repeated in horror. "You gave him his fingers."

Hunter tamped down the musket ball with a firm hand. "The Indians have this thing about being buried with all their body parts. From what I can gather, when the time comes, if they don't have all their appendages, their souls can't get to heaven." He shrugged. "I guess it was foolish of me to bother to find 'em for him. The Shawnee say the Mohawks haven't got souls anyway."

Alexandra just stood there and stared at him in wide-eyed shock.

Without thinking, he reached out to brush a lock of hair from her cheek. "You could bathe if you want," he said softly. "Neither Jon nor I will do you any harm and Two Crows'll certainly not be back."

She pushed away his hand. "You're saying I'm dirty?"

"You are dirty. Not that I mean it's your fault. Renegades like Two Crows are not known for their hygiene. If a little grit beneath your nails is all you came out of this with, you're a damned lucky woman. Jon says you've been with Two Crows nigh on a month. You're fortunate to be alive, Alex."

"It's Alexandra. Only my friends call me Alex, and you sir, are not a friend." She dropped her hands to her hips. "And who, might I ask, are you, to be making commentaries on my appearance. At least I have an excuse. Look at you." She threw up her hand. "From your speech, you obviously weren't raised in a dairy. But look at yourself. You're a disgrace to your family, whoever they might be, with . . . with your tangled hair and nasty beard!"

Hunter watched her stomp past him in the direction of the camp. He lifted his hand to stroke his red beard. "I should have given you back to Two Crows when I had the chance," he muttered, falling in behind her.

*   *   *

"By the king's cod, what are you doing, Hunter?" Jon came down to the stream's edge and bent over to splash cold water on his morning face.

Hunter adjusted the tiny piece of mirror he'd propped on a tree stump. "Shaving my beard, what's it look like?" he answered gruffly.

"Phew!" Jon shook his head. "Shaving your beard and washing your hair all in the same year? The fever taken you?"

Hunter frowned and went on scraping the whiskers from his cheek. "Did you wake up the woman?"

"Her name is Alexandra. Fine piece of fluff, don't you think?"

Hunter looked up. "Fluff! I think not. Hell and fire is more like it." He shook his head and went back to shaving. "Way out of your league, friend. She's neither a slut nor some wealthy man's forgotten country wife."

"She said she was a serving girl in Annapolis."

Hunter gave a laugh. "And I'm the Queen of the May."

"No. I didn't believe her either. Speech is too good. Clothes too fine, or at least what was left of them." Jon smiled. "She did paint a pretty fetching picture though, didn't she, with all that long leg and just a touch of white ass showing?"

Hunter splashed his face with water, washing away the remaining soap suds and whiskers with it. "The woman's just escaped a pack of Iroquois and all you can think about is tumbling with her! For God's sake! You're a sick man, Jon."

"And what? You're totally immune to a comely

face? A shapely thigh?" Jon's voice lowered an octave, softening. "Christ, Hunter. Laughing Rain's been dead more than a year. It's time you got on with your life."

"The Shawnee say it is bad medicine to speak the name of the dead," Hunter murmured.

Laughing Rain. God, he'd loved her. From the first day she'd rode into the Delaware camp of the turtle clan, Hunter had known he would marry her. She was a tall woman, for a Delaware, but still a mite of a thing in comparison to his own hulking stature. She'd had the blackest eyes, eyes a man could lose himself in. They were married only three months to the day from their first meeting. What plans they had had. A cabin. A trading post where they would deal fairly between the white and red men. Children . . .

But then she'd gone hunting for honey in a grove of trees beyond the camp. She'd asked Hunter to go, but he'd been busy repairing a friend's musket. He remembered how she had teased him that the honeymoon must be over when he was no longer inclined to follow her alone into the woods.

Hunter closed his eyes, still tasting her lips on his. Then she was gone. When she didn't return at dusk, he went out looking for her. He found her beneath a tree, honeycombs littering the ground. He winced at the thought of the sight of her violated body. God in heaven, what the beast had done to her. Tortured . . . raped . . . murdered.

To judge from the signs in the grass, she had fought bravely, even wounded her attacker with her knife, but in the end she had lost the battle and her life. The life of their child.

Hunter averted his gaze from the mirror, not wanting to see his own face, not wanting to see his own tears.

Laughing Rain. He'd loved her so much. He'd find her killer and see justice done—or die trying. That was what this journey was about. He and Jon were traveling west to seek information on the English soldier known as Blue-Green Eyes to the Shawnee and the Delaware. Word was that the man claimed to be in the trade of buying and selling women, both red and white. Word was, that he was Hunter's man.

"Here she comes," Jon said, breaking Hunter from his reverie.

"Who?"

Jon punched his friend in the arm. "Alexandra, of course. I'm telling you, she has her eye on you. Best apply your charms while she's still all thankful you rescued her from the savages. I'll be more than happy to step aside and let you have a go."

Hunter snorted. "I'm not the rutting boar you are, Jon. Not interested."

"Then she's mine?"

"I'll wager you put one hand on that lily flesh and she'll take it off."

Jon arched a sooty eyebrow. "Is that a challenge?"

"No, it's not. And mind you, if she injures you, I'll not tend to your wounds."

The two men looked up to see her come through

the trees and approach them.

Alexandra was a tall woman with long dark wavy hair and an olive complexion darkened by the sun in her weeks of travel. Even with her haunting dark eyes and perfect cheekbones she'd not be considered handsome by the standards of London. But to Hunter, who had grown accustomed to dark skin and nut brown eyes, she was a striking beauty.

Irritated by his thoughts, Hunter stood and reached behind his head to tie back his hair with a leather thong. This morning, on impulse, he'd trimmed his hair, shortening it to shoulder length. When he saw Alexandra and realized he'd done it for her benefit, he felt foolish. He thought he'd left his vanity back in London. His hair had been something to hide behind; if only he could have it back. Now the birds would use the bright red locks left on the ground to line their nests come spring.

"Good morning." Alexandra nodded in the men's direction, but didn't bother to look at them. Then she stopped short. "Heavens!" She broke into a smile. "What happened to you?" She dropped a graceful hand to her hip, addressing Hunter. "You don't look like the same man!"

Hunter grabbed his straight razor and the piece of mirror and stuffed them into the leather knapsack he carried his personal belongings in. "A man has a right to shave his face without becoming a spectacle, doesn't he?"

She shook her head, still staring at him. With his hair trimmed and pulled back she could see a copper earring in one lobe. "I can't believe it! Why you could get into the queen's drawing room with a face like that.''

Hunter felt his cheeks begin to burn and then he became irritated at the thought that this chit could embarrass him like this in front of Jon. There'd be no living with the man now.

Jon cackled. "Fair, isn't he?" He took a step back, turning to stand beside Alexandra so that he, too, could study Hunter. "I vow he could catch himself a wealthy man's daughter with those features.''

"That he could." Thinking of the man who had left her, Alexandra turned away suddenly. "If you gentlemen have completed your morning ablutions, I'd ask that you leave me to mine.'' She ran a hand through her dirty hair. "I thought I might bathe in the river, if there's time before we go.''

Hunter picked up his knapsack and started toward the camp. "Take your time. There's plenty of daylight left to this day." He looked back over his shoulder. "Call if you're in need of something. I don't expect to see Two Crows again, but we'll not go far.''

She opened her mouth as if to say something, and then closed it again.

Hunter waited until Jon passed him, not wanting to have to put up with any more of his friend's harassment than necessary. "What is it?" he asked Alexandra when Jon had disappeared through the trees.

Alexandra tugged at the remnants of her blue gown and shirt. "My clothes. I'm showing more than I'm covering. Do you . . . could you . . .''

She lifted her gaze. "Have you anything suitable for traveling I could borrow?"

"I don't carry lady's hoops on my mule, but I might have something."

She smiled a smile that seemed to Hunter to light up the morning. "Thank you . . ."

"Hunter, it's Hunter," he said, not knowing why it was so important to him that he hear her say his name.

". . . Hunter." She paused, looked down and then back at him again. "Hunter, despite my jests, I do like the change."

"What?"

She gestured. "The clean face and neat hair. It becomes you."

Hunter felt odd to be standing there talking to this stranger in such a manner, but part of him liked it—enjoyed her compliment. Their gazes locked and for a moment he held her captive. "I'll see what I can find in the packs in the way of clothing for you. Be right back." He walked away.

As he trudged through the trees toward the camp, he contemplated the mystery of women. He couldn't figure them out. This Alexandra, one minute she was all tooth and claw, then the next she was smiling like an angel sent from the heavens. They were all like that, every blasted one of them!

For some reason Hunter's thoughts shifted to a woman from long ago. He remembered his betrothal back in London. It had only been six years ago, but it seemed like six thousand.

He'd never regretted deciding to come to

America rather than marry as his father had bid him, but he was sorry for the way he'd gone about it. He was sorry he had hurt her the way he knew he must have. He should never have signed that betrothal agreement. But once he'd signed it, he should have had the decency to go to her and break off in person. It didn't matter that he'd never met her, he still had owed her that courtesy. He shouldn't have run off like that. He should have said his good-byes. He should have tried to explain to his father why he had to leave . . .

Hunter knelt on the ground and began to go through his bags on the ground. He wondered what had become of the child he'd been betrothed to. No doubt her father had found her another man and she was now married with a brood of children. He was quite certain she was better off. He'd have made a poor excuse for a husband to a proper lady. He'd never have been happy there in London . . . he'd have made her life miserable.

"Ah, hah . . ." He pulled out a doeskin tunic and shook it free of wrinkles. It was his own shirt, but it would do, tied with a belt at her waist. It would be short, but not too short, and certainly more practical than what Alexandra was wearing now.

Grabbing a small cotton blanket from another bag, he went back down toward the stream.

As Hunter cleared the trees, he spotted Alexandra in the center of the stream. Even in the middle it was shallow, but she had somehow managed to lower herself into the water until nothing showed but her head and the linen straps of her shift.

Hunter averted his eyes, not wanting to embarrass her—not wanting to allow himself to dwell on the way he knew the wet shift must be molding to her firm, round breasts. He held up the clothing. "Here's a blanket to dry off with and a tunic to wear. Belt it with the leather and it will work well enough."

"God's teeth, it's short," she called from the water, her teeth chattering. "Have you nothing else?"

"I told you. I'm no rag and bone man. I carry no ladies' undergarments. Now wear it or don't. It makes no difference to me, but I'm packing up the mule." He turned and started back for the camp. "We leave in ten minutes' time." Passing through the trees, Hunter wondered why he had suddenly turned so caustic with Alexandra.

How shocking it must seem to her to go from a gown that covered her from bodice to slipper, to a sleeveless, bare-legged leather tunic. But he had no time to care for tender feelings or modesty. He'd done enough for her. He had more important things on his mind. He had that murderer, Blue-Green Eyes to be concerned with. He'd saved Alex from Two Crows. He'd send her back to Annapolis with a guide as soon as they reached the Shawnee village. That would have to be enough.

Chapter Four

For the first few morning hours, Alexandra walked alone, following in the two men's footsteps. While they ignored her, conversing with each other, she hung behind, trying not to feel sorry for herself.

She knew she had much to be thankful for. She was alive and relatively safe. Two Crows was miles from here by now. These men were taking her home to her uncle's house. In a day or two she'd be back in Annapolis. Aunt Sally and her cousins would be there to comfort her. She'd have a real bath. She'd put on that new apple green organza gown she'd never gotten a chance to wear, and she'd sit and have tea in one of Aunt Sally's twin parlors.

Alexandra knew she just had to hang on a little longer. So what if she was wearing some animal's skin shamefully hiked up above her knees? So what if there were mosquitos buzzing around her head? So what if her savior was the rudest man in the colonies? She had to ignore the inconveniences, including Hunter.

Hunter. His name rang in her head.

He'd startled her this morning by shaving and cutting his hair. He was such a handsome man without all those tangled tresses, that she wished now that she'd kept her mouth shut and that he'd left himself be. He was entirely too attractive without his long hair and beard.

Alexandra nearly groaned aloud.

She didn't like the warm feeling in the pit of her stomach he'd given her when she first laid eyes on him this morning.

His image flickered in her head. Standing there by the river without his shirt, he'd made a fetching sight, indeed. Certainly she'd seen men nude from the waist up—her father and brothers . . . and once even her friend Martha's cousin Charles. But she'd never seen a man like Hunter.

His shoulders and biceps seemed to be shaped from a potter's wheel or da Vinci pen with their fluid lines and shaped muscles. Power emanated from his suntanned flesh. His chest was broad with a sprinkling of red hair that ran in a line down his flat stomach to disappear beneath the waistband of his leather breeches. Her first impulse when she'd seen his bare chest was to touch it, to feel his flesh beneath her fingertips.

Alexandra felt her cheeks grow warm at the thought of him. She knew she should be ashamed of herself. Heavens, her thoughts were bordering on lustfulness. But she was nearly twenty-two, well past the age of a blushing maiden. Long in the tooth, her mother—a woman entirely too blunt—had called it.

So what harm could a little fantasizing do? She was in the middle of the wilderness struggling to keep her sanity. Once she returned to Annapolis and a suitable time of mourning was observed for Uncle Charles and Cousin Susan, no doubt Alexandra would be married off to that Mr. Comegys Aunt Sally had been speaking of. Mr. Comegys was said to be a suitable match, kind and only twenty years her elder. Of course Cousin Molly had said he was short and had a bulbous nose and a twelve-year-old, pinched-faced daughter. But what could Alexandra expect at this point? Any husband was better than the shame of none at all.

Alexandra lifted her gaze until it came to rest on Hunter's broad back. She ground her teeth. The man was infuriating. One moment he was kind to her, the next he was shouting like a madman. Now he'd taken to ignoring her. She didn't know which of the three made her angrier.

Jon slowed his pace, obviously waiting for her to catch up. Hunter walked on, leading his mule.

"Tired?" Jon asked.

"No."

He nodded. "I wanted to apologize for my behavior last night. I shouldn't have laughed." He looked up, his black-eyed gaze meeting hers. "A delicate creature like yourself could certainly not be familiar with such a task as cleaning a rabbit."

The brandy-smooth tone of his voice sent off warning signals in her brain. Jon wasn't the first man to cast his wiles in Alexandra's direction. Many a man in the past had been willing to tumble in the sheets with her. Alexandra had never had any trouble getting those proposals. It was marriage proposals she was sorely lacking in. "I warrant you I'll do better with the next rabbit."

He reached out to brush his fingertips against her bare arm. "I warrant you will. But please let me do the honor. It was wrong for my crude friend there to expect you to see to such a menial task. A woman of your beauty surely must have talents of a more civilized nature."

She cast a sideways glance at him, amused. "Tell me, Jon. Did the two of you flip a coin to see who was to have my favors?"

Jon brought a palm to his chest. "Pardon?"

She smiled, turning away from him. "Don't act the innocent with me. I know when a man is inviting me to sleep with him. The manner is the same with all men, apparently, be it on one continent or another, red man or white."

Alexandra heard a chuckle out of Hunter, who was still walking ahead of them but had slowed his pace so that the distance between him and Alexandra and Jon was shorter.

"What I want to know, Jon," Alexandra went on, "is—when you two flipped the coin to see who would go for me first, were you the winner, or the loser?"

Hunter slapped his knee, making no attempt to hide his laughter now.

Jon looked up at Alexandra, feigning innocence. "I assure you I don't know what you mean, Alexandra. I was simply—"

"You were simply making illicit advances toward me." She stopped and turned to him. "Now let me tell you, Jon, so that there is no further misunderstanding. I appreciate your aid back at the trading post. If you like, I can pay you handsomely for your time, once I reach home. However, I will not offer my body as payment, no matter how charming you might be."

Jon began to walk again, appearing nonplussed. "So you admit you do find me charming." He flashed her a grin.

"As charming as any Jack of Dandy in London."

"You see that, the lady does find me charming," Jon called to Hunter.

"She's telling you to knock off," he called back, still walking.

Jon looked back at Alexandra. "Are you telling me to knock off, madame?"

"That I am. Else I'll skin you like I did that rabbit, beginning between the thighs." She smiled sweetly.

Jon grimaced.

"Best be warned," Hunter threw over his shoulder. "You'd not be a comely sight skinned, my friend."

Jon shrugged to Alexandra. "You can't blame me for trying."

She lifted her chin a notch. "I'll not hold it against you. Just keep your hands to yourself and we'll get along fine." She stepped over a log that lay across their path. "Tell me, just why are you out here in the middle of nowhere?" She eyed him from head to toe. "You obviously have an education. Access to money as well. Tell me your tale. I'm certain it's a good one."

Jon sighed. "If you must know, I'm the heir to a

great fortune in England, run from my father and his talk of responsibility and a child meant to be my wife." He nodded. "Yonder is my serving man, though I have to admit I allow him liberties."

"You're a rogue." Her eyes narrowed. "But something makes me think there's a glimmer of truth to all your lies."

Again Hunter chuckled. Alexandra took notice that though he obviously didn't wish to take part in the conversation, he was listening to every word.

Jon reached back to adjust his queue. "You accuse me of telling falsehoods, but what of yourself? You're obviously no lady's maid."

"It's not any of your affair who I am." She pointed. "Ahead lies Annapolis. Get me there safely, and I'll be on my way. I told you. You'll be well paid for your assistance." When her gaze met Jon's, she realized something was wrong.

He looked away.

"What?" she asked softly.

He slid his jaw back and forth as if stalling for time.

"What?" she repeated more loudly. "What is it? What haven't you told me?"

He cleared his throat. "Annapolis, Alexandra?"

"Yes."

"It doesn't lay ahead."

"Well . . . well what do you mean?" She felt her heart skip a beat. Remain calm, she told herself. "You're not taking me to Annapolis? Well, any large settlement will do. I can have my aunt contacted. She can send someone for me. I'm certain I can find a place to—"

"Alexandra, we head west, not east." He looked away guiltily. "There are no settlements in this direction. Nothing but Indian camps."

"What?" She came to a halt. "What?" she demanded. "You're not taking me home?"

"Eventually someone will see you home. But not now. Hunter—"

Alexandra ran forward, hurling herself into Hunter's broad back. "You maggot-brained whoreson!" she shouted, beating him with her balled fists. "You said you were taking me home! You said—"

Hunter dropped the mule's reins and spun around, trying to shield himself as Alexandra pummeled him.

"Whoa, whoa, there!"

"You lied! You lied to me!"

"I didn't lie. Ouch, damn!" He pulled back his head but not before she managed to strike him in the nose, spewing blood. "Damn, that hurt!"

Alexandra was out of control. She was nearly hysterical. She beat him with her fists, kicking his legs at the same time. "You were supposed to take me home! You were supposed to take me to Annapolis! To my aunt! I have to tell her what happened to my cousin and uncle! I have to go home now!"

Hunter caught one of her wrists and then the other. "I never said I was taking you home to Annapolis! Never once did you hear those words from these lips!"

Letting out a string of curses that would have made a sailor blush, Alexandra brought up her knee between Hunter's legs with all the strength she could muster. He groaned in pain and buckled, going down on his knees, but taking her with him.

"Cease your grappling, blowze!" he warned beneath his breath. "Cease!"

"Or what?" She struggled to free herself from his grasp, still batting at him. Her limbs were tangled in his. His face was so close to hers that she could feel his heaving breath on her cheek. "You'll what? You'll kidnap me? You'll tie me to a tree? You'll rape and murder my twelve-year-old cousin in front of my eyes?"

Hunter suddenly released her wrists, shoving her backward into a pile of dry leaves.

Jon came running toward them. "Ad's-blood, Hunter!"

Alexandra shoved her doeskin tunic down over her bare thigh. "Stay out of this!"

"Back off," Hunter echoed, scowling at Jon.

"You said you would take me home," Alexandra accused, staring venomously at Hunter. "You said you would! Liar!"

"I said I'd see you to safety!" He got up off the ground, not bothering to brush away the dry leaves that clung to the fringes of his tunic. "I never said I was taking you directly to Annapolis. I would never have said that."

He threw out his hand to help her up, but she swatted it away and stood on her own. "All right, so maybe you never actually said we were going straight to Annapolis," she conceded hotly. "But you let me think I was going home. You made me think I was safe."

"You are safe. Jon and I'll see that no harm

comes to you until we can find a guide to take you back." He wiped at the blood that trickled from his nostril. The corner of his mouth was bleeding as well. "Safe enough, if I don't throttle you, that is."

She crossed her arms over her chest. "I can't believe you did this! After all I've been through! By the king's cod! I was better off with Two Crows!"

"So go!" Hunter swept his hand. "Go back to Two Crows. Let him sell you to the soldier. You'd probably enjoy being a whore—that big mouth of yours will come in handy!"

Alexandra's jaw dropped in shock. "You son of a stinking—" She hurled herself at Hunter's massive frame again, but this time he caught both her arms and twisted her around until her back was pressed against his chest, her buttocks planted intimately in his groin.

"Let me go! Let me go!"

"Then cease this tantrum!"

"I'm not having a tantrum." Tears stung her eyes and she fought them. "I'm angry. I thought you were taking me back to Annapolis." She sniffed. "I thought I'd be home in another day drinking tea in my aunt's parlor."

"Headed west with us?"

She glanced over her shoulder. Now that she had calmed down a bit she realized what a compromising position she had gotten herself into. She was trapped in Hunter's arms. He smelled of pine needles and raw masculinity. His nearness was making her lightheaded.

She suddenly knew that she was more attracted to this man than she'd first thought.

"West?" She panted. "I don't know what you

mean. How was I supposed to know which direction we were going in? Everything looks the same out here in this swanking wilderness!"

"Now who's the addlepated one?" Hunter's voice in her ear was husky with anger. "We've been walking west with the rising sun on our backs since we left the trading post."

Now she really felt stupid. He was right. They had been walking into the setting sun. How could she have been such an imbecile as to have not realized it? "Let me go," she said quietly.

"You going to behave yourself?"

She was silent for a moment. She exhaled. "Yes."

"Pardon?"

"I said yes, now release me!"

Slowly, Hunter loosened his grip on Alexandra's arms. She stumbled forward, as alarmed by her physical attraction to the sot as she was by the altercation. She spun around to face him, dropping a hand to her hip. At this distance she would be able to think more rationally—she'd be able to reason with this lunatic. "If we're not headed east to Annapolis, where are we going?"

"Instead of being so blessed demanding you could express a little gratitude," Hunter chastised harshly. "I saved your tail, remember?" He reached back to brush off his shoulder a lock of long red hair that had come loose in the tussle.

"Where are we going?" she repeated, looking to Jon who stood near the mule, then back at Hunter. "I have a right to know where I'm being taken."

"West into Ohio country. I'm looking for a man, a Shawnee medicine man."

"Indians?" Her lower lip trembled. "We're

walking halfway across the continent to find an Indian? You couldn't find enough of them on the Chesapeake?''

"Not that it's any of your concern but I need some information from him. I'm looking for someone else."

"You're looking for someone else? And that couldn't wait?" She shook her head in disbelief. "This someone is so important that you couldn't get me, a woman who's been kidnapped by savages, back to civilization first? So important that you have to drag me with you? Who in God's holy name can be that important? Surely King George has not been kidnapped by red heathens as well!"

Hunter's face seemed to darken. He turned and strode away.

"Don't turn away from me when I'm speaking!" Alexandra ran after him. "Did anyone ever tell you how rude that is?" She grabbed his arm. He flinched.

"Let it go," Jon warned softly. "Just let it go, Alexandra."

"Who are you looking for?" she repeated, ignoring Jon. "If I'm being forced to be a part of this, I at least have the right to know why."

Hunter shook his head, looking away. "It doesn't matter."

She laughed, but there was no humor in the tone of her voice. She still had her arm on the sleeve of his tunic. Beneath the soft, supple leather she could feel his biceps tighten. His reaction to her words was so strong that she almost backed down. Almost. "Why have I been dragged into this? I demand to know who's so important!"

Hunter turned to face her, his piercing hazel eyes boring down on her. "The man who murdered my wife and unborn child," he whispered.

Alexandra released his sleeve, mortified by her own behavior. Hunter strode away. "Going scouting," he said as he passed Jon. "Take the mule and keep heading west."

"I'm sorry," Alexandra murmured beneath her breath as tears clouded her dark eyes. The pain in Hunter's eyes had been so strong at that moment, so real, that her own heart ached for his loss. "Heavenly Father, I'm so sorry, Hunter—"

But he was already too far away to hear her.

Two Crows struggled against the strength of the two English soldiers who half carried, half dragged him into the room. The entire left side of his face ached from the beating the men had given him in the fort prison. One eye was swollen shut, his nose broken, his cheek slashed and his lower lip split.

One soldier released him and the other gave him a vicious shove. Two Crows hit the dirt floor tucking his arms and legs up as best he could considering the fact that they were tied. His head hit the log and mud wall and for a moment he lay still, catching his breath. Then he rolled onto his side and glowered at the uniformed soldiers.

"Now don't go anywhere," the taller of the two soldiers warned.

A woman's scream echoed somewhere in the fort.

The solder smiled to his companion. "The captain wants to see you, just as soon as he's done, redskin."

He left the room and a few moments later returned on the heels of Captain John Cain. The captain was impeccably dressed in a red uniform, the breast of his pressed coat lined with medals of commendation. The only thing that seemed slightly out of place was his flushed face and the dots of perspiration above his upper lip.

Two Crows watched from the floor as the captain strode by. Two Crows could smell the leather of his shiny black boots and the smoke of his tobacco. But there was another smell that enveloped him. One more subtle. Was it madness?

"Dismissed," Cain ordered with a flip of his hand. He was a small man, but well built with bulky shoulders and obvious strength.

"You certain you want to be left alone with the red bastard?" the taller soldier said.

"I said you're dismissed, Mitchell. He gives me any trouble and I'll shoot him between his eyes." He turned to smile at Two Crows. "Fair agreement, wouldn't you say?"

Two Crows made no response.

Cain nodded. "There we have it." He looked back to his men. "Dismissed, I said. I'll call you when I'm ready for you to come back for him." As if on second thought, he then said, "Why not clean up the room down the hall? You know which one I mean. Take the woman back to her cell."

"Yes, sir," the soldiers echoed. They made a hasty retreat back through the door the captain had entered by. Back in the direction of the woman's screams.

Cain walked across the sparsely furnished room and propped one booted foot on a camp stool. He gazed out a tiny window as he reached for his pipe tucked inside his shirtwaist.

Two Crows eyed him uneasily. This cap-i-tan was a madman. He could smell it on his breath. Two Crows had been a fool to let the soldiers take him alive. He should have died a warrior's death. It was what his father would have done. But he wasn't his father, was he? He would never be the man his father was. It was his mother's white blood that tainted him.

Cain tapped a little tobacco into the bowl of his pipe and turned his gaze on Two Crows. "So, I understand there's been a little trouble with our trade agreement."

Two Crows stiffened his back. "The redbeard stole her."

"One trapper, and what, five or six of you? Surely you could have overtaken even the fiercest of men."

"There were two of them."

"Two, five—" his voice rose in volume until he was shouting. "Ten! It makes no difference. You and I had an agreement."

"I'll get you another woman. Two."

"I wanted the white woman. I tire of the red bitches. They never scream loud enough. They never beg." He glanced out the window. "I can never get them to beg," he murmured.

"Then white women. I will give two for the loss of the first."

Cain shook his head. "No good. I want that woman. My man said she was uncommonly handsome. She'll bring a good price further north. The Mohawks love white women, don't they? That's why he purchased her. Alexandra, was that her name?" He poked his pipe between his teeth. "Alexandra. That's who I want." He turned to glare at Two Crows. "That's who I'll have . . ."

Two Crows nodded his head. "Yes. The Alexandra woman. I'll find her." At this point he would promise anything to gain a chance at freedom. "Bring her to you."

"How will you find her?"

"She travels with a white man. A man who calls himself the Hunter of the Shawnee."

Cain turned, his interest suddenly tapped. "Hunter of the Shawnee you say? The name is familiar."

For the first time Two Crows realized the captain had one blue eye and one green eye. An evil omen. "You know this redbeard?"

"I know of him."

Two Crows nodded. "I will track him and take the girl. I will bring her to you."

Cain smiled to himself as he turned back to stare out the window. "I know you will, redskin. Else you'll come to regret the day your whore white mother ever whelped you . . ."

Chapter Five

Alexandra studied Jon carefully. "The truth?"

He lifted his right hand. "The honest God's truth."

She turned her gaze toward the small campfire. Darkness was closing in quickly and still Hunter hadn't returned. Jon said he often scouted ahead and that he would find them, but she was concerned. After all, wasn't it her fault he'd walked off like that? She was the one who had pried into his personal life. She was the one who had made him tell her his wife and baby were dead.

She looked back at Jon who was stretched out in front of the fire, one hand tucked behind his head. Alexandra's own plight was forgotten for the moment. All she could think of was Hunter and the unfairness of life. "But how could his wife's family have accused him of such a horrendous crime? The man is certainly not filled with social graces, but he's not a murderer. I've only known him two days and I could tell you that much."

Jon shrugged. "They found him with the knife in his hand. He was covered in her blood. Circumstantial evidence. They needed a killer, someone to blame. In their minds he was the most logical person to accuse."

"But he loved her." Alexandra picked up a stick and poked at the fire in contemplation. "You said he had agreed to remain among the Indians just to have her as his wife. You said he was willing to give up a title and lands in England to have her. Why would he kill a woman he loved that much?"

"Her family accused him of being angry that she was pregnant. They said he killed her because the rich white man wanted no half-breed child."

The mention of Hunter being rich didn't go unnoticed, but that didn't matter to Alexandra right now. "Where were you when all this took place? You're one of them. Surely the Indians would have listened to you."

"I was in a card game in Annapolis when Laughing Rain was murdered. Hunter and I were supposed to meet at a tavern the following week. I didn't see him for nearly six months. Besides, they're Delaware, I'm Shawnee. We're related but not one and the same. And then,"—he slapped the leather shirtwaist he wore—"I'm not much of a Shawnee, not with my white man's ways."

She shook her head. "What a tragedy. Hunter must be a remarkable man to be able to withstand it all. A lesser man would have committed suicide or just run from his pain. I think it's admirable that he's trying to catch his wife's killer."

Jon cracked a charming smile. "Don't tell me

you're smitten with that grouchy old bear. I warn you. He's too wild for your delicate nature. He'll offer nothing but heartache." He reached out and took her hand. "Better to lay your coppers with me." He winked. "I'm a hell of a man! Give me a chance and I'll prove it to you, Alexandra. I vow I will!"

She snatched her hand from his, but she wasn't offended. Actually, she was just a little flattered. Even though she knew Jon was one of those ladies' men that couldn't be trusted any further than a woman could toss him, he was harmless . . . as long as you didn't get involved with him. "I told you. I'm not interested. Not in you and certainly not in Hunter. My aunt has a fine match for me back in Annapolis. A wealthy man. A gentleman."

"Hunter's wealthy and I'm a gentleman. Combined, doesn't that count for something?"

Alexandra tossed a stick. It glanced off his shoulder and fell into the campfire. "Very amusing. Now tell me, why didn't you wed one of these beautiful Indian maidens like Hunter did?" It was odd, but she felt a twinge of jealousy as she spoke.

Jon grimaced and turned his attention back to the fire. "I'm not cut out for colonial life and certainly not cut out for Indian camp life. I'm not like Hunter. My life is at the theater, at the gaming tables, in Whitehall if I could find my way in. My home is in London and just as soon as Hunter finds Laughing Rain's killer, I'm going back to London, with or without him. I came to these godforsaken colonies nearly six years ago. He swore we'd only stay a year. I figure my duty to him is done."

"Him." She drew up her legs to ward off the chill of the autumn evening. "And just who is Hunter to you?"

Jon shook his head slowly, watching the flames lick at a piece of wood he'd tossed into the fire. "A companion. A friend since childhood." He chuckled. "No. He's more." He stretched out on the ground again, tucking his hands behind his head.

"His father brought me back from the colonies when I was three. Apparently I was an orphan from one of the Shawnee villages. No one wanted me. Shortly thereafter the earl married Hunter's mother and she gave birth to Hunter. I think I was supposed to have been a manservant to Hunter, but it didn't turn out that way. The earl was very good to me. Hunter and I shared the same schoolmasters. I was taught the ways of a gentleman at Hunter's side. He and I have been inseparable since Hunter's governess cut his apron strings."

Alexandra smiled as she listened to Jon. "It does the heart good to hear of such friendship." She rubbed her arms for warmth, wishing *she* had had a friend as she was growing up. Of course her household had been full of sisters, but no one had ever been her friend. Not the kind of friend that Jon talked of. She lifted her gaze until it settled on Jon's face. "Who is he, Jon? You speak of title and lands . . . money. My family may well have known his. Tell me who he is," she implored softly.

"Not my position to say."

"What isn't?" Hunter asked, as he stepped into the circle of light.

Alexandra jumped involuntarily. "God's teeth, how do you do that? I never heard you!"

"He's always sneaking up like that. Drives me to distraction, too," Jon commented, reaching for the flask of brandy at his side.

"Lucky I wasn't a Mohawk or I'd have had your scalps on my belt by now," Hunter said. His tone was light and playful. The darkness Alexandra had seen on his face a few hours earlier was gone. "You both need to be more observant of your surroundings."

"No need." Jon flashed him a grin. "Not when I've got you around."

Hunter slung the bow and quiver of arrows off his back and laid them on the ground. He acted as if he wanted to say something to Alexandra, but just couldn't find the words.

She looked up at him, speaking before she lost her courage. "I . . . I'm sorry I provoked you. It was none of my business." His hazel-eyed gaze settled on her face and her voice wavered. "You . . . you were right that I should be more grateful. I'd have died in the hands of Two Crows or the man he was going to sell me to."

"No, you wouldn't have." Hunter sat down on the ground between her and Jon. "You're a survivor. You'd have to be, to have made it three weeks in the hands of the likes of that half-breed." He snatched the brandy flask from Jon who was in midswallow, and took a long pull. "You'd have found a way to escape. That or talked one of them into letting you loose. Hell, with a tongue like yours, you could talk a man out of his soul. He'd give it to you just to shut you up.''

Alexandra knew she should be offended by his words, but she chose not to be. He had said she was a survivor, and she knew that in his mind that was a high compliment. So what if he said she was sharp-tongued? It was the truth, wasn't it? Hadn't her father and mother said so, often enough? Hadn't they said that was a good part of the reason why she couldn't catch a husband?

Alexandra dared a glance at Hunter as he took another sip of the brandy. "There's rabbit left for you there beside the fire. It's safe enough. I didn't skin it. Jon did.''

Hunter shrugged. "'Tis an easy enough task to learn, to skin a rabbit. The children in the Shawnee camps learn to clean game by the time they're old enough to toddle.'' He took a bit of the succulent dark meat. "I told you I wouldn't mind teaching you. All you have to do is ask.''

She smiled to herself thinking that this man could be quite pleasant when he set his mind to it. Was this the side of him that his wife, Laughing Rain, had fallen in love with? A hundred questions tumbled in her mind as she watched him pick at the rabbit. What kind of husband had he been? A smitten lover, or a cool provider? What kind of father would he have made?

Then she wondered what brought such thoughts to her head. She lay back on the skin bedding, listening to the men's low comforting voices. Exhaustion, no doubt was what brought on such silly notions about Hunter.

I'll have to be careful, she warned herself. *Else I might find myself liking this virile creature.*

But as she drifted off to sleep, her last thoughts were of Hunter and his long red tresses blowing in the autumn wind.

Dawn came all too quickly and once again, Hunter, Jon, Alexandra, and the mule, were on the trail. They walked at a grueling pace set by Hunter, with the rising sun on their backs and the cool fall breezes on their faces. The canopy of trees over their heads was painted with an artist's brush from a palette of browns, reds, and golds, and the air was filled with brightly colored leaves drifting to the ground.

"How much farther is the village?" Alexandra asked. She had vowed to herself that she'd not complain about the arduous travel but she was tired to the bone. It seemed as if her head barely hit the cradle of her arms and Jon was shaking her awake, telling her Hunter was up and ready to start west again.

Jon picked up a stick and began to drag it along the scattered leaves. "Hunter says we'll reach there today if we can keep up the pace."

She exhaled slowly.

"Why?" he continued. "You tired? Want me to tell him to slow down? We could rest. I know I could sure as hell use it."

"No." She lifted her hand. "No, I'm all right. We're not moving any faster than Two Crows did.

I swear by the king's cod, he dragged me over most of the Maryland Colony." When she looked up at Jon, she could see a silly grin on his face. "What? Why are you laughing at me?"

He shook his head. "Nothing. It's just been a long time since I've heard a young Englishwoman speak."

"Young? My mother thinks me haggard. Nearly past the age to be pawned off. No prospective husbands left for me but the feeble minded grey-hairs with bad cases of the gout."

Hunter's baritone voice rang out in laughter.

Alexandra looked to Jon. "Does he always eavesdrop on other's conversations?"

"Always."

On impulse, Alexandra hastened her pace until she caught up with Hunter, who was leading the mule. "You find my plight so amusing?"

"To be unhindered by the bonds of marriage, that's a hindrance?"

"Perhaps not to a man but to a woman, yes. I'm my father's property until I take a husband. As a wife I might have few rights, but they'd be a damned few more than I have now."

"You deserve better," Hunter said quietly.

"What?" She looked up at him quizzically. "I deserve better how?"

"I mean that a woman like you shouldn't be passed off to the first man who comes along just so that your father doesn't have to feed you."

"An odd opinion for an Englishman."

"Among the Shawnee and Delaware, women are men's equals."

"No?" Alexandra's face lit up. "You jest."

"I don't. My . . ." He lowered his head so that she couldn't see his hazel eyes. "When I married my wife, I married into her family. She owned our wigwam and everything inside it. Had we had any children,"—his voice seemed to strain as he spoke—"they would have been hers as well. Among the woodland tribes women are voting members of the village, of the clan, of the entire Algonquian-speaking nation. Not only are they the mothers of our children, but often the chiefs and medicine women of our people."

"Our," Alexandra said softly. "You said *our people.*"

"My friend here considers himself one of them," Jon offered. "The Shawnee adopted him."

"Adopted?"

"He became one of them, as if of their blood. It's a strange notion these native Americans have. They think that by saying a man is their brother, it makes it so."

"I never knew such things! I'm impressed."

Hunter had an odd look on his face, as if he was greatly surprised by her words. "You really are, aren't you?"

"I've never known anything about any other cultures before," she said as Hunter lifted a low-hanging branch to keep it from striking her in the face and she ducked beneath his arm. As she straightened, his hand brushed her back in a strangely intimate way. "These people seem rather civilized for naked heathens."

"Naked they may be in midsummer, but

heathens, certainly not. Many of them have been Christianized. They seemed to have managed to accept the white man's God while still retaining their own ancient culture.''

"So why did they adopt you? Why do they call you one of their own, these Shawnee?''

He reached out to scratch the mule behind the ears. "No reason in particular.''

"No reason, hell.'' Jon tossed the stick he'd been carrying. It made a terrible racket as it whirled end over end through the treetops. "He saved the lives of an entire village a couple of winters ago.''

"Did you?'' Alexandra found herself staring up at Hunter's handsome broad face again.

"I didn't save their lives, I just helped them out a little.''

"The whole bunch had come down with the smallpox and no one was well enough to fetch food and water. They were dying. Hunter nursed them back to health. He fetched water for them to drink, bathed them, hunted for them and fed them until they were well enough to care for themselves.''

She saw Hunter's cheeks grow pink. She couldn't resist a smile. A modest man! She had thought the two words contradictory in meaning! "It was a noble thing to do.''

"No it wasn't.'' He looked at her, his eyes seeming to gaze deep into the soul of her thoughts. "It was the right thing to do. You'd have done the same, put in the situation. As would Jon. As would any decent human being.''

"The hell I would have. I've never had the

pox." Jon rapped a tree with his knuckles. "Knock on wood. I'd have swept my tail out of there."

Hunter pointed to his companion. "Jon likes to think of himself as a bit of a rogue, maybe even a little crazy. He doesn't want anyone to know he's a good man at heart."

Alexandra nodded, a smile playing on her lips. She was enjoying this easy banter. No one had ever spoken with her like this before. No one had ever made her feel so comfortable. The relationship Jon and Hunter had was obviously good, and she was jealous. They loved each other as she always imagined friends should love. Why hadn't she ever had a friend to love? Was it her sharp tongue, as her parents observed, or was it because she wasn't the kind of person anyone could truly care for?

"There's a small spring up ahead." Hunter shifted the weight of his bow and musket, both of which he carried on his back within easy reach. "We'll stop there for a drink and a few minutes' rest. We're still going to have to move along at a good clip if we're to make it to the village by sunset."

The spring Hunter spoke of was barely more than a bubble of water coming up out of the rocky ground. There was a low streambed stretching out from it, but it obviously had been dry a long time.

Alexandra kneeled and cupped her hands, drinking greedily. The water was so cold that it was sharp on her tongue, but it tasted heavenly. She splashed some on her face and neck as she turned to watch the two men start off into the woods.

"Where are you going?" she asked uneasily.

"Just going to take a quick look around," Jon answered. "Sit down and rest. It's going to be a long day. We'll be right back." His voice was calm and easy, but as he spoke he lifted a spare musket off the pack animal's back and checked to be certain it was loaded.

"Don't leave me long," Alexandra murmured, trying not to sound frightened. "Two Crows could be lurking out there."

"Two Crows is gone, I told you," Hunter said as he disappeared into a hedge thick with greenbriars. "He's taken his fingers and hightailed it home."

Alexandra took another long sip of water and then sat up to wait for the men. She could still hear Jon moving through the brush. Hunter, as usual, made not a sound.

A whippoorwill called out from somewhere high in the tree limbs and Alexandra smiled at the sound of its shrill voice. She had never thought she would admit it, but this wilderness forest was breathtakingly beautiful. At every turn there seemed to be something new to see, to hear, even to taste.

Now that she had accepted the fact that it would take her a little longer to get back to Annapolis, she was actually beginning to enjoy the journey. So what if it was going to take her a few more days to reach home? What was there waiting for her anyway? Only an old man with a bulbous nose and bad breath.

Alexandra heard the snap of a twig and looked

up. The sound had come from somewhere down the dry streambed. "Hunter? Jon?" She rose. "Is that you?"

For a moment there was silence, but then she heard movement again. She was certain of it this time.

Alexandra took a few steps back and bumped into the mule. She brushed her hand over the packs on his back, wishing one of the men had left her some sort of weapon to defend herself.

"Hello?" She strained to see what or who was approaching and then gave a sudden strangled cry of fear.

A bear. It was a bear, headed straight for her, not more than a hundred feet away.

"H . . . Hunter. J . . . Jon," she called out.

She stumbled backward and tried to push the mule out of her way. The bear caught sight of her movement.

"No," she whispered. "No, bear. I won't hurt you. I won't—"

The black bear suddenly reared on its hind legs, standing over seven feet tall, and opened its massive jaws in a thundering growl. The mule behind Alexandra brayed in fear, kicked up its heels, and took off, plowing into the thick brush. Alexandra had a mind to follow, but she knew she'd never make it through the thick greenbriars she had backed her way into. Behind her she could still hear the mule braying as it pushed its way through the seemingly impenetrable wall.

Alexandra took the last half step back, her gaze locked on the bear's snapping jaws. It was close enough now for her to smell its strong, musky scent. She could swear she could feel its hot breath on her face.

The enraged animal was now stalking her, staggering back and forth on its hind legs as it came closer and closer.

There was no way for Alexandra to escape. No way to defend herself against the animal she had provoked in no way. It was going to kill her, she knew that. It was going to tear her limbs from her body with its steel jaws and sharpened yellow claws . . .

"Hunter!" Alexandra screamed one last time. "Hunter! Help me!"

Alexandra heard a blood-curdling scream and then suddenly Hunter was behind the bear, waving his arms and babbling like a rabid madman. Hunter had on nothing but his moccasins and one of those revealing loincloths all of the Indians wore. He carried no pistol, no knife, no weapon but a stick that was as big around as his wrist and the length of one sinewy arm.

"*M'kwah! Mat ath eeth ee, M'kwah!*" he screamed, waving the stick. "*M'kwah!*" He struck the animal on its rear quarters and it bellowed in almost humanlike protest and whirled around.

Slowly the black bear moved away from Alexandra to face the red-haired man that taunted him.

Alexandra's eyes widened. "Hunter! Take care!"

Jon appeared out of the brush and slipped past the bear and Hunter who were now slowly turning in a circle, determining who was to be prey and who predator.

"Shoot him!" Alexandra cried at Jon. "Shoot the bear before he kills Hunter!"

But Jon kept his musket lowered, putting himself between Alexandra and the bear. "Hush," he whispered. "Don't want to break his concentration." He turned to give her a silly smirk. "The bear's."

"Are you both madmen?" she shouted in fury, striking him in the shoulder. "The damned thing's going to kill him! For the love of God will you shoot?"

But all he did was lift an arm to defend another blow. "Let's see how he does," he told her, seeming to think the entire situation was somehow funny.

"M'kwah!" Hunter taunted, circling the bear. "M'kwah mat ath eeth ee!"

Alexandra tried to advance forward, to somehow help Hunter, but Jon held her back. "What's he saying?" she demanded above the howls of the bear.

"I'm not sure, my Shawnee's rather poor, but I think he's calling him an ugly son of a dog-faced whore." Jon laughed aloud, striking his knee with his hand as he watched.

"I can't believe this is happening," Alexandra muttered, left with no choice but to watch. "I just can't believe it."

Hunter was now moving in toward the bear in a slow, graceful action that seemed absurdly out of place here in the wilderness. Every muscle beneath his nearly nude sun-bronzed skin rippled with his movements so that it seemed almost like a dance. His thick, sinewy arms, his broad chest, even his muscled legs leading up to his bare buttocks moved together in fluid motions.

"Hunter," she whispered.

Now it seemed the man was stalking the bear . . .

Another step closer and Hunter tossed the stick aside.

Alexandra bit down on her lower lip to keep from crying out. The bear was a full head taller than Hunter and was now pressing down on him.

Then Hunter lifted his arms. He drew back his lips to bare his teeth and roared much like the bear.

Alexandra could do nothing but stand back and watch in awe as the black bear roared back.

Then Hunter did it again. He growled like the beast.

The bear took half a step back. Hunter growled again. The bear growled again, but with less conviction this time. Hunter shouted something in the strange tongue he had spoken in before and growled once more.

Then, to Alexandra's utter amazement, the bear dropped down on its four feet.

Hunter growled one last time, his voice frighteningly primal, and the bear turned and ran back in the direction it had come.

Alexandra ran toward Hunter. "Hell's bells!" she cried before she even reached him. "What in God's living name did you think you were doing?"

Chapter Six

Hunter took a deep breath, his mouth widening into a grin as he slapped his bare chest with his palm. "Damnation, I love to win!"

"Are you daft?" Alexandra demanded, circling him. "You could have been killed! No, no, that would have been simple, that would have been easy. You could have been maimed! That bear could have ripped your arms and legs off! You could have lain here in the grass and died bleeding from your belly!" She dropped her hands to her hips, panting. "Why didn't you kill it? Tell me that, will you?" She stared at him, determined to get an answer.

Hunter touched the shiny copper-band earring in his ear, as she noticed he often did when taking his sweet time in answering her. Standing in front of her nearly nude in the heat of the day, his muscular chest heaving from exertion, his hazel eyes bright with adrenalin, she found him strangely attractive. It was crazy. She knew it was crazy. For God's sake, he was crazy! But as she stood an arm's length from him waiting for her answer she wondered what it would be like to be this man's woman, his wife . . . his lover.

"Well," she demanded, alarmed by her thoughts. "What have you to say for yourself?"

Hunter threw back his head and laughed, his rich voice echoing in the sumac treetops above. "If I didn't know better, I'd think you were concerned for my welfare, you mouthy wench!"

"Concerned for your welfare, the blast! I didn't want to have to help Jon dig your thumping grave!" she shouted, infuriated again.

Jon came up behind her and tossed Hunter a water skin. "You're getting better," Jon told his companion, a lazy smile on his face. "Only took you, two, two and a half minutes this time."

Alexandra's eyes widened. She looked from Jon, to Hunter who was pouring water into his mouth, letting a little dribble down his bare chest, and back at Jon again. "You mean he does this all the time?"

Jon shrugged. "Not all the time. I mean he doesn't seek them out . . ." He looked at Hunter, his forehead crinkling. "You're not out looking for these damnable bears are you, Hunter?"

He grinned, wiping the water across his chest with a sweeping hand. "Of course not," he joked. "Bears are dangerous. Ferocious. They can rip a man limb from limb!"

Alexandra spun around. He was making fun of her. She knew he was. "Crazy," she muttered beneath her breath, stretching her legs into long strides. "The both of you are crazier than May butter. Crazier than a pair of bedlamites, crazier than, God, I don't know!"

"Where are you going?" Hunter called after her, his laughter mixing with Jon's.

"To find the mule," she shouted back over her shoulder. "Because the sooner we can get to that village, the sooner I can get away from you two lunatics!"

Alexandra could still hear their laughter as she disappeared into the brush, following the mule's trail.

For the remainder of the day, Alexandra walked in a silence that echoed in her own ears. Several times Jon tried to make conversation, but she told him to leave her alone. She was tired and she was confused.

Hunter was crazy. That was obvious; after all, only a crazy man would fight off a charging bear by growling at it. But the thought that she found this growling man attractive was what was really bothering her.

Alexandra brushed back a lock of tangled hair, forcing herself to keep walking. She had reached a point beyond exhaustion. When she took into consideration the time she had spent wandering through the wilderness with Two Crows, she figured she'd been walking around in circles in the middle of nowhere for nearly a month.

How could her life have taken such a turn so quickly? Six months ago she had been in her father's house, bored, but comfortable. She still had parties to attend—no one dared not invite the Earl of Monthrop's daughter, whether they liked her or not. She had chambermaids to draw her bath, manservants to make her tea, ladies' maids to dress her. Her only concern in life had been her lack of a suitable prospect in marriage. Now suddenly she was thousands of miles from home, fighting for survival.

What would the men who had turned down her father's handsome dowries think of her now? She almost smiled at the thought. They'd probably have been more adamant in their refusals. After all, wouldn't any decent young Englishwoman have lain down and died that morning on the boat on the river? No decent woman would have fought the way Alexandra did. No decent woman would have come with men like Hunter and Jon.

Suddenly Alexandra realized that the two ahead of her had stopped in their tracks. They were listening, though for what, she didn't know.

She stopped too. All she could hear was the sway of the trees, the rustle of the leaves, and a squirrel scurrying across a branch over her head. All she could hear were the sounds of the forest around her, and her own breathing.

"What is it?" she called in a loud whisper.

Jon brought his finger to his lips and then reached for a musket protruding from one of the leather packs on the mule. A shiver crept up Alexandra's spine. Jon didn't usually carry a weapon. It seemed that was Hunter's role. So why did Jon suddenly see the necessity?

She glanced around. She saw nothing unusual. They were traveling on a game path, as they had since the morning they left Two Crows at the trading post. The usual blend of deciduous and evergreen trees stretched high above their heads, bending to block out part of the sun's light as well as its warmth. She saw the usual assortment of rabbits, squirrels and birds that she had grown used to in the last weeks, animals she actually took pleasure in seeing as of late.

But something had set the forest out of balance. Something was different. She could almost feel it.

Alexandra walked up to Jon. "What is it?" she whispered.

"Hunter thinks—"

Jon's words were silenced by a spine-tingling screech. Suddenly, an Indian appeared out of the treetops above. He descended through the air and landed on Hunter's back. Hunter hollered, startled as he swung around, the wild Indian latched onto his back.

Alexandra almost screamed, but she clamped her hand over her mouth, afraid the sound of her voice would distract Hunter.

Jon grabbed Alexandra's arm and pulled her back out of the way of the tussling men, but made no attempt to aide his friend.

"Aren't you going to do something?" she cried, watching as the Indian wrestled the musket out of Hunter's arms and threw it to the ground. "Help him, for God's sake! It's not a bear! He can't growl at him! He's going to kill him!"

With the half-naked Indian still on his back,

Hunter whirled around and around, trying to use his momentum to dislodge the heathen. The redskin was babbling in his own tongue and whooping loud enough to wake the dead.

Hunter shouted and grunted, his own voice matching his opponent's.

Alexandra shoved Jon forward. "Help him! Get the beast off his back!"

Jon lowered his musket, butt down, and leaned on it. "Best just to let Hunter handle himself. Bears and wild Shawnee. He gets aggravated when I intrude. Besides"—he shrugged—"there's just one of them. I join in and it would be an unfair fight."

Alexandra looked at Hunter, fighting for his life and then back at Jon. What was wrong with him that he wouldn't help his friend in such grave danger?

Without thinking Alexandra lunged forward.

"Alexandra!" Jon called, "Stop!"

But she was too fast for him. She darted across the game path and grabbed the musket Hunter had lost in the scuffle. She contemplated shooting the redskin off his back, but only for an instant. If she missed, she'd kill Hunter.

Instead, she swung the heavy musket around and brought the carved wooden stock down on the Indian's black-haired head. He fell like a stone.

"Jesus!" Hunter swung around to see Alexandra place one foot square on his attacker's chest and raise the musket butt to strike him again. "I don't know if you understand English, but I don't care," she threatened. The Indian stared up at her with round, dark eyes, slightly dazed by her blow. "But, you move, and I'll brain you, I swear to God I will."

Hunter burst into laughter. Then Jon. Then the black-eyed Indian.

Alexandra pulled her foot off the laughing Indian's chest and took a step back, the musket still raised over her shoulder.

She'd missed something. Why were the men laughing? Why was the redskin laughing? Was everyone in these godforsaken colonies as mad as May butter? Was she the only person in the wilderness that still had any sense?

Hunter came up behind her and gently took the musket from her hands. His voice was oddly soft in her ear. "It's all right, Alexandra. I think I can take over from here." He was obviously amused, but his tone was not unkind.

"What's going on?" She looked at the Indian who was trying to sit up. There was a gash above his left ear that was oozing blood. She looked up at Hunter. "You know him?" she asked, her voice suddenly deflated.

Hunter grinned. "Creeping Turtle, this is Alexandra." He swept a hand as if making a court introduction. "Alexandra, Creeping Turtle."

Alexandra brought her fingers to her lips. "Oh, God," she muttered. "He's your friend."

"A good friend." Hunter offered his broad palm and Creeping Turtle took it, rising to his feet.

"Greetings." Creeping Turtle nodded, running a hand over his wound, blinking to clear his head. "You are strong for a white woman. The bear clan could use you on their next hunting party."

Alexandra was mortified. He spoke English—well. She looked back at Hunter. "Well, how was I supposed to know! I . . . I thought," she stammered. "I thought he was one of Two Crows's men. I thought you were in danger. I thought he was trying to kill you. Jon . . . Jon wasn't going to help. I thought . . ." She let her words trail off into silence.

Hunter was still smiling. "You surprised me, Alex." He touched her cheek in a tender gesture that caught her completely off guard. "As foul a mood as you've been in all day, I'd have thought you'd have helped someone do me in." He was looking straight into her eyes, completely oblivious to the other two men. "Could it be you've taken a liking to me?"

It was the same soft, intimate tone he'd used the day before.

She tore her gaze from his, now completely confused, not just by Hunter's attention, but by her own physical reaction to him. Her stomach was suddenly filled with butterflies. Her mouth was dry, her palms damp.

"I'm so sorry . . . Creeping Turtle . . ." she apologized. "I thought you were trying to kill him. First the bear this morning. Then you. He's crazy, you know. He thinks he's immortal. I didn't mean—" Then a thought struck her and her tone changed to one of agitation. "Say, if you're his friend, why in heaven's name did you jump out of the trees and scare him like that? Why were you trying to hurt him?"

Jon stepped into the conversation. "Some kind of male thing, Alexandra. I've never understood it myself. The more one man likes another, the more often he tries to send him to his maker. Hunter once let a party of soldiers capture me thinking I was some renegade, Shawnee, hatchet murderer. They carried me back to their fort and locked me up. He left me in a horse stall for two days while he played cards with the soldiers before he finally sprang me."

Hunter and Creeping Turtle laughed as if it was still a good joke.

Alexandra shook her head. "You all deserve to be whacked in the head," she muttered.

Creeping Turtle nodded at Alexandra. "A brave woman, Hunter of the Shawnee. Is she yours?"

Hunter looked at Alexandra, his gaze seeming to pierce her soul for a moment's time. He looked back at the Indian. "Aye."

She sank her elbow hard into his side. "I am not! What makes you think you have the right to—"

"Want to buy her?" Hunter asked, lifting an eyebrow. "Give you a good price. A few otter pelts, a pouch of tobacco. Maybe a bear-claw necklace . . ."

Alexandra opened her mouth to speak again, but then thought better of it. Hunter was teasing her again. She didn't appreciate it, but she'd not let him bait her this time. He seemed to take too much pleasure in it.

When Hunter realized he'd not bested her this time, he laughed easily, his baritone voice echoing in her ears. He winked at her and then turned back to the men. "No takers? Guess I'm stuck with her then. No?"

Creeping Turtle and Jon laughed with him until Alexandra was chuckling too. God, it felt good to laugh. It felt good to be included like this.

"So tell me what brings you to my forest," Creeping Turtle said when their laughter had subsided. "You have promised for a long time to come, but I doubted I would ever see you so far west. You are like a blue crab, Hunter of the Shawnee. You like to stay near your great bay."

Hunter sobered. "Business, friend. I need to speak with your shaman, He-Who-Wishes."

Creeping Turtle lifted his red palm. "He-Who-Wishes is not here. He's gone across the great river to tend to a sickness, but he is expected home soon. I will escort you to my village and make you honored guests while you wait for our shaman. We will eat and dance and smoke my father and mother's pipe."

Hunter nodded in agreement and then touched Alexandra's arm lightly. "Not much farther," he assured her. "Once we reach the village I'll see that you have a bath and a comfortable place to sleep." He paused, but she knew he wanted to say something else. "I'm sorry to have had to drag you so far from home, but it's imperative that I speak with He-Who-Wishes. Winter is setting in and I vowed not to let another season pass with my wife's death yet to be avenged."

Without thinking, Alexandra found herself reaching out with her finger to touch the drop of drying blood in the corner of his mouth. His hazel eyes seemed green at this moment. His gaze held her spellbound. What was it about this man that drew her to him? Why against all reason did she like him, a man so unconventional? It made no sense.

Jon and Creeping Turtle had taken the mule and started down the path. Alexandra could hear them in the distance. Yet Hunter made no move to follow. He just stood there staring at her, a strange light in his eyes.

"Scary isn't it?" he whispered, his voice meant only for her ears.

"What?" she breathed, their gazes still locked in an embrace.

"This. Between you and me."

Her first impulse was to deny his words and the feeling that stirred in her belly, but she didn't. "I don't really like you," she said. "You're unstable. Maybe crazy."

"I don't want to like you. You talk too much. And you're too dangerous. I loved once. I vowed never to love again. Hurts too damned much."

"I loved once, in a silly girlish way."

"What happened?" he asked softly.

Alexandra was oblivious to her surroundings. It didn't seem to matter that she was in the middle of the wilderness with two Indians and a stranger. All she could hear was Hunter's soft, rich voice. All she could feel was the magnetism of his gaze that drew her in and enveloped her in a tingling warmth.

She shook her head. "I was supposed to marry him, though we never really met."

"You were in love with a man you never met?"

"I told you. It was girlish. An infatuation more than a love."

"He died?"

She thought of Geoffry Rordan, Viscount Ashton and smiled. "He left me at the altar in a manner of speaking. I never saw him again."

Hunter suddenly turned away. "That's unfortunate. We'd best hurry. The sun is setting."

Alexandra watched him walk away, trying not to be hurt by his sudden reserve. But the spell was broken and once again she felt the chasm between them.

"Wait! I'm coming," she called. And as she ran to catch up, she wondered if that tender exchange between her and Hunter had really taken place. Or had she just imagined it all?

The sun was just beginning to set over the treetops to the west as Alexandra and the men entered the Shawnee village. She was immediately surprised by the bombardment of sound and sights of the busy encampment.

There were dogs everywhere, barking and racing in circles at the sight of the new arrivals. Children ran in groups, much like the pups, laughing and all shouting at once as they approached the strangers to have a look.

The village swarmed with people as busy as bees in a beehive, all attending to evening chores. Two young women walked by just as Alexandra and the men stepped into the clearing. Both carried water in skins in each hand. They nodded to Creeping Turtle and then to his guests, then put their heads together and giggled as they went on. Several men walked out to meet Creeping Turtle and immediately fell into conversation with him. To Alexandra's amazement, Hunter spoke the Shawnee language and became an integral part of the conversation.

Jon hung back, standing beside Alexandra.

"He speaks the Indian language, but you don't?" she asked.

Jon shook his head. "A little, but he always had a gift for languages, even when we were children. The king's tongue is all I need." He lifted an eyebrow. "That and a few decent French oaths."

"Hunter said you were Shawnee. You didn't want to learn your own people's language?"

"Hunter speaks to them when communication is necessary. Besides, a good deal of them speak English these days anyway."

Alexandra nodded in fascination. She found herself constantly amazed by Hunter and Jon. It seemed as if their personalities were reversed. Hunter, the white man with his aristocratic nose and supposed fortune was the native American at heart. Jon, with his bronze skin and coal black hair, was the loyal Englishman.

Hunter took a step back. "We have been invited to stay. The accusations of Laughing Rain's family don't seem to matter. Creeping Turtle's uncle says the turtle clan of the Delaware were always a contrary bunch anyway." He glanced at Alexandra. "Creeping Turtle says his widowed sister would be more than happy to have you stay with her. The Shawnee are great ones for hospitality. I'm sure she'll make you comfortable."

Alexandra nodded, offering a faint smile. "I just want a place to sleep."

Creeping Turtle nodded to the two braves he had been speaking to and then turned to Alexandra, Jon and Hunter. "You must come meet my parents and then I'll see to finding you a meal. I know you must all be starved." He outstretched a hand. "This way to the wigwam of my father."

Creeping Turtle led them through a maze of dome-shaped huts, waving and speaking to friends and family as he went. Alexandra was amazed by the friendliness of the people as she made her way through the camp. Women and children stopped to speak. Someone pushed a tin cup of cool water into her hand. Another offered a wooden bowl of sweet dried berries for Alexandra to nibble on. The Shawnee seemed not to be in the least disturbed by the arrival of the white man and woman, in fact, they seemed to be excited by the thought of visitors.

On the outer edge of the camp, Creeping Turtle stopped. "Let me get my mother. Father will be home from his fishing trip soon."

He ducked inside the wigwam and a moment later came out leading an Indian woman. She was not particularly pretty in any usual sense of the word, but Alexandra thought her striking. She had the same dark eyes and black hair as everyone else in the camp, but there was something about her face that glowed with an inner beauty. She appeared to be no more than forty, which Alexandra knew was impossible, considering that Creeping Turtle had to be at least thirty.

"This is my mother, She-Who-Whispers-To-The-Wind," Creeping Turtle said proudly. He turned to his mother and began the introduction in Shawnee, but suddenly the woman drew her hands to her face and wailed.

Alexandra's eyes widened in surprise as the woman began to fling her arms wildly, babbling in her native tongue.

Creeping Turtle and Hunter both turned to Jon. Both appeared to be shocked by the Indian woman's words.

"What is it?" Alexandra asked Hunter. "What is she saying?"

Hunter nodded to his friend standing a few feet to his left. "She says," he murmured in disbelief, "that Jon is her long-lost son."

Chapter Seven

"Her son?" Alexandra whispered.

They all stared at Jon.

For a moment Jon didn't move. A myriad of emotions flashed across his face. Alexandra saw joy as well as sadness. But then he put on that charming smirk of his and the moment was lost.

"I'm flattered," he said, just a little too sure of himself. "But tell your mother she is mistaken. My parents are dead. Hunter's father found me wandering in the woods near Annapolis and took me home with him to England. I have no family."

Creeping Turtle took his mother's hand and spoke quietly in their native tongue. The woman listened without interruption, but then shook her head firmly. She spoke again. Hunter translated for both Jon and Alexandra.

"She-Who-Whispers-To-The-Wind says it is you who are mistaken, son. What mother does not know her own child, even if she has not seen him in thirty-odd years? She says a woman does not forget the blood of her blood she brought into this world in pain and joy and suckled at her breast."

Jon's dark eyes narrowed as he studied Creeping Turtle's mother. He crossed his arms over his chest defensively. "Ask her this—if I am her son, how is it that I was abandoned and left to die alone in the forest."

Hunter repeated Jon's words.

She-Who-Whispers-To-The-Wind brought her hand to her cheek to brush away her tears. She spoke softly.

Hunter turned back to Jon. "She says that you were not left, but taken."

"Taken?"

The Indian woman went on, adding hand signals to her explanation.

"She says," Hunter watched her as he spoke, "that their village was once much closer to the Great Bay than it is now. She says their village was raided by white men when her son Konah was but two winters. They were separated by fire and men on horses. She was carrying her sister's twins and her Konah disappeared in the smoke." Hunter's gaze met Jon's. "She says she never saw him again, but she knew he would be back one day."

Jon gave a little laugh, but it was obvious he saw nothing funny in the woman's words. "Could it be true?" he asked Hunter, still staring at the woman. "Could this be my mother?"

"I suppose she could be, Jon. All Father ever said was that he found you in the forest near Annapolis."

"But he said he looked for my parents," Jon murmured. "He said he tried to find them."

"Maybe he just couldn't find them," Alexandra offered gently.

Jon looked at Creeping Turtle. "If this old woman is my mother, then you and I are brothers?"

"Half," Creeping Turtle answered, resting an arm across his mother's shoulder. "My father, Listening Man, is not your father. He married my mother after you were lost."

Jon's gaze met that of the Indian woman's. "Who was my father, if you are indeed, my mother?"

Creeping Turtle asked the question in the Shawnee language. She-Who-Whispers-To-The-Wind answered hesitantly.

Creeping Turtle turned back to Jon. "She says your father is a white man. She loved him, but she was young and did not understand the consequences of falling in love with a man not of her own religion."

"And what became of my father?"

She-Who-Whispers-To-The-Wind spoke and Creeping Turtle translated. "She says he went away after you were born. She says he was ashamed of the color of his son's skin."

Jon turned away.

She-Who-Whispers-To-The-Wind walked to her son's side and laid a hand gently on his shoulder. She spoke softly, her words meant for no one but Jon.

Alexandra felt tears gather in the corners of her eyelids. It didn't matter that she couldn't understand what the woman was saying, and she knew that it didn't matter that Jon couldn't understand either. Her words were the words of a mother who thought her child lost forever, only to find him years later, a man.

Alexandra turned to Hunter. "She is his mother."

"What makes you say so?" Hunter questioned.

Again Alexandra felt the intimacy between her and Hunter that she had felt before. He honestly wanted to know what she thought. He honestly cared.

"A woman doesn't mistake her child." Alexandra spoke softly, from her heart. "Not even if she hasn't seen him for thirty years. A mother's intuition is very strong."

"And how would you know?" he teased. "You've never been a mother, have you?"

"No. But I'm a woman and women know these things." She smiled to herself. "I'd like to be a mother." Alexandra didn't know what it was about this man that made her feel so comfortable that she felt she could express such feelings. "I'd like to feel the way She-Who-Whispers-To-The-Wind must feel now."

"You, a mother?" Hunter caught her hand, surprising them both. "Somehow I didn't see you as the type of woman who would want of passel of brats at her heels."

"Just goes to show you that you might think you know me, but you don't."

Hunter wove his fingers through hers, studying the differences in skin color and texture. "I almost like you when you're like this."

She smiled. "Like what?"

"Thoughtful. Honest."

"I'm always honest."

He laughed, his rich voice pleasant in her ears. "I don't doubt you are, but it's hard for a man to get past that shrewish tongue of yours. You lash out and I automatically take a step back. It keeps me from hearing what you have to say."

She looked down at the ground. Creeping Turtle and his mother were now speaking quietly to Jon. Jon stood apart from them, listening, his arms crossed over his chest. Alexandra had Hunter all to herself and she liked it.

"My tongue. My father always claimed it was my greatest fault," Alexandra answered Hunter. "He said no one would ever marry me. He said no man wanted a harridan for a wife."

"I don't know. Perhaps a woman as beautiful as you could make a man see past the sharp tongue. We forget that the benefit of a sharp tongue is often a sharp wit."

"Something you may see as a well-liked quality," she quipped, "but most men see it as a fault. Men don't like women who are smarter than they are. I found that out the hard way."

"Depends on the man, and how smart he is."

When she looked at Hunter, he was smiling at her, a smile that made her stomach flutter nervously. Heavens, but he was a good-looking man when he was being nice.

"You just haven't found the right man," he went on softly.

"Maybe there isn't one for me."

He let go of her hand. "Nonsense. I found Laughing Rain in the middle of the wilderness, thousands of miles away from my home. I have a feeling God guides us in the right direction when it comes to these things."

At the mention of his wife, Alexandra felt herself stiffen. She was ashamed of herself. Jealous of a dead woman—how terrible. But jealous she was.

She looked at Hunter, who was watching her. Who was she kidding, with these silly word games and innocent flirtations? This man wasn't any more interested in her than any of the others had been. She was going to get herself into trouble if she didn't back off, she knew it.

"I really am tired," Alexandra said, looking away. "You said there would be a place for me to stay. Could you find out where?"

With a nod, Hunter went to Creeping Turtle. The men spoke briefly and then came back to her. Jon excused himself from the woman who claimed to be his mother and he walked with the others.

"Let me take you to my sister's wigwam," Creeping Turtle said, leading Alexandra through the maze of wigwams. "She will be pleased to have you as her guest." Creeping Turtle looked at Jon. "Wait until I tell her I have found our brother. Now our mother's heart is complete. You know, our people say a woman who loses her child can never be whole again."

"No offense meant to you or your mother, Creeping Turtle,"—Jon pulled a flask from beneath his buckskin waistcoat and took a long pull—"but I'm not convinced your mother is my mother. Seems pretty far-fetched to me."

Creeping Turtle chuckled. "It is not necessary for you to believe in us. Only for us to believe in you, my brother."

Jon rolled his eyes heavenward and took another drink from the flask. "Christ, I hope we're not staying here long," he muttered under his breath.

Hunter slapped his shoulder. "A day or two, no more and we'll be on our way. I swear it." He looked to Alexandra. "In the meantime we'll see what we can do about finding someone to escort her back to the world."

For some reason Alexandra felt hurt by the cool way he was suddenly referring to her. God, but she was confused. All reason told her to stay away from Hunter. But a part of her wouldn't seem to listen. She found herself wanting to be near him, to hear his voice, to feel his touch. *Just get me home safely,* she prayed silently. *Just get me away from here and him before I do something stupid.*

"Here is my sister's wigwam," Creeping Turtle declared, stopping at a hut that looked just like the others. He stuck his head inside. "She is not here, but go in. I will find my sister and send her to tend to you."

Alexandra hesitated at the doorway.

"It's all right," Hunter assured her. "I told you, the Shawnee are great ones for hospitality. His sister really will be glad to have you."

Alexandra ducked to walk in, but then turned back to Hunter. "Where are you going?"

"Just to Creeping Turtle's wigwam to smoke his tobacco. I'll come by and check on you later." He reached out and brushed her cheek with his fingertip. "You'll be all right, Alex. I swear it."

She gave him a half smile and let the doorflap fall.

The wigwam seemed bigger to Alexandra once she was inside. The structure was built from tall saplings bent to form a frame, and the walls were constructed from woven saplings and bark shingles. It was cozy inside, made warm by a fire that glowed in the center of the room. A thin whisper of fragrant smoke rose and escaped through a small hole in the bark roof.

Alexandra turned to look at all the dried vegetables and herbs that hung from the ceiling. A section of the wall was lined with baskets filled with squash, shelled corn, and assorted tubers. Along another part of the wall was a platform bed piled with thick furs and covered, oddly enough, with an embroidered counterpane that looked much like the one covering Alexandra's own bed back in Annapolis.

Alexandra heard the faint tinkling of bells and swung around. "Oh!"

"I'm sorry, I startled you," said the woman dressed in a leather vest and leggings standing in the doorway. "I didn't mean to." When she spoke, her bell earrings tinkled with the movement of her head. "I'm Judith."

Alexandra stared at the woman in the doorway. She was a white woman! A white woman with long red hair braided like the other Indian women's in the village. "I . . . I'm Alexandra. I . . . Creeping Turtle said for me to wait here for his sister."

She smiled. "I am his sister. Sister by marriage. My husband was his brother. He's dead now, but among the Shawnee we will always be family. Please sit." She indicated a small mat made of rabbit skins that had been sewn together. "I know you must be hungry."

Alexandra sat down. "Just a little maybe." She still stared at the woman.

Judith smiled as she knelt in front of the fire and stirred a small metal pot. A delicious, meaty aroma rose in the air. "Yes, I am a white woman," she said as if reading Alexandra's thoughts. "But I'm also Shawnee." She took a wooden spoon and began to dish out a healthy portion of chunky stew. She pushed the plate into Alexandra's hand and handed her a pewter spoon. "Surprised to see another white woman here, are you?"

Alexandra nodded. "We're so far from the bay and any towns. How did you get here? Are you a prisoner?"

Judith laughed and the bells in her ears rang. "Heavens no! My husband has been dead nearly a year. I could have left the day he died, could have left sooner. No, I choose to live here among the Shawnee."

Alexandra took a bite of the stew. It was a delicious concoction of tender meat and vegetables with a touch of an unfamiliar spice. She took another bite. "You came here to marry an Indian?"

"Not quite. I was captured by Mohawks north of Penn's colony. My husband saved me. I was nearly dead. He brought me here and healed me."

"But he wouldn't take you home to your family?"

Judith shrugged, dishing out a bowl of stew for herself. "By the time I had recovered enough to travel I didn't want to go home." She smiled a bittersweet smile. "I had fallen in love with a Shawnee brave."

Alexandra shook her head in amazement. "I cannot imagine loving someone so much that you would stay here with him, live like this for him."

"You mistake my intentions. They were clearly selfish. The truth was that I did love my husband. But the best thing about staying here was that my life among the Shawnee was better than the life I'd had in Philadelphia."

"You were bonded?"

She laughed. "No. Worse, I think. I was a shipping merchant's eldest daughter. I had more gowns than I could wear in a season. I went to every tea, every ball, every horse race, within ten square miles of Philadelphia." She added another heaping spoonful of stew to Alexandra's empty bowl. "But I was unhappy. My life was without purpose." Alexandra popped a chunk of dripping meat into her mouth. "Here I have a reason to exist. I'm teaching the children the white man's language so they can become a part of the world they're being forced to become a part of. Here I have friends and family who love me. Here I'm happy, something I could never say about Philadelphia."

Alexandra took another bite of stew, not knowing what to say. She couldn't imagine an educated Englishwoman choosing this kind of life. It seemed an impossibility, yet here Judith was.

"Tell me how you come to be in our village." Judith set aside her bowl and reached out for a tiny china teapot resting on a rock near the edge of the fire.

"I was captured and rescued too, only they, Hunter and Jon, were supposed to take me back to Annapolis. But Hunter said he had to come here first. Someone killed his wife, a soldier, and he's trying to find him." Finished with her stew, she set her bowl down next to Judith's.

Judith handed her a delicate handle-less teacup filled with steaming tea. "The villagers speak of a white called the Hunter of the Shawnee. They respect him a great deal. I've never had the pleasure of meeting him. He's here?"

"With Creeping Turtle."

"He has quite a reputation among the Shawnee. They say he is a very brave man."

Alexandra gave a little laugh, sipping from her teacup. "Brave? Insane I would say. As wild as weeds in a rose garden. He's impulsive. Without manners or any sense of decorum. It's no doubt they like him. He's more of a savage than any other savages I've come across." Alexandra knew that wasn't quite true. Not when she took into consideration the way Two Crows and his men had butchered her cousin and uncle.

Judith smiled. "I think I'd like to meet this Hunter of the Shawnee."

"Alexandra," Hunter called from outside the wigwam. "May I come in?"

Alexandra looked at the woman sitting cross-legged across the campfire from her. "It's him," she said.

Judith got up and laid aside her teacup. She swept back the animal-skin covering on the door, greeting Hunter with a warm, friendly smile. "Come in, Hunter of the Shawnee. We were just speaking of you. I was telling Alexandra of the respect our people have for you."

Hunter stepped in. "I'm sure you exaggerate." He nodded. "You must be Judith. I just came to check on Alex. She's had a difficult journey."

Alexandra watched as Judith's green-eyed gaze settled on Hunter's handsome face. "She was just telling me how fortunate she was that you came along and saved her from the Iroquois." She smiled a smile Alexandra had seen many a time in drawing rooms across the city of London. And she didn't like the smile. Not one bit.

"Come in and join us for tea." Judith swept her hand. "I have something stronger if you like."

Hunter smiled casually at Judith, seeming to take an immediate liking to her. Alexandra couldn't remember him smiling at *her* like that. "No. Thank you. I'd like to, but Creeping Turtle and Jon are waiting for me. I guess you heard from Creeping Turtle that She-Who-Whispers-To-The-Wind thinks my companion is her son."

"Amazing how life makes its turns on the game path, isn't it?"

"I suppose it is." He pushed back a lock of red hair that had fallen loose from his queue. "Well, guess I'll be on my way. I just wanted to make sure you were settled, Alexandra."

"Judith has been very kind," was all she could think to say in response.

Hunter backed out of the door. "Just get a good night's sleep." He nodded to Judith. "Thank you for seeing to her. I would take it as a personal favor if you see she's well cared for. She's been through a hell of an ordeal. It would be good for her to speak with another woman."

"I'll see to her every need, I can promise you."

Alexandra listened irritably as they spoke about her as if she weren't there, or as if she were an infant.

Judith was still smiling at him.

"Good night," he said as he backed out of the wigwam.

Judith let the flap fall over the doorway and then swung around to face Alexandra. "He's a fine specimen of a man, indeed. Is he yours?"

Alexandra nearly choked on a mouthful of tea. "My what?"

"Your man."

Alexandra gave a laugh. "Certainly not."

"You're sure? I'm not a woman to take another woman's man, not even a man as fine as Hunter."

Alexandra gulped down the last of her tea. "I said he's not *mine*." She didn't mean to sound cross. It was just that she was tired. When she spoke again, she softened her voice. "I told you. He was kind to me, and for that I'm grateful. But we're only traveling together."

Judith broke into a grin. "Then that means I'm free to seek his company?"

Alexandra let her eyes drift shut, rubbing her forehead. Suddenly her head was pounding. "Certainly. I wouldn't have that man." She exhaled. "Not for all the sugar cane in the West Indies."

Chapter Eight

Despite Judith's attempts to make Alexandra comfortable, Alexandra slept fitfully that night. Her dreams were filled with swirling visions of Hunter and the black bear, of Uncle Charles and Cousin Susan, of Two Crows and his filthy comrades. And in the misty shadows of her mind, Alexandra saw Geoffry Rordan dancing, dancing with woman after woman, laughing . . . laughing at her. His laughter echoed in her mind, mixing with the sound of Cousin Susan's tortured screams, of Two Crows cackling, of Hunter's voice until her head was filled with madness.

Alexandra bolted upright, clutching Judith's counterpane to her chest. She could feel her heart pounding beneath her breast. Sweat beaded on her forehead, despite the chilly morning air. The music of the ballroom still reverberated in her head.

Pale light seeped through the hole in the wigwam ceiling, illuminating Judith's sleeping face. She slept naked, her attractive, slender body curled comfortably in a ball on the center of a pile of skins, a light coverlet thrown over her body.

Alexandra rolled onto her side, away from Judith, and closed her eyes again. But sleep evaded her. Her mind was too filled with thoughts for sleep.

Hunter said that he would find an Indian guide to take her back to Annapolis, but did she trust an Indian to see her home safely? How did she know her guide wouldn't surrender her to the first unfriendly man, red or white, they came upon in the forest?

Alexandra wondered if once Hunter talked to the medicine man, he wouldn't head back toward Annapolis. Maybe he would take her home. She trusted him, though she didn't know why.

Because he had rules he lived by. They were not her rules; they didn't make sense to her, but they were the rules he guided his life by. If he agreed to see her home safely, he'd keep his word. And once they reached Annapolis, Alexandra could see that Aunt Sally paid him handsomely for his trouble.

Of course if he was as wealthy as Jon hinted, would the money be enough to convince him to see her home himself? Maybe, maybe not.

Then she wondered why she wanted Hunter to take her home. Was it because she had trusted him this far and felt she could trust him all the way back to Annapolis? Or was it because she wanted to prolong her time with him? The thought, of course, was absurd. Or was it?

Alexandra sat up, swinging her legs onto the

leather flooring. It was obvious she wasn't going to be able to go back to sleep. She glanced at her hostess, still sleeping, her arm thrown casually across her forehead, her naked body barely covered by the coverlet, stretched out in plain view.

Alexandra pushed aside the counterpane and rose quietly. What she needed was a walk. She had always been an early riser. In her father's home she had often risen even before the house servants so that she might have a few minutes alone in the house or garden before they became overrun with footsteps and voices.

Slipping her feet into her moccasins, Alexandra lifted the flap covering the doorway of the wigwam and stepped into the morning light. The autumn air was refreshingly brisk and smelled faintly of pine and wood smoke. There were a few villagers just beginning to move about, but for the most part the Shawnee village still slumbered peacefully.

Alexandra stepped over a sleeping spotted dog in Judith's doorway and started toward the river she had been to last night. She thought she'd wash her face in the cold water and then just sit for a while. The spot in the river, a tributary of the Ohio, Judith had explained, had seemed tranquil last night, even in the darkness.

As Alexandra passed a wigwam, an older woman in a long buckskin dress called to her.

Though Alexandra didn't understand what the woman said in the Shawnee tongue, Alexandra could tell by the tone of her voice that it was a greeting. She nodded, pleased that everyone seemed to be going out of their way to make her feel welcome. "Good morning to you."

The Shawnee woman went back to stirring a pot and Alexandra smiled to herself as she walked on. *How comfortable life must be for these people,* she thought. *Everyone seems so relaxed and content. Everyone is so friendly, even to me, a stranger and a white woman.*

Alexandra passed between the many wigwams, through the village, and followed the path cut through the undergrowth that led down the riverbank. Sparrows fluttered overhead as she stepped into the clearing. Ahead, the moving water gurgled and splashed as it made the bend in the riverbed, flowing south.

Kneeling by the water's edge to splash her face, Alexandra thought about how, in many ways, this Indian garb of Hunter's she was wearing was quite sensible. True, it left one's legs shamelessly bare, but Alexandra could never have managed to kneel so easily in one of her gowns. With her stays laced as tightly as her mother expected, it was all she could do to manage a breath of air!

Taking a drink of water from her cupped hands, she sat back on a flat stone, apparently left for just that reason.

Heavens but this forest was beautiful! She chuckled at the sight of a pair of squirrels fighting over half a walnut.

When she heard rich laughter from behind, she turned around. She knew it was Hunter.

"Startled you again?"

She shook her head. "I think I've gotten used to

your sneaking about."

He made his way down to the riverbed, a small basket swinging from his hand. "You've paid heed to my warnings. You've become more observant. I just wish Jon would as well." He set a piece of mirror on a tree branch and then pulled out a cake of soap and a long razor.

Alexandra watched, strangely fascinated by his morning ablutions. She'd never watched a man shave before. He splashed water on his face, soaped his chin and cheeks, and began to scrape away his red whiskers.

"I think I may have found someone to take you to Annapolis," he said in an offhand manner after several moments of silence.

"You did?"

He glanced at her in the reflection of the piece of mirror propped on the branch. "You don't sound as anxious as you did yesterday. Sitting rooms, boned stays, and tight shoes not quite as inviting as they once were?"

"Oh, it's not that. It's not that I don't want to go home." She toyed with the fringe of her tunic. "It's just that I'm a little . . . concerned about going off in the woods with some savage, even if he is a Shawnee." She glanced back up to see that he was still watching her. "You know, after what I've been through with Two Crows I don't know if I would feel comfortable crossing this wilderness with an Indian."

"So, what?" He arched a dark eyebrow. "You're going to find your own way home? Or have you decided to remain here with the Shawnee as Judith has? She seems to have made herself very content."

Alexandra didn't like the tone of his voice when he spoke the woman's name. He was attracted to her.

"Remain here? Certainly not!" she huffed. "But you brought me all the way out here, don't you think you ought to see that I get home in one piece?"

He laid aside his razor, done shaving, and knelt to splash water on his smooth cheeks. "I thought you couldn't wait to rid yourself of my company."

"I can't." She let out an audible sigh. "It's just that at the moment . . . at the moment you seem the lesser of the evils. I already know what kind of man you are."

He turned around, his hazel-eyed gaze settling on her face. "No, no you don't," he said sharply. "You don't know me at all."

She looked down at her hands folded neatly in her lap. "I know that you're tracking some man down so you can kill him. But I also know that you saved me from Two Crows, twice," she conceded quietly.

"So?"

"So, I figure my best chances of getting back to Annapolis alive are with you—and Jon."

He shook his head slowly, his cheeks glistening with water. "I'm no escort. I told you, I'm searching for my wife's killer."

"I know that, but he's a soldier, isn't he? Surely he's not this far west. Surely once you talk to this medicine man, you're going to have to head east again. Couldn't I just . . . tag along?"

"I don't think so, Alex." He began to put his shaving things back in the basket. "I think you'd best just go alone with Creeping Turtle's cousin."

"Why?"

Picking up his basket, he walked up to her. She rose up off the rock. For a moment they said nothing, their gazes locked.

"Why?" he asked.

"Why?" she repeated softly. "Why don't you want me with you?"

He exhaled slowly, as if measuring his words. She could tell that he wanted to look away, but he didn't. "All right, hell's fire, I'll admit it. I'm attracted to you, Alex. That's why I want you to go. I'm attracted to you and I don't want to be. The sooner you're gone, the sooner I'll forget you."

She glanced down at her moccasined feet, completely taken off guard by his words—and just a little flattered. "I don't know what to say."

"For once in your life, don't say anything. Just go with Creeping Turtle's cousin. It's like Jon said, I'm trouble."

"A man who says he's attracted to a woman so he wants her to go away. What an oddity." She laughed a little and when she looked up he was reaching out to touch her.

He stroked the curve of her chin with his index finger. "This . . . it just wouldn't be a good idea, Alex."

"Why?" she asked softly, not knowing what made her so bold. "Why isn't it a good idea?"

He dropped his hand. His hazel eyes were piercing. Alexandra's hand ached to reach out and touch a lock of the brilliant red hair that fell across his broad shoulder.

"I'm not Jon. I'm not interested in dalliances."

"Neither am I," she answered. "I've been a part of that dance one too many times."

"I'll not have another woman," he said. "I loved once and I lost her. It just hurt too damned much, can't you understand that? I'm just not cut of the cloth a man must be for romance."

"Better to leave that to me," Jon called, seeming to appear from nowhere.

Alexandra took a step back, annoyed by Jon's presence; annoyed that he'd broken the spell between her and Hunter. What was Hunter trying to say? That he was attracted in more than a sexual way? That he liked her enough to . . . no, that couldn't have been what he was saying. She must have misunderstood.

Hunter cleared his throat. "Jon—wondered when the hell you were going to get out of bed. Day's half over already."

Jon smiled lazily as he came to stand between the two of them. "Creeping Turtle sent me to find you. The shaman is back."

Hunter turned away. "Guess I'd best get back then. I'll speak to Creeping Turtle about that guide," he called to Alexandra over his shoulder.

She watched him disappear into the trees. Once again, she felt the twinges of jealousy. She knew it was crazy, but she wanted Hunter to care about her and her plight, not the dead woman.

Jon shook his head and headed down toward the water. "I warned you, Alex."

Reluctantly she turned her gaze from the direction in which Hunter had disappeared, and she watched Jon kneel and wash his face. "Warned me how?"

"Hunter. I told you. He's no ladies' man. Not like me."

She gave a little laugh. "What makes you think I'm interested in Hunter? The man is completely unsuitable, rich and titled or not—which I have to admit I question the validity of."

"Pretend you're not attracted to him if you like, but I'm telling you, you're only going to get hurt going for a man like Hunter." He stood and dried his face with a square of linen he carried over his shoulder. "Now me. I'm a man you can lay money on." He gave her a sideways grin. "I'd have you in a minute."

She laughed at the absurdity of his statement.

"Go ahead, laugh, but consider this. I'm headed back for England. Hunter can stay and play Indian if he likes, but I've had enough. Hunter's father has graciously given me a handsome allowance. With good luck at the gaming tables you and I could live quite comfortably in a nice apartment in Covent Gardens. Fine clothes, the best wines, important friends . . ."

She couldn't help smiling. The man was mad! "You're asking me to be your wife?"

It was his turn to laugh. "Of course not! I think both of us are too smart for that. Be my mistress. I'll treat you well. Better than any man treats a wife. You know I would."

She shook her head in disbelief. A few weeks ago

she'd have been shocked. Appalled. But after all that had happened, it was just funny. Even a half-breed Indian bastard didn't want her for his wife!

"So what do you say?"

"You're serious, aren't you, Jon?"

"Damned serious. I told Hunter I'd stay with him until he catches Laughing Rain's killer, but then I'm a free man. If this shaman knows where to find the bastard, you and I could be sailing for England in a matter of a couple fortnights."

"I don't think so."

He walked toward her. "And why not? You like me, don't you?"

She couldn't resist his charm. "Of course I like you."

"So why not give it a whirl?" He stopped only a foot from her. "I'm a damned fine lover. Take you to the stars and back."

She felt her cheeks color. She looked away. "Jon, it's not that I'm not flattered, but, but I want to marry. I want to have a home, children."

She heard him sigh. He reached out and gently touched her arm. "Don't take this the wrong way, sweetheart. I wouldn't hurt you for the world. But let's face the reality of your situation. What do you think the chances are some titled skip-Jack's going to marry you now?"

When she didn't say anything, he went on. "You were carried off by renegade scum. God knows what they did to you. Another man would care, but I don't. I don't even want to know."

"I told you. Nothing happened. They never touched me. Not that way."

He waved his hand as if to say the truth didn't matter. "Just listen to me. Then if that wasn't enough, you've been traveling with two rogues like Hunter and me. What will people think? What will they say?"

Alexandra felt a lump rise in her throat. She didn't want to hear this, not from Jon, not from anyone.

"It's just not going to happen, Alex. It's just not. You get back to Annapolis and that aunt of yours'll ship you back to papa to live out your life as an old maid. If he won't take you, which is likely if he's got other daughters to marry off, then you'll most like be bumped from distant relative to distant relative the rest of your days, always the topic of hushed whispers." He stroked her arm. "I just think that would be a waste of all that spirit you've got inside you."

She stook a step back. "No, Jon. I'll be no man's wagtail. Not yours, not anyone's."

"We'd make a hell of a pair. Turn London town on its ear. Just think about it, will you?"

She turned away and started for the path that led back to the camp. "I have. The answer's no. I'm not a trollop."

Jon ran to catch up with her, seemingly unoffended by her turndown. "Well, think about it just the same. You'd be making a big mistake not to. You might not get a better offer. You certainly won't from Hunter."

Afraid she would break into tears in front of Jon and embarrass herself, Alexandra broke away and ran for the village. God knew she wanted someone to love and be loved by, but damned if she'd be whore to any man! She'd die an old spinster before she did that!

Hunter inhaled deeply, filling his lungs with the fragrant, enveloping smoke of the clay pipe, and then handed it to the shaman's wife. She smiled, showing white teeth ground down by the years, as she accepted it.

He-Who-Wishes, the shaman of the village, watched his wife take a puff of the pipe.

Hunter had to smile. He thought of Laughing Rain and wondered if this was how he would have looked at her when they were well into the seventieth winter. It was funny, but as he watched the old couple, he felt none of the pain he had grown so used to feeling each time he was reminded of his dead wife. Did time truly heal the wounds of life as the Shawnee said?

Oddly, Alexandra's comely face flashed in his head. He heard her laughter echoing in his head. Alex? Was that it? Was that brave young woman a salve sent by God to heal his heart? He had to consider it a possibility. The Shawnee always said that Wishemoto worked in puzzling ways.

He-Who-Wishes tapped his clay pipe and Hunter looked up.

"Lost in thought?" the old man asked in his native tongue.

"Aye," Hunter replied, his Shawnee impeccable. "Lost in memories of the past. Good memories."

"Your wife." It was a statement, not a question.

Creeping Turtle had told Hunter that the old man knew things he shouldn't know. "My wife," Hunter echoed. "My dead wife." He lifted his gaze to meet the shaman's. The man's dark eyes had faded to the palest steel gray. "That's why I've come to you, sir. To ask for your help. I seek the man who raped my Laughing Rain, then murdered her and our unborn child."

"Yes, yes, all in time." He-Who-Wishes fluttered a wrinkled hand. "But first let us speak of the living. Tell me of the other woman."

"Other woman?" Hunter shook his head in confusion. "What other woman?"

"The one who now tugs at your soul. I know not her name but I see her eyes in yours. She troubles you?"

Hunter lowered his gaze. He didn't know that he was comfortable discussing this with a man he'd never laid eyes on before a few minutes ago. But He-Who-Wishes was a shaman, and that put him in a class above others. If the shaman was going to help him, he knew he must be open with him. It was the way of the Shawnee. "There is another woman."

The shaman's wife grinned. "What is man without woman?" She cackled. "Nothing. Nothing."

Hunter's gaze cut back to He-Who-Wishes. "Her name is Alexandra. A white woman."

The old man shrugged. "It is not her fault Wishemoto put her soul in the body of a white," he said with good humor. "Do not hold it against her just as I do not hold it against you. Not all can be as lucky as *The People.*"

Hunter had to smile. "I guess not. She was captured by a gaggle of Iroquois. They had her tied to a tree at a trading post off the Tuskit River. I rescued her and brought her along because I didn't have time to take her back to her home. I wanted to see you and head east again before the first snows."

"So what is it that troubles you about this white woman? Wishemoto has given her to you. You know it. I know it. Even this stupid old woman knows it."

The shaman's wife cackled and tossed a stick at him playfully. To her, his harsh words were endearments.

"I—" Hunter shook his head. The shaman made it sound so simple. But, of course he didn't understand. It wasn't simple. It wasn't possible. "I—I'm not worthy of another woman to love. Had I gone with my wife that day, she and my child would not be dead."

"Hah! You cannot change fate so easily and you are a fool if you think you can, Hunter of the Shawnee. What happens to us each day is written in the stars long before we are babes in our mother's wombs. Do not forget that, my fierce warrior."

Hunter nodded. "Just the same. I don't want another woman."

"You are afraid you would dishonor Laughing Rain to take another wife, to love again?"

"Yes," Hunter answered simply.

The old man smiled with his wrinkled face,

casting a bright white light that seemed to emanate from within. "What makes you think that your wife did not ask the great Wishemoto to send this Alexandra to you? What makes you think it was not she that did not want to see her lover sleep alone the rest of his days?"

Hunter wiped the back of his mouth with his hand. He was confused. The shaman's words made sense to the Shawnee in him, but not to the white man in him. The white man in him told him to walk away from Alexandra.

The old man waved a hand. "Think on it, Hunter of the Shawnee. You will do the right thing. This man knows it. Now tell me what you know of your wife's killer and I will see if I can help you."

Hunter exhaled, glad to change the subject. He drew closer to the shaman and started to repeat the tale of his wife's death. Talk of Laughing Rain would make him forget about Alexandra and her dark, haunting eyes, or at least he hoped it would . . .

Chapter Nine

The vibrations of the hollow, pounding, Shawnee drums shook the ground beneath Alexandra's feet. The sound was completely foreign to her English ears, yet something about the driving rhythm drew her in.

The sun was just beginning to set over the treetops in the western sky. A cool breeze blew in from the northwest.

"The harvest song," Judith said, coming out of her wigwam to stand beside Alexandra. "Our crops are in. Our dried fish and meat are stored. We're ready for Father Winter once again and we give thanks."

The sweet sound of bone flutes, many joining as one, melded with the throb of the drums and for a moment Judith and Alexandra just stood there in the failing sunlight listening.

"It's so beautiful," Alexandra breathed, brushing back a lock of hair off her cheek. She had bathed in the river this evening with the other women and scrubbed her hair clean with the sudsy pith of some unknown plant. She could still smell its faint, pungent scent in her damp hair. "The sound is so . . . so hopeful." She laughed, thinking how silly she must sound. How could music be hopeful?

But Judith didn't laugh. Instead, she smiled. "I hear it, too. You must be a musician."

"No. My music instructor declared me hopeless at twelve years old. I always found the sound of the spinet cold and uncaring. But this . . ." She searched her mind for the right words, her heart for the right feelings. "There's just something about the sound that makes me feel good inside."

"These are the sounds of the rejoicing of the Shawnee. It's meant to bring joy to the heart. I'm told these drums have been beating the harvest song for more years than there are stars in the heavens."

The Shawnee villagers were now beginning to emerge from their wigwams. The men, women and children were dressed in their finest clothing. They wore buckskins decorated with seashells and porcupine quills. They wore white dresses of butter-soft tanned leather. They even wore an occasional pair of man's breeches or waistcoat. Their hair, as black as crows' wings, was adorned with feathers, beads, and seashells.

The villagers laughed and chatted with their neighbors as they headed toward the center of the camp where the sounds of the drums originated. There, Alexandra knew, from earlier in the day, were two great campfires with roasting venison halves hanging above stoked coals.

"A party," Alexandra murmured, delighted.

"Yes. A party." Judith smiled.

Alexandra had to smile back. As much as she hated to admit it, she liked Judith. The woman was kind and thoughtful. But more importantly, Alexandra found her in the last two days to be very forthright in her words, a trait seldom seen in the finer social circles of London. Judith said exactly what she thought, without ulterior motives. The trait was refreshingly admirable. Somehow Alexandra thought Hunter would think so as well.

"Winters are always long and often hard for these people," Judith went on. "This is one last chance to dance and sing before they settle in for the snows."

The tempo of the drums had again changed and Alexandra found herself tapping her foot to the rhythm. The sounds reminded her of a country dance she'd seen a long time ago.

"Join us," Judith encouraged. "There's good food, good drink. We'll dance until dawn. Harvest night is magical." She winked. "Perhaps you'll find a handsome brave to warm your bed."

Thinking of Jon and his outrageous proposal, Alexandra rolled her eyes. "I think not. My luck runs poorly with men. I think I'd best swear off them while I'm still ahead."

Judith laughed, her silky voice rich with a woman's intuition. "You just haven't found the right man, that's all. But speaking of the right man . . ."

Alexandra followed Judith's gaze. Standing

beside a wigwam, halfway across the camp was Hunter.

Alexandra suppressed a gasp. He was shamefully dressed in his leather loincloth again, his long muscular legs left bare, as well as a considerable portion of his buttocks. The sleeveless tunic he wore was quilled and adorned with feathers and shells. He was talking with Creeping Turtle and completely unaware of the two women who now watched him.

"As fine-loined a brave as I've ever laid eyes on," Judith remarked. "A comely specimen of a man."

Alexandra felt her cheeks grow warm. She looked away from Hunter. Imagine, dressing up like one of these savages! Still, she felt a silly nagging sense of jealousy at Judith's reaction to his obvious maleness. "I understand he's not looking for a wife," Alexandra said, forcing herself not to look back toward Hunter.

Judith shrugged, the bells in her ears tinkling. "So maybe I'll just have a pleasurable roll in the sleeping mats with him." She laughed as she walked away. "Enjoy your evening, Alexandra."

With a sigh, Alexandra watched Judith stroll between the wigwams toward Hunter, but she turned away before she reached him. Alexandra didn't want to watch. She didn't want to know. Hunter's personal life was certainly none of her business. Nor was Judith's.

Just the same, it irked her to think of the two of them together.

Alexandra started back for the wigwam she

shared with Judith, but as she ducked through the door, Jon came around the corner. "Where are you going?" He grabbed her by the hand.

"Inside."

"And miss a night like this?" He flashed a handsome grin. His thick black hair was recently combed and slicked back over his head in a devil-may-care manner. "Come on!"

She could hear the sound of chanting now. "I don't think so. I'd rather be alone." Of course she wouldn't rather be alone, but she didn't want to have to sit and watch Judith work her womanly wiles on Hunter.

"Just have something to eat and then you can hibernate." He started to pull her along. "There's something I want you to try. A little Shawnee liquid refreshment Hunter introduced me to."

She laughed, swept up by Jon's enthusiasm. "I'm not a drinker, Jon. I can hardly keep my wits about me now. I've no need of hard drink."

"It's not what you think. Now come along. I'll not take no for an answer."

"I can't." Alexandra's hand went to her unbound hair, remembering that Judith had obviously taken great care with her appearance this evening. "I look a sight. My hair's not even combed."

He squeezed her hand. "You look beautiful to me."

She looked up at him, offering a quick smile. "Thanks."

He looped her arm through his and led her toward the center of the village. "Just stick with me, sweet. I can show a woman a good time at a party, even a heathen party."

Alexandra chuckled. Why not go and eat and drink with the others? She didn't care what Judith did, or what she did with Hunter for that matter. She had a right as a guest of the Shawnee to join in the festivities. She fit in as well with these people as she'd fit in anywhere. The strange truth was that if she would allow herself to admit it, she fit in better here.

Jon led her through the camp, weaving in and out among the wigwams until they reached the center clearing. The sound of the beating drums and the chants of the men dancing round and round in two interlocking circles was deafening. At another point in her life, she might have been frightened by the frenzied activity, but tonight she took it all in and was fascinated.

"Drink this," Jon shouted above the din.

Alexandra looked down into the gourd cup he'd pressed into her hand. "What is it?"

He shrugged sipping from his own. "Some heathen concoction. Better than rye whiskey. Doesn't leave you with a splitting bean the next morning."

She sipped the drink cautiously. To her surprise the taste was not bitter, as she'd expected, but sweet and fruity. She took another sip. The warm liquid left a tingling sensation on the tip of her tongue as it went down.

Jon accepted a wooden trencher of roasted venison and squash an older woman offered, and then led Alexandra around the circle to take a seat beside a teenaged boy and his mother. Polite nods were exchanged. The boy grinned at Alexandra and she laughed instead of turning away. She didn't know what was in the drink, but it was definitely having an uplifting effect on her.

Sitting down cross-legged on a deerhide mat beside Jon, Alexandra reached for a slice of venison. The meat was hot and savory. She hadn't realized just how hungry she was until she took the first bite. Then she was ravenous.

"Look at that," Jon said loudly in her ear.

She followed his line of vision.

There was Hunter in the circle of dancing men, pounding his moccasins into the dust with the same motions as the other braves. Alexandra chewed her venison slowly, mesmerized by Hunter's movements.

Every muscle in his nearly nude body flexed as he swung his arms and danced to the beat of the drums, his feet following invisible intricate patterns in the dirt. He moved with the others around in a tight circle, while still remaining part of the larger moving circle. The men threw back their heads in unison and howled and Hunter howled with them.

Alexandra couldn't tear her eyes from him as the music picked up rhythm and he danced faster, whirling in circles, stamping his feet and clapping to the sound of the drums that now seemed to rise up out of the earth. Light beads of perspiration rose on his forehead, and then his entire body began to glow with a thin sheen as he exerted more and more energy.

"Where did he learn to do that?" Alexandra breathed.

Jon shrugged his shoulders. "Beats the hell out of me." He stood. "More drink?"

She nodded, still hypnotized by Hunter's exotic, almost erotic dance. "Yes."

"Be right back."

She barely noticed when Jon returned again, except to know that her cup was again filled.

Finally the men's dance ended with an ear-splitting whoop of the dancers and Hunter disappeared into the crowd of men.

Jon offered to get her a third cup of refreshment, she accepted.

"What the hell," she told him. "Why not?" Her head felt light, her lips tingly. She wasn't drunk, not like that time she and her brother Jeremy had drunk too much of her father's brandy wine. This feeling was different. She still had command of her senses. Her speech wasn't slurred. She wasn't sick to her stomach. She just felt good from the tips of her toes to the shell earrings that bobbed in her ears. She kept thinking of Hunter and the way he had moved his hard muscular body, the way the muscles of his buttocks had flexed, the way he had swayed his broad hands to and fro.

As she waited for Jon's return she watched new dancers gather. First the men had danced and now it seemed to be the women's turn. Women young and old began to whirl to the sound of the beating drums as the men clapped and sang and called to their lovers.

As Alexandra watched she thought about the

differences between the Shawnee culture and her own. These people seemed genuinely to care for each other. Married couples were free with their physical displays of affection, even in public. And just as Hunter had told her, the men saw the women as their equals. Alexandra saw it everywhere. Men carried water for their wives' cooking pots. Women hunted and fished with their men. Judith, a white woman, had been invited to partake in a village meeting the night before and had actually been permitted to vote on the decision!

Yes, life was very different here among the Shawnee for the women. And as much as Alexandra hated to admit it, she could understand why Judith would choose to remain here instead of returning to so-called civilization.

The rhythm of the drums picked up and the men clapped louder as the women danced faster, whirling round and round, their moccasined feet beating the ground.

Across the campfire Alexandra spotted Judith. Her long, shapely, lithe body moved to the ancient rhythm of the drums and bone flutes, her movements one with the sounds. Slowly she made her way around the circle of firelight until she stopped in front of Hunter who had just appeared out of the darkness. The other women all stopped before their mates and began a slower, tantalizing dance as one of the older women began to chant.

Alexandra tried to watch the others dance, but she couldn't take her eyes off Judith and Hunter. She danced. He smiled and sipped from the gourd cup in his hand.

Alexandra glanced about for Jon. She spotted him beyond the light of the adjacent fire. He was whispering in the ear of a young Shawnee woman. The woman was laughing and brushing her fingertips across Jon's chest. Alexandra turned her attention back to the dance before her.

An old woman's voice rose above the sounds of the drums. She was obviously telling a story. The Shawnee women swayed to the sound of her voice, their hands signing the words.

Judith turned slowly in a circle, smiling up at Hunter, her body beckoning him with each sway of her hips.

Is he yours? Judith's words echoed in her head.

No! Alexandra had answered.

What was it Hunter had said the other day at the stream about being attracted to her but not being willing to love again?

Of course the thought was absurd. She, the Lady Alexandra, and this wild man, Hunter. But he was a lord, wasn't he? Wasn't that what Jon had said. Hunter was simply *playing* Indian? He had land, money, and a title across the ocean in England.

If Jon was going to return to England, why not Hunter? Once his wife's death was avenged what would keep him here in the colonies? Nothing.

Slowly Alexandra rose. The drums were still beating. The old woman's tale had come to an end but the younger women still danced. Alexandra felt herself swaying her hips to the sound of the hollow instruments. The music was hypnotic.

She knew the drink Jon had given her was

influencing her thoughts, her behavior, but she didn't care. The old Alexandra would certainly not have danced a seductive heathen dance, but the old Alexandra had died that sunny morning on the boat the day the Iroquois had attacked. Life could never be the same after that carnage. Why did she keep thinking it could be?

Slowly she made her way around the circle of the campfire, copying the other women's movements. The sweet drink and the rhythm of the drums swept her up and carried her around the circle toward Hunter. He was the first person who had made her feel truly alive in a long time. He made her heart beat faster, her stomach tie in knots, her mouth go dry.

Alexandra spun around and suddenly found herself beside Judith, in front of Hunter. He lifted an eyebrow, surprised but seemingly not shocked.

"Glad to see you join in the festivities," he said, his voice warm with the drink of the Shawnee. The light from the campfire reflected off his handsomely chiseled face. As Alexandra moved to the beat of the gourd rattles, she took note of the peacefulness she saw on Hunter's face. Tonight he seemed to carry none of the burden of his wife's death. He seemed to be open to the magic of the night.

The tempo of the song changed, and suddenly Indian braves were joining the women in their dance. Judith put her hand out toward Hunter.

He hesitated.

"No, let me, Judith," Alexandra murmured.

Judith looked at her face, then Hunter's. She

smiled and laughed as she danced away. A moment later she was swept up in the arms of a tall Shawnee brave. Alexandra heard her laughter as she looked up at Hunter.

Around them the Shawnee danced, clapping and singing in rising frenzy. For a moment there seemed to be no one on the earth to Alexandra but Hunter.

"You're asking me to dance?" Hunter asked, a hint of amusement in his voice.

Throwing caution to wind, she smiled up at him. "If you'll have me."

Tossing the gourd cup carelessly to the ground, he grabbed her hands and swung her into his arms. Moments later they were in the middle of the dancing villagers, matching footstep to footstep, their bodies brushing against each other.

Alexandra laughed and threw back her head as Hunter spun her until she was dizzy. Everything was suddenly a whirl of glorious confusion, the heat of the campfire, the pounding of the footsteps, the scent of Hunter's masculinity, the feel of his breath on her cheek.

Finally, the dance ended and the men and women collapsed in each other's arms. Alexandra looked up at Hunter, relieved the dance was over, but not wanting to part from him. Hunter's arm rested on her shoulder, partially bared by the leather dress that had shifted to one side. His fingertips were hot against her skin.

"So the lady is multitalented," he murmured in her ear. "Not many Londoners who can do the Shawnee *Tah-mee Men-ya-lo-wai.*"

She threw back her head to look up into his green eyes. She was breathless but she didn't know if it was because of the physical exertion or the nearness of this man. "The what?"

"Roughly translated, the corn dance." He led her away from the center fire, but didn't lift his arm from her shoulder.

"Something to drink?"

"More?" She laughed. "I don't think so. I've already nearly taken leave of my senses, dancing like a Fleet Street strumpet."

"Taken leave of your senses?" They reached the pot of drink and he accepted a cup from a man who was dipping several. "That, or found them?"

When she didn't reply for lack of anything substantial to say, he brought the cup to her lips and she sipped. When she pulled away, he brought the cup to his own lips and drank heartily.

Somehow they found themselves beyond the light of the campfire. The sound of the hollow gourds and bone flutes faded a little. Alexandra stared up at Hunter's face. His earring glimmered and she was tempted to reach out and touch it.

She could tell by the look on his face that he was going to kiss her.

Is this what I want? she thought wildly.

Yes!

When his lips touched hers, she nearly recoiled. She was not an innocent to a man's kisses, but no one had ever affected her like this. As their mouths met, a physical energy arced between them. Alexandra lifted her arms to rest on his massive shoulders and leaned into him, wanting to taste him.

His kiss was gentle, but probing. It was gentlemanly, yet immensely sensual at the same time.

"I shouldn't be doing this," he whispered against her lips.

He was kissing her cheek now, the tip of her nose, the length of her neck. Shivers of pleasure reverberated through her body.

"No, no you shouldn't. *I* shouldn't," she somehow managed.

"But it's been coming to this, hasn't it, Alex?"

"Yes, yes," she answered, returning his kisses. "It doesn't make any sense, but—"

"Of course it makes sense." He brushed his fingertips across her breasts and she felt her nipples pucker beneath the soft leather. "It makes sense because we're two people in need. In need of each other."

Alexandra covered his hand with hers. This was all going too quickly. Her breasts were tingling. Her woman's place ached. She looked up at him and touched her finger to the copper earring in his ear. "You'll take me home, won't you, Hunter? You won't make me go with Creeping Turtle's cousin?"

"I'll take you back to Annapolis, but I warn you it'll be the long way home. He-Who-Wishes had some information for me. I head for a fort in Penn's colony."

She shook her head. "I don't care. I don't care how long it takes. There's nothing for me in Annapolis. Nothing that can't wait."

He smiled a roguish smile to beat Jon's best. "Are you certain you won't regret your words in the morning after the wine has worn off and the sunlight hits my ugly face."

She bit down on her lower lip. How could a savage man in such a savage country be so gentle? "No," she whispered. "There'll be no regrets."

"For a handful of coppers I might take you here and now," he said, nuzzling her neck. "For the first time in a very long time, I want to make love. I want to make love with you, Alex."

She smiled. Tonight was a night to hold back nothing. She might not get the chance tomorrow. "For a handful of coppers I might do the same."

"But we won't," he whispered.

She shook her head. "Not tonight. Not like this."

He dropped his hand on her shoulder and began to lead her away from the commotion of the dancing. "Jon said he asked you to go back to London with him . . . to be his mistress."

"Did Jon tell you I said no?"

They walked between the shadowy wigwams. Somewhere a baby fussed and then was quieted by his mother's breast. The light of the full moon beat down on them with its golden rays. "He said he tried to warn you against me. He said he told you I'm not a man to count on, not for—"

"If you're trying to tell me that you're not willing to marry me, just as he isn't, it's not necessary." She stopped in front of the wigwam she and Judith shared. "I'm no fool. It's just that . . ." her voice trailed off for a moment and then she spoke again. "It's just that I've enjoyed these last few days as I've never enjoyed life. I've seen things in myself and in others I never knew existed. I somehow get the feeling that it's you that's changed me."

"No, it's not me, Alex. It's this land." He took a deep breath of the crisp autumn air. "It's the land that changed me, and you as well I'd wager."

She laid her cheek against the soft leather of his tunic. The rise and fall of his breathing was strangely comforting.

"Hunter's moon," he mused.

She lifted her head to look up at his face. "What?"

He pointed to the sky. "A hunter's moon. A full moon. It always seems to be there in the sky at turning points in my life." He brushed his lips against her forehead. "Is this a turning point in my life?"

She sighed. "I don't know. I don't know anything, not anymore I don't." She brushed back a lock of his magical hair with her fingers. "Good night, Hunter."

He kissed her one last time, his lips lingering on hers. "Sleep and I'll see you in the morning. Things always seem to make more sense by the light of the day."

The morning, she thought and she forced herself to step out of Hunter's arms and go into the wigwam. Would morning change what she and Hunter had shared tonight? More importantly, did she want it to?

Chapter Ten

"What do you mean she's going with us?" Jon took a pinch from his silver snuffbox and inhaled deeply. "I thought Creeping Turtle's cousin was taking her back to Annapolis in the morning!"

Hunter leaned against the rough bark of a tree, crossing his arms over his chest. In the distance he could hear the pulsing of the Shawnee drums. He knew they would play until dawn's first light before they finally grew silent. "She was going with the boy, but she asked me to take her back. After all she's been through, she just doesn't feel safe heading back through the forest with an Indian."

Jon lifted a feathery black eyebrow. "And she feels safe going with you?" He grimaced. "Surely you jest?"

Hunter shrugged. "The woman's scared, Jon. She could easily have died at the hands of Two Crows. I'm a white man. She thinks she can trust me."

Jon swore softly. "You'd best back off, friend.

You're going to hurt her."

"Hurt her?" Hunter scoffed. "What the hell are you talking about? I'm just going to take her back to Annapolis. I told her we would be heading for the fort He-Who-Wishes said Blue-Green Eyes has been seen near, but then once I deal with him, I'll take her home."

"And tumble her along the way? Is that it, Geoffry?"

Hunter scowled. "Don't call me Geoffry. Geoffry's dead, long gone."

"I know, I know, and now you're the great Hunter of the Shawnee, right?"

Hunter stared up into the sky. A canopy of stars twinkled overhead, piercing the darkness of the forest with the rays of white light. "I wouldn't hurt her, Jon. Not for the world."

Jon chuckled. "Smitten on her, are you? Imagine what your father would think if you brought her home with you. Here's my wife, Papa. Yes, she was kidnapped, raped, and tortured by Indians in the colonies, but isn't she lovely? Yes, I can see how your father would be overjoyed to meet your new wife."

"She says she wasn't raped. And you're blowing this all out of proportion. No one said anything about marrying anyone. I just said I wouldn't hurt her. Not like you would, Jon."

"I made as honest a proposal to her as she'll get anywhere. She'd be a fool not to take me up on it. Better to be a wealthy man's whore than a pauper's wife I say. And a pauper is all that will have her now and you know it. Once she gets back to Annapolis, it doesn't matter who she really is, no decent man will have her. No respectable man's family would approve of the marriage."

Hunter ignored Jon's ranting. He always got like this when he had too much to drink. "She has been secretive about who she really is, hasn't she?"

Jon swept off his cocked hat and ran his fingers through his black hair. "Maybe she's an heiress, in which case," he added thoughtfully, "I might marry the wench, myself. The two of us would make a fine couple in London town. Hell, if her papa's got a title I might yet find my way into the queen's drawing room. Imagine that!"

An owl flew overhead and Hunter watched it soar. "So you're still determined to go back to England?"

"I told you. I've had enough of ticks, the hard ground for a bed, and no decent wine to drink. I'm ready to go home."

"Even now that you've found your mother?"

"She could be lying."

"Why would she, Jon?" Hunter turned to stare at his friend's masked face. "She wouldn't. She'd have no reason to. She-Who-Whispers-To-The-Wind is your mother and you blessed well know it."

Jon glanced down at his boots. "I asked her about my father. She said it didn't matter. She loved him, but they were too young, too different. She said he went back to England shortly after I was born."

"She gave you no name?"

"No. Creeping Turtle made some explanation about speaking the name of the dead or those long gone. Another silly Shawnee superstition."

Hunter sighed, crossing his moccasined feet, his back still planted firmly against the tree trunk. "Would that I could have been born to She-Who-Whispers-To-The-Wind and not you. Think about it, Jon. You should have been Rordan's son, not me. You're perfectly suited for the life of a lord. You're all he wanted in a son, all I'm not. Me, this is where I belong. It's funny that such a twist of fate could leave a man so torn between two worlds."

"Ah, hah. So you have thought about your father. I thought maybe you'd come to your senses. I thought maybe you just needed a little time to play the wild man and then you'd be ready to go home and take up your duties. It's what your father did, isn't it? He came here, knocked around with the savages for a few years and then he went home and married the woman his father had chosen for him."

Hunter smiled ironically. "I'd say that's out of the question, wouldn't you? I practically left Mary Lambert at the altar. By now she's long-married with a handful of runny-nosed earl's children."

"So your father will find you another maid. With the lot you'll inherit any man would pay well for you to take his daughter."

Hunter sighed. "Christ's bones, Jon. I know that once I deal with Laughing Rain's killer I ought to go home. I've already caused my father too much pain, but—"

"But what? You've played Indian. You married for love, something few ever get a chance at. Now it's time you saw to your duties and left this all behind."

"You just say that because you don't want to go back to England alone."

For a long moment Jon was silent, but then he spoke with a gentle, open honesty Hunter rarely heard in him, but knew him capable of. "I'm saying that, because that's the best thing to do. You know it and I know it. I'm saying it because I love you like a brother."

Hunter stepped away from the tree, rubbing his temples. He was tired. Too tired to think now. Tomorrow he would make ready to leave the Shawnee camp. The following day he and Jon and Alexandra would set out for the fort in Penn's Colony. In a few weeks' time he hoped this nightmare with Laughing Rain would be over. Once he saw her death avenged, then he would be able to make a responsible decision about returning to London with Jon. In the meantime he had to concentrate on finding Blue-Green Eyes. He didn't have energy or time to worry about his father or the dark-eyed Alexandra who haunted his dreams.

"Good night, Jon," he said softly. "See you in the morning."

"Don't wait up for me," Jon called after him. "Got myself a widow waiting on me in her wigwam."

Hunter laughed, his rich voice echoing in the trees. He waved a hand over his shoulder and was still laughing as he walked around a wigwam and lost sight of Jon.

It was early morning, barely daylight. Alexandra, Hunter, and Jon, had their belongings packed on the mule and were ready to set out for Penn's Colony and the fort the shaman had directed Hunter toward. A small group of Shawnee well-wishers huddled near the edge of the camp, bidding farewell from the folds of the blankets they wore around their shoulders.

She-Who-Whispers-To-The-Wind stood beside her son, Creeping Turtle. She spoke softly, directly to Jon, even though it was necessary for Creeping Turtle to interpret. Alexandra stood back, beside Hunter, listening.

"Our mother wishes you a safe journey and happiness the rest of your days," Creeping Turtle repeated after his mother. "She says she will pray for her son who was once lost, but is now found."

Jon scuffed one booted foot on the frozen ground. When he spoke, his breath formed clouds of white in the frosty morning air. "Tell She-Who"—He looked to Hunter, then back at the old Indian woman—"Tell my mother I thank her for her prayers and . . . I thank her for giving me an identity. For that I will always be grateful."

Creeping Turtle translated quickly and tears welled up in his mother's eyes. She stepped up to Jon, raising her arms. He lowered his head to allow her to drop a leather necklace over his head. His hand went to the perfectly shaped black stone that hung from the leather string. The old woman spoke again.

"Our mother says she picked up a jagged black stone the day her first-born son disappeared," Creeping Turtle translated. "She carried the worry stone in her bag all these years and each time she thought of the son she had lost, she rubbed the stone. Now it is worn smooth with the love of a mother's hand. Wear it, and it will protect you as she was unable to protect you that terrible day you were lost to her."

Tears came to Alexandra's eyes, but she didn't brush them away. Hunter rested his hand on her shoulder as they watched Jon lean forward and kiss his mother's dry cheek.

"Let's be on our way," Jon said gruffly, turning away from his mother and brother. "If we must journey to Penn's colony, let's make haste. I can smell the blasted snow in the air." He brushed past Hunter and Alexandra, obviously touched by his mother's gift, but not wanting anyone to know it. "You know how much I hate the damned snow!"

Alexandra smiled to herself as she waved to Creeping Turtle and his mother and to Judith who stood behind them. "Thank you," she said, "for the hospitality you showed me. I'll never forget your kindness."

Judith stepped forward, carrying a rabbit-pelt cloak with grey foxtails hanging from the collar. She draped the beautiful cloak over Alexandra's shoulders. "May the God Wishemoto guide you in your journeys," she leaned to whisper in Alexandra's ear, "and in love. He's a good man, Alexandra. Don't let him go."

Alexandra felt her cheeks grow warm with embarrassment. "Thank you for the cloak," she whispered, kissing Judith on the cheek. "I've never owned anything so fine, nor so beautiful. To be sure, I'll treasure it always."

Judith stepped back into the crowd of those who

had braved the cold of the early morning to say good-bye to the visitors. The shaman and his wife pushed their way through the group. He-Who-Wishes extended his wrinkled, suntanned hand to Hunter. He spoke a few solemn words in the Shawnee tongue, and then turned and walked away.

Alexandra could have sworn she had heard her name spoken. "What did he say?" she asked Hunter as they waved farewell to the villagers and started after Jon.

"Nothing of importance," Hunter mumbled gruffly. "Now let's get going. We've a long day of traveling ahead of us."

Alexandra watched him walk away, confused by his gruffness. Deciding that the man was impossible to figure out, she ran to catch up with him and Jon, her new rabbit cloak wrapped tightly around her shoulders.

The campfire flickered, casting long fingers of light across the faces of the weary travelers. Jon had already turned in for the night, rolling up in a bearskin near the fire with a flask of whiskey nestled in his arms.

Alexandra and Hunter still sat up, staring into the depths of the flames, content to listen to the quiet sounds of the surrounding forest. It had been a long, but pleasant day of travel and both seemed to be reluctant to let the day end.

Alexandra held a pewter cup of brewed tea in her hands, rolling it between her palms to savor the warmth. Hunter was stretched out beside her smoking an Indian pipe given to him by Creeping Turtle. They had talked all day long as they walked, mostly about unimportant things, but somehow the day's conversation had drawn them closer.

Alexandra found that despite Hunter's wild ways, she liked him. He was quite a story-teller, making her laugh as he told about his years at Oxford, and touching her heart as he told about the Shawnee and their ways. He was a man who seemed to live each moment to its fullest, something she found quite admirable, something she had vowed to begin doing herself.

Hunter rolled onto his side on his deerskin sleeping mat and pushed up on one elbow so that he faced Alexandra. "Tell me something," he implored softly. "Who are you . . . really?"

She took a sip from her cup, savoring the taste of the herb tea he had brewed for her. "You know, the reason I didn't tell you two rogues to begin with was that I feared if you knew the truth you'd hold me captive for ransom."

"So now you know differently."

She turned to look at him, a smile playing at the corners of her mouth. "I know no such thing. The fact of the matter is that now that I know you, I'm certain I shouldn't tell you who I am."

He scowled. "Why would I do such a thing?"

"The same reason any other man would. To line your pockets with coin."

"Money means nothing to me, Alex. I've more than I could spend in a lifetime already and I've yet to inherit."

"So you tell me," she teased.

"I'm serious. I want to know who you are." His hazel eyes narrowed. "Who's looking for you at this very moment? Who weeps for your return? A mother? A father? . . . A lover?"

She turned back to gaze into the flames, suddenly sad. "No one," she whispered.

"No one? I find that hard to believe."

She felt him rest his hand on her knee and she was touched by his gentleness. "No one," she repeated. "I told you. Twice I was meant to wed. Neither time it came to be. My father sent me to the Maryland Colony in disgrace. My aunt and uncle were supposed to marry me off to anyone they could find willing."

He chuckled and squeezed her knee. "Surely it's not all that desperate. I mean, you seem a suitable enough match for a man. Your teeth are decent, you're not sickly. I've yet to hear you howl at the moon."

She smiled. She knew he was trying to make light of her situation and she appreciated it. "It seems my rejections have marred my reputation. That and my sharp tongue. Not an eligible man of my station in London would have me, or so my father said when he put me on the ship to the American Colonies."

"Your father? And who might he be?"

She turned to study his face. The firelight played off the planes of his high cheekbones and set the red hair that brushed his shoulders aflame with red light. "Why are you suddenly so curious? You looking for a wife?"

God Almighty! The moment the words came out of her mouth, she was sorry for them. She didn't know what could have possessed her to say such a thing. If Hunter was the man Jon hinted he was, he certainly wouldn't be interested in her.

Alexandra lowered her lashes, waiting to hear his laughter ring out, waiting for the mortified embarrassment she knew was coming.

But Hunter didn't laugh.

After a moment he said, "Actually Jon says that after I see to the man who killed my wife, it's time I think about returning to my *responsibilities* in England. I suppose responsibilities include a wife."

Relieved to have the chance to turn the conversation to him, she looked up at his face. "And what do you think of these *responsibilities?*"

He sighed. "Good question." He brushed his fingers across the rabbit fur of the cloak that lay across her crossed legs. "I left suddenly, hurting my father a great deal."

"And now you're sorry?"

He shrugged. "Not sorry that I came here. Not sorry that I loved Laughing Rain."

Alexandra heard his voice tighten as he spoke of his wife, but then he went on.

"I am sorry that I left in the manner I did. I should have told my father I wasn't ready to marry the woman he'd chosen for me and settle down. I should have told him I wanted to come to the colonies as he once had. Christ, I was nearly thirty years old. I should have had the guts to face his anger instead of running."

Alexandra covered his hand with hers. "Mary Alexandra Lambert."

Hunter felt his heart fall. He looked up at her,

certain he'd heard incorrectly. He entwined his fingers in hers. "What did you say?"

She was smiling down at him. "I said Mary Alexandra Lambert. You wanted to know my name. I just told you. My father is the Earl of Monthrop."

"Mary Lambert," Hunter murmured beneath his breath. *Christ, it couldn't be!* The odds were one chance in a million that this could be the woman he had been betrothed to! He was too stunned to speak.

"My father? Do you know him?" he heard her say.

Hunter looked up to see her staring at him quizzically. "Your father is the Earl of Monthrop?" He thought of the short, stout Earl of Monthrop and his sour disposition. Hunter had never thought much about little Mary Lambert he'd left behind without having ever met her. He just assumed her father had married her off to some other reluctant earl's son. But suddenly he realized the travesty of his deed. Suddenly he had a face to go with the name. That night he'd not appeared at the betrothal party, it was Alexandra who had been left with the shame of abandonment. It was Alexandra who had been left with the anger of her father and his own father's most likely as well.

"Hunter, I said, did you know my father?" he heard her say again.

He glanced back at her innocent face feeling like an ass. "Why yes, yes as a matter of fact I met him once. Pleasant gentleman," he lied.

She laughed, withdrawing her hand. "Must not

have been my father you met, then."

For a moment Hunter didn't know what to say. He knew he should tell her the truth of who he was, what he'd done, but he just couldn't bring himself to do it. Instead, he reached for her hand, taking it in his larger one.

When he spoke again, his voice was light and teasing. "I don't know, maybe there's something to your suggestion."

"What suggestion?"

He grasped her arm and pulled her down until she was stretched out beside him, facing him. "The two of us wedding."

"Us marry?" Alexandra sputtered. "I never suggested such a thing! I was being sarcastic and you well know it!"

Alexandra looked surprised, but she couldn't possibly have been as surprised as he was when he realized what he'd said. God's teeth! He wasn't going to marry this chit. Laughing Rain was his wife. She would always be his wife. He'd let her go into the forest alone and now she was dead. He didn't deserve a woman like Alexandra. He didn't deserve any woman.

"Us wed," she went on. "That's absurd."

"Of course it is." He laughed, brushing his fingertips beneath his chin. "Imagine you and me in a big stone house in London. You shouting at me from the banister like a fishmonger's wife."

She laughed at him. "And you dancing round my cherry dining table stark naked save for a feather headdress!"

Her voice rang in his ears and suddenly he felt

the urge to kiss her laughing mouth. Before he reasoned himself out of it, he leaned forward and brushed his lips against hers.

Her laughter ceased and for a moment she lay very still, staring up at him. "I thought we weren't going to do this again," she whispered, making no attempt to move away.

His hand found the dip of her waist and he pulled her a little closer. He kissed the tip of her nose. "Who said?"

"The other night, remember? We . . . we agreed it wasn't a good idea."

"Feels like a good idea to me," he answered, kissing her again, this time on her trembling lips. "Tastes like a good idea."

Her eyes drifted shut. "Exactly," she breathed. "Exactly why we shouldn't. Feels too good."

Hunter threaded his fingers through her fresh, clean hair and brought his mouth down on hers. She sighed against his lips.

God in heaven, she was sweet! Her lips were so soft and yet as she pressed her mouth to his, he tasted a fire in her kiss that shot shivers of pleasure through his body. Already he could feel a stirring in his groin. How long had it been since he'd felt this heat?

"Alexandra," he whispered. "Alex."

She rolled onto her back and he pressed her into the deerhide sleeping mat. He caressed her cheek with his fingertips as he touched her upper lip with the tip of his tongue.

She laughed, stroking his shoulder with her hand as she lifted up to kiss him back, her tongue touching his in innocent enthusiasm.

Hunter heard himself groan.

Laughing Rain had always been a willing lover, soft and yielding, but she'd been passive. He'd made love *to* her many times, but never made love *with* her. This woman, this woman here in his arms was rising up to meet him, to take pleasure as she gave it. As Hunter thrust his tongue into her mouth, caressing her breast with his hand, all thoughts of his dead wife blew from his mind like the leaves blown free from a rocky crevice in an autumn storm. All that seemed to matter at this instant was Alex and her sensual mouth, her inquisitive touch.

He kissed her again and again, exploring the soft pale flesh of her shoulders and neck, tickling the lobes of her ears with his tongue, tasting her mouth, unable to get enough of her. She moaned softly in his arms, arching her back to meet his every move, beckoning innocently with the pressure of her hips against his groin.

His fingers found the knot of her tunic belt and he tugged on it until it came free. Kissing the hollow of her throat, he slipped his hand beneath the butter-soft leather and caressed the full roundness of her breast.

Alexandra moaned softly in his ear, sending shivers of desire through him.

"Hunter," she whispered. "I shouldn't be doing this; we shouldn't."

"Want me to stop?" he forced himself to say, though all he could think of was touching her nipple with the tip of his tongue.

"Yes," she breathed. "No . . . I don't know." She ran her fingers in his hair. "It feels so wonderful. No man has ever touched me before. No man—"

He silenced her with another kiss. "I'll stop," he told her, glorying in the feel of the weight of her breast in his hand. "Just tell me."

She groaned in indecision. "Yes." She lifted her head to kiss him full on the mouth. "Stop, else I'll have my underskirts over my head in a minute . . . that is if I had any."

He groaned as he reluctantly slipped his hand out from beneath her tunic and the warmth of her silky flesh. "All right." He ran a hand through his hair, trying to catch his breath. "I'll stop, but you'll damned well be sorry in the morning."

"No doubt I probably will." She sat up, her breath still coming faster than normal. "But this can lead to nothing but trouble." She tried to straighten her tunic, flustered.

He reached out and pushed her hands away and straightened the folds for her. "It's all right, Alex. I understand." Of course he didn't, not really. But at this point he was as confused as she was. He didn't understand his uncontrollable attraction to her. Not with Laughing Rain barely cold in her grave. Not with her killer still running free.

She looked up at him, her dark eyes awash with emotion. "No, you don't. How can you when I don't understand myself. I want you, Hunter. It's stupid. It's out of the question. But I do. I—"

"Hush," he soothed, drawing her into his arms. "You talk too damned much, you know that?"

She rested her cheek on his chest. "I know. I know. I always talk when I'm nervous."

"Or when you're content, or sad or happy or—"

She covered his mouth with her hand. "You're embarrassing me, shut up."

He kissed the top of her head. God in heaven. He wanted to make love to her. Now even more than he had a few minutes ago. It didn't make any sense, he knew it didn't, but tonight he was too tired to even care.

With a sigh, Hunter lowered himself down on his sleeping mat, Alexandra's soft form still in his arms.

"What are you doing?"

"Just lie with me," he whispered in her ear. "Let me sleep with you in my arms." He smiled down at her. "Just sleep."

She lifted her head to look directly into his eyes. She was going to say something, going to argue, but then stopped herself. "All right," she answered softly, lowering her head to rest it on his shoulder. "But what will Jon—"

"The hell with Jon, the hell with the world." He pulled a wool blanket over the both of them and drew her close to him. "The hell with them all," he murmured, closing his eyes, ". . . at least for tonight."

Chapter Eleven

For a week the trio traveled northeast without mishap. The wind blew cooler and the leaves began to turn color, showering the travelers in the reds, oranges and yellows of autumn. The mornings were so brisk that when Alexandra spoke, her breath was frosty in the air. But the afternoon sunshine was still bright and warm.

Although they traveled swiftly, she seemed not to tire. The night she and Hunter had kissed in the Shawnee village had been a turning point in her life, if not in his. After the words they had exchanged, the kisses they'd shared, she somehow felt different. For the first time in her life she no longer felt on the outside looking in. For the first time in her life she had a friend—two friends.

Alexandra didn't know what would come of this relationship she and Hunter were developing. She didn't even know what she wanted to come of it. All she knew was that he made her feel alive and vital. He angered her, but he also made her happier than she could ever remember being. He frustrated her, but he made her look beyond the walls of the world she had never glanced beyond before. In these last few days she had learned more about herself and mankind than she'd learned in her lifetime.

Jon kept up his private crusade to try and convince Alexandra to go back to London with him, but he did it in such a way that she was now amused rather than offended. Hunter had toned down his extravagant manner and behavior so as to be pleasant company.

In midafternoon of the third day, Alexandra was walking between the two men, with the pack mule following behind them. The rolling hills of the western Shawnee country had flattened, making the walk easy enough to carry on lengthy conversation. The three were discussing what delicacy each would enjoy when they reached Annapolis. Hunter wanted a slice of beef cooked rare with wild mushroom sauce, Alexandra a cup of real English tea, and Jon a bottle of expensive French brandy and a blond tavern wench all to himself. The three were laughing at their differences when Hunter suddenly ceased speaking in midsentence.

The moment he brought his finger to his lips, Alexandra was instantly silent. She now knew Hunter well enough to know when danger was imminent. Jon grabbed a musket from the pack animal. Hunter slid a feathered arrow from his quiver and notched it in his bow.

Alexandra listened to the sounds of the forest that first were simply a cacophony of confusion, but as the seconds passed they began to filter in her mind and she was able to distinguish one sound from another. She heard the trees swaying in the breeze and the leaves fluttering to rest on the rich ground. She heard the chatter of squirrels building their nests. She heard the late-afternoon song of the swallow.

Then, suddenly a flock of quail burst from a hedgerow just off the game trail ahead. Hunter raised his bow and pulled back the arrow in one fluid motion. Jon cocked his musket with an ominous click.

Alexandra's mouth went dry. She was afraid, but not paralyzed by fear. She wished she had a weapon so that she might fight beside the men. She'd come too far to be killed by an Iroquois arrow now.

"Ne she!" a voice called from the brush. "No. This man comes in peace."

Two Crows. Alexandra recognized his voice immediately. She turned to Hunter as she found that in these last few days she often did when she was uncertain or afraid. *"Two Crows,"* she whispered harshly. "Don't believe him. It's a trick. I won't go with him! I'll die before he takes me again!"

Hunter gestured with his bow. "Step out where you can be seen, He-Who-Wishes-To-Die!"

Two Crows appeared above the hedgerow, his hands raised above his head. His face was bruised hideously, his jaw slightly off center. Where his two front teeth had been, was a gaping hole. He wore bloody rags wrapped around the hand that was now missing fingers.

Alexandra's first instinct was to step back, but she didn't. She stood her ground beside Hunter.

"Are you alone?" she demanded. "Or do your dog companions wait in the trees?"

"No. This man is alone. No *len ah wai.*"

"Dog Companions," Jon muttered. "Christ, Alex you sound like Hunter! Hunter, do you hear—"

She shot him such an angry look that he shut up in midsentence.

"Why are you here?" Alexandra questioned, turning her attention back to Two Crows.

He still held his hands high above his head. "I come to warn you, to warn the Hunter of the Shawnee."

"What the hell's he talking about?" Jon sighed loudly. "Just shoot him, Hunter. You told him that if you saw his ugly face again you'd kill him. I'd do it, but I'd prefer to save my musket ball for a deer. I can't eat Mohawks. Just never had the stomach for them."

"Let him speak," Hunter said quietly.

Alexandra glanced sideways at Hunter. Seeing that he was content to let her question the half-breed, she went on, feeling even more confident than before. "You come to warn Hunter? Warn him of what?"

Two Crows licked his lips, his gaze never straying from Hunter's drawn arrow. "I come to warn him of the cap-i-tan. He and his soldier-men look for the Hunter of the Shawnee. They look for the white *equiwa* called Alexandra. You must not go further north into the rising sun. He camps there."

Hunter motioned with his bow for Two Crows to step out of the brush and approach them. He did so, but cautiously. As he walked, he limped. His leather tunic and leggings were torn in shreds and blood-stained.

"Put down your hands," Alexandra said. "But you move and he'll kill you, you know that, don't you?"

Two Crows slowly lowered his hands. Hunter relaxed his aim, letting his bow fall to his side.

"I am without a weapon. They took them all. If this Hunter tries to kill me, I am without defense," Two Crows said. "This I know. The Hunter of the Shawnee already gave me life when he could have given me death."

She laughed but she saw nothing funny in his words. "So why do you give up this chance at life? Why did you come back when you knew he would kill you? Why didn't you run when you had the chance?"

"Listen to my words. I come to warn the Hunter. The cap-i-tan looks for him. The cap-i-tan freed me because I said I would bring him the woman, Alexandra. The woman he paid me for." His black eyes sparkled with sudden defiance. "But I will not."

"I don't get this. Is this some kind of trick? Why do you warn me?" Hunter asked quietly.

"No trick. No trick. I warn you so that you will not die."

Hunter listened carefully to the half-breed's words. "It's obvious this captain beat the hell out of you to convince you to see things his way. Why didn't you run north when you had the chance? Or why didn't you try to take Alexandra back to him now?"

Two Crows glanced down at his tattered

moccasins. "My father was a man of honor. This man"—he tapped his chest lightly—"has none, but . . ." He looked up at Hunter. "But . . . you give this man without honor the chance to live when you did not have to. My father would have warned you if you had given him that chance."

It was Hunter's turn to laugh. "An Iroquois with a conscience! I'll be damned straight to hell and back. Never heard of such a thing!"

Two Crows hung his head. "I warn you now. Do not go in this direction. To the northeast lies death for you, worse for the white woman. The cap-i-tan will sell her to my people, as he has sold other white *equiwa*."

"You're serious, aren't you?" Alexandra asked, studying his battered face carefully. "You really did come to warn us."

"Yes, and now the task is done. This man has warned you. Kill me if you wish. If you do not wish, I go home to brothers and sisters on the lakes."

"You've warned me and now you're going to run?" Hunter grimaced. "This captain catches your tail and he'll kill you, Two Crows." He nodded. "Looks like he already tried."

"He will not kill me." He gestured with his bloody bandaged hand. "This man will run like the wind, invisible to the red-bird soldiers."

Jon leaned against a tree and pulled a silver snuffbox from his coat. "It's probably a trap. There's no captain looking for us. Two Crows has got a covey of redskins waiting in the trees for us. I say kill him now and be done with it."

"Kill this man if you wish," Two Crows

repeated solemnly. "But these lips speak the truth."

"And what?" Jon asked sarcastically. "You never lied before, Two Crows?"

Again, he hung his head. "These lips have said many lies, many half truths, but I tell you, I speak the truth today."

Alexandra crossed her arms over her chest and glanced at Hunter. It was obvious he, too, was carefully weighing the words and motives of Two Crows.

"What do you think?" Hunter asked so quietly that only Alexandra could hear him.

She stepped closer to him. "I think he's telling the truth."

"Why do you think so?"

She shrugged. "Just an instinctive feeling."

Hunter nodded. "Those are the ones to go by. Listen, watch, rationalize, but in the end you've got to go with what you feel in your belly."

She studied Hunter's handsome face. His earring sparkled in the late afternoon sunlight. "So we don't go northeast?"

He set his jaw. "We have to."

"Hunter—"

"Where is this cap-i-tan, and his soldiers?" Hunter asked Two Crows, cutting Alexandra off.

"Two days' easy walk." Two Crows pointed in the direction Alexandra, Hunter, and Jon were headed. "An English fort. The fort is supposed to protect English land, but I think these soldiers do not protect. Mostly they eat, drink, play the playing cards, and futter women."

Hunter nodded. "We thank you for your warning. You can go."

"You will go this way now?"

"We have to," Hunter answered. "I seek a man. I head for another fort three or four days from here. Fort Maurice. Fort Bend-In-The-River to *The People.*"

"Then take the white woman back if you want to save her. Send her with the Shawnee." He nodded at Jon who was busy picking through the mule's packs muttering to himself about being hungry.

"No." Alexandra spoke up. "We travel together." She looked at Hunter and then back at Two Crows. "We won't separate. The Hunter of the Shawnee seeks the man who killed his wife. *We* seek him." She didn't know what had made her say that. She wanted no part of this vengeance of Hunter's. She didn't care about his beloved Laughing Rain. She just wanted to get home. Didn't she?

Hunter looked at her and she saw something flash in his eyes, though what, she didn't know. Then he looked back at Two Crows. "The fort I travel to is farther north. I will take heed of your warning and stay clear of the soldiers you speak of."

"It will not be enough." Two Crows shook his head emphatically. "This cap-i-tan, he is evil. He no longer follows the English rules. He has no fort, but many soldiers. There are men of the Iroquois nation who walk with him. I tell you, he will find you, he will take the woman, and kill you for taking what he thinks is his."

"We'll be all right, Two Crows. Now you take

yourself and get out of the colony. Run as fast as you can. Run home to your family and never return to the land of the Delaware and Shawnee again."

Two Crows turned to go.

"And Two Crows," Hunter called to him.

The half-breed Iroquois turned back. "This man thanks you. We are even. Now go before I lose my patience and kill you as I said I would."

Without another word Two Crows took off into the trees and disappeared before their eyes.

Alexandra watched him go.

Hunter touched her shoulder. "You afraid to go on?"

She looked up at him. "Yes."

He brushed her cheek with the back of his fingertips. "You understand I can't turn back?"

She could feel herself trembling, though whether it was from fear or his touch, she didn't know. "I understand."

"You and Jon could—"

"I said I'd stay with you until you could see me home."

"Ah, Christ," Jon muttered from where he now sat on a rock beside a tree chewing on a piece of smoked, dried venison. "What? Have you both got a death wish now?"

Hunter looked at Jon, but made no response. "Let's move on," he said quietly. "There's still a few hours of daylight left."

Alexandra walked to where the mule stood and picked up his lead-line. "Let's go, Jon."

Jon rose, shaking his head. "The man tells us there's someone out there waiting to kill us and we go anyway. I don't like this, not one bit." He lifted his musket onto his shoulder and fell in behind Alexandra and Hunter. "The two of you are crazy, I'm telling you. I just can't figure out for the life of me which one's crazier!"

Hunter, Alexandra, and Jon traveled until dusk and then set up camp in a clearing near a small bubbling stream. Once the campfire was lit and the mule hobbled for the night, Jon settled back on his sleeping mat to nurse his brandy bottle.

Both too restless to turn in, Hunter and Alexandra decided to try to catch a few fish to grill for a late-evening meal. With some fishing line and hooks from one of the mule's packs, the two journeyed up stream just out of sight of Jon and sat down on the bank to try their luck.

Using grubs found under a rotting tree stump Alexandra and Hunter sat in comfortable silence for a while, jiggling their lines in the hopes of catching the first fish. Though silence had once made Alexandra uncomfortable, she had grown used to it out here in the wilderness and found that she liked it. As ridiculous as it seemed to her, she just enjoyed being with Hunter. Sometimes words didn't seem to be necessary.

It was Hunter who finally broke the peace of dusk. "I've been thinking about what Two Crows said," he mentioned casually. "About this captain." He glanced at her. "Maybe it would be a good idea if you and Jon headed south. You could be back in Annapolis in a few days' time."

She jiggled her fishing line. The sun had set

over the horizon to the west, but the sky was still lighted by the brilliant afterglow. "You trying to get rid of me?"

"Yes. No." He groaned, seeming to try to find the right words. "Alexandra—"

"We agreed I'd go with you to find Blue-Green Eyes and then you'd take me home."

"But—"

"*You'd* take me home. Not Jon." She watched the grub on the end of her line bob up and down below the surface of the water. "I like Jon well enough, but I don't know that I can trust him with my life. He can be a selfish man."

"That he can be. But a lot of it's an act. If I asked him to, he'd die for you, Alexandra. He'd die for me."

She didn't want to get into an argument with Hunter over Jon. He was his friend, more than a friend, more like a brother. But the fact remained that it was Hunter she knew would see her home safely. "I said I'll go with you and I will. I'm not afraid."

"Of course you're not afraid. You're the bravest damned woman I think I've ever met. I thought I was going to have to defend Two Crows against you today the way you were interrogating him." He smiled. "It's just that there's no need for you to go with me. This is my battle."

"Jon agreed to go with you to find Blue-Green Eyes. I agreed." She made eye-contact with him and was immediately drawn in by the deep color of his hazel eyes. "I meant what I said today when I said *we* had to go on. *We* have to find Laughing Rain's killer."

Hunter tied his line to a tree root protruding from the dirt bank and slid over to sit beside her. "I heard you say that, but I don't understand. You never even knew her."

"No man has a right to do that to a woman. To take a woman's life like that. That could have been me, Hunter."

He smiled, catching a lock of dark hair that had escaped the leather tie at the nape of her neck. He twisted the lock around and around his finger. "I want to kiss you," he whispered so softly that she felt his words more than heard them.

She turned her face toward his. "So kiss me." On impulse she leaned forward and brushed her lips against his. "Better yet, I'll kiss you."

She watched his eyes drift shut as she pressed a kiss to his sensual mouth. She was exhilarated as she found this power to make a man feel as he made her feel.

"I've been wanting to do this for days," he murmured.

"So why didn't you?" She traced the line of his jaw with her finger, not knowing what made her so bold. "Why didn't you kiss me, Hunter?"

"Because I don't want to become involved. I don't want to care about you. I can't."

"But you already do," she whispered. "Don't you?"

He slipped his hands around her waist and drew her into his lap. Alexandra let go of her fishing line, too caught up in the moment to care.

"Yes. I do. I do care. But it doesn't make any sense. It would never work. We're too different."

Their lips met again, hungrily. She tugged the

leather tie at the nape of his neck and freed his shoulder-length red hair, his magical hair. She ran her fingers through the thick tresses, amazed that a man's hair could be so soft, so sensual, yet so masculine at the same time.

"Things don't always make sense, do they, Hunter?" She was questioning herself as much as she was him. "And things don't always happen the way you think they're going to, either."

He slipped his hand inside her rabbit cloak to cup her breast through the soft doeskin tunic Judith had given her. "Doesn't make sense," she repeated, her thoughts blurring with the sensation of his mouth on hers and the heat of his hand.

Hunter kissed the hollow of her throat as he unlaced the bodice of her doeskin tunic. When his hand touched her bare breast, she groaned, amazed by the sensation. He touched her nipple with his thumb and immediately her nipple puckered against his rough flesh.

His tongue delved deep in her mouth and she strained against him, reveling in the taste of him and the shivers of pleasure he sent through her body.

"Alexandra," he whispered hoarsely in her ear. "Let me make love to you, sweeting. It's what we want, both of us."

Somehow her fingers had found the laces of his tunic. Somehow she had found her way to the crispy hair of his broad muscular chest. "No," she murmured, her hand exploring his hard, male body. "I can't."

"I'll not hurt you. I swear by the Christ, I won't. I just want to touch you. Like this." He rolled her nipple between his thumb and forefinger in a slow, deliciously agonizing way. "I want to kiss you like this." He buried his head between her bare breasts and pressed his hot mouth to her responding flesh.

She shook her head. She was breathless. Her mouth was sore from his kisses. Her mind was a whirl of confused thoughts. She physically ached, but for what, she didn't know. "I can't," she repeated. "I want to, Hunter, but I just can't."

"Why not?" He lifted her breast with his hand. His tongue touched her nipple and she leaned back, awash in glorious sensation. His hand was still touching her in that delicious way, caressing every curve of her body. She could feel herself growing moist between her thighs.

"Why not, Alex?" he repeated, lifting his head to stare directly into her hooded eyes. "Why won't you let me? We've both been hurt. We both need healing. Let us heal each other as only a man and a woman can."

She wanted to say yes. She wanted to make love with Hunter. It was all she'd thought about since the last time he'd touched her. She wanted to know what it was between a man and a woman that men fought wars over, that men killed for, but . . . "I can't," she said again. She buried her face into the hollow of his shoulder, trying to gain control of herself and the situation. "I want to. I don't mean to lead you on. But . . . but I can't, Hunter."

He slid his hand out from her tunic. "Why not?"

"Because . . ." She couldn't look up at him. "You're going to laugh."

"Tell me why."

She forced herself to look him in the eyes. "Because it's all I have to give to my husband someday. If anyone will ever marry me, that is."

He swore softly and looked away.

"No. It's true. Think about it. Try to see it from my point of view. It's all I have, Hunter. It can only be given once."

His muscles suddenly tensed. The tenderness was gone from his voice when he spoke again. "You mean you expect me to marry you?"

"No!" She was completely taken off guard by his words. She held the bodice of the doeskin dress closed with one hand. "No. Of course not. I just meant—"

He pushed her out of his lap and rose. "You're just like all other women, aren't you, Alexandra?"

"No! No, I'm not." She leaped up to stand before him. To face him down. No man would speak to her like this. No man would make her do what she didn't want to do. Not ever again. "I'm not like everyone else. I wouldn't be alone like I am if I was. My papa wouldn't have shipped me off, ashamed of me. If I was like all other women I'd not have been kidnapped, and survived, would I?"

"You're just like the women who try to trap a man into marriage."

"Trap you into marriage!" She laughed at the absurdity of his words. "I'm not trying to trap you into marriage. I'd sooner marry Two Crows than marry you. What makes you think I would want to marry you?"

"You let me touch you. You kissed me like a woman who wanted to be made love to."

"I let you touch me like that because it felt good.

Because you made me feel good. That doesn't mean I want to marry you, you stinking, arrogant, jackanapes!"

"This is why I'm never getting involved with another woman," he said hotly, pointing an accusing finger. "This is why! You want the world, but you don't want to give anything in return."

She dropped her hands to her hips, not caring that she was baring her breasts. The night air was cold on her bare skin, but she didn't notice that either. "What are you talking about?" she shouted furiously. "What the hell are you talking about? You're not making any sense. I hate men! They never make any sense."

"Keep your honey lips," Hunter thundered, walking away. "Keep your soft breasts."

"Son of a stinking cur!" she shouted at him. "I hate you. I hope the cap-i-tan does come after you!"

He disappeared around the bend in the stream, putting an infuriatingly abrupt end to the shouting match. "Knave," she murmured to herself, wrapping her arms around her waist to ward off the sudden chill of the evening. "It didn't feel that great anyway!"

Chapter Twelve

"Come on, where's that sense of adventure you're always nagging me about?" Jon prodded. "The fort is barely two hours' walk directly east. It won't put us far behind, and we could get a decent meal and soft cot to sleep on."

Alexandra walked behind the two men listening to their conversation, trying not to appear sulky. After the incident with Hunter last night, he'd been in a foul mood all day. He had argued for hours with Jon over pointless matters. Worse yet, he'd simply ignored Alexandra.

"I don't want a soft bed to sleep in," Hunter snapped. "I want to find this damned Blue-Green Eyes. I've grown tired of the chase. I want to see this through, Jon."

"A good night's sleep and a hearty meal will fortify you." Jon glanced over his shoulder at Alexandra taking up the rear, leading the mule. "Tell him, Alexandra. He looks like hell, doesn't he? The man needs a decent brandy and a hand of cards."

She shook her head. "Don't get me into this. He could care less what I think."

"Lovers' spat," Jon teased. "Nothing more." He turned back to Hunter. "Come on, friend. I'm dying for a brandy and some companionship. Just one night at the fort and we'll be on our way."

"Last time we stopped at Potter's Fort you stayed three weeks," Hunter grumbled. "I haven't got three weeks till the snow flies."

"What can I say? The twins? Vega and Frieda? What man could resist a pair of long-legged blondes?" He ran to catch up with Hunter, who had increased the length of his stride. "But it won't happen again. One night, I swear to God, and I'll go on north with you. We'll find Blue-Green Eyes. I'll kill the murdering pettifogger myself."

Hunter looked over his shoulder at Alexandra. "I suppose you'd like a hot bath and a soft tick to sleep in." It was the first civil thing he'd said to her all day.

She shrugged. "It makes no difference to me. Do what you want. I can bathe in a stream and sleep on the ground. I've been doing it this long, haven't I?"

Jon slowed up, letting Alexandra catch him. "Come on! Roasted beef. Pastry tarts. Wine. A bath. I bet they've soap. Bubbly lady's soap. The fort does trading. Their storehouse is enormous. Tell Hunter you want to stop for the night. He couldn't give a lick for my comfort, but he'll stop the night for you, Alexandra."

She looked at Jon. "I said I don't care." Honestly, she didn't. She was so miserable after the fight with Hunter last night that even the prospect of a hot bath and a hearty meal didn't sound inviting. "It's Hunter's decision. It's his quest. I'm just trying to get back to my aunt's in Annapolis with my scalp attached, remember?"

She heard Hunter sigh. "All right," he finally said. "But one night."

"Yes!" Jon leapt in the air, swinging a fist in excitement. "One night of heaven!" He ran to catch up with Hunter again. "One night!" He lowered his voice. "One night with the Swedish twins?" He elbowed him with a cackle of glee.

"One night," Hunter repeated, threatening him with a stern finger. "But then I move on, Jon. I'm warning you. With or without you."

Less than two hours later, Hunter, Alexandra, and Jon arrived at Fort Potter. They were welcomed by two red-uniformed English soldiers and escorted through the gate of the garrisoned wooden fort that jutted up out of the pine-forest floor.

Inside the log and mud-mortared walls, Alexandra was amazed to find a small town. Though it was a military outpost, Jon had explained to her, many of the men had either married Indian women or simply brought Indian women into the fort to help pass the lonely hours. Through the gates was a large open muddy area and then beyond the yard were one- and two-story log cabins attached by a maze of connecting covered walkways. There were several small children running about the compound, along with a pack of yapping dogs, two flocks of geese, and several bleating goats.

The soldiers, who seemed to know both Hunter and Jon, led them through the gates and into the *office*, the first doorway they came to, in the haphazardly built inner log walls.

Alexandra hung behind Jon and Hunter as they entered the large room that seemed to her more like the common room of a tavern than a military facility. It was sparsely furnished with several battered English pieces and two dozen or so crude wooden stools. Two large dining tables dominated the smoky room. Uniformed men sat at both, some eating, others playing cards. A lone red rooster strutted down the center of one of the plank tables.

At the far wall was a large stone fireplace. A young, mob-capped girl stirred a pot of some sort of soup or stew. A leggy dog ran in its circular cage on the hearth, turning a large hunk of roasting meat on an iron spit.

Alexandra felt her stomach rumble. "Nice place," she murmured sarcastically in Jon's ear. "This was the civilized establishment I walked two hours for?"

He turned back to grin at her. "What did you expect out here? The queen's drawing room?" He shrugged. "The drink isn't sour and the food lacks maggots. What more could a man ask?"

Hunter leaned to whisper in her other ear. "My, how the mighty have fallen. This *is* civilized to Jon-boy."

Alexandra looked up to see Hunter smiling at her. His anger was gone, the black cloud that had shadowed his face all day, absent. She smiled back. "If this suits you, gentlemen, it suits me."

Hunter was still smiling. "That's the spirit."

Spotting Hunter and Jon in the doorway, one of the officers rose. "Hunter! Jon! How the hell are you two? I heard just last week your scalps were hanging from a Mohawk lodge pole somewhere north of here!" The bearded, blond-haired man slapped Hunter on the back, laughing heartily. "I should have known that lying half-breed Joseph was full of crap. I pay the man to bring me back information and all he does is tell tall tales and drink my whiskey!"

Hunter laid his hand on Alexandra's shoulder. "Joshua, I want you to meet the Lady Alexandra Lambert. Alexandra, Captain Joshua Potter. King's servant and one hell of a soldier. He runs this sorry excuse for an English fort. Carved it out of the forest nearly ten years ago."

The captain took Alexandra's hand, bowed and brushed his lips against it. "A lady. You're the first to grace these humble walls, madame. Pleased to make your acquaintance."

"Pleased to meet you, Captain."

Still holding her hand, he nodded toward Hunter. Jon had beaten a hasty retreat to the far table and had already been dealt into a hand of cards. "So tell me how such a beautiful woman could get caught up with these nitty muck-worms?"

Alexandra looked to Hunter for support. She

really didn't want to have to go through the entire tale of her uncle's and cousin's death and her kidnapping by Two Crows. She just wasn't up to it.

As if sensing her thoughts, Hunter took her hand from the captain's. "Long story, Josh. One meant to tell over a hot meal and a cold ale. You think we could find this young lady a bath and a little privacy? We've been traveling hard."

"I'll have Martha see right to it, ma'am." He spoke directly to Alexandra, ignoring Hunter. "But please, promise that once you've been refreshed you'll grace us with your company again. Come and sup with us. It's been a long time since I've enjoyed a lady's supper conversation."

She nodded. "That would be fine. But first a bath."

"And tea," Hunter stipulated. "The lady would like a true cup of English tea."

"Tea it is, then!" Captain Potter turned back toward the fireplace. "Martha!"

The girl dropped her spoon in the cast-iron pot and came running. "Captain?"

She was barely more than a child of ten or twelve, her face still dimpled with the roundness of a girl who was not yet a woman. Alexandra wondered what she was doing out here in the middle of nowhere. What terrible fate had befallen a girl so young? But Martha was clean and appeared to be in good health.

"This is Lady Alexandra. I want you to take her to the guest's quarters and see she has water for a bath and a clean change of clothing. Hot water,

Martha. Have Allen haul it up."

Martha nodded with each instruction as she wiped her hands on her apron. "Yes, Captain."

"And, most importantly, a cup of tea. Have Allen fetch the tea chest from my private quarters. The lady will instruct you on how to make it."

She bobbed her head. "Yes, sir. Right away, Captain." The girl turned shyly to Alexandra. "This way, ma'am, if you please."

"Go on," Hunter murmured in Alexandra's ear. "You're safe enough here. I won't be far. I'm going to sit right here with Joshua. You call me, and I'll come."

His voice was strangely affectionate. She just couldn't figure this man out! How could he have been shouting at her the way he had yesterday and now be so sweet. "Thank you," she murmured.

He gave her a little wave as she followed Martha through an inner doorway. As she disappeared from the view of the room down the dark, musty, hallway, she heard Hunter's rich, husky voice and she smiled to herself. When he was kind, like this, when he was laughing, she almost felt as if she was falling in love with him.

Heart's wounds! Wasn't that a ridiculous thought. She, Lady Alexandra Lambert, in love with the Hunter of the Shawnee. Alexandra laughed aloud in the dark hallway and Martha turned around to glance at her suspiciously.

"No, I've not taken leave of my senses," she assured the young girl. "Not yet at least."

* * *

Not half an hour later Alexandra lay perfectly still in a large wooden tub, hot water to her chin. With her eyes half closed, she sighed in utter contentment. Never had a bath felt so good. She took a sip from her teacup and then rested her head on the cotton towel again. She'd forgotten how glorious a hot bath, and a hot cup of tea, could be. The only thing that felt better was—

She sat up.

Hunter. There she was, thinking about him again. Remembering what his hands had felt like on her breasts. Remembering the taste of him. She groaned aloud. Did all women fall into this wanton trap so easily, or was it just her?

She rose out of the tub and grabbed the towel Martha had left for her. Standing in a puddle of water in the tiny room, she dried herself off. Across the narrow wooden bed lay a plain blue sprigged gown Martha had brought for her. Beside the gown was a pile of ladies' underclothing, including stays and woolen stockings. Martha was cleaning her leather traveling clothes, so she had to put on the gown, but the thought of all those tight undergarments made her shudder. All she wanted to do was to go downstairs and have a bit of supper with Hunter. Then she wanted to crawl onto the goose tick and sleep.

She reached out to finger the soft but sturdy material of the gown. What if she were to skip the underclothing and just go down to supper in the dress, stockings and her moccasins? Who would know? Who would care?

Without another thought to the propriety she

had once been so concerned with, she dressed, brushed out her clean hair and tied it back, still damp, with a grosgrain ribbon. After finishing the last sip of tea, she went out the door, down the stairs and down the long dark hallway back the way she and Martha had come. The night air was so cold in the narrow hallway that she wished she'd worn her rabbit cloak, but she knew the common room would be warm from the fireplace and that thought made her hurry.

She stepped through the door into the dining room and Hunter immediately rose and came toward her. "Feel better, sweeting?" When he leaned toward her, she could smell the ale on his breath. There he was, smiling at her again. It was almost as if he was smitten with her. *Has to be the strong drink,* she thought.

"I feel much better, thank you."

"I had Martha keep you a warm plate." He led her back to the table where he'd been seated. "Hungry? The stew is delicious. A damned sight tastier than Jon's."

She looked up at him, smiling. He'd shed his outer tunic in the heat of the room and now wore his fringed leather leggings and a sleeveless doeskin vest that tied up the front. Here in such a crude setting, so far away from home and all that was once familiar, he seemed shockingly attractive to her with his brilliant red hair pulled back in a queue and in his ear the copper earring that sparkled in the firelight.

She sat down on the stool he indicated and at his signal, Martha immediately brought her a plate heaped with food, and a mug of cool ale. The bear stew was hearty, the bread flaky, and the ale surprisingly sweet.

As Alexandra ate, she listened as the men talked. Hunter, the captain, and several other men were just finishing their meal. On the far table, Jon was concentrating on the game of cards he was playing with several red-coated soldiers. Once he leaned back in his chair and winked at her, but then went right back to the game at hand.

After a second helping of stew and a third cup of ale, Alexandra pushed away her plate and rose to stretch her legs. Hunter and the captain had begun a friendly game of knap and slur. They invited her to play, but she declined. She'd never been much for the gaming tables. Instead, she just stood back and watched.

The heat of the room and the potency of the ale made her mind pleasantly fuzzy. She was sleepy. She knew she should turn in, but instead, she lingered in the room, listening to the men tease and prod each other as they played their games . . . listening to the sound of Hunter's voice.

He called to her and leaned over his shoulder to hear his voice in the noisy room. "You look tired," he said, his hazel eyes sparkling. He had had a lot to drink, she could tell by the tone of his voice. He wasn't drunk, but there was hint of amusement in every word he spoke. "Let me see you to bed."

She rested her hand on his shoulder. "No. Stay where you are. Play your game. You're winning. I can find my room on my own."

"You certain?" He touched her hand where it

rested on his shoulder. Their gestures were innocent enough, but with each touch some sort of energy arced between them.

Suddenly she wished she was alone with him. She wished . . . "I'll be fine. Good night."

She almost hoped he would get up and follow her, but he didn't.

"I'll check in on you later before I turn in," he called after her as he lifted his mug of ale to his lips.

She smiled back at him and went out the planked inner door. Upstairs in her little loft room she slipped out of her dress and into the shift she'd left on the bed. She climbed into the bed, which indeed sported a feather tick, and she pulled the quilts up high to ward off the chill. She closed her eyes, but sleep eluded her.

All she could think of was Hunter. The smell of him. His touch. The sound of his voice in her ear. For a long time she lay listening to the distant sounds of the men talking and laughing. Chairs scraped the wooden floors. A dog barked. Somewhere in the maze of buildings a woman laughed. A small case clock on the mantel above the tiny fireplace in her room chimed midnight, then one in the morning. Still she couldn't sleep.

Then, just as she was finally beginning to doze off, she heard her door squeak.

"Alex?"

"Hunter?" she called drowsily.

"You asleep?"

"Not yet. Come in," she murmured, rolling onto her side. If she'd been more awake perhaps she'd have thought twice about inviting him into the bedchamber, but this late at night, after the long day of travel and the ale, she saw no reason for concern.

She felt the bed sink as he sat down on the corner. He reached out to brush back the hair from her face. "Feels good to be in a bed, does it?"

"Um-hmm," she murmured. He continued to stroke her hair and she nestled deeper into the goose tick. His hand was so warm, his touch so relaxing.

"I just wanted to say good night. I'll bunk with the men tonight but if you need me—"

"I'm fine." She rolled onto her back and looked up at him. By the light of the glowing coals in the fireplace she could see the outline of his expressive face. Somewhere he'd had a bath. His hair was still so damp that it curled at the nape of his neck. He'd changed into a pair of cotton breeches and a plain white muslin shirt. He smelled of shaving soap, ale, and that exquisite masculine scent that always seemed to cling to him.

He leaned down to brush his lips against her cheek. She turned her head and then his mouth was on hers.

"Alexandra," he murmured.

"Hunter . . ."

His innocent kiss deepened and she found herself reaching out to him, pulling him closer. He stretched out beside her on the bed, slipping beneath the heavy quilt. Without consideration for the consequences, she molded her nearly nude body to his. She sighed audibly as he slipped his hand into her bodice and caressed her budding nipple.

Her hands found the corded muscles of his shoulders and then his back. As they kissed, their mouths melted into one; their bodies entwined. The past slipped from Alexandra's mind. All that mattered was this man and the way he made her feel deep inside. All that mattered was the excitement she felt as she grazed his hardened male muscles with her fingertips.

Heavens what a creation of God's a man's body was! How distinctly different from her own. Where her flesh was soft and rounded and smooth, his was all hard and rippled, sprinkled with hair.

They kissed again and again and when he moved above her, she did not protest, not even when he lifted her gown.

"I want you, *ki-ti-hi*," he murmured, his voice hot in her ear. "I want to make love to you. I want to take you to the heavens and back."

"Yes," she whispered, panting. "Yes, Hunter. Love me. Please love me. It's what I want. I'm sure of it."

He lifted his hand, gliding it up her calf, to her shapely thigh . . . higher. She threaded her fingers through his damp hair, having yanked it free from its leather binding. She groaned aloud as he touched the soft nest of curls at the apex of her thighs.

"Ah, Hunter," she cried. "Hunter—"

Then suddenly he stiffened. He ceased his movement, dropping his head to rest it on her bare breast.

She was breathless. Confused. Was this it? Was she supposed to be left with this empty aching inside? "Hunter?"

"Stay here," he said in an odd voice.

"What?"

He slid out of bed and ran for the door. "I said stay here. Put on your dress. Or at least your shift. Light a candle. I'll be right back."

He slammed the door behind him.

Alexandra shook her head to clear the cobwebs in her mind. She slid her bare feet over the side of the bed, letting them dangle in midair. She still hadn't caught her breath. What was he doing? Had he lost his mind?

She rose and straightened the shift that had tangled around her waist. Going to the mantel, she lit a single beeswax candle. Just as she pulled on the flannel wrapper Martha had left for her on the chair, Hunter came back through the door. He was half carrying, half dragging a balding man in a night dress.

"Hunter?" she cried.

"Marry us, good Reverend," Hunter insisted.

"Hunter!" Alexandra wrapped her arms tightly around her waist, utterly bewildered.

"What?" the reverend gentleman mumbled, equally confused by Hunter's request. He squinted to see Hunter in the dim light of the room.

"You heard me. I said marry us," Hunter demanded, brushing back a lock of red hair off his shoulder. "Now!"

Chapter Thirteen

"N-now?" the man stammered, scratching his stomach sleepily. "In the m-middle of the night?"

"Marry you?" Alexandra exploded, the meaning of Hunter's words finally sinking in. "Marry you! I'm not going to marry you!"

Hunter turned his head. "Yes, you are." He looked back at the minister standing in the doorway. "Yes. Marry us. Tonight. Now. This instant."

"This . . . this is highly irregular. W-well, I-I'm not even dressed." He lifted a dark eyebrow. "The bride is not dressed, the groom . . ." He indicated Hunter's bare chest weakly.

Alexandra crossed the tiny bedchamber in three determined strides. "It doesn't matter if you're dressed, I'm dressed, he's dressed, or not. This entire discussion is preposterous!" She prodded Hunter's bare chest with her forefinger. "I'm not marrying you. Not tonight. Not dressed, not undressed. Not ever."

Hunter tried to put his arm around her. "Now, sweeting—"

"Get your hands off me." She shoved him away. "Have you gone stark raving mad? If this is a joke I don't see the humor. Maybe you're stumbling drunk! Is that it?"

He leaned toward her so that the reverend couldn't hear him. His breath was warm and husky in her ear. "Not any madder than you. Not a joke. Just a little drunk, else I wouldn't have the nerve, but I realize what I'm doing. Now be agreeable for just once, Alex, and let us get this over with. I mean to bed you tonight and bed you well. The ceremony will take but a moment and then we can get back to what we were about in yonder bed." His eyes cut to her bed with the crumpled bedcovers.

She grasped his head with both hands, practically shouting into his face. "Don't you hear me, you pig-headed jackanapes? I tell you I'm not going to marry you!"

He grabbed her by the collar of her dressing gown and drew her even closer. "You are going to marry me and marry me now. It's the best thing for you and you'll realize it by morning." He winked. "I can promise that."

She turned in utter bewilderment to face the minister still standing in the doorway. If Hunter couldn't be reasoned with, certainly a man of the church . . . "Surely you wouldn't wed a woman against her will?"

The holy man's eyes widened. "Surely . . . surely no." He looked at Hunter as if for support. "N-not if she *positively* didn't wish to be married."

Hunter grabbed her by the elbow and steered her toward the minister. "She does wish to marry me. She's mad in love with me. Left her father's home to run away with me. I have to marry her, tonight, else her reputation will be ruined."

"Liar!"

Hunter clamped his hand down on her mouth and smiled with exaggeration. "It's just wedding jitters. Do what a clerk of the cloth does. See to the words, man!"

Alexandra tried to back up, but Hunter's grip was too steady. His hand still covered her mouth.

Her mind was swimming. Surely he wasn't serious. Surely he wasn't really going to marry her without her consent!

"Come! Come!" Hunter insisted. "Let's get to it, good sir! As you can see, I'm an anxious bridegroom."

The reverend stammered for a moment and then lifted a hand. "B-Brethren, we are gathered—"

Alexandra clawed Hunter's hand from her mouth. "No! It won't be legal." She was grasping at straws now. Anything to stop him. "It's not binding! There are no witnesses! No legal document." She grabbed Hunter's arm. "You can't marry like this. It would never hold up in court!"

Hunter looked at Alexandra and then back at the reverend who appeared rather relieved by her declaration. "She's right." Hunter let out a loud sigh and bit down on his lower lip. "Damnation! I want it legal. I want no one to claim our children to be bastards later."

"Children!" Alexandra tightened her grip on

his muscular arm, trying to remain in control of herself. "Hunter, you can't—"

"Would you hush, woman? Just for once in your life, keep that sweet mouth of yours shut. Can't you see I'm thinking here?"

"Hunter—"

"Ah hah! I've got it!" He grabbed her by the wrist and dragged her past the reverend at a gallop. "Five minutes, Reverend. I'll give you five minutes to get a piece of paper, a quill, and ink and be back in this room. My betrothed is right. This has to be legal in the English courts!"

Before the reverend could respond, Hunter had turned down the drafty hallway and led her into the darkness. "Come on, Alex! This really is the best for you considering all that's happened. You'd know it was true if you'd just consider it for a moment."

Alexandra tried to pull away. She tried to escape, but he was too strong for her. He was too determined. Her bare feet scraped the splintered plank floor as he half carried, half dragged her along. "Don't do this, Hunter. Please," she begged.

He came to an abrupt halt in the hallway and pushed her up against the log wall. He brought his face so close to hers that in spite of the frigid air, she was suddenly warm again. "Tell me you don't want me, Alex," he whispered harshly. "Tell me you don't want to lie with me. Tell me you don't like it when I touch you." He brought his hand up beneath her breast, his thumb caressing the bud of her nipple through the thin material of her dressing gown. "Like this." He lowered his mouth to the hollow of her throat. "Like this. Just tell me!"

She threw back her head, all too aware of the cold, unhewn wood at her back and Hunter's overwhelming sexuality. She was trapped. She squeezed her eyes shut. Yes, yes, she wanted him . . . desperately. She wanted him even now when his touch was a little too rough, his kiss just a little too insistent. She wanted to make love with him. She wanted to know what it meant truly to be a woman, to have experienced what it was between a man and a woman that the poets had been writing about since the dawn of mankind.

But marry him? No. She was afraid of him. Afraid of his unpredictability. Afraid of the emotions he stirred in her, the good and the bad.

"Alexandra!" He lifted her wrists above her head, molding his body to hers as he brushed his lips against the lobe of her ear. "I'm waiting."

"Yes," she whispered miserably.

"What?"

He was kissing her again. Confusing her. Making her senses reel until logical thought was impossible.

"I can't hear you, sweeting. Speak louder."

"Yes . . ."

"Yes, what?"

"Yes, I want you." She fought back a sob. "I want you, Hunter."

He touched his mouth to hers gently. "**And I** you. There's nothing wrong with that, sweeting. We're both of legal age. Neither is married to another. It's all right to want me, and I you."

"But I don't want to marry you," she lamented.

"Why not?" His voice was harsh again. "Tell

me, damn it! Because you've gotten a better offer?"

"No."

"Because you're saving yourself for a nunnery?"

"No."

He ran his fingers through her hair. "Look at me."

She opened her eyes. Even in the darkness she could see his hazel-eyed gaze, a gaze that pierced her very soul.

"Then why?" he asked.

"Because . . . because—"

"Ah hah! You don't have a reason other than the fact that you're a female and females never know what they want or why!" He grabbed her arm and started down the hallway again. "So let's do it and be done with it before I sober and change my mind!"

"Hunter." She ran with him to keep from tripping. "Hunter, please—"

He stopped and slammed his fist into a door. "Coming in Jon, ready or not." He turned the doorknob and flung it open.

Pale yellow candlelight illuminated the tiny room. On the far wall, which was not far from the doorway, Alexandra spotted Jon's dark head of hair, a twist of long, naked limbs, and a flash of bare breasts. She huffed a breath of shock, but Hunter seemed to pay them no mind. She tried to turn away, knowing her face must be burning with embarrassment, but Hunter refused to let go of her wrist.

He marched up to the bed and tugged on the muslin sheet. "Jon."

"God's teeth!" Jon mumbled thickly.

A high-pitched feminine giggle came from the lumpy bed.

Hunter grabbed a corner of the sheet and pulled it back to reveal Jon's face. "I've need of you, friend. Just a moment of your time and you can get back to your recreation."

Jon rolled onto his back to stare up at Hunter. "Have you bloody taken leave of your senses?"

"Hunter?" came a voice from beneath the sheets. "Zee Hunter uf the Shawnee?"

Alexandra's mouth dropped wide open as a woman's face appeared from beneath the sheets. The woman smiled, her lovely young heart-shaped face framed by a head of blond hair.

"Frieda!" Hunter nodded in a mannerly fashion. "Good to see you again. How's your sister Vega?"

"Hunter! Iss that you?" There was another string of giggles as the sheet moved again and another blond head bobbed up. The women were identical twins, as alike as two peas in a pod.

Alexandra clamped her free hand across her mouth, mortified. "God's teeth, Jon!" Then, suddenly coming to the realization that the twins had immediately recognized Hunter, she jerked the hand he still had wrapped around her wrist. "You know these trollops?"

He grinned sheepishly. "Alexandra, meet Frieda and Vega." He cleared his throat. "Friends."

The second twin reached out and caught Hunter's hand. "Jon said you vould not join us. But you come now." She giggled slyly.

"No. No, sorry, Vega." He gently disengaged

himself. "Alexandra is my betrothed."

Vega looked up with wide blue eyes and reached for Alexandra. "Oh! So sorry. You are most velcome to join us too, Al-ex-andra, betrothed."

When the girl reached out to touch her, Alexandra drew back as if she'd been burned by a candle flame. Surely Hunter had not participated in such debauchery! "I think not," she managed to murmur.

Jon slid his legs over the side of the bed and Alexandra caught a glance of his nakedness before she was able to turn away.

Hunter's soft laughter filled her ears as he released her. "You're more of a man than I thought, Jon, to take the twins on all by your lonesome."

Alexandra heard Jon slip into his breeches.

"Just tell me what the hell you want, will you, Hunter?" Alexandra turned to see Jon reaching for half a glass of whiskey left sitting on a camp stool. He took a long swallow. "I mean, this is crazy, even for you."

"You've got to stop him, Jon," she sputtered. "He's making me marry him! He won't listen! He—"

"Marry *her*?" Jon screwed up his face, looking to his companion. "You can't marry her! Your father will have a cow!"

Alexandra dropped a hand to her hip, insulted by Jon's tone of voice. "What? You don't think I'm good enough for him? I'll have you know my father is the Lord of Monthrop. My family has been respectable for a thousand years." She gave a derisive snort. "And I can tell you one thing, no one in my family ever traipsed off to the colonies to pretend he was an Indian!"

Jon took another swallow from his cup, running one hand through his tangled black hair. He squinted, obviously confused. "I thought you didn't want to marry him."

She wrapped her arms around her waist. "I . . . I don't, but don't make it sound like I'm not fitting enough to be Lord Redman's wife here! He's the lunatic! Not me! My father would be the one with the vapors if I came home toting him as husband!"

Hunter grasped Alexandra's arm. "Why don't you two discuss this tomorrow. Right now, we need you down the hall, Jon."

"Christ! I'm not marrying her. What do you need me for?"

"Witness." Hunter started for the door, taking Alexandra with him. "I want this wedding legal and binding. You can be my best man if you like."

Jon followed them, trying to reason with Hunter. "You're making a big mistake. You'll regret it in the morning."

Hunter flashed him a lopsided grin over one shoulder. "But I'll have had one hell of a night, won't I!"

"Have one hell of a night here." Jon hooked a thumb in the direction of the twins. "Take one, take both. All to yourself. I'll sleep in the hall."

"I'm going to marry her." Hunter started down the narrow, dark hallway with Alexandra in tow. "You're not going to stop me, Jon."

"But I don't want to marry you," Alexandra protested.

"You're not going to stop me either."

Jon groaned, running to keep up. "Is this out of a sense of guilt, Hunter? Is that it? Because if it is—"

"Shut up, Jon!"

"Hunter—"

"You with me, Jon?" Hunter never broke stride, but his tone was steely. "You going to help me out here? Because if you're not, you can go back to the twins. My mind is made up. It has nothing to do with the past. I'm going to marry her with or without your blessing. I just wanted you to be there."

"I'm not dressed. And damn, it's cold out here!" Jon slapped his bare chest.

"I can't believe you're going to go along with this, Jon," Alexandra argued. "I can't believe you're going to let him force me into marriage!"

Jon shrugged as the three entered the dim light of Alexandra's bedchamber. "What can I say, sweetheart? Hunter's the best friend I have in the world. The only one that's saved my life. If he wants to get married, I'll be here to witness it."

Alexandra saw the reverend standing near the fireplace in a flannel nightrobe warming his hands. An ominous sheet of onion-skin along with a quill and ink bottle lay on the small table by the bed.

"I can't believe this is happening," she muttered, dizzy with fear.

Hunter rested his arm around her waist and ushered her toward the reverend. "A witness! A bit of paper to sign." Hunter slapped his bare chest. "Damn well sounds like a marriage to me!"

Alexandra covered her face with her hands.

What need was there to fight him? To fight any of them? They were going to do what they wanted with her. Wasn't that always the way with men?

Hunter made a motion for the ceremony to begin and the reverend started to chant his obligatory words. Alexandra was so numb she couldn't think. She squirmed to get away, but Hunter held her fast. When the sorry excuse for a man of the cloth got to the point where it was necessary for the bride to give her sanction, Alexandra pressed her lips tightly together. They might marry her against her will, but be damned if she would consent to anything! But Hunter gave her a sharp prod in the side and she gave an involuntary squeak.

The minister took that to be a sign of her approval.

When they arrived at the part in the ceremony where the groom was to provide a wedding band, the minister started to pass over it, but Hunter stopped him.

"No wait! I've a ring."

Alexandra watched in total astonishment as he pulled the copper ring from his earlobe and, grasping her shaking hand, slipped it over her ring finger.

"And with this ring, I thee wed : . ."

Hunter's voice was still ringing in her ears as he led her to the table to sign the document. He signed with a scrawl of illegible names and then pressed the quill into her hands.

"Be damned if I'll sign," she muttered from clenched teeth.

Hunter grabbed her hand and guided it across

the onion-skin page making a X on the appropriate line. "She doesn't write," he explained to the minister.

"Don't write! How dare you—"

Hunter clamped his mouth down on hers, refusing to budge until she thought she would suffocate. When he withdrew, she was gasping for breath. "Didn't yet kiss the bride, did I?" he remarked. "Now if you'll excuse us, gentlemen, my wife and I would like to become better acquainted. I'll bring payment to your room on the morrow, good Reverend." Hunter snatched up the still-wet document and handed it over Alexandra's head to Jon. "Take this for safe-keeping and lock us in, will you?" He grinned at Jon.

"You're going to regret this," Jon muttered, following the minister out the door. "You know you are."

"Good night," Hunter called. "Don't expect us early. We'll get on the trail after we break the fast." He gave a wave.

Jon stepped out of the room and closed the door behind him. It was not until Alexandra heard the bolt slide that Hunter finally let her loose.

"To us, wife," he said, lifting a pewter mug of ale apparently left by the minister. "May our days together number many and our sons more."

Alexandra swung her fist and knocked the mug from his hand, splattering the contents across his bare chest.

Chapter Fourteen

Hunter slammed the mug down on the table and touched his bare, broad chest. Foamy ale ran in rivulets to the waistline of his broadcloth breeches. "Damnation woman! What's wrong with you?"

"What's wrong with me?" She took a step toward him, too angry to be afraid of him. The weight of the copper band on her finger was heavy. "What's wrong with me? You just forced me to marry you and you ask what's wrong with *me?*"

He grabbed from a chair the dress she'd worn that evening and began wiping the ale off himself. "I've heard nothing from you for weeks but prattle about how you have to have a husband. I provide you with one and you're hot with me!"

"You didn't provide me with a husband! You married me yourself!"

He shrugged, throwing the dress to the floor in a damp heap. "What's the difference? You're a respectably married woman now. A bride with her maidenhead still intact! A rarity indeed in London society!"

She balled her fists, bringing them to her face in frustration. "You're missing the point!"

He shook his head, wide-eyed. "And just what is the point, pray tell?"

"The point is," she spoke slowly, as if to a child, "that the marriage was not of my choosing."

"And what?" he scoffed. "You chose the last two men who dumped you?"

She thrust out her jaw.

"Did you?" he asked.

"No!"

He lifted his hands heavenward. "Then there you have it. Women don't choose their spouses." He pointed an accusatory finger. "But I've got news for you, men don't either. It's all politics. The decisions are left up to the family. A man is lucky if he's ever met his bride when she comes to him at the altar! Then dog-faced or old as his mother, he's stuck with her the rest of his born days."

The circumstances of her first betrothal flashed before her. It was true enough. Their families had drawn up the betrothal papers. Geoffry Rordan had never laid eyes on her. She, at least, had had the opportunity to see him close enough to know he wasn't infirm or disfigured. He, on the other hand, had never had that option. Geoffry Rordan was to have met her at the betrothal party. It had never occurred to her until this moment how unfair that was to both of them.

Alexandra turned away. She was so angry, so confused. She didn't know what to say.

"At least we've met each other, Alexandra," Hunter said, his tone softening. "We've talked together. We've laughed together. We've spent enough time together to know that we at least have a fighting chance at being happy with each other." He came toward her and she felt his hand on the curve of her shoulder. "We know that despite our differences we can make each other's blood boil with a single kiss. That's a hell of a good start to a marriage, I'd say."

When he turned her around so that she was facing him, she squeezed her eyes shut. She didn't want to look at him. She didn't want to admit that somewhere in his senseless words was a tiny thread of truth. She didn't want to admit, even to herself, that somewhere deep inside she was excited by the thought of being married to this wild, unpredictable, virile man.

"Kiss me, Alex," he said softly, lifting her chin with the tip of his finger.

"No," she whispered, her eyes still shut. "I'm still mad at you. You should have asked me."

"And what would you have said if I'd gone down on one knee and begged for your hand?"

She lifted her lashes to stare up at him. His breath was warm on her lips. "I'd have said no, of course."

His mouth touched hers. "Of course," he murmured. He grasped her wrists and raised her hands, leaving them to rest on his bare shoulders. "You'd have done the logical thing, the thing a decent Englishwoman would have done. But the path of logic is not always the best path to take. Sometimes you have to follow your gut instinct, remember?" He nibbled at the lobe of her ear. "Sometimes you have to go with your heart."

He kissed her again, but this time she couldn't help herself. She responded. She touched his tongue with the tip of hers. She tasted the ale and the intoxicating flavor of passion on his mouth.

"Ah, sweet Alexandra," he whispered in her ear, bringing his hand up to cup her buttocks through her night robe. "Tell me you'll let me make love to you. Tell me you give your consent."

She brushed her fingertips over his bare chest, still damp with the ale she'd splashed on him. She was fascinated by the hardness of his muscles and the crispness of the dark red hair sprinkled across his chest.

"Tell me," he whispered, pressing his mouth to the hollow of her neck. "Let me love you, Wife. Let me teach you the ways of a man and woman. Let me show pleasure you've never known."

Her hand fell to his hard, muscular buttocks and she kneaded them as he had kneaded hers. She leaned back as he kissed a trail down between her breasts, peeling away an inch of dressing gown at a time.

"Tell me," he repeated.

"Yes," she heard herself say in a voice so filled with sensuality that she didn't recognize it as her own. "Yes, love me. Show me."

With one sudden movement he swept her into his arms and carried her to the narrow bed. He laid her down and then, drawing the candle closer on the small table he slid in the bed and stretched out beside her, his hand gliding over her quivering body.

"Blow out the candle," she whispered. She could feel her cheeks burning. She'd said yes. She'd given her consent. There was no turning back now.

"No, no," he murmured in her ear. "Making love is an act meant not just to feel, but to see, to hear." He brought his mouth to hers, sliding his hand down the curve of her side. "Now lie back and relax. I'll not rush you. We've all night."

Following his instructions, she relented and lay back on the soft goosedown tick. She pushed all thoughts of fear or embarrassment far from her mind. She was married now, wasn't she? She had a right to take her pleasure with her husband.

Hunter slowly opened her nightrobe to her waist, then untying the drawstring bodice of her shift, he pushed aside the delicate material and brought his mouth down to take her nipple. He teased the pink nub with the tip of his tongue and she arched her back, sighing softly.

She ran her fingers through his shoulder-length red hair, still intensely aware of the copper ring she wore on her finger. As waves of pleasure washed over her the word *husband* echoed again and again in her head.

When Hunter pulled the nightclothes off her shoulders and slipped them down around her ankles, she made no protest. The caress of his labor-roughened hands felt too good against her flesh. His kisses were too enticing. All that mattered now was the stroke of his hand and the soft, tender endearments he whispered in her ear.

He caressed her with his fingertips, flesh barely brushing flesh, sending chills of anticipation through her veins. When he wove a trail across her flat stomach toward the bed of soft curls below, she stiffened involuntarily, but he kissed softly, whispering assurances. Against her will, she felt her muscles relax. She had never known such exquisite pleasure.

When Hunter slipped off the edge of the bed to drop his breeches, she opened her eyes to watch him by the light of the candle. A smile played on her lips as she watched him lower the broadcloth material to reveal to evidence of his ardor.

Perhaps she should have been shocked by the sight of his engorged member. She'd heard enough servant chatter to know that some delicate women were known to faint at such a sight, but to her, at this moment, he was shamelessly beautiful.

He smiled a silly smile as he climbed back into the bed and lowered himself over her. "Not as shy as you thought," he teased.

She lifted her hips to meet his, shifting beneath him until she felt his hardness pressing against her woman's mound. A sweet, burning, aching had spread through her, an aching she knew only he could ease.

Hunter pressed his hips to hers in a rhythmic motion again and again, covering her face, her neck, her breasts with soft, fleeting kisses.

How perfectly our bodies mold together, she thought, as she spread her legs in what seemed a most natural gesture. How flawless this act of love between a man and a woman.

"I've tried to control my lust," he rasped in her ear, "but I'm sorely getting ahead of myself." He brushed his lips against her cheek. "Are you ready, sweeting?"

Alexandra could feel her heart pounding. No

matter how fast she breathed, she seemed unable to fill her lungs. "I'm ready," she answered.

With the aid of his hand he parted her soft folds and slipped inside her. Her first reaction was one of surprise. "Oh," she murmured. She had expected pain or at least discomfort. There was none, only an overpowering sensation of a task yet to be completed.

"You all right?" he whispered.

"Yes, yes . . ." Instinctively she lifted her hips to accommodate him.

Hunter was breathing heavily in her ear now. She could feel his heart pounding. Slowly he moved, rising and falling, filling her.

"Hunter," she called, lifting her hands behind her head, writhing in the ecstasy of his well-timed movements.

"Alex, sweet Alex," he crooned.

Time seemed to stand still as she felt her skin grow flushed with excitement. Higher and higher her expectations rose. Faster and faster they moved, once separate, now rising and falling as one. She felt herself sinking her fingernails into the flesh of his back, driving herself harder against him, all thought but to reach some unreachable pinnacle gone from her head.

Then, without warning she lifted up in a cry of ultimate ecstasy. She was so surprised by the sudden, violent pleasure that her eyelids flew open. There was Hunter, staring down at her . . . smiling.

He was laughing, softly, all-knowingly. He gave her a moment to rest and then he began to move again. Alexandra clung to him, moving with him, wanting to give him the same joy he had given her. Finally with one long thrust he groaned, burying his face in her hair that spilled across the pillow. Then his movement ceased and nothing could be heard but their erratic breathing.

After what seemed a long time to Alexandra, Hunter lifted off her and rolled onto his side, drawing her into his arms. When he spoke he sounded sleepy but content. "With a wedding night like this, I'm going to have to work hard to best it," he murmured.

She smoothed his stubbled cheek with her fingertips, wanting to hold on forever to the feeling she had at this moment. "So this was a decent first effort, hmm?" She was as pleased with herself as she was with him, certain she had given as well as taken pleasure.

"Damned decent." He lifted up, kissed her soundly on the mouth and then rested his head on her pillow again. "Now cease the chatter and sleep, Wife. Give me a little rest and perhaps in the morning I'll show you a trick or two."

Alexandra raised her hand. The candle had nearly burned out and was now sputtering in its wooden stand. But even in the semidarkness she could make out the outline of the copper wedding band on her finger. She lowered her hand to his bare chest and closed her eyes, snuggling against his shoulder. She wouldn't think now of the consequences of tonight's events. She was too exhausted, too utterly satisfied.

There would be time enough in the morning for regrets.

Seated at a table, Hunter rested his forehead on the heel of his hand and slid his mug out to be refilled with thick, dark coffee. The serving girl, Martha, filled it to the brim and backed up and out of his way. He took a loud slurp.

Jon entered the room dressed in a freshly ironed linen shirt complete with a stock, and a pair of durable but finely cut breeches. He carried a coat over one shoulder. "Good morning, lover." He slapped Hunter good-naturedly on the shoulder and plopped down beside him. "What you drinking?"

"Coffee."

"Coffee? Gag. Sweetheart!" Jon clicked his fingers, signaling to Martha who was serving breakfast to several soldiers at the other table. "Ale for me and for my friend."

The girl nodded that she'd heard and went on doling out biscuits.

Jon turned his attention back to Hunter seated beside him. "Headache?"

"It's pounding."

"Too much fine fort ale?"

"Too much futtering."

Jon grinned. *"But you wanted to marry her,"* he mimicked. *"You knew what you were doing."*

Hunter lifted his head and wiped his mouth with the back of his hand. He'd been certain last night that he'd made the right decision in marrying Alexandra. It was the least he could do to make up for leaving her back in London. But this morning, watching her sleep in his arms, her soft hair spilling across his chest, he wondered if he'd made a mistake. Not enough time had passed since Laughing Rain's death. It was unfair to Alex . . . unfair to Laughing Rain. "Who said I regret it?"

"You don't sound like the happy bridegroom."

Hunter sipped his coffee. "How many happy bridegrooms have you known in your life?"

The serving girl brought two ales and a plate of fresh-baked biscuits. Jon picked up one and dipped it in his ale. "So just tear up the evidence. It's safe in my pack. Tell her it was a joke." He bit down on the soggy bread.

Hunter refused the ale Jon slid toward him. "I wouldn't do that to her."

"Damnation." Jon took another bite of his biscuit. "Must have been one hell of a wedding night."

Hunter stared into the thick coffee. "That it was," he said more to himself than to Jon. He looked up, his eyes unfocused. "But it's time to move on. Time to see to Blue-Green Eyes. I've tired of the chase. I'm ready for the kill."

Jon lifted his booted foot, resting it on the tabletop. "Heard some rather interesting gossip last night. No need to go on to Fort Maurice."

"No?"

"Overheard two sentries talking when I went out to relieve myself. Interested?"

"Yes."

"Seems the army's lost control of one of its men. He no longer reports to his superiors. No longer follows orders. He's apparently decided the army isn't profitable enough so he's gone into his own business."

Hunter lifted a dark eyebrow. "And what business might that be?"

"The buying and trading of women."

Hunter swore softly. He looked away. "Who is he?"

"Someone important, or his family is at least. Important enough that no one's yet been sent to stop him."

"His name, Jon," Hunter said softly. "What is the man's name?"

"John Cain. Captain John Cain."

"Where is he?"

"That's part of the army's problem. He keeps moving from one fort to the next. They can't catch up with him. Apparently he's got quite a reputation with the Indians. They despise him. I think our government keeps hoping some savage will just scalp him and everyone will save face." He crammed the rest of his biscuit into his mouth. "So far luck hasn't run with the army. The captain has been quite busy. It seems that the Iroquois desire for women is so great, Mr. Cain has been selling white women as well."

"Alex . . ." Hunter murmured under his breath. That was what he wanted her for. That was why he'd bought her from Two Crows—to sell to the Iroquois . . .

Jon picked up the biscuit Hunter had left untouched. "That would be my guess." He took a bite. "And get this. I asked around a little this morning. The son of a bitch has one blue eye and one green one."

Hunter pushed back on the bench. "You mean to tell me the bastard who murdered Laughing

Rain is the same man Two Crows warned us about? The same man Two Crows supposedly sold Alexandra to?"

Jon shrugged. "It's a hell of a coincidence, but the pieces fit. How many English captains can there be out there capturing and selling women?"

Hunter glanced at Jon. His head was suddenly clear, his thoughts in order. He'd not lose another wife to that butcher—not Alex. Not his hell and fire Alex. "Where is he, Jon?"

"I told you, the army's not sure. But you're going to love this. The last sighting was two days ago, just west of the Chesapeake. Guess he broke camp, or Two Crows lied."

"Back into Shawnee country."

"Looking for Alexandra would be my guess."

Hunter rose. "He might be looking for Alex, but what he's going to find is me." He started for the inner door, his stride long and determined. Suddenly he wanted to hold Alexandra in his arms again, to feel her heart beat against his chest. He had to assure himself she was safe. "Get the mule saddled and say your farewell to the twins, Jon. We head south in half an hour's time."

Hunter closed the door softly behind him.

Chapter Fifteen

Self-consciously Alexandra pulled the coverlet to her bare breasts as Hunter walked into the bedchamber they had shared last night. Last night had been magic, a night she would remember the rest of her days, but by the light of the sun pouring in the two tiny, crude windows near the ceiling, she wondered how it would be between her and Hunter. The copper band around her finger caught a ray of sunlight and glimmered. She looked up at Hunter, trying not to appear nervous.

"Sorry to wake you, sweeting."

"No, it's all right. I was already awake." She smiled hesitantly. "I know I should have come down to break the fast with you, but I was lying here being lazy."

He sat down on the edge of the bed and caught a corner of the bedsheet. He tugged on it and she let the material slip through her fingers. He kissed the swell of her breast and then looked up at her. "I want you to stay here for a few days."

She drew her bare legs up beneath her and sat up

on her knees. "Without you?" She lifted the sheet to cover her nakedness. She couldn't think reasonably with him looking at her like this, touching her . . . "I won't do it."

"Alexandra—"

"I'll not discuss it. I've come this far with you. I'll not be left behind now. Not in a fort full of soldiers. You go north, I go north."

He looked away. "It's not north I travel."

Her brow creased. "What do you mean? I don't understand. You're not going after Laughing Rain's killer?"

Hunter rose off the bed. He began to pace the floorboards of the tiny room. "Oh, I'm going after him. Now he even has a name. Captain John Cain."

"You've gotten information on where he is?" She watched him pace. Four long strides across the room, four back.

"Vague information. It seems . . ."

When he didn't complete his sentence she got out of the bed, dragging the sheet behind her. "What? It seems what?" She laid her hand on his arm, forcing him to stop and look at her. "Tell me."

"It seems Two Crows may have been telling the truth. The captain may be looking for you." He paused. "And I think he may be the man who killed Laughing Rain."

"He's Blue-Green Eyes?"

"Aye."

For a moment both were silent. Fingers of chilling fear crept up Alexandra's spine. For the briefest moment she wondered if perhaps it would be better for her to stay here. But Hunter was her husband now. She belonged with him, no matter what. If they were to have even a fighting chance at making this mismatched marriage work, they had to remain together. She had to be with him when he dealt with his first wife's killer. It was the only way to put Laughing Rain to rest in Hunter's mind and in Alexandra's. That was one thing she was certain of.

She slid her hand up and down his arm in a soothing caress. He had already dressed in buckskins and knee-high moccasins. His hair was pulled back in a neat queue and tied with a band of leather. A single eagle's feather dangled from the knot of fiery hair. "I can't stay here, Hunter."

"Why not? Joshua will see to it you're not harmed. The men wouldn't dare touch you. Not when you're my wife. You could rest a few days. Once Cain is dead, I could come back to get you. We could go to Annapolis together." He tried to make light of the conversation with a half smile. "You can introduce me to your family."

She shook her head. His face was so wrought with underlying fear, fear for her, that a part of her wanted to concede just to spare him the pain. But she knew she couldn't. If Hunter was going to walk into the face of danger for her, for Laughing Rain, then Alexandra knew she had to be at his side.

Her mind suddenly made up, she dropped the sheet and walked nude across the room. She picked up her leather tunic and leggings left on a chair by Martha and began to dress. "I can be ready in five minutes. Is Jon packing the mule?"

Hunter spun around and snatched the sheet up off the sand-washed floor. "I said you weren't going."

He hadn't exactly shouted at her, but he had come very close. She spoke softly, but her words were steely. "And I say I am."

He threw the sheet onto the bed. "You're my wife and you'll do as I bid!"

She stepped into her legging and began to lace the leather ties with sharp, jerky movements. "The hell I am! You didn't hear me repeat any vows last night, did you? We may be wed, but I never agreed to obey you. You wanted me as your wife. You've got me, Hunter. But you get me as I am. I'll never be controlled by another man, not ever again, not by my father, not by scum like Two Crows, not even by you." She jerked hard on a leather tie, lowering her head to secure the knot. She gave him a moment to let her words sink in. When she spoke again, it was matter-of-factly. "I'll meet you out in the yard. Don't forget to pay the minister."

"I could lock you in this room," Hunter threatened.

"Perhaps. But if you have an ounce of sense, you won't." Her right leg propped on a chair, she looked up, the leather ties of her leggings still laced through her fingers.

Both were eyeing each other now, assessing the other's words, the other's motives.

"I just want you to be safe," he said finally. "Don't you understand that?"

When she made no reply, he went on. "I lost Laughing Rain to him." He touched his chest. "It's my fault she's dead. I didn't protect her from that animal. I didn't—"

"I understand what you're saying. Maybe I can even understand how you must feel. But you should understand that if this Captain Cain really is looking for me, I'm probably safer with you than anyone else." She lowered her gaze to her leggings again. "After all, at this point, you've got more interest in my life than anyone else, haven't you?"

Hunter exhaled angrily. She was right. Damned if she wasn't right! Slowly he walked to the door. "Five minutes, Wife." He held up five fingers as he walked out the door. "Five minutes and I'm gone."

The door swung shut behind him and Alexandra was left alone in the room to dress hurriedly.

"Do you get the idea our friend here is leading us on a wild-goose chase?" Jon questioned Alexandra as he lifted a pine bough, letting her duck under it.

As she led the mule through the thick brush she looked up at Hunter, who walked a dozen yards ahead of them, his head bent in concentration.

She was worried about him. Since they'd left Fort Potter two days ago, and headed toward the Chesapeake, he'd been withdrawn and silent, speaking only when spoken to. He treated Alexandra with the utmost respect and consideration, but he wasn't treating her like his wife. The emotion she had witnessed the night of the wedding was gone. Though the kid-glove treatment was pleasant, she was beginning to think she preferred the rougher side of him. It was that side that she had shared passion with. It was that side she yearned to share passion with again.

"You heard the scout yesterday," Alexandra finally answered Jon. "He said Captain Cain was headed for the fort on the Noniack River. Hunter seems to think we can catch up with him there."

Jon groaned. "I don't know about you, sweetheart, but I'm sick to death of this revenge. These feet of mine have traipsed over half of this continent and for what? Killing this murdering whoreson isn't going to bring Laughing Rain back to life. He's got himself a new wife now." He nodded in Hunter's direction. "He's an important man back in London or will be in a few years time. Why doesn't he just forget the past and go with the future?"

Alexandra yearned to ask Jon who this man she now called husband really was, but she didn't. That was now between her and Hunter. He would have to tell her.

She looked at Jon. "It's not that simple and you damned well know it." Though she was exhausted, she trudged forward, knowing she had to keep up with Hunter's grueling pace or he'd leave her behind. "Sometimes you can't begin a new life until you've ended the old one." She paused. "Besides, if Hunter doesn't stop him, who will? How many women, red and white, will be taken from their homes to be sold? How many women will have died rather than be captured as Laughing Rain was?"

"Laughing Rain." Jon sighed, shaking his head. "I'm curious. Aren't you just a little jealous of this obsession he has with her? You're his wife now. He ought to be concerned with your safety. You're still alive.''

Alexandra stopped in her tracks. She placed the palm of her hand firmly on Jon's chest. "Now you just wait one minute! Hunter wanted to leave me behind at Fort Potter where he thought I'd be safe. I refused.'' She whipped around and started forward again, keeping her gaze on Hunter's broad back. "I come by my own choice. You remember that. I'm responsible for any danger I might put myself in.''

"God's bowels! You needn't get so riled with me!'' Jon stepped over a fallen tree, quickening his pace to keep up with her and the mule. "You sound like him now.''

Alexandra turned back to reply, but out of the corner of her eye, she saw Hunter stop in the center of the game path. She immediately dropped into a crouch. Once she would have spoken, questioned him, but now she just waited in silence.

For a minute or two all three of them held perfectly still, listening to the sounds of the forest. A V-formation of geese flew overhead, the haunting cries of their migration song filling the air.

After a moment Hunter walked back to Alexandra. "You and Jon stay put. Jon, load your musket. Anyone who comes near her, shoot first, question later.''

"Where you going?'' she whispered, touching the fringe of his winter tunic. Her breath made frosty clouds in the air. God, she wanted to touch him so badly. She wanted him to want to touch her.

"We're very near the fork in the Noniack River where the fort lies. Maybe only a mile, maybe two. I'm going to catch the river and walk upstream. I'll come back for you as soon as I know it's safe. This fort is notorious for being one the soldiers just can't hold. It's right on the north-south road the Mohawks take. They raid it at least twice a year. Two years back they held it for an entire winter." He looked at her. "Every time they take control, they kill every man, woman, child, and mangy dog inside the walls."

She nodded. "We'll wait here. Give me a musket."

He cut his eyes at her. "You know how to use it?"

"Load it for me. I know how to pull a trigger. I'll just wait till someone is close enough for me to be certain I can't miss."

Hunter hesitated for only a moment and then reached into a pack on the mule. He brought an oak-butted wheel lock with an engraved barrel. He loaded it with a ball and powder and pushed it into her hands. "It's like you said. Just pull the trigger."

She offered him her brightest smile and then lifted up on her tiptoes to press a kiss to his lips. "Take care," she murmured. His gaze locked with hers. She missed seeing the earring in his ear, but she liked the weight of it around her finger. "Promise me," she whispered.

"Promise," he answered.

For two hours Jon and Alexandra waited on the

game path for Hunter's return. They huddled together for warmth beneath a bare sumac tree, resting and talking.

Jon told her she'd made a mistake in marrying Hunter. He told her it would never work. He told her she should have taken him up on his offer. He could have had her in London by now. She told him to shut up or she'd use the musket on him.

Just as the sun began to set Alexandra heard the cry of a bobwhite, Hunter's signal that he was approaching. She rose and was waiting for him when he came around the bend in the path.

"Is he there? Have you found him?"

"He's not there, but he's been there in the last day."

"They expecting him back?" Jon slid his musket into the mule's pack and reached for the flask of whiskey he'd purchased at Fort Potter.

"No. I don't think so. They sent him away."

"Sent him away? I don't understand." Alexandra drew her cloak closer. "Why didn't they take him into custody? Why didn't they arrest him? It's not right that our government should allow a man to continue—"

"Alexandra," Hunter said gently. "What's right is not what's always done. There's apparently been no order to arrest Cain as of yet."

"But everyone must know what he's doing! How many women must die before he's stopped."

"Apparently others do know what he's doing. That's why the commanding officer at this fort sent him on, but he had no jurisdiction to arrest him."

"And why not?"

"He's someone important. That's all I know. I didn't ask more. I didn't want to appear suspicious. I want no one to suspect what I'm about. This has got to be handled delicately. I want to be certain I find the right man. Laughing Rain's killer will die, but I'll make no mistakes. I'll kill no innocent man. There's already been too much bloodshed in the country." He grabbed the mule's lead line.

"So we go to the fort?" Alexandra asked.

"We go. We'll spend the night so as not to look suspicious. I'll find out just where the bastard's gone and then Jon and I'll see the deed to the end."

Alexandra fell in beside her husband as he started toward the Noniack River. The sun was beginning to set and a biting wind was beginning to blow. Winter was descending quickly on the Tidewater. The thought of a warm fire and a soft bed to share with Hunter was invigorating. They'd not made love since their wedding night and she was anxious to feel his touch again.

They arrived at the fort—a structure which looked much like Fort Potter—just as the last red glow of the setting sun disappeared below the line of treetops on the horizon. The only difference between Fort Potter and this one was that this fort on the Noniack River was smaller and the spiked log walls were higher. Everywhere Alexandra looked she spotted signs of previous Indian attacks. One wall was scarred with embedded musket balls, another had been partially burned and then rebuilt. On one of the corner palisades a single feathered arrow protruded from the bark roof, jutting into the air as if it were a symbol of survival.

Alexandra pushed her hand into Hunter's. He squeezed it. "It's almost over," he told her as they walked through the massive log gate and it swung closed behind them. "A few more days and it will be our turn, Alex. I swear it."

The three were greeted by a low-ranking officer who was the acting commander in his captain's absence. The dark-haired man, Lieutenant Winslow, was pleasant, but not chatty. Hunter asked him a few questions about the fort and the hostiles. The soldier answered, but only halfheartedly. He seemed more concerned with getting back to Annapolis by Christmastide than with protecting the wilderness fort and the few civilians living within the fort walls or in the area.

Alexandra was escorted to the only private room in the fort. Hunter gave her a quick peck on the cheek and promised to return later. He followed one of the red-coated enlisted men to the bunkhouse where Jon would sleep. Hunter told her he would play a few hands of cards and see what information he could glean from the men's conversation. He warned to keep the door locked and not let anyone see her. There was always the possibility that Captain Cain could have left some of his own men behind.

Hunter had been gone barely half an hour when Alexandra heard a scratch at the door. "Yes?" she called, rising off the hard plank bunk. "Who is it?"

"Food," came a graveled accented voice. "For the Missy Lady."

Alexandra cautiously slid back the iron bolt and

peered through the crack in the door.

A haggard Indian woman stood with a plate and mug in her hand. "Food for the Missy Lady," she repeated.

Even through the crack in the door Alexandra could smell the pungent aroma of venison soup. "For me?" She pulled the door open. "Thank you."

The old woman bobbed her silver head. "Your *neet-il-se*, Hunter of the Shawnee tell me to come. Bring you food. Make sure room warm."

Alexandra watched her put the plate and mug down on the only table in the bare room. "You know my husband?"

She clasped her hands bringing them to her left breast. "Hunter of the Shawnee, he was married to my *nuxans n-dah-nes*."

Alexandra shook her head and the woman closed her eyes in search of the correct words.

"Bro-ter . . . bro-ter's d . . . doh-ter."

"Brother's daughter? Laughing Rain was your niece?"

The old woman shook her head, waggling a shriveled finger. "It is not a good thing, this to speak the name of the dead."

"Oh. I'm sorry." Alexandra sat down on the corner of the bunk and patted the flat tick beside her. "But you are of the Delaware nation?"

"I am *Lenni Lenape*, what English *manake* call the Delaware."

"Sit with me a moment."

The old woman shook her head.

"Please," Alexandra coaxed. "I'm hungry for a woman's company." When the old woman appeared to be considering the invitation, Alexandra patted the bed again. "You look tired. Please sit, just for a minute."

The old woman nodded and came toward the bed slowly, her back hunched over by years of hard work and poor nutrition. "This old woman's bones, they hurt. This is true. A girl will give baby tonight. This old woman must be strong to cut the girl's pain."

"There's a woman in labor here in the fort?"

The old woman shook her head sadly. "Little girl. Too few summers to carry a soldier's seed." She lifted her lined palms heavenward. "But what Manito gives us, we do not question."

Strangely taken by this Indian she had known only a few moments, Alexandra studied her lined leathery face. It was obvious that this old Lenni Lenape woman had once been very beautiful. "What's your name?" she asked. "What do your people call you?"

"Ah. My people, they are dead. I have no people. I live here because I have no sons to care for my old bones. Here the soldiers feed me and bring me wood for my fire. I care for their wives, for the little children." She looked up, her eyes unfocused, a bare hint of a smile on her face. "But once, the Lenni Lenape once called me—" She sighed, searching her mind for the English words, then she made a fist. "They called me She-Who-Stands-Strongly." She smiled at the memory, then shrugged, the smile fading. "Now I am called Old Esquawa if I am called a name at all."

Alexandra watched her rise and walk slowly to the door. "I don't know much about childbirth, but if you need a woman's help, come for me."

The old Indian woman gave a nod as she shuffled out the door.

Not twenty minutes later, She-Who-Stands-Strongly was tapping at Alexandra's door again. "Come," she called through the rough-hewn door. "Come, wife of Hunter. This old woman has need of you."

Alexandra swung open the door. "Is something wrong? Has the girl had her baby?"

She-Who-Stands-Strongly nodded. Her wrinkled suntanned face was beaded with perspiration. "The baby will not come. I have need of help." She grasped Alexandra's hands and turned them palm up, studying them carefully. After a second she nodded and dropped her hands. "Yes, strong hands. Good heart. You can help this old woman and this child who will be a woman." The Indian turned abruptly and started back down the dark corridor.

Alexandra grabbed her rabbitskin cloak off the bed. She knew she should find Hunter and tell him where she was, but by the look on the old woman's face, she was afraid there wasn't time. "I don't know anything about birthing," she said as she followed the Lenni Lenape woman.

For someone so old and frail, She-Who-Stands-Strongly now walked quickly.

"It does not matter. I need only another pair of woman's hands."

Chapter Sixteen

Following She-Who-Stands-Strongly down the maze of log-walled corridors that connected the inner cabins of the fort, Alexandra learned from the old woman that the girl about to give birth was Sara. She was a half-breed left abandoned as a small child by her Shawnee mother. Sara had grown up at the fort where the father she had never known had once been stationed. She was thirteen or fourteen years old. The baby's father was one of the soldiers. Sara didn't know who.

The old Indian woman said the baby was breech but could be born safely with skillful hands and the help of God Almighty, known to her people as Manito.

When Alexandra hinted at her concern for who would care for a child's child, She-Who-Stands-Strongly jutted out her bony chin and declared that she could certainly care for a babe. Alexandra smiled in the darkness of the dank log-walled corridor. She had no doubt at this moment that the old woman could.

Alexandra found Sara's birthing room to be nothing like an Englishwoman's birthing room. There was none of the stinking cloistered feeling Alexandra was familiar with. The room Sara and She-Who-Stands-Strongly shared was bright with candlelight. The two tiny windows were thrown open to allow the crisp night air to fill the room. A sweet smell of pungent burning herbs hung in the cool air.

Rather than lying back in a bed, Sara was seated on a chair, her legs drawn up beneath a billowing night gown.

"Up! Up!" She-Who-Stands-Strongly ordered as she entered the room. "Up! Up! Sara, girl. This baby will come faster!"

Alexandra hung in the doorway. She was shocked by how young this girl with her huge rounded belly appeared. Sara was barely more than a babe herself. Alexandra couldn't imagine what man would want to bed a girl whose breasts were barely budding. How cruel the world was to some . . .

She-Who-Stands-Strongly pulled the door shut behind Alexandra's back, as if to be certain she wouldn't escape. "Help me!" She fluttered her fingers. "This Sara girl must get up. She must walk! Big baby must come down!"

Alexandra tossed her rabbitskin cloak on the floor and walked to the chair where the girl sat. Sweat beaded on the child's pale face, black matted hair stuck to her cheeks and neck in clumps. "My name is Alex," Alexandra said, going down on one knee as she took Sara's hand.

Sara's eyes were half closed. She was obviously exhausted.

"Sara, She-Who-Stands-Strongly says you have to get up. She says it's the only way your baby will come."

Sara shook her head. "Too tired," she mumbled. Just then another contraction overtook her and the girl clutched her swollen middle, groaning.

"Holler," the old Indian woman said from the fireplace where she was throwing a handful of dried herbs onto the fire in the hearth. "No one to hear you, girl. No one to care!"

Alexandra waited until the contraction passed and then she tugged gently on Sara's arm. "You have to get up," she insisted.

Slowly the girl rose. She-Who-Stands-Strongly took Sara's other arm and the three began to pace the uneven floorboards. At each contraction they stopped and Sara leaned heavily on Alexandra, but when the wave of pain passed she walked again.

An hour passed and then another. Twice the old woman examined Sara. The labor was progressing, but slowly. Alexandra lost all concern for time and for herself and her own problems. All that mattered was helping She-Who-Stands-Strongly bring this baby alive into the world.

Sometime in the middle of the night a pounding knock came at the door. "Alexandra! Alexandra! Are you in there?"

"Hunter?" Alexandra pushed back the hair off her face. It had been hours since she'd thought of her husband and the reason they were here.

"Alexandra!"

"Go! Go, to your husband," She-Who-Stands-Strongly commanded. "We will let this girl rest."

"Just a minute!" Alexandra helped Sara into the chair and went to the door. She swung it open and slipped out, pressing her back to the closed door.

"What the hell do you think you're doing? I went crazy looking for you!"

Alexandra wiped her forehead with the back of her hand. She was exhausted and wrought with fear for the young girl inside. "I'm sorry," she murmured. "There wasn't time. There's a little girl in here having a baby. She-Who-Stands-Strongly needed my help. What was I supposed to do?"

"You could have let me know where the hell you were!"

Alexandra smiled. In the darkness of the corridor she could make out the lines of Hunter's face. He had been afraid for her. He really did care. She reached up and caressed his beard-stubbled cheek. "I'm sorry," she whispered.

He covered her hand with his. "Alexandra, I have to go."

"Cain?"

He nodded. "I know where he's headed. I can catch up with him on the trail, but I have to go now."

Alexandra turned to look at the closed door. She could hear the rumble of She-Who-Stands-Strongly's soft voice. Alexandra looked back at Hunter. "I can't go now."

"I can't wait."

She looked at him, torn in indecision. "I can't

go," she said finally. "I have to stay here. I can't leave Sara now. She might not live, Hunter."

He took her hands, sighing as he contemplated his choices. "It sounds logical," he thought aloud. "Logically you'd be safer here anyway, but . . ."

She chuckled. "You wanted me to stay behind at Fort Potter. Now you don't?"

"Afraid to let you out of my sight, I think."

"I'll be all right here. She-Who-Stands-Strongly has been kind to me. Sara needs me. They both need me."

Hunter grasped her around the waist and pulled her against him. He kissed the nape of her neck. "It seems we have no choice," he murmured in her ear. "I'll go with Jon and come back for you."

Alexandra rested her cheek on his chest, feeling the rise and fall as he took each breath. He really didn't want to leave her. His muscles were tense, his tone anxious.

Suddenly, as if hit by a bolt of lightning, she realized she was in love with Hunter. It wasn't just an infatuation. It wasn't just lust. It wasn't a childish attraction to the unseemly. It wasn't even that desperate yearning to be wanted. She loved Hunter. She didn't care what he'd done in the past, or who he really was, she loved him. The words hung on the tip of her tongue, but she bit them back, afraid to admit them to him.

He buried his face in the hollow of her neck. "I'm going to kill him and then I'm going to come back to you, sweeting. I'm going to make you glad I made you marry me."

She smiled up at him. "I'm sorry you have to go

now. I was looking forward to spending a night in a bed with you." She didn't know what made her so bold. The exhaustion perhaps. Or maybe it was just this revelation that she was glad he was her husband. At least tonight.

He chuckled, brushing his lips against hers. "I have to admit I was considering the same possibilities."

The husky catch in his voice and his warm breath in her ear made her giddy. It felt so good to be wanted by this man. She lifted up on her toes and kissed him, not as a wife kisses farewell but as a lover bids *until next time* . . .

Hunter groaned, twisting his fingers through her hair as he pressed her against the cold, rough logs of the corridor. Alexandra molded her body to his, pressing her breasts to his chest, her hips to his. Her tongue flicked out to taste his upper lip and then she deepened the kiss, suddenly desperate to be part of him again.

"Promise me you'll be careful," Alexandra whispered, her voice husky with desire she knew must go unfulfilled for now. "Promise me!"

"If I didn't know better, I would think you approved of my attentions," he whispered, cupping her breast with his hand.

"Promise me, Hunter!"

"I promise. No chances. No heroics. Find Cain, kill him, and be done with it."

She pressed her lips to his, one last time, knowing she had to get back to Sara, knowing Hunter had to go. "I'll be waiting right here for you."

Hunter pulled away from her. "I've left the musket in your room. Also powder and ammunition. There are only a few soldiers here. This time of year the fort's filled with women, children, and old folk looking for a warm, dry place to winter. The lieutenant assures me you'll be safe. It's past the season of Mohawk raids. They've all gone home for their harvest feasts and to dig in for the winter. If you need anything, you tell the lieutenant."

She nodded her head, touching her lips, still feeling the rough, sensual feel of his mouth on hers. "Go. I'll be all right." She touched his broad chest with her hand, afraid to see him go. "See you when you get back."

He caught her chin with his hand and stared into her eyes for a moment, then released her and walked away. Alexandra listened to the sound of his heavy footsteps until they died away and then she returned to the birthing room.

"He looks for me?" Captain John Cain gave a laugh. "You jest!"

"No, sir." Charles Mattle shook his head. "Heard him say so myself, back at Fort Potter."

Cain drew on his cigar and stared into the flames of the campfire. The smell of snow was in the air tonight. He was uncomfortable, restless. "How long ago was this?"

"Three days ago, sir."

"Three days!" He kicked at a log protruding from the fire and sparks flew. "Why the hell didn't you find me sooner? I told you if you heard anything you were to come straight to me, Mattle!"

The young man cowered. "I . . . I did, sir. Soon as they left I came." He swallowed. "I was afraid to leave the night they came, else someone would suspect something."

Mattle's words tapped Cain's attention. "They? They who? He's still got the woman?"

Mattle nodded. "Her and some Indian dressed in Englishman's clothes."

"Tell me about her. Beautiful like that red bastard Two Crows said?" Cain's gaze wandered to the darkness surrounding them. He could have sworn he'd just heard something in the brush beyond the circle of light that protected them from wolves. After a second, he went on with his conversation, thinking he must have been mistaken. "Will she be worth my trouble?"

Mattle nodded. "Dark hair. Dark eyes. Striking. But, but Captain, there could be a problem."

"Problem? What the hell you talking about, Mattle? Speak up!"

The young man stared at his dusty boots. "He married her."

"Married her?" Cain made a face. "Who married her? You not making any damned sense, Mattle!"

"The redhead. Hunter, he calls himself. He married her that night at the fort. I heard so the next morning. Seems he had some reverend up in the middle of the night. Married 'em stark naked the boys at the fort said."

Cain twisted his cigar in his mouth, his gaze

wandering to the campfire's flames again. "He can't marry her, she's mine," he said, more to himself than to the soldier. "I paid for her."

"Yes, sir. I know that. The thing is—"

Cain suddenly turned to stare into the shadows beyond the light of the fire. The boy stopped in midsentence. "Sentry!" Cain called, feeling the hair rise on the back of his neck. Was someone watching him?

"Yes, sir," came a voice out of the darkness.

"Just wanted to be certain you were at your post and not dreaming of your wet nurse," Cain answered.

"Yes, sir! No, sir. Awake, sir."

"Have you seen anything out there? Heard anything?"

"Just the wind, sir."

Cain looked back at Mattle, not wanting to appear skittish in front of one of his men. "Now what were you saying? There was something else?"

"Ye . . . yes, sir. He . . . Hunter was asking questions about you."

"About me?" Cain looked back at Mattle. "I'm flattered. What about me?"

"Wanted to know if you'd been seen."

"Why?"

"I don't know, sir. He was tightlipped about it. Just asked a few questions whilst playing cards. He was at another table so it was hard for me to hear. I had to be careful so no one would suspect. You told me that."

Cain removed the cigar from his mouth and

turned it between his thumb and forefinger thoughtfully. "So the Hunter is looking for me, is he?" He smiled. "Gone to the Noniack has he?"

"Yes, sir. That's my guess. That's the direction the boys at the fort sent him."

"And he took my woman? You're certain of that?"

"Yes, sir. Saw them leave with my own eyes. Him, the girl, and the Indian that fancies himself a gentleman."

Cain tossed the butt of the cigar into the campfire and strode away. He had a bit of soft flesh waiting for him in his tent and suddenly he was anxious to have her. "Excellent," he murmured, dismissing Mattle with a wave of his hand. "Excellent."

"Hunter, do you really find it necessary to run?" Jon panted, coming to a halt and leaning over, his palms pressed to his thighs. "Surely you don't think Cain has his soldiers *running* through the forest like a pack of Iroquois!"

Hunter stopped in the middle of the game path and turned to face his companion. Only the thin sheen of perspiration across his forehead indicated the grueling pace he'd set since dawn. He looked up at the bright sun rising in the east to burn off the powder of snow that had fallen during the night. "You've grown soft, traveling with a woman," he teased.

"Alexandra! Hah! She's nearly as bad as you are. The two of you get a thought in your head and you can think of naught else!" Jon walked toward Hunter, swinging his water skin off his shoulder to take a drink. "Either of you would kill a man walking if he let you." He shook his head. "Sacred blood, what I wouldn't do for a carriage and a pair of footmen right now."

Hunter chuckled as he grabbed the water skin from Jon's hand and took a long pull. Jon made a face, crossing his arms over his chest. "And that's another thing, how's a man to keep warm with no liquor to heat his blood? I can't believe you poured the last of my brandy on the blessed ground!"

"I want you clear-headed when we come upon Cain. I don't know how many men he travels with. Could be soldiers, could be Mohawks, could be both."

Jon snatched back his water skin. "We going to kill them all?"

"Only if we have to. They turn Cain over to me and they can all go free."

Jon exhaled loudly. "Fat chance I should think."

"Enough rest." Hunter repositioned the bow he carried slung over one shoulder and started down the path. "Let's get moving. I don't like leaving Alexandra behind. Not one bit."

"God's bowel, listen to you! You sound like a smitten husband." Jon jogged to catch up. "I still can't believe you married the chit. I understand you're a man with a conscience. I can accept that. I understand you felt bad for leaving her at your betrothal party like that," he grimaced, "but for God's sake, did you have to *marry* her? I mean, that's for life, until one of you dies." He shrugged. "That, or one of you kills the other."

Hunter cut his eyes in Jon's direction, failing to see the humor of his words. "If I recall correctly it was you no more than a month ago who told me I was in need of an English wife to take home to my father and the family estates."

"A wife, yes, but not Alexandra Lambert! Where is your head, man? A wife must be a woman who can be easily manipulated, easily handled. A wife is to be impregnated once a year and sent off into the country for her lying-in." Jon tugged at his black queue. "I doubt your Lady Alexandra will be easily manipulated. I think I had the right idea. She'd have made a far better man's whore than wife."

Hunter elbowed Jon hard in the side. "Shut your mouth. She's my wife now and you'll not speak that way, else I'll cut out your tongue."

Unintimidated, Jon went on. "What I want to know is when are you going to tell her who you are? Surely before we see the white cliffs of Dover."

Hunter scowled. "I said nothing of returning to England. Perhaps I intend to remain here and raise my sons as colonials."

"And the Lady Alexandra's going to wear buckskin and sleep in a wigwam, right?" Jon slapped his thigh with a guffaw.

Hunter couldn't resist a smile at the thought. It was rather ludicrous to expect Alexandra to live out the rest of her life here in the colonies. Of course the other night when he'd married her he'd given no thought to the future. It had never occurred to him that he would have to return to England. All that mattered that night was Alex — the thought of possessing her, possessing her totally as only a husband and lover could.

"I'm waiting," Jon prodded. "When are you going to tell her you're the bastard who left her at the altar?"

"You make it sound overly dramatic, Jon, as always." Hunter grabbed a stick off the ground threw it end over end into the brush. "I just have to find the right moment. When I explain to her the circumstances, she'll understand."

"And now I'm Queen of the May."

Hunter opened his mouth to make a retort, but a sound in the brush off the side of the path silenced him. Jon froze. He'd heard it too. For a moment both men held perfectly still, listening, waiting, their hands on their weapons.

There it was again, very distinct this time. A moan.

Jon pointed into the brush in the direction the sound had come from. Hunter slipped his knife from his belt and cautiously walked off the path.

Jon swung his musket off his shoulder, aiming it into the brush to back Hunter up.

Silently, Hunter crept off the path. With a sudden motion he parted a tangled web of dying greenbriars and nameless underbrush, his knife held high. Immediately his knife fell to his side. He swore softly.

Crouched on the ground was an old man, a Shawnee by the appearance of his torn clothing. A dying man.

He turned his head toward Hunter, bloody holes where his eyes had once been. *"N-xilt-o-wah-kun,"* he cried. "Kill me and be done."

"No, no, it's all right," Hunter soothed in the man's native tongue. He returned his knife to its place in his belt. "I am not your enemy, brave warrior."

The old man slumped to the ground, his energy exhausted. "Who is that? Who is that speaks to me?"

Hunter pushed his way through the thicket and knelt. "I am the Hunter of the Shawnee," he said, reaching out to take the old man's shaking hand.

"White man?"

"Only of the skin, not of my heart," Hunter answered honestly. "Tell me who has done this to you? Who?" he demanded furiously.

The brave shook his head. "I do not know. They shamelessly attacked from behind. My nephews, they were taking me to see their mother. We carried no war weapons. We were but travelers."

"Were these men red or white who did this to you?"

"I do not know for sure. It happened so quickly." The old man held tightly to Hunter's hand. "I know only that I heard the cry of the Mohawk."

"Jon! Help me!"

Jon pushed his way through the brush. "Ah, Christ," he moaned when he saw the old Indian.

The old man shrank back at the sound of Jon's voice, but Jon put up his hands. "It's all right," he murmured in his best Shawnee. "I'll not harm you." He reached to help Hunter lift the man.

The old man looked up with unseeing eyes. "You are one of us," he murmured excitedly. "Not a white man."

Jon looked to Hunter and then back at the Indian. "It's true. I am Jon of the wolf clan of the Shawnee." He stumbled to find the right words. "My mother . . . my mother she is She-Who-Whispers-To-The-Wind of the wolf clan."

Hunter looked up at Jon, showing the slightest smile. This was the first time Jon had acknowledged his mother. "Let's get him out in the open where we can get a look at his other wounds."

The old man looked bad. Besides the obvious loss of his sight he had multiple stab wounds. Part of his scalp had been lifted. His flesh was cold, his bones stiff. It was a miracle he was still alive.

"How long ago did this happen, brave warrior?" Hunter asked.

The old man hung his head. "I am not brave. I did not save my nephews. I do not deserve the honor of your words. I am called Joseph Three Blankets. My people—what is left of my people— live on the Misicack."

Hunter and Jon carried Joseph out into the game path and gently laid him in the leaves. "How long ago?" Jon urged.

"Two nights. I think." Joseph rolled his head in confusion. "This old man is not sure."

"You've lain here for two days?" Jon asked in disbelief. He took off his outer cloak to use as a pillow for Joseph's head. "You're certain?"

The old man nodded. "Twice the mother sun has come and twice it has fallen. I asked the great Manito to take my soul, but he would not." His voice broke. "He would not."

"Where are your nephews?" Hunter stood to gaze at their surroundings.

"I do not know," Joseph answered. "I crawled away. I meant to hide only until they were gone and then I would have gone back to help my sister's sons." Tears seeped from his eye sockets to roll down his bloody cheeks. "But this stupid old man lost his way."

Jon slung his pack off his back and began to dig through it. Pulling out a linen towel he tore off a strip and wrapped it around the old man's eyes and tied it behind his head to keep the insects out of the wounds. Already the eye sockets were festering. Jon took his water skin and offered it to Joseph's lips. The old man drank a sip and then laid back, his strength sapped from speaking.

Hunter stood with his hands resting on his hips. "Jon," he said quietly.

Jon tried to stand, but Joseph grasped his hand. "Don't leave me," he said, only half lucid now. "Don't leave this old man to die alone, Jon of the turtle clan, son of She-Who-Whispers-To-The-Wind."

"I won't leave you," Jon vowed, amazed at how easily the Shawnee words came to mind when he wanted them to. "I'll be right here. I just have to speak to my friend." He squeezed Joseph's hand and then released it. Rising, he went to stand next to Hunter, out of earshot of the old man.

"One of us will have to go for help. He must have come from what's left of that village on the north side of the Misicack."

"We can't carry him?"

Hunter looked at Joseph and back at Jon. "He won't make it. It'll be faster to run for help."

"He's not going to make it anyway."

"No," Hunter answered, touched by Jon's concern for the old man. "But at least he can die in the arms of someone he knows."

"I doubt he'll even make it till tonight, Hunter."

Hunter shrugged. "Then someone can come to retrieve the body. It's all we can do. It's what we have to do."

Jon studied Hunter carefully. "And what about Cain? You run for this man's family and your captain might well escape again."

Hunter shrugged. "The bastard will have to wait, won't he?" He sighed. "You stay here with Joseph Three Blankets. It can't be more than half a day's run to his village. I can be there by nightfall. I'll find Joseph's relatives, then I'll take the river by dugout, hook up with the Noniack and go back to the fort to get Alexandra. Once you see to the old man you can meet me back at the fort."

Jon nodded. "I'll move him off the game path and into a clearing. I'll find the nephews' bodies and cover them with brush. They've got to be nearby. How far could he have crawled?"

"Good enough." Hunter's gaze met Jon's. "You surprise me friend, all this concern for a stranger."

Jon looked away, uncomfortably. "Yes, well,

just don't go repeating the story, all right? My reputation will be ruined."

Hunter watched Jon walk back to Joseph and kneel at his side. He listened as Jon quietly explained that Hunter was going for help and confirmed which village the old man was from. Joseph seemed grateful to know that the men would find his family for him.

Hunter unloaded his pack. He would travel light and fast. With only his bow and quiver of feathers on his back, and a skin of water flung over one shoulder, he turned west and began to run. He knew he had to do this for this old man he didn't know; it was the right thing to do. But he wanted to get to the Indian village and then on to the Fort on the Noniack as quickly as possible. Suddenly he wasn't comfortable with the thought of Alexandra being there alone. He had to get back to her. And this time he'd not leave her behind again.

Chapter Seventeen

Alexandra walked down the long hallway, a lantern swinging in her hand. She massaged the back of her neck, exhausted, but filled with a sense of accomplishment.

Sara had finally delivered a baby girl at noon. Both the mother and babe were well and sleeping comfortably. Alexandra smiled to herself. This was not the first time she'd witnessed the birth of a child. Her older cousin Natalie had two, her sister Margaret, twins. But this was the first time the birth of a child had touched her heart like this. Seeing that little baby suckling at her mother's breast had brought tears to Alexandra's eyes.

Secretly she wanted a baby of her own. Hunter's.

She pushed through the door to her room and closed it behind her. Sliding the bolt to lock it, she set down the lantern and went to the tiny fireplace to warm her hands.

She thought about Hunter and all the reasons why their marriage was doomed. For heaven's sake! She still didn't know his real name. For all she knew he could be a pauper, a runaway bondservant, a murderer!

And then there was the matter of the two of them being so different. He was so unconventional, she so conventional. She chuckled to herself as she looked down at the Shawnee doeskin tunic and leggings she wore. Perhaps she wasn't quite as conventional as she'd once been.

Then lastly, and probably most importantly, was the subject of the future. Hunter had married her without saying where they would live or how. Surely he knew that eventually she would be pregnant. Where did he intend to raise his children? Obviously he didn't expect her to spend the rest of her life moving from fort to Indian village to fort to Indian village as he'd apparently done since Laughing Rain's death. Or did he?

She picked up a plate of stew left on the mantel for her by She-Who-Stands-Strongly. She took a bite and then another, not really hungry, but knowing she should eat.

Her life at this moment seemed as uncertain as it had the day Two Crows had kidnapped her, but for some reason she wasn't afraid. She had had the will to survive. Hunter had rescued her. He'd protected her. He'd made her his wife. And though she had protested at the time, knowing it wasn't sensible, a part of her had been thrilled at the thought of marriage to a man like Hunter. And now with him gone, with him somewhere in the wilderness of the forest stalking a killer, she was glad he was her husband. Somehow they would find their way—together.

Finishing her stew, Alexandra slipped off her tunic and leggings and got into bed in the manner of the native American she was very quickly coming to respect a great deal—naked. Pulling the muslin sheet and pile of soft fur blankets up to her nose she rolled onto her side and blew out the oil lantern. She murmured a prayer asking God to protect Hunter and bring him home safely to her and then she fell into a deep sleep.

Sometime in the middle of the night something woke Alexandra. Her eyes flew open. Though she saw nothing in the darkness, she could feel her heart pounding in her chest. Embers in the hearth glowed, casting an eerie light against the log and chink walls of the tiny room.

"S . . . someone there?" she called.

She looked at the door. She could see that the bolt was still as she had left it when she climbed into bed. No one could possibly have gotten in, no one human . . .

Ghosts? Was she losing her mind? Or was it just the exhaustion and her fear for Hunter's safety?

She shivered violently. She was freezing cold, despite the furs she nestled under. Her nerve endings were raw with primal fear. But why? A nightmare she couldn't remember? A childish fear of the dark?

No. There was something in the room—someone. Instinctively she knew.

She lay perfectly still for a minute, listening. There was an icy breeze coming from some-where . . .

Then she smelled it—the dank stench of uncured animal hide, the scent of an unwashed body and sour whiskey breath.

A man.

Alexandra was frozen in terror. How had he gotten in?

The window? But how could he possibly have gotten through such a tiny space, cut that size just to prevent intruders?

The important thing was, where was he?

Alexandra had to muster every ounce of strength she possessed to keep from leaping out of bed and running for the door.

She forced herself to breathe evenly.

Where was he and what did he want?

The musket Hunter had left her rested beside the fireplace out of arm's reach. The only other possible weapon she possessed was the dinner knife left on the mantel with her empty plate and that also was too far away to be of any comfort.

Suddenly Alexandra realized there was something familiar about the odor she smelled. Something about the intruder that was familiar.

Two Crows!

She bolted upright just as he wrapped his filthy hand around her mouth.

"Silence!" he hissed.

She struggled, clawing at his hand, trying desperately to call out to someone, to anyone.

"Silence, I said! I will not harm you!"

When she didn't cease her struggling, he shook her so hard that her teeth rattled.

"I said I would not harm you," he whispered

harshly in her ear. "I come to warn you, but you call the soldiers or your man and you will not hear my words! I'll be gone before they make it to your door."

Alexandra's first instinct was to continue to fight, but to what end? she realized. She was alone with her enemy, Two Crows. She had no weapon. If he wanted to, he could slit her throat before she ever managed a word. She ceased her struggling.

"You will not scream?" he asked.

She shook her head no.

Slowly he lifted his hand from her mouth.

Despite her vow, it was all she could do to keep from screaming out. Hunter had said Two Crows was gone! He'd said he was far from here by now. He'd said he'd gone home to his people.

"What do you want?" Alexandra demanded, rising up on her knees and dragging the furs with her to cover herself. Even in the darkness she could see the outline of his face. She could make out his bandaged hand.

"I told you I come to warn you."

"Warn me of what now? You already warned us."

"He came south for you. The cap-i-tan. He knows where you are. He comes for you. He brings Iroquois, men without law. Men who kill for the joy of the sight of blood. You must tell the Hunter of the Shawnee to take you far from here. Tonight. Now."

She looked at Two Crows. Apparently he didn't know Hunter wasn't in the fort. He didn't know Hunter had gone out after Captain Cain. She certainly wasn't going to tell him. She didn't trust him, not as far as she could throw him. "Why would you warn us again?" she asked suspiciously. "Why would you put yourself in this kind of danger to save me?"

He glanced up at the tiny window he had squeezed through. The clouds shifted and moonlight poured through the opening, illuminating his scarred face. "I know this man has no conscience." He sighed. "This man has no conscience left, but his father, his father was a man of great honor."

"You speak of *your* father?"

Two Crows nodded. "My father was a great shaman respected by his people. He was a trusted man. I am glad that he is dead that he does not know what his son has become."

She almost laughed aloud. "You mean to tell me that you risked your life to come here out of a sense of honor for your dead father? You who played a part in the rape and murder of my cousin?" She felt a hysteria rising in her voice. "You who murdered my uncle? You, who sold me to some soldier to be sold as a whore or slave to other men!"

"Enough!" He raised his fist to her. "Why I have come does not matter. All that matters is that your man takes you from here, tonight."

She watched Two Crows creep around her bed, headed for the window. She still didn't trust him, but for some reason she believed him. His story was too absurd not to be believed. Somehow this really did have something to do with this sense of honor among the Indians that Hunter had tried to explain to her. Two Crows honestly had come to warn them. He did have a conscience buried somewhere in his heart. He regretted his past. He was trying to save face.

Two Crows swung up into the window and balanced on his palms in the sill.

"Thank you," she murmured.

"Go. Run. Fast. Save your lives."

She watched him squeeze through a space that seemed impossible to fit through and suddenly Two Crows was gone as quickly as he'd come.

Alexandra lay back in her bed, the blood in her veins racing with adrenalin. She listened, certain the Iroquois would not be able to make it out of the fort without being detected. Once she heard a dog whine, but then silence. After several minutes, she knew he had somehow gotten back over the fortress walls and had slipped into the darkness of the surrounding forest.

Gradually Alexandra's heart slowed to a normal beat. Of course she couldn't go back to sleep. Her mind was too filled with thought. If what Two Crows had said was true, then Hunter had not caught him . . . or Hunter was dead.

She immediately dismissed that idea. Of course Hunter wasn't dead. He was too intelligent to let a man like this Captain Cain outsmart him. He was too fierce a fighter to lose.

But what had happened then? If Two Crows was telling the truth and Cain was approaching the fort, where was Hunter? Why wasn't he here? Who would protect her now? Certainly not that mealy-mouthed Lieutenant Winslow.

She looked at the musket leaning against the stone of the fireplace. She'd protect herself. Cain wouldn't take her out of this fort. Not alive.

She rose and dressed quickly, her teeth chattering in the frigid air. She looked up at the external wall. The first rays of dawn were just beginning to spill into the tiny room. Two Crows had broken the glass pane to squeeze through the window and now an October breeze blew through it. She tossed the last log from the hearth onto the red coals. Then she picked up the knife Hunter had left her as an eating utensil and slipped into her leather belt. She brushed her hand against the carved hilt, wondering if Hunter himself had made it.

She left the room with determined strides. First she would check on Sara and the baby and see if She-Who-Stands-Strongly needed her, then she'd speak with Lieutenant Winslow. Serving as commanding officer with his captain gone, it would be Lieutenant Winslow's duty to protect her against Captain Cain.

An hour later Alexandra walked into the officer's dining room. Lieutenant Winslow sat at a crude trestle table eating a bowl of corn mush. He was the only person in the drafty room.

"Lieutenant," she called from the doorway.

He turned. His eyes were bloodshot. "Madame?"

She wondered to herself just how the English army had gotten itself into such a position that they had men like Winslow and Cain serving as commanders of the outposts. It was no wonder Mother England was losing its grip on the

American Colonies. "Lieutenant, it's necessary that I speak to you immediately."

"Is there something you need? See the old woman. She'll tend to it." He turned back to his bowl and pushed a spoon of mush into his mouth.

Alexandra shifted her weight from one foot to the other. She was caught between remaining the proper lady she had been brought up to be and being the forceful woman it was obviously necessary to be here in the colonies. "Lieutenant."

She heard him sigh. "Yes?"

She approached the trestle table. "Lieutenant, I have reason to believe that a man will try to forcefully take me from this fort."

He frowned. "What was that?"

She rolled her eyes heavenward. "I said, someone's going to kidnap me. A man my husband is tracking."

The dark-haired lieutenant picked up a small pewter pitcher and poured a healthy serving of honey over his half-eaten bowl of corn mush. "And what man is that?"

She stared at him, forcing him to look up at her. "Captain Cain."

He immediately dropped his gaze to his bowl. He laid down his pewter spoon. It clinked as it hit the corner of the bowl. "I—"

She almost laughed. He was afraid of Cain. She could tell by the look on his pale, hungover face. "You sent him away last time he came, you told my husband so. Just send him away again. Don't allow him within the confines of your walls. Better yet, arrest the whoreson."

The lieutenant blinked in reaction to her sharp words. "I . . . I have no orders to arrest Captain Cain . . . no authorization. My captain, he . . . he'll return within days."

"Are you telling me that you'll not protect me against this man? You gave my husband your word as an Englishman that I would be safe within these walls and now you tell me you have no authorization to do so?"

Winslow pushed his bowl away and rose in a halfhearted protest. "No. No, of course not. It's . . . it's my duty to protect the citizens of England. I'm simply saying Captain Cain still remains a fellow officer."

"A fellow officer who's gone wrong. You know it, every Englishman for a hundred miles knows it. Someone's got to stop him, why not you, Lieutenant?"

"Again, I must say that despite the accusations—"

"Accusations?" Alexandra came around the table toward the lieutenant, who immediately began to make a retreat. "I'm not talking about accusations! I'm talking about facts. He kidnaps and sells women, for God's sake! He rapes and murders!" She prodded him with her finger. "This Captain Cain says he owns me. He's going to try and carry me off, a defenseless woman! My husband has gone after this very same man. I don't know if he's dead or what's happened to him, all I know is that right now you may be the only thing standing between me and Cain. You may be the only one who can save my life. Now are you or are you not going to do so?"

"Of . . . of course. Yes." He stared at her as if unsure whether or not she was of stable mind. "If . . . if the captain comes to the fort, I'll simply turn him away as I did earlier in the week. I . . . I'll tell him that due to the accusations I . . . I cannot give him asylum."

"You'd better do more than that! You'd best close up your gates and set out guards. You'd best—"

The door swung open and a young soldier stepped into the common room. He saluted the lieutenant and then nodded in Alexandra's direction. "Sorry to interrupt sir, but a sentry says someone is approaching, at least two dozen men, maybe more, some of them Indians."

"It's him!" Alexandra exclaimed. "It's Cain, I tell you!" She grabbed Lieutenant Winslow's sleeve. "I told you he was coming!"

The lieutenant tried to gather his composure. "Did the sentry say if it was Captain Cain and his men?"

"He didn't say, sir."

The lieutenant walked around Alexandra and picked up his uniform cap off the trestle table. "I want my most experienced men at the gate in two minutes, Corporal." He pulled his cap over his head. "If this is indeed the captain, we'll meet him outside the walls. I'll not permit men of his ilk to threaten the peacefulness of this fort while I'm in command."

Alexandra stared at the officer in disbelief. "Lieutenant, have you heard nothing I've said? This man is dangerous!"

"Ma'am, I would suggest you return to the safety of your quarters until I've dealt with this matter."

Alexandra could do nothing but stand and stare as the two men left the room. A sob rose in her throat. Where was Hunter? Who would protect her from Cain now? But she was only paralyzed for a moment by the commanding officer's stupidity, and then she raced for the door. If Winslow wouldn't protect her, she'd protect herself. She had too much to live for to die now.

Down the maze of dark hallways she ran. She ducked into the room of She-Who-Stands-Strongly, spoke rapidly and then raced for her own room.

With her musket in her hand, the ammunition bag thrown over her shoulder and her knife in her belt she burst through the outside door and into the fort's courtyard. A powder of snow lay on the muddy ground and the air was frigid, but even without her cloak, Alexandra took little notice.

Lieutenant Winslow had about a dozen men mustered and was just marching through the open gates when Alexandra came around the corner of the log building. In the distance she could see a flank of soldiers and Indians approaching. A handsome man in an English uniform led them.

He had to be Cain.

"Captain Cain," Winslow called as he led his men outside the gates. "I must ask you and your men to halt."

Alexandra crouched behind a rain barrel. From here she could see and hear but not be seen. Out of the corner of her eye she saw She-Who-Stands-Strongly running along the far wall toward the gate.

Cain halted as did his men. "Lieutenant, so good to see you again. I must ask you if you have within these walls a woman by the name of Alexandra. A tall white woman. Dark hair. Comely I'm told."

"I do."

"Then I must ask that you hand her over."

"I'm sorry, I cannot do that," Winslow responded, his voice wavering. "Her husband has left her in my care."

"Turn her over to me and I'll take my men and go in peace."

Even from this distance Alexandra could see Cain's men tensing. Their hands were moving to their weapons. Winslow was a fool. He was going to die. They were all going to die.

Alexandra looked across the compound at She-Who-Stands-Strongly. The old woman had reached the gate and now hung in the shadows of the wall, her ragged hooded cloak all but obscuring her withered frame.

"I must repeat myself, Captain. I cannot turn over any woman to you."

"Where's this Hunter of the Shawnee? Send him out here!"

Winslow straightened his spine. "I am the commanding officer of this fort and I make the decisions. Now leave, Cain, before I'm forced to take measures against you."

Alexandra didn't know what happened next.

Did Winslow move to draw his weapon? The next thing she knew a war hatchet was whirling end over end toward the lieutenant. It struck him in the forehead with a sickening thud.

Alexandra bolted as the Iroquois standing behind Cain broke into a frenzy of macabre hoots. The two lines of men dissolved and the first musket shots were fired. Feathered arrows whistled through the air.

Alexandra dropped her musket and ran up behind the gate door, hitting it with full force. She-Who-Stands-Strongly already had her side of the gate halfway closed.

"The gates! The gates!" Cain shouted above the din of shouting men and firing muskets. "Get the gates! They're closing them!"

An Indian shaved bald save for a long black forelock sprinted for the fort gateway. The two women met and ran side by side as they raced to slam the heavy hinged doors shut. The Indian thrust one hand through the opening and Alexandra screamed. The only way to close the gates and secure the fort was through these doors.

Without thinking she drew the knife from her belt and sliced at the Iroquois's hand, carving a long gash and spilling his blood into the snow.

He howled and pulled back.

The moment he withdrew his hand, the two women pushed the gates shut and threw down the iron latches. The Iroquois on the far side of the gate was still howling and cursing as Alexandra dropped the last iron gate latch and ran for her musket.

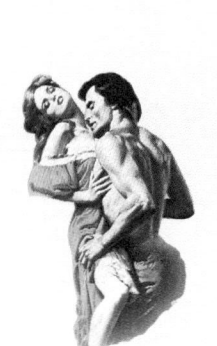

Chapter Eighteen

Alexandra snatched up her musket from the muddy ground and raced for the ladder that led up to a narrow walkway high on the fortress wall.

Several soldiers came running into the courtyard from within the fort living quarters.

"What the hell's going on?" a young man with blond hair and half-buttoned breeches called.

Alexandra took the ladder rungs two at a time. "Captain Cain and a band of Iroquois," she called over her shoulder. "We're being attacked."

Spotting no one else who seemed to be in charge, the young man came after her. "The gates secured?"

"Yes!"

He followed her up the ladder, buttoning up his breeches. "What about the lieutenant?"

"Dead."

"Jesus!" He clamped his hand over his mouth. "Pardon me, ma'am."

"It's all right."

"Where're the other men?"

"Outside the walls."

Alexandra reached the walkway and peered over the jagged points of the fortress wall. She squeezed her eyes shut and swallowed against the bile that rose in her throat. She could almost smell the sickeningly sweet scent of blood. Thoughts of the slaughter of her cousin and uncle flashed in her mind but she pushed them aside. There was no time to feel sorry for herself. There were women and children inside these fortress walls to be protected.

Alexandra took a deep cleansing breath and forced herself to peer over the wall. Below, men fought hand-to-hand. Crimson stained the soft white snow in angry splashes. Lieutenant Winslow's body lay in an unnatural heap, kicked aside in a struggle, his eyes staring heavenward, glassy and unseeing. Three more bodies littered the ground.

Lieutenant Winslow's men were losing . . . badly.

The remaining three soldiers still fought Cain's men and the Iroquois, but were backed against the wall now and had nowhere to go. The same scalp-locked savage that had tried to push his way through the gate tossed a spear, striking a dark-haired soldier in the chest. It sliced through his body to sink into the mushy ground behind him. The man screamed, then gurgled and was silent. Steam immediately rose from the wound and Alexandra turned away in horror.

"Ma'am." The young soldier who had followed her up onto the walkway touched her leather-fringed sleeve hesitantly. "Ma'am."

She opened her eyes. "He wants me. Captain Cain has come for me."

The young man peered over the side of the wall. A feathered arrow whizzed past his head and he drew back. "The name's Eli, Eli Jacobs."

"I closed the gate on the men. I didn't know what else to do," she said, dazed. She looked at the boy. "Now they're all going to die."

"You did the right thing. Those redskins come into this fort and more men will die. They'll carry off the women. The Mohawks do it every time they pass through here." Eli glanced over the spiked wall again. "Now what?" he said when he looked back at her. "Those were all the officers. They're all dead now."

Alexandra pressed her back to the rough bark that had been left on the logs when they'd been cut down. She panted, trying to catch her breath and get her wits about her. "All of them?" she asked, unable to bear looking over the wall again.

"All of them," he breathed.

She exhaled. "We defend her then," she said firmly. "We defend the fort. What other choice do we have?"

Eli touched his chest. Though he was probably sixteen or seventeen, he still had the body of a boy. "Us? We're going to hold off a madman and a band of murdering Iroquois?"

She nodded. "My husband will be back. I know he will. We just have to hold on. He was going after Cain. When he realizes the captain's doubled back, he'll be here.''

Eli took another look over the wall. The unholy cries of the Iroquois had slackened. A man groaned but then was silenced with the echo of a musket ball. Eli looked back at Alexandra. "But the officers are dead. Who's going to tell us what to do?"

She didn't even consider the matter. "I am," she said, heading for the ladder, her musket still in her hand. "Come on. We've got work to do."

Eli followed her down the ladder and across the yard. The sun was beginning to melt in the morning sunshine, melting the snow and turning the entire compound into a mire pit. "Assemble every man, woman and child here in the yard," she commanded, walking through a gaggle of geese and scattering them as she went. "Now."

Eli lifted his hand to salute and then dropped it sheepishly. "Yes, yes, ma'am."

"Alexandra," she called after him as he ran for the living quarters."

"What?" he hollered back.

"Alexandra, that's my name. Alexandra—" She felt silly when she realized she still didn't know what her married name was. "You can just call me Alexandra," she finished.

Eli walked away and she shook her head. Once she got through this, once Hunter returned and Cain was dead, she would find out what her name was. She'd sit Hunter down and make him tell her his true identity. But right now she had more important things to worry about.

"Hey, you," she ordered across the compound at another soldier.

He turned around. "Me?"

Good heavens, she thought, *there's no one left here but children*. This boy appeared even younger than Eli. "Yes, you! Take your musket and go up there." She pointed at the ladder. "Keep a watch on Captain Cain and his men, but keep your head down or you'll catch a musket ball between your ears."

The boy stood staring at Alexandra, as if questioning her authority.

She didn't have time to explain herself to anyone right now or to consider how she must look ordering them around. Though this young man was an English soldier, he was still barely old enough to have had his apron strings cut. "Did you hear me?" she demanded, taking a fast step toward him.

Startled, the boy jumped and raced for the ladder. "Yes, ma'am!"

A few minutes later Alexandra stood in front of a line of people in the compound. Eli swore this was every living soul inside the fortress walls. There were twenty-three in all; six boy-soldiers, one soldier with a broken leg, six wives or whores of the men who had died outside the walls or gone to Annapolis with the commander of the fort, four Indian women, She-Who-Stands-Strongly, Sara and her new babe, and three small children.

"Sara, you needn't have come out here in this chill," Alexandra said quietly.

The young girl had her baby tied safely in an

Indian sling beneath her beaver-pelt cloak. "I'm right as rain," she said, standing proudly. "I can help, I swear I can. Little Matthew, he's happy as he can be, long as he's got his mama's teat."

Alexandra couldn't resist a smile. Despite the girl's crude words, she found her admirable. She also couldn't help thinking how sensible the Indians were about their children. A baby was content as long as he was allowed to sleep against his mother's breast, wasn't he?

Alexandra nodded, giving Sara's hand a squeeze. "Well, if you're certain, I could use you."

The girl smiled back. "I'm certain. I got to protect my son. He's all I got."

With a nod, Alexandra stepped back to face the others. For a moment she studied their faces. Everyone looked scared, even the seasoned soldier with the broken leg . . . that was, everyone looked scared but She-Who-Stands-Strongly. The old Indian woman stood proudly, her sagging breasts thrown out, an Indian spear with feathers dangling from the hilt clutched in her hand.

"All right," Alexandra said quietly, hoping her voice didn't reflect the stifling fear she fought in her chest. "This is the way it is. Captain Cain has come for me. But you all know that if he gets inside these walls with those Iroquois, someone else might die or at least be injured."

The old soldier murmured some words of agreement beneath his breath.

"Now the way I look at it," she went on, "is that all we have to do is keep them from scaling the walls. Help is coming. My husband will be here, today, I hope, tomorrow at the latest. Then there's the commander of this fort."

"Robertson," someone offered.

"Robertson," she said. "I understand he and the men he took with him to Annapolis are expected back any day, so all we have to do is hang on."

"My husband." A pregnant woman in a red wool cap stepped out of the line. "Where's my husband, Samuel? He was with the lieutenant."

"Dead," Alexandra said. She didn't know how else to say it, except to come right out and tell the truth. "I'm sorry."

The woman fought a sob as she stepped back into the line, comforted by another woman.

"I'm sorry," Alexandra repeated. "They're all dead, every man who walked outside these walls with the lieutenant."

Someone else began to cry.

Alexandra fought the tears that threatened to choke her. She didn't want to be in charge here. She didn't want to be the one responsible for protecting these people, but who else was there? The soldiers left were no more than children and the older man seemed unable or unwilling to give any leadership. So Alexandra had no choice.

"Now listen to me," she said. "We're going to have to get up on this wall and keep watch. We've got to keep those savages outside until help comes. We'll all take turns on watch and that means the women too. Someone starts to scale the wall and we kill them, all right?"

Several of the women nodded their heads. The soldier-boys all murmured in agreement.

"All right," Alexandra said. "There's already one man up there. You, you, and you," she pointed to three more soldiers. "Get up on those other walls and take your weapons."

The soldiers broke from the line and ran for the fort walls.

She walked to the soldier with the broken leg. "Can you coordinate the sentries?"

He nodded his head. "I can't walk with this bum leg, but you prop me against a barrel and I'll sit out here and keep the boys sharp."

Alexandra nodded her head. "Thank you."

She pointed to one of the women. "You and your friend here," she indicated the woman whose husband had been killed, "and you take an inventory of how much food we've got. I want every sack of flour, every hogshead of dried pork, every keg of ale counted and marked down."

"I can do that," the woman said. "Come on, Dorcas. No time to mourn now, you got to protect that baby of yours and Samuel's."

Alexandra moved down the line giving each person a job. "You see to firewood. You too. Gather every stick you can find. We'll all move into that common room where the officers ate. That way we can keep everyone accounted for and save on firewood." She moved on down the line. "You take the children inside. Gather their belongings and take them to the common room. You be sure the livestock is fed."

Alexandra moved to another woman. "How do we get water in here? Please don't tell me you walk out to the river."

"No. This ain't the first time we been laid to siege. Water comes in around the back by way of a stream dug in off the river."

"Good. Then you start storing water in rain barrels in case they get clever and dam up our flow."

Alexandra reached Sara. "You see to a meal cooked for everyone. Make sure the sentries are fed and given something warm to drink. Take those women without anything else to do and get them on it with you."

Sara nodded. "I can see to it, Alexandra." She spoke to several Indian girls and they headed for the inner fort.

Alexandra looked up to see that everyone had been assigned a job now but She-Who-Stands-Strongly and Eli. She approached her Indian friend first. "I know you have medicinal supplies. Gather them. We may have injuries. Then come back to me and I'll give you something else to do."

The woman nodded. She gripped Alexandra's shoulder in a reassuring gesture. "This day I am proud to be your friend. Hunter of the Shawnee has chosen well his new mate."

Before Alexandra could respond, the old woman was gone. Only Eli was left now. He stood at attention.

"Eli."

"Ma'am?"

"I've got some questions, about the fort, about Captain Cain. Can you sit down inside and help me out?"

He grinned. "That I can."

"Good, now—"

"He wants a Hunter," one of the soldiers called from high on the fort wall. "You know a Hunter?"

Alexandra ran for the ladder. She was freezing now and needed her cloak badly, but she didn't have time to run back for it. She scaled the ladder, her musket still in her hand. She took a quick look over the wall to see Captain Cain standing, waiting. She ducked back down.

"What did you tell him?"

"Told him nothin'. He just keeps saying he wants to speak to someone called Hunter. I don't know who he wants."

"Hunter!" Cain called from the ground below. "Give her up and no one else need die."

Alexandra listened to the grating sound of the captain's voice. He didn't know Hunter wasn't here!

"Do you hear me? I say give her up!"

Alexandra grabbed the boy's arm. "Tell him we give up no one. He's talking to my husband. He mustn't know he's not here. He mustn't know how many of us are in here."

"Hunter!" Cain bellowed again.

The boy raised his head above the wall calling out between two jagged spikes. "We give up no one!"

Alexandra watched from between two spikes farther down the wall.

Cain's head snapped in the direction of the boy. "I want to speak with the man who calls himself Hunter! The woman is mine. I'll take what's mine and then I'll go on. No one else need get involved."

He indicated the bodies that littered the muddy ground. "These men didn't have to die."

"Tell him again," Alexandra told the boy.

"We give up no one," he repeated.

"Oh, you will," Cain answered, his voice taking on an odd tone. "I'll have her. I'll have her because she's mine. The question is, how many of you will die in the process? How many will give their lives before one of you turns her over to me?"

Alexandra stood up, no longer able to control her anger. "You'll have me in hell!" she cried.

An Indian standing behind Cain spun around and shot an arrow through the air. Alexandra ducked and watched it whistle over her head.

As she started for the ladder she heard Cain chastise the savage for shooting at her. He wanted her alive, he said. Alive to regret crossing him like this.

"Come on, Hunter," she murmured silently and she climbed down the ladder. "I need you, husband. I don't know how long I can hold on here."

"I have to go." Hunter accepted the Shawnee woman's hand. "I thank you for your hospitality, but I must go," he repeated in the Shawnee tongue. "I have to return to my wife."

Twice Mended smiled all-knowingly. "The home campfire burns for you, no?"

Hunter accepted the small pack of food Twice Mended was insisting he take. "Something like that."

She handed him his bow and quiver of arrows. "This woman thanks you again for coming to tell us of my great-uncle's injury. Our men will bring him home, even if it is only the shell of his body. We thank you from the depths of our hearts for caring enough not to let an old man lie to rest so far from those who love him."

Hunter pulled a leather headband down over his head and tucked back the last stray locks of red hair. When he left the village, he would travel straight through to the fort on the Noniack. He wouldn't rest until he held Alexandra in his arms again and knew that she was safe. He told himself that he had lost one wife to Cain, he'd not lose another, but the truth was, he missed Alexandra. He missed her sharp tongue; he missed her fiery kisses.

"He's a brave man, your uncle," Hunter went on. "This man is thankful to have known him in this life, if only for a few moments."

Twice Mended nodded. "Well, do not let me keep you from the wife that calls. Goodbye to you, Hunter of the Shawnee. Your dugout waits down by the river bank."

Hunter turned to go. It had taken him longer to get to the village than he had hoped. It was further than he had remembered. He'd now not slept in more than two days, but he wasn't tired, just edgy and anxious to be on his way. "I'll try to get the dugout back to you somehow. I appreciate your lending it to me."

She waved her hand in farewell. She was a pretty woman in her midthirties, a widow, a woman who might have interested him a few months ago. But suddenly he had no eyes for anyone but the dark-haired white woman, Alexandra.

"May the wind always be at your back and the luck always at your heels," she called after him.

Hunter left the small village and followed a path down to the river's edge. Just as promised, a dugout canoe waited for him. He dragged it off the bank and waded into the icy water. With one easy movement he swung into the boat and dropped to his knees. He tossed the food bag into the bow and grabbed the single carved wooden paddle. "I'm coming, Alexandra," he murmured to himself as he turned the dugout and headed out into the open water. "I'm coming, sweeting."

"Four days," Alexandra said softly. She stood in the fort's compound, her cloak tied tightly around her neck. It was almost dusk, and the October air was sharp and stinging. Tonight she could almost smell the salt water of the bay. "Four days and still you don't return. Where are you, husband?"

She-Who-Stands-Strongly laid her hand sympathetically on Alexandra's arm. "He will come."

"He won't. Something's happened to him. I know it has. He went after Cain. At some point he had to have realized Cain turned back to the fort. Hunter reads the trail signs too well to have missed it."

"He will come."

Alexandra laughed, but without humor. "How do you know? He could be sick. He could have been eaten by a bear. He could have been killed by Mohawks." She shrugged. "He could have decided not to come back for me. He didn't really want to marry me, you know." She looked up at the older woman. "He did it on a lark. He did it because I wouldn't sleep with him without the bonds of marriage."

She-Who-Stands-Strongly smiled a crooked smile. "You were smarter than most maids. Luckier to have caught such a catch. Now do not speak words you will later wish had not been spoken. Have faith in the heart, I tell you, Alexandra, wife of Hunter."

Alexandra crossed her arms over her chest. How much longer could they go with this standoff? How much longer before Cain realized there were no soldiers inside the fort, and that Hunter was gone? How long before he realized that if they all attempted to scale the walls at the same time, it would be impossible for her to fight them off? How long would it be before he realized it was a woman holding the fort?

In the three days since Cain had arrived, he'd cut off their water supply by damming it up, just as she had feared he would. He'd made trade offers to anyone who would listen, offering guns, whiskey, even gold, to the man who would hand Alexandra over. Cain had sent several Mohawks to try to scale the wall. Eli had managed to kill one. Another boy severely injured another.

But Cain seemed to be a patient man, and determined as well. He wasn't going to leave without her. She seemed to have become an obsession with him. No one took what was his, he repeated over and over again. No one.

Alexandra hugged herself for warmth. Above, on the narrow walkways two women, a boy, and Eli, paced, keeping the watch. Alexandra figured that they had enough food to last indefinitely, but their water supply would run short in another three days. Even rationing it, it would be depleted in a week.

Unless, of course, it snowed and there was enough to collect and melt for water. She peered up into the blue, cloudless sky that hung in a canopy above the treetops. "Please let it snow, hard," she prayed.

But even if it did snow—they couldn't go on like this forever. Something had to happen.

She hoped the commander who had left Winslow in charge would return, but what if he did? What if he came with only a few men? They would die at the hands of Cain's renegade Mohawks before they ever reached the fortress gates. They would—

"Hunter," came Cain's now-familiar voice from the other side, tearing Alexandra from her thoughts. "I'm losing patience. It's cold out here." There was a pause. Then he spoke again. "Last chance, Hunter, or whoever is listening. Send her out or we burn down the place and we come in after her."

"We give up no one!" Eli called from his post.

A slew of arrows flew through the air in response.

Alexandra crossed the compound in a few long

strides and started up the ladder. At the top, she walked to where Eli stood, taking care to keep her head below the jagged posts of the log wall.

"Last chance," Cain repeated. "And if we burn the place down we'll kill every living thing inside! I swear by the father God Almighty we will."

Alexandra felt her heart fall. She had been afraid of this, afraid since the beginning. She'd just not allowed herself to consider the matter.

"Why?" she shouted.

Eli grabbed her hand to try and keep her from showing herself, but she was too angry to allow logic to control her now. "Why?" she asked Cain again. Looking over the top of the wall, their gazes locked.

He lifted a dark eyebrow. He was a handsome man dressed in a fur cloak and an officer's cap. "Why, indeed?"

"This is between you and me. Not my husband. Not the people inside this fort."

Cain smiled a courtier's smile at her.

She could see his soldiers and the Indians at their campfires. They were dipping arrows into a small pot of black ooze and then lighting them. Pitch. They were going to bombard the fort's main building and walls with arrows of pitch! The fires would be nearly impossible to put out.

"Tell me," she demanded. Her heart felt leaden in her chest. She would never see Hunter again, never see her family or England, never give birth to a child like little Matthew.

Cain was still smiling up at her. "He isn't here, is he?" Cain asked. "Your man, the one they call

Hunter of the Shawnee. If he were here, he'd have shown his face. He'd not be sending you up. Not unless he was ready to give you up."

"My husband is none of your concern. I want to know why you would harm these people because of me."

"Spite." He was still smiling.

Alexandra could feel Eli's grip. "Don't do it. Don't go. He wouldn't kill us all. Not women and children."

Alexandra watched as the first arrow of fire arced over the wall and struck home in the roof of the building. One of the young soldiers in the compound clambered up the wall to try and put out the spreading fire.

"I'm waiting." Cain nodded his head and another arrow flew through the air.

Alexandra couldn't catch her breath. She could feel her heart pounding in her chest. Her palms were wet, her hands shaking.

How could she give herself up to this man, this man who had raped and murdered Hunter's Laughing Rain?

Yet how could she give up the lives of all the people inside the fort? She had gotten to know these people in the last few days. They weren't just names or faces. They were people with families to go to, futures to be made.

"Don't do it," Eli begged. "How do you know he's telling the truth? How do you know he won't kill us all anyway?"

"I'll have to take that chance," she heard herself whisper. She started for the ladder.

"Don't go," She-Who-Stands-Strongly cried as Alexandra's feet touched the ground. "This woman is ready to die for you. Don't give yourself up."

Slowly Alexandra walked toward the massive gates. "I can't ask you to do that," she said softly. "I can't ask that of any of you."

She-Who-Stands-Strongly wept. "Alexandra . . ."

She kissed the old woman on her wrinkled cheek. "Take care of Sara and the baby." She looked into the old woman's teary eyes and then looked away, afraid she would break down herself.

"Alexandra," Cain called from the opposite side of the wall.

Another arrow arced high overhead and struck an inner wall.

"Light the gates!" Cain commanded.

"No," Alexandra shouted. "Don't! I'm coming!"

Everyone inside the fort had spilled out into the compound now. They were running to put out the fires with wet rags and animal skins.

"Don't do it," Mary Masten cried as she ran for the far wall that was already blazing. "You'll not survive."

"Joey!" Alexandra called.

"Yes, ma'am," one of the young soldiers said, running toward her with tears in his eyes.

"When I say so, lift the latches and let me through. Close them behind me. You understand?"

"Yes, but—"

"Just do it!" she said sharply between clenched teeth. "Let me out. My husband will come for me," she said weakly. "I'll be all right."

Tears ran down Joey's face, but he followed her to the gate.

"If anyone tries to push through as I go out, you shoot them with your musket, you understand?"

He nodded.

"Good." She forced a smile and turned to face the gate. She took a deep breath. She knew Cain was waiting for her on the other side. She could feel him.

"I'm coming," she called in the loudest voice she could muster. "Stand back or the boy will shoot."

She nodded her head and Joey lifted the iron latches one at a time, each one making a hollow clanking sound. She took one step forward and felt a hand clasp her arm and yank her through the opening. Against her will she opened her mouth and screamed.

Chapter Nineteen

When Hunter heard Alexandra scream, he bolted. He ran blindly through the underbrush, oblivious to the greenbriars and branches that tore at his face.

He was too late! Cain had beat him here! Cain would take Alexandra from him just as he had taken Laughing Rain . . .

Hunter was so out of control that he was unaware of the shadow of the man ahead of him. He never saw the man's moccasined foot until he tripped over it and fell flat on his face.

Hunter cried out, but his voice was smothered by the solid ground as his attacker climbed onto his back and forced his face into the wet humas.

"Silence!" the Iroquois ordered. "Silence or they will hear us and we will both die."

Instinctively Hunter struggled against the weight on his back. How could he have been so stupid to have fallen into a trap like this? How could he have lost sight of the basic instincts of survival? How would he save Alexandra when he was lying dead and scalped in the underbrush?

"I said *silence* or the others will not have to come for you. I will slit your throat myself," the voice hissed in his ear. "The woman is safe for the moment. They have not harmed her—not yet."

Realizing his limited choices, Hunter let his entire body go limp. This was not the way to fight a man, face to the ground, his weapon out of reach. Better to play along, and wait for a chance to take the upper hand. *Pray for a chance*, Hunter told himself.

"I will let you up if you vow to keep silent, but I swear, this man will not be given away by a fool."

There was something familiar about this Mohawk's voice. Hunter's nerves were raw. He knew him. He knew this brave.

The moment the attacker moved off Hunter, Hunter leapt to his feet. Even in the shadows of twilight Hunter recognized the man. "Two Crows!"

The Indian lowered his gaze. "You are a fool, Hunter of the Shawnee, to run through the forest like a spooked deer. You are one and they are many. You cannot save the woman of yours without forethought."

Hunter stared at Two Crows. His facial wounds inflicted by Cain and his bullies were healing. The Iroquois still wore rags tied around the hand Hunter had shot the fingers off of. "What in God's holy name are you doing here and what do you know of my wife?"

Two Crows dropped into a crouch and pointed in the direction of the fort. The smell of burning tar and charred wood was sharp in the air, but

Hunter saw no signs of fire. Whatever had been burning, the walls of the fort, he surmised, had been put out. He knelt on one knee beside Two Crows. He still didn't trust the renegade, but the man had spared his life and he knew something about Alexandra. "My wife," Hunter urged. "Tell me what you know of her capture."

"The cap-i-tan, he came for her only a day after you left. I followed him here. The cap-i-tan and you, your paths did not cross."

"I got held up. Someone attacked an old Shawnee man in the forest, wounded him fatally, and killed his escorts. A good guess would be that they were Cain's men. I understand he travels with Iroquois."

Two Crows nodded. "He brings my brothers with him to this fort."

"Three days. You said he came to the fort three days ago." Hunter stared through the underbrush trying to catch a glimpse of Alexandra, of anything. Campfire smoke rose and curled heavenward. Oddly it appeared to be coming from outside the fort walls. "If he took her three days ago why is he here? Why didn't he carry her off and why the hell are they camped outside the walls?"

Two Crows looked at him, a silly smirk on his face. "The white woman, the woman you call your own now, she held the fort."

Hunter looked in the direction of the fort; most of the north wall was obscured by the trees, but he caught a flash of red uniform. He looked back at Two Crows. "The soldiers, you mean. The soldiers held the fort."

Two Crows gave a quick shake of his head. "The

fort soldier-leader walked outside the gates with his men. I watched the fool. Cain's men killed them all, but someone closed the gates from the inside. I see only boys for sentries. Your woman gave the orders."

Hunter swore softly. "So where is she now? That was her. I heard her scream."

Two Crows laid his hand on Hunter's to keep him from leaping up. "I tell you, she is safe for this moment. Cap-i-tan will not harm her. Not yet. He sells the women. He can get nothing for a corpse."

Hunter knew what Two Crows said was true. He was one man and they had many. He couldn't just barrel in. If he did, odds were, he would lose his life. Most likely Alexandra would die as well, or worse, live to wish she had died. Hunter had to have a plan. "How many men?" he asked. Before Two Crows could respond, he grabbed his arm. "Wait. How do you know all this? How is it that you come to stand here and not with your brothers, the Mohawk dogs? A trap?" He tightened his grip. "Because if this is a trap I will kill you, Two Crows. I'll strip your hide from your bones and hang it from the trees as carrion for the turkey buzzards."

Two Crows lifted his black-eyed gaze to meet Hunter's. "No trap. No trick. I went into the fort to warn your woman. She did not tell me you had gone." He nodded. "But when she closed the gates I knew you were not among the soldiers inside."

Hunter released his grip. "You warned her?"

He nodded. "But she would not listen. She thought I spoke lies. She knew when the cap-i-tan came that this man did not speak lies."

"None of this tells me why, Two Crows. Why did you warn my wife? Why did you come here at all? Cain will kill you when he finds you have betrayed him."

"Why does not matter." Two Crows turned away. "We must make the plan. Darkness will fall. We will take her from them when the night spirits come."

Hunter watched Two Crows for a moment. All reason told him not to trust the renegade. He was without scruples, without honor; he was a thief and a murderer. Yet something in the man's tone of voice made Hunter think he could trust him, even with his own life. "We? You say we will take her? You intend to help me?"

He nodded. "Enough of this talk. You want my help or you do not. Tell me."

Again, logic warned Hunter not to trust him. Send him away, a voice echoed inside his head. "Yes, this man accepts your help and he thanks you. Now I have to see my wife. I have to know she's all right."

Two Crows crooked a finger, beckoning Hunter to follow him. "These brothers, I would not call brothers. They have grown lazy and stupid. For three nights I stand within paces of them and they do not hear me. They do not see me." He ducked beneath the boughs of a pine tree and dropped to his knees and began to crawl toward the fort. "Come and you can see your woman, but I warn you, do not speak or she will die. My brothers thirst for blood. We will both die if they know we are here before we wish them to know."

Hunter nodded.

Keeping his body flat to the ground, he crawled behind Two Crows, oblivious to the cold wetness of the ground or the branches and briars that snagged on his buckskins. Two Crows had somehow beaten a path through the seemingly impenetrable undergrowth. Closer and closer they drew to the fort until he could hear individual voices. He heard Cain and another soldier, then an Iroquois, then finally the sound of Alexandra's voice.

He almost smiled. She wasn't sobbing, or pleading for her life. He couldn't tell at this distance exactly what she was saying, but he could tell by the sound of her voice that she was lashing out at her captors. *Good,* Hunter thought. *Hang onto that anger, sweeting. It will keep you alive, at least for a little while . . .*

They drew closer until Two Crows turned back to Hunter and brought a finger to his lips. He moved aside and parted the pine boughs. Hunter rose up in instantaneous anger, but he checked himself before he drew attention to their hiding place.

Alexandra was bound hand and foot and seated on the ground beneath a sycamore tree. A soldier in a tattered blue uniform was tying her to the tree. Cain stood only a few feet from her, arguing with several of the Mohawks. They were discussing whether or not they should break camp tonight.

One Mohawk, a man with a human fingerbone threaded through his earlobe, stepped up to Cain. Obviously he was the leader of the renegade Iroquois. In broken English he warned Cain of the foolishness of remaining here all night. Cain argued that he didn't care what the Mohawks wanted. He needed a hot meal and a good night's sleep before they started north into Iroquois country.

The conversation became more heated. The Mohawk made a sudden advance toward Cain and shouted in his own tongue. Cain whipped a pistol from his coat and pulled the trigger before the Indian had the chance to back down. The echo of the shot was followed by the muffled thump of the Mohawk's body as it fell. Even at this distance Hunter could smell the acrid black powder mingled with the sickeningly sweet scent of fresh blood and bits of brain tissue. In the cold air of late afternoon, steam rose from the crack in the dead Mohawk's skull.

"Settles that discussion, doesn't it?" Cain said, glancing up at the other Indians. "Anyone else have any comments on the matter?" Spooked, the Mohawks scattered to their assigned posts. Cain shrugged. "There you have it then."

Hunter felt his stomach lurch. He was a Shawnee warrior. He had seen many deaths, but one so cowardly made him physically ill. Cain was a bully. God, but he hated a bully worse than anyone else on God's green earth.

"Murderer," Alexandra shouted from beneath the sycamore tree. "May your bones rot in bloody hell."

"No," Hunter whispered. "Hush, sweeting. Just once, keep your pretty mouth shut."

He wanted to call out to Alexandra. He wanted her to know that he hadn't abandoned her. He wanted her to know that she only need bide her time and not antagonize the bastard. But here she was again, speaking before she thought, riling the man who could kill her as easily as he had just killed the Mohawk his friends were now dragging away.

"What did you say?" Cain said, a hint of disbelief in his voice. He turned to face Alexandra whose hands were tied behind her back.

"I called you a murderer," she shouted. "Son of a poxed whore! Coward!"

Cain took the four steps between them. "Do not perturb me, lovely thing, or you'll lose your life as quickly as the man before you."

She laughed at him. "So kill me. Why not? Do it now," she dared, thrusting her chin at him, glaring with hatred-filled dark eyes. "Kill me like you killed Laughing Rain!"

"Laughing Rain?"

"My husband's first wife. You murdered her."

He smiled. "Ah, yes." He shrugged. "Hunter of the Shawnee. I make the connection now." He took a knife from his belt and slowly drew it back and forth across his leather pants leg. "Didn't mean to kill her, you know. She'd have brought a pretty price. But the bitch fought me. Cut me. I had to open her end to end. It was self-defense." He smiled. "Two of this Hunter's women. What a coincidence."

"He'll come for you," she taunted. "Hunter will come for you and you'll die. Kill me if you like. You'll still die and burn in everlasting hell."

Cain brought the tip of the hunting knife to her lower lip.

Every muscle in Hunter's body tensed. He was

too far away to make a kill by bow or spear. If he had to, he would make a run for her. As he watched Cain, Hunter was poised to leap.

"Now why don't you close that mouth of yours before I have to cut your tongue out," Cain cautioned Alexandra.

A dot of blood rose on Alexandra's lip.

She opened her mouth to speak. Then closed it. Hunter heaved a massive sigh of relief.

Cain smiled at her. "Excellent. I like a woman who knows how to obey her man. Wait another night or two until I'm able to provide us with some privacy and I'll teach you what a woman can do for a man when she's willing to obey. I'll make you forget your Hunter, I vow to that."

A soldier called to Cain, and the captain walked away from Alexandra, leaving her be, at least for the present.

Two Crows touched Hunter's shoulder lightly. He signaled with a bob of his head for Hunter to follow him again. Hunter hated to leave Alexandra unguarded, but he knew he and Two Crows must make plans. They had to have a carefully laid course before they went into the camp.

On their hands and knees they crawled through the tunnel of greenbriars until they reached a safe distance from Cain's camp.

"Son of a blind cur," Hunter muttered as he rose and stretched his long legs. "We have to go in now. We can't leave her tied like that. I can't do it."

"No."

Hunter glared at Two Crows. "No? Who the hell are you to be telling me *no*? Misbegotten prick!" He slammed Two Crows in the chest with his palms. Two Crows dropped his spear. Hunter gripped him by his leather vest and shook him. "If it hadn't been for you, Alexandra would never be in this position to begin with! I ought to kill you now and be done with you!"

Two Crows refused to make eye contact with Hunter. "Kill me if you wish, Hunter of the Shawnee," he said, his voice steady and without emotion. "But it would be better to wait and kill this man after he had helped you save your wife from the men this man calls brothers."

He was right. Hunter knew he was right. He needed help. He shoved Two Crows backward, wondering where the hell Jon was. If Jon were here, he wouldn't need Two Crows.

Hunter panted, trying to gain control of his emotions. He would be of no help to Alexandra this way. He had to remain calm and go about this in a logical manner. There wasn't much time, and there would only be one chance.

He looked at Two Crows. "You think we should wait until dark?"

The Mohawk nodded. "The sun already begins to set. This cap-i-tan and his men, they are lazy. They will not break camp tonight."

"We wait until most of them go to sleep and then we slip in? The coward's way?"

"The way to save the woman," Two Crows responded.

Hunter gave a sigh. Cain had at least two dozen men, more, counting sentries. He and Two Crows, no matter how fierce warriors they were, would be hard-pressed to beat two dozen men in open battle.

If they could sneak in when most of the men slept, they would have a much better chance at getting out alive. The question was, could Alexandra hold on that long? "Cain may try to rape her," he said, his own voice sounding hollow in his head.

Two Crows nodded. "We will watch and wait. If we must, we attack early. Now we prepare ourselves."

Hunter slipped his quiver of arrows off his back. "I can't believe this," he mused aloud. "I swore I would kill you if I set eyes on your face again and now I agree to fight at your side."

"This man fights at *your* side." Two Crows began to disrobe. "Now we go down to the riverside. We make our bodies invisible. We make our hearts worthy."

Hunter studied the man he had considered his adversary. "You're serious, aren't you? You'll die to help me get her back?"

He made the hand sign of peace. "To die fighting is to die honorably." He lowered his gaze. "It has been a long time since this man knew honor."

Hunter dropped his bow to the ground and began to strip down. He was trying to understand Two Crows, but he couldn't. Why would a man who had sold a woman now try to rescue her? A Mohawk with a conscience? It was hard to believe. "Is that what this is all about? Honor?"

Now nude, but seemingly unaffected by the falling temperature, Two Crows strapped his belt around his waist again, checked for his knife, and took up his spear. "I told you. Why, does not matter. You take this man's help, or you do not."

He shrugged. "It is your choice, he who the Shawnee call the Hunter."

Stripped down to nothing but a leather loincloth, Hunter shivered as he leaned over to take his beaded belt and his quiver and his bow. "I will take your help, but be warned. You betray this man and you and yours will be cursed for a thousand years."

Two Crows gave a nod and then turned and ran off into the forest in the direction of the Noniack River. Hunter followed.

Darkness set in. The full moon rose bright in the sky, and still Hunter and Two Crows waited, crouched on the cold ground.

"A full moon, an evil omen," Two Crows whispered.

Hunter shook his head. "A hunter's moon, always a good sign for me." He ignored Two Crows as the Indian made a sign against bad luck. The Shawnee always said the Mohawks were a superstitious lot.

Hunter watched through the cover of underbrush confident of the magic of the paint he wore. Down by the river he had covered himself in freezing riverbed mud. Then he had dug deep into his medicine bag and found the tiny pots of battle paint he carried with him always. Mixing the pungent, colored scrapings with water, he had painted his body and face in the manner of a Shawnee brave about to go to war. Across his torso he wore streaks of camouflage, but down his arms and across his cheekbones he painted the symbols that signified the Shawnee family he had been adopted into and the history of their bravery. With each symbol his confidence grew, his power grew. As he made each streak of paint he absorbed the strength of his Shawnee ancestors. Hunter knew he would be triumphant over the enemy. By the time he had completed the ritual, he was confident he would save Alexandra; he knew he would accomplish the vengeance that was rightfully his.

Now he needed only to choose the right moment to set the inevitable sequence of events in motion.

Hunter glanced at the man he had once considered his enemy, who now offered his own life to aid Hunter in his cause. Two Crows had also stripped naked and painted himself, but the paint of the Iroquois was bold and boastful. Angry red streaks covered his face and chest.

"The men sleep," Hunter said, his voice as soft as the whisper of the October wind. "Four sentries—two Mohawks and a bluecoat. We take them one at a time. Quietly. I get Alexandra out and then go back in for Cain. He dies and we move out."

Two Crows nodded as he slipped his hunting knife out of his belt. "May the spirits of the war gods be with you," he offered.

"God be with you," Hunter echoed.

The two men parted, fanning out, nearly invisible to the naked eye. Hunter crept up behind the first Mohawk sentry. The brave, either half asleep, or his instincts clouded by whiskey, never turned. Hunter cut his throat clean and let the body slip to the ground.

The second man was a little more difficult. Hunter had to approach him nearly head on. He took his bow from his shoulder, nocked an arrow and called softly in Iroquois to the brave, who carried a belt heavy with human scalps. The man spun around. Hunter's arrow flew clean, piercing the Indian's heart and stopping it in midbeat. The leaves beneath his moccasins rustled as he fell to the ground.

With the two men dead and Two Crows taking the other two, Hunter was free to walk into the firelit camp. He cut around the circle of wavering light, moving hesitantly toward Alexandra. She was tied to the tree, huddled inside her cloak for warmth, her head hung in exhausted sleep. Cain slept on a bedroll beneath a bearskin only a few feet from her.

Hunter crept behind the sycamore tree, left leafless and skeletal by the autumn winds. He murmured a prayer vowing to make this marriage work if only God would set Alexandra free unharmed.

He took a deep breath and carefully brought his hands around the back of the tree and covered her mouth. Alexandra bolted awake, clamping her teeth down on the soft flesh of Hunter's palm. The barest squeak of a cry escaped the muffle of his hand.

Chapter Twenty

For hours Alexandra had fought sleep, fearful Cain would attack her if she relaxed her guard, but finally she had succumbed. She awoke the instant the hands clamped down on her mouth. She tried to scream but the hands that smelled of stinking bog bottom smothered her voice. She bit down hard on the soft flesh of the palms.

A face appeared in front of hers, a savage face painted in frightening streaks of blue and black and green. Terrified, Alexandra tried to escape the hideous apparition. She struggled, but to no end. Her feet were still bound, her hands tied behind her back around the tree trunk. She was defenseless against the night apparition that was all too terrifyingly human.

"Shhh," the form hissed as he drew a long knife from his belt. Alexandra cringed, certain he was about to slit her throat. Instead, keeping one hand still clamped over her mouth, he drew the blade to her feet and cut the leather bindings. Then he freed her hands.

Just as he swept her into his arms, one of the soldiers sleeping near her called out an alarm. Suddenly Cain's camp was alive with confusion. A volley of musket shots sounded in the night and the sky rained with arrows.

"Run," a voice shouted in the darkness. "Take your woman and run, Hunter of the Shawnee. This man will defend you."

Hunter? Where was Hunter? Alexandra was frighteningly confused. Who was calling out to Hunter? Was she being rescued? Who was this creature who carried her in his arms?

She heard her kidnapper groan as a feathered arrow sunk into his forearm. Seemingly unaffected by the wound, he leaped over the burning campfire, and ducked into the overgrowth at the edge of the clearing. Just inside the tangle of greenbriars he dumped her.

"Run, sweeting," the kidnapper ordered as he grabbed the shaft of the arrow embedded in his forearm and broke it off at the skin. "Run deep into the forest and hide."

"Hunter?" She grabbed the painted man's bare arm, realizing for the first time that he was almost completely naked. "Is that you?" she sobbed.

He grasped the folds of her cloak and pulled her up against him, crushing his lips against hers. "Not Hunter, the Queen of the May," he whispered.

She smiled through her tears and then suddenly remembered the arrow in his arm. "Oh, God, you're hurt."

"Let go, sweeting." He gently took her hand from his shoulder.

"Go? Where are you going?" She watched him as he pulled away from her and turned to go. "Don't leave me, Hunter."

"Do as I say, and you'll be safe, Wife. Run and hide. I'll find you. I have to go back for Cain and Two Crows."

"Two Crows? What are you talking about?" But he was already gone. She watched Hunter disappear into the darkness as a sob rose in her throat.

Run, he had said. Run from Cain, from the Mohawks. But how could she run when he had gone back?

And what was he talking about, going back for Two Crows? What did Two Crows have to do with all this? Did Hunter intend to kill him as well? She couldn't let him do it! Two Crows had warned her of Cain's approach. Because of him she had been able to protect the women and children inside the fort.

Alexandra dropped to her hands and knees. She couldn't let Hunter kill Two Crows, no matter what he'd done in the past. He had helped her, maybe saved her life. She crawled through the greenbriars, realizing now that it was a man-made tunnel Hunter had brought her through. Reaching the end of the tunnel, she crouched, getting her bearings.

By the light of the campfire she could see bodies strewn everywhere. Mohawks and soldiers alike lay in heaps, staring up with unseeing eyes.

Someone had opened the fort gates and the young men Alexandra had gotten to know so well were charging Cain's camp, their muskets flashing and echoing again and again in the darkness.

Near the fort walls Alexandra spotted Hunter fighting a soldier and a Mohawk at the same time. He swung a pole in his hands, fending off their attacks. With one swift movement he caught first one man and then the other beneath the chin, sending them both reeling backward.

Stepping over a dead body, Hunter raced across the clearing. Two Indians wrestled on the ground, both with glinting knives. Alexandra suddenly realized one of the Indians was Two Crows. Her heart leapt in her chest, but everything was happening too quickly. Before she could shout to Hunter to let Two Crows live, her husband released his knife, letting it turn end over end through the air. To Alexandra's relief, it sank into the back of the Mohawk that had Two Crows pinned to the ground. The dead Indian flopped to the dirt and Two Crows bounded to his feet. To Alexandra's amazement her husband and the man who had once kidnapped and sold her, exchanged looks that could have been interpreted as nothing but a strange kinship between warriors.

"So you're the one," Alexandra heard a voice say.

It was Cain.

Hunter turned around to face the man who was calling to him. "Cain," he said.

"You have taken my woman. Surely you know the consequences of your actions."

"She's mine," Hunter's voice was frighteningly even. "Alexandra is my wife, as was Laughing Rain."

"Ah yes, the redskinned bitch I had to kill. Come now. Are you still angry with me over that, *Hunter of the Shawnee?*" He spoke Hunter's name with a hint of sarcasm.

"Then you admit your guilt?"

"Don't tell me you would let a heathen whore stand between two English gentlemen. God's bowels, Hunter, my uncle, the lord chancellor, knows your father."

Alexandra studied Cain carefully. He knew who Hunter was? She watched the captain lower his hand to his belt. A pistol rested on his hip. It was a cat-and-mouse game now.

"Guilty or not guilty?" Hunter demanded.

"Surely—"

"Guilty or not guilty of the crime of which you're accused?"

The corner of Cain's mouth turned up in a hint of a smile. "Guilty, and you want to know something? I enjoyed killing the minx."

Hunter stood utterly still except for the nervous movement of his fingers on the carved hilt of his knife. Soldiers and Mohawks still fought around them, but the two men seemed oblivious to the carnage. "She was my *wife*," Hunter murmured through clenched teeth. "She carried my *child*."

Cain sighed dramatically. "I suppose you think I should return this jade in exchange for the savage whore's life." He nodded in Alexandra's direction.

Alexandra thought to back up further into the shadows of the forest, but what was the point now? Cain had seen her. She remained crouched, not wanting to disturb Hunter's concentration.

"An exchange?" Hunter's gaze never wandered from Cain's face. "Not hardly. I'll have your life, instead."

The handsome captain threw back his head in laughter. "You can't kill me. Did you hear me? My uncle is the Chancellor of England, for Christ's sake!" He smiled an arrogant smile. "No one can hurt me. No one can stop me. Why else do you think they've not sent anyone to *curtail* my activities? Because they can't. They wouldn't dare."

Alexandra wasn't certain who made the first move, Hunter or Cain. Cain's pistol cracked and a streak of light blew from the muzzle. Hunter dove for the ground, rolled, and came up only a foot from Cain unharmed. Cain cursed at his bad luck and threw the pistol aside. There would be no time to reload now. With one fluid motion he withdrew a short saber from beneath his coat.

Alexandra closed her hand over her mouth to keep from crying out. Hunter had only his knife and the captain a sword. How could Hunter possibly best him?

The two men turned slowly, summing each other up. Hunter moved in a crouched position, his gaze riveted to the enemy's face. By the glint in his hazel eyes she could tell that he would make only one move and that would be to kill.

Growing restless with Hunter's patience, Cain brandished his saber. "What kind of Englishman are you anyway? A man to marry a redskin? A man to run through the forest naked like some heathen? A man to marry a white woman who's lain with every redskin on the Chesapeake?"

At that barb, Alexandra expected Hunter to pounce. But he didn't. It was what Cain wanted. He wanted him to attack with his hatred rather than his clear head. Every soldier knew that emotions weakened a man.

Alexandra's legs began to cramp and she stood. There was less fighting now. Many dead and wounded lay on the cold ground. Several of the Mohawks and Cain's soldiers had disappeared into the forest.

Twice Cain lashed out at Hunter with his saber. Both times Hunter leapt backward, then dashed forward again. Still the men circled each other.

Alexandra's nerves were taut with fear. If something didn't happen soon—

Alexandra saw a sudden flash of movement behind Hunter and heard an unholy war cry. She looked up to see a Mohawk running straight for his back. She screamed out his name. "Hunter! Behind you!" she cried.

Hunter half turned, knowing he couldn't turn his back to Cain. It all happened so quickly and yet standing there in the shadows of the pine trees, everything seemed to Alexandra to move at quarter time.

The Mohawk raised a hatchet above his head and hurled it into the air. Two Crows appeared out of nowhere. "Nooo!" he screeched.

Two Crows's body met the cold steel of the Indian hatchet in midair. It struck his breast, splitting flesh and cracking bones as it sank deep into his chest cavity.

In the confusion of that split second, Hunter dove forward and sank the blade of his knife into Cain's stomach clear to the hilt.

Cain's eyebrow arched in startled shock. Hunter twisted the knife and pulled it out. The saber fell from Cain's hand. He touched his hand to the oozing wound and looked up at Hunter in utter disbelief. "You can't harm me," he whispered, his voice barely carrying in the night air. Blood bubbled from his mouth and he fell to his knees. "No one can harm me. The chancellor is my uncle."

Hunter wiped his blade on his bare, muddy leg and thrust it into his leather belt. He walked away from Cain, who was now extending a hand to him.

"Don't leave me," Cain sobbed pitifully.

Alexandra watched as Hunter walked to Two Crows and knelt. She wanted to go to them, but she didn't. She only stood and watched.

Hunter lifted Two Crows's body and held him in his arms. Two Crows was still breathing, but barely. Hunter leaned and whispered something in the Mohawk's ear.

Alexandra took a few steps closer, unable to resist hearing what her husband would say.

"This man thanks you for his life."

Two Crows shook his head. "This sorry man owed the Hunter of the Shawnee. To take the woman. It was not right."

Hunter forced a smile. "Then we're even."

Two Crows closed his eyes and for a moment Alexandra thought he was dead, but then he opened them again. "Tell me, Hunter of the

Shawnee. Have I taken back the honor that was once my family's?"

"Aye," Hunter answered. "You die a warrior's death and I will bury you with honor. I do not know the rituals of the Mohawks, but a Shawnee ceremony will take you to the heavens just as well."

Two Crows coughed, his entire body convulsing. When the spasm passed, he spoke again. "My fingers. In the bag at my waist. Do not forget them, Hunter of the Shawnee."

Tears ran unchecked down Alexandra's cheeks as she watched her husband cradle in his arms the man who had been his enemy. What man would hold his enemy with such respect, she wondered, even if he was dying?

Two Crows's chest rose and fell one last time and then his body went limp. Hunter lowered him to the ground and he stood. "Alexandra," he called, his voice cracking.

Alexandra ran toward him. The fighting had ceased. The last of Cain's Mohawks and soldiers still alive had run into the forest when their leader had fallen.

"Hunter!" She threw herself against his mud-caked naked body. "Oh, God, Hunter, I thought he would kill you! I thought—"

"Hush," he soothed. "Hush, sweeting. It's done. Done now."

She smoothed his cheeks with her palms, not caring that she covered herself with his war paint. All she cared about was that he was alive. She kissed him again and again. When she touched his arm, his face paled.

"Oh, God," she murmured. "Your arm. You've still got the arrowhead in it."

He draped the other arm over her shoulder and started toward the fort. "Easy enough to fix," he assured her. "It doesn't hurt."

As they passed Cain, he half sat up, reaching out to Hunter. "Please kill me," he begged, clutching his oozing stomach wound. "Please. Don't leave me here to die like this. Finish me off. I beg you . . ."

Hunter stopped and stared down at the pathetic man who had boasted only moments ago how he had enjoyed raping and murdering a pregnant woman. "I'll do you a better turn than you did Laughing Rain," he told Cain coldly, looking him straight in the eye. "I'll let you live . . ."

Cain fell back onto the ground with a moan, and Hunter walked off, taking Alexandra with him.

Inside the walls of the fort, Alexandra had hot bath-water brought to her room and poured into a copper tub for Hunter. She-Who-Stands-Strongly came with a knife and a needle and thread and cut out the metal arrowhead embedded in Hunter's arm. He never flinched as he sat submerged in the tub and allowed the old Indian woman to do her surgery and stitch him up.

Alexandra hovered over him, wanting to help, but knowing her friend knew what she was doing. Once the wound was cleaned and stitched, She-Who-Stands-Strongly took up her medicine bag and left with a wave of her hand.

"Thank you, She-Who-Stands-Strongly," Hunter said. "Now see to the other injured men."

"I must prepare the dead for burial."

"They can wait until morning, Aunt. Now is the time to deal with the living. Tomorrow will be soon enough to give our brave fighting men a proper burial."

"How many died?" Alexandra asked.

"Only two of the boy-soldiers, and then the Mohawk the Hunter called friend," the old woman answered.

"Eli?"

"A cut on the arm. A black eye. A happy young man to have fought his first battle."

Alexandra couldn't resist a smile as she accompanied She-Who-Stands-Strongly to the door. "What should I do for Hunter?" she asked.

She-Who-Stands-Strongly shrugged. "The warrior needs sleep." She smiled the barest hint of a smile. "And what all young virile warriors need when they have come home from battle."

Alexandra felt her cheeks color with embarrassment, but she laughed. "Good night, friend. Thank you."

She-Who-Stands-Strongly gave a wave over her shoulder as she shuffled down the corridor. "Do not thank me. Bring a son or daughter into the world. That is how you may thank an old woman."

Alexandra stepped back in her room and dropped the iron bolt. Hunter had climbed out of the tub and was now drying himself off. When she approached, he opened the cotton towel and drew her in against his wet skin. She laughed as she ran her finger down the bridge of his nose, wiping away the last streak of warpaint.

"Are you tired?" she purred.

"Not tired." He bent and kissed her lower lip.

"Hungry?"

He drew his warm lips across her cheek and down the length of her neck. "Not for food."

"You've been injured." She lifted her hands and rested them on his bare shoulders, kneading them. "You should rest."

"Can't rest until I've kissed you." He kissed her again, but this time his lips lingered on hers, sending shivers of anticipation through her veins. "Can't rest until I've touched you."

He brought his hand up her rib cage and she covered it with hers, guiding him up to the swell of her breasts. She sighed as his warm hand touched her. Even through the leather of her tunic, she could feel his caress. Her nipple puckered against the brush of his fingertips and she pressed closer to him, molding her hips to his.

"I don't want to be accused of forcing you," Alexandra teased. She drew an imaginary line with her finger, starting between his breastbone and moving lower.

Hunter groaned as she brushed her finger past his navel and lower still. She laughed, a soft rumble deep in her throat. Already she could feel him growing hard beneath her hand.

"Too many clothes," he chided. "Take them off."

Her fingers found the leather ties that ran the length of the front of her tunic. As she unlaced top to bottom, he followed with his tongue, painting a wet path of shivering delight.

"Witch," he accused. "Enchantress."

She undressed herself slowly, tantalizing him, reveling in the pleasure she could give him. When her tunic finally fell to the rough-hewn plank floor, she started on her leather legging. Finally she stood in the center of the room, wrapped in Hunter's arms wearing nothing but her moccasins.

She threaded her fingers through the wet locks of auburn hair that fell across his shoulders. Lifting herself up on her bare toes, she pressed her lips to his and kissed him deeply.

"Alex, Alex," he murmured in her ear. "Let me love you."

She took his hand and led him to the narrow wooden cot. "Let me love you," she whispered, pushing him gently backward onto the bed and straddling his legs. "Let me take away the pain." She brushed her fingertips lightly over his freshly sewn wound. "The physical pains and the emotional."

"My pain has ended," he assured her as he pulled her down beside him. "Laughing Rain can now rest. It's time for us, sweeting, for you and for me."

He lowered his mouth to her breast and teased her nipple with the tip of his tongue. She laughed a sensual laugh, arching her back in encouragement.

"Good?" he asked, turning his attention to the other nipple.

"Good," she responded, letting her eyes drift shut as the waves of pleasure washed over her. "Too good!"

"Too good? Ah, there's no such thing as too good when it comes to the flesh, sweeting."

Instinctively Alexandra lifted her hips as he kissed his way down her stomach and even lower. She threaded her fingers through his hair, drawing up her knees, thinking just one kiss. But when the tip of his tongue touched the moistness at the apex of her thighs, she could feel her flesh melting with pleasure.

"Hunter, Hunter," she moaned.

"Love me?" he teased between strokes of his tongue. "Tell me you love me, Lady Alexandra."

She tried to twist away, half laughing, half sobbing with pleasure. "Let me go! Beast!" she accused. "Savage! Heathen! Torturer."

"Say it and I'll release you. Tell me you love me, savage or not." His voice had a husky catch to it. "Better yet, tell me you love me for the savage in me."

She hesitated for only a moment. She did love him. She was certain of it now. "I love you," she cried, breathless, wanting him to stop what he was doing to her, wanting him never to stop. "I love you. I love you for the man you are."

He laid his cheek on her stomach for a moment. "And I you," he said softly.

She took his chin with the tip of her finger and lifted it until she could stare into the depths of his hazel eyes. "You don't have to say it."

He rose and stretched out over her, pushing his knees between her legs. "You're right, I don't," he answered softly.

He was prodding between her thighs now. She could feel the stiff hot flesh of his manhood. She lifted her hips, needing to feel him inside her, needing to be fulfilled.

"But I do love you," he told her as he reached down with his hand. "I do love you, you mouthy wench."

Alexandra arched her hips, accepting the length of him. She moaned, lifting her hands over her head.

"Alex, Alex," he groaned, his voice hot in her ear. "You've made me love when I never thought I could love again."

She rose and fell to the rhythm of his thrusts. "Hush," she told him, covering his mouth with her hand. "You talk too much."

His laughter echoed in the tiny bedchamber as he molded his body to hers and picked up the rhythm of his movements. Together they rose and fell, joining as one until finally, when Alexandra thought she could stand the frustration of the pleasure any longer, her world burst into a shower of white light and slowly she fell to earth in the aftermath.

For a long time Hunter lay still on Alexandra, nuzzling in the crook of her neck, but when her breath finally slowed to a more normal rate he began to move again.

"Not again," she moaned, already lifting her

hips to meet his.

"Yes, again," he whispered, threading his fingers through hers above her head. "And then maybe again, Wife."

This time it was her laughter that filled the bedchamber. Twice more he brought her to the pinnacle of ultimate ecstasy before he finally gave way to his own pleasure and together they drifted off into contented sleep.

Chapter Twenty-one

Alexandra sat cross-legged in front of Hunter on the deck of the single-masted skiff. Hunter had hired the owner of the small boat to take them up the Noniack River, into the Chesapeake Bay and then into Annapolis. If the winds didn't alter their course, they'd be at her aunt's doorstep by late afternoon.

Hunter draped his arms around her and pulled her against his chest. He rested his chin on her shoulder. They were sitting on the bow of the boat letting the salt spray carry over their heads as they watched the skiff gracefully cut through the water. Both were oddly pensive.

"Anxious to get home?" he asked her. "To put on lady's clothing?"

She sighed. "Yes." She snuggled inside her rabbitskin cloak with the foxtails hanging off the collar. Once she arrived in Annapolis she knew she would have to give up her Shawnee buckskin clothing, her soft comfortable moccasins and the cloak.

She would go to her room and have a maidservant dress her from the skin out in boned stays, hoops, stockings, a gown and stomacher. Her hair would be tugged, crimped and curled into an appropriate coiffuer for a married woman. She would powder her cheeks and rouge her lips. She'd dab expensive perfume at her wrists and neck. Of course she would be elated to be dressed properly again. Of course she would . . .

"Aye, I was thinking myself it would feel good to put on a pair of man's breeches that weren't made of leather that still had bits of hair stuck to it."

She laughed with him. "I am anxious to get home again, to have the life I had before, but . . ."

"But what?"

"But a part of me isn't."

He lifted her dark hair and kissed the nape of her neck. "And what part is that?"

She stared out at the blue-green water of the Chesapeake and then up at a gull that sailed overhead. Behind her she could hear the flap of the mainsail as the wind changed direction. "The part of me that likes my moccasins." She wiggled her toes inside the soft leather. "The part of me that likes to wake up in the morning snuggled inside a bear hide, trapped in your arms. The part of me that likes to hear the songbirds as I wash my face in the river at dawn."

"We could stay here on the Tidewater," he suggested.

She laughed.

"No, I'm serious. Why go back to Annapolis? Why consider London? We could get a land grant, build a house, hell, we could grow tobacco."

"You don't know anything about growing tobacco."

"I could learn."

"And what of your father?" she chided softly. "You said yourself last night that you had to go home and set things right with him. Remember all that talk of responsibility and it being high time you owed up to it?"

He groaned. "You can't make a man accountable for the words he speaks when he has a naked woman in his arms, even if she is his wife. Don't you know that?"

She leaned back and looked up at him. "You mean we're not going back to London?"

He ran a hand through his hair that he wore loose today. It fell to his shoulders in a fiery curtain and blew in the salty breeze. "I don't know, sweeting. I don't know what I want. More importantly I don't know what's best for you and me."

"To go to London, of course. It's your home, my home too."

"I don't know, Alexandra. I know what sounds logical, but I get a bad feeling when I think about it."

"I thought you'd already made your decision, we'd made our decision. You left a message at the fort for Jon to meet us in Annapolis. You left a message that you'd be buying us all passage back to London on the first boat you could find. He'll be expecting us to return home with him, Hunter."

"Then let him go."

She turned back around and leaned against him, staring out again at the bay waters.

For several minutes they sat in silence and then Hunter spoke again. "If I decided to go back to London, I'd have many duties to fulfill as my father's son. I'd not have the time to spend with you as I have now. There would be duties for you to tend to as well. Do you understand what you're getting yourself into?"

"You're my husband now."

"That doesn't answer my question."

"We'll return to London. We'll both fulfill our responsibilities." She squeezed his hand. "Oh, come on Hunter, it'll be fun. You've forgotten all the suppers and balls, the riding to the hounds, the horseraces and the theater." She took his hand, leaning back against him to look up into his eyes. "Laughing Rain's death has been avenged. You can't spend the rest of your life wandering about without purpose."

"Why not?"

"Because it's not what adults do. We're adults now. God willing, we'll be parents. Someday you'll be speaking to your own sons of responsibility."

He sighed and rested his chin on her shoulder again. "You're right. I know you're right," he said without much enthusiasm.

"Of course I am. It will all be all right. You'll see." She kissed his cheek. "I love you Hunter of the Shawnee."

He closed his eyes. "And I you, sweeting."

"You ready?" Hunter murmured in Alexandra's ear.

Her hand trembled in his. They were standing in the front hallway of Aunt Sally's Annapolis home. Servants had let them in and run to find Aunt Sally and the cousins. Sounds of confusion came from the back of the house. Alexandra could hear children running on the slate floors and the sound of one of Uncle Charles' hounds barking. The house smelled of cleaning soap and herbs Aunt Sally had sprinkled on the Turkey carpets to keep them smelling fresh. All the sights and sounds were so familiar, so why was Alexandra suddenly so apprehensive?

For weeks she had dreamed of this moment—returning home to Aunt Sally's home where she would be safe. And now that the moment had arrived, she wanted to turn and run.

Aunt Sally came bursting through the parlor doorway, her heavy black skirts rustling as she walked. "Oh my dear Jesus in heaven," she sobbed. "Praise be! You're alive!"

Hunter released her hand, allowing Aunt Sally to pull her to her ample bosom and hug her tightly. "Good heavens child, I never thought I'd set sight on your face again in this lifetime!"

Alexandra felt her aunt's tears on her own cheek. "I'm sorry I couldn't send you a message. I know this must be a shock."

Aunt Sally took a step back, clasping Alexandra's hands so that she could look at her. "With

Susan and Charles dead, I was certain—"

"It's all right, Aunt Sally. I'm fine." She smiled, but she didn't feel very happy. That dear Aunt Sally should have known before, suddenly seemed overpainted, overly dramatic and just a little insincere. "I'm safe, really I am," she told her aunt. "It just took me a while to get back."

Aunt Sally shook her head. "Heavens, child. Look at you. You've lost weight. You look simply horrid in those hides. Have you been among the savages all this time?"

Alexandra released her aunt's hands. Of course Aunt Sally would think she looked terrible in her buckskins. What else was she going to think?

"I—"

"Let me call someone to get you changed into something decent. I'll have supper delayed." For the first time she glanced at Hunter, who had stepped back to the rear of the hallway to allow the reunion to take place privately. "Oh, goodness. Excuse my manners. Did this trapper bring you home? Thank you," she called, fluttering her hands that were covered in black lace fingerless mitts. "You'll be paid handsomely, I can assure you, man."

Alexandra laughed, holding up the finger she wore her copper wedding band on. "No, no, you don't understand, Aunt Sally." She went to Hunter and took his hand. "This is my husband, Hunter."

Aunt Sally's eyes grew round, seeming to protrude from her face. "Your . . . your husband?" she choked.

Hunter stepped forward and bowed smoothly from the waist. "Pleased to meet you, mistress. Geoffry Rordan, the Viscount Ashton."

Aunt Sally's mouth dropped.

Alexandra felt as if the floor had been pulled out from under her feet. For a moment she feared she'd swoon.

"*The* Geoffry Rordan?" Aunt Sally managed in a high-pitched voice.

He gave her a handsome devil-may-care smile. "I'm afraid so, madame."

"Well!" Aunt Sally breathed with an excited puff of air. "I can't wait to hear how you found him and managed to marry him, Alexandra." She touched her rice-powdered cheek. "No one will believe this tale, I can vow to that."

Still in shock, Alexandra managed a weak smile. Of course she couldn't tell Aunt Sally that she hadn't realized this was Geoffry Rordan, the fiancé who had run out on her six years ago. She couldn't tell her the whoreson had tricked her, that he'd known all along who she was because she'd told him. She'd look like a fool!

Alexandra cut her eyes at Hunter. He flashed her the same grin he'd offered her aunt, but it had no effect on her.

How could he have done this to her! Lying cur!

Aunt Sally was talking again, calling servants to draw baths, calling others to escort Alexandra and Hunter to their chambers.

Hunter slipped his arm through hers and steered her toward the grand staircase, chatting with Aunt Sally. It was all Alexandra could do to keep from knocking him in the head. She wanted to scream, to stomp her feet, to throw Aunt Sally's precious Chinese vase at the deceitful louse. But instead, she smiled sweetly, nodding as if she agreed with whatever Aunt Sally was babbling about now.

One of the maidservants, Chastity, who had been Alexandra's personal maid, led them up the staircase, down one hallway and then another, to two connecting bedchambers. This was the first time that Alexandra had ever known her aunt to use these rooms. They were meant for visiting dignitaries, she'd been told. Of course no dignitaries ever visited Aunt Sally, to Alexandra's knowledge.

As they stopped at the first door, Aunt Sally rattled on about being flattered to be hosting a viscount in her very own modest home. Hunter was speaking like some court dandy, saying all the right things. He had her aunt, who was supposedly in mourning, laughing like a giddy dairy maid.

It made Alexandra ill.

Chastity curtsied to Hunter as she pushed open the paneled door that led to his bedchamber. "Your room, sir."

Hunter winked at Alexandra, promised to head Aunt Sally's dining table for supper, and closed the door behind him.

Alexandra managed to keep her smile plastered on her face until Chastity showed her into her room. "The tub will be up directly, mistress," Chastity said, going to close the draperies. "I'll bring one of your gowns directly." She hung on the azure brocaded draperies. "God Almighty, he's a handsome man, your husband," she bubbled.

Alexandra dropped a hand to her hip and stared at the freckle-faced girl. "Not when I finish with him, he won't be," she muttered.

Chastity's eyes grew wide. "Can I . . . I'll help you with your bath and dressin' if you like." She eyed Alexandra's buckskins as if expecting them to walk on their own at any moment. "I know you must want to get out of those heathen clothes."

"See to my bath, Chastity. I'll have the cranberry gown with the quilted overskirting." She opened the door leading to the hallway. "Now if you'll excuse me, I'd like to speak with my husband in private."

The girl ran for the door. "'Course, mistress." She took one last look at Alexandra and fled.

Alexandra closed the door behind her and then turned to look at the cross and Bible door that led into Hunter's chamber. It took her six long strides to reach it. She flung it open.

Hunter turned in surprise. He was already half undressed. Barefoot, he stood in nothing but his leather breeches.

"Sweeting."

"Don't you sweeting me!" She slammed the door behind her so hard that a tiny portrait of Aunt Sally's grandmother flew off the wall. "How could you do this to me!" She stalked him. "How could you have deceived me! You son of a—" She raised her hand to strike him and he caught it in midair.

"Never ever hit me," he ordered through

clenched teeth. "I don't believe in hitting a woman, but there could always be a first time."

He held her wrist in an iron grip still poised in midair. She felt tears sting behind her eyelids. This was the first time he had spoken to her in that tone in weeks. That was the voice of the man who had taken her from Two Crows at the trading post, the man she hadn't liked very well.

She pulled her hand from his and turned away. "I apologize," she whispered.

For a moment there was a long silence. She heard him sigh and move across the room to pick up his buckskin tunic he'd dropped to the floor. "Alexandra, this is all very complicated."

"When you said you'd left a woman behind, you were talking about me," she choked.

"Not that it's an excuse, but I didn't know at first. Not until you told me your entire name. I only knew you as little Mary Lambert. No one told me you went by Alexandra."

She turned slowly to face him, certain she hated him at this moment. "You've made a fool of me. I'll never be able to show my face again."

"I haven't. You were very good downstairs. No one will ever know."

"*I'll* know."

"Look, sweeting," he tried to reach for her but she shrank back.

"Don't touch me," she spit. "Don't you dare lay your filthy hands on me."

"Alexandra—"

"It was just a big joke with you and Jon, wasn't it? You felt guilty for leaving the girl behind, for leaving me, so you married me to satisfy your own remorse.''

"No, well, yes." He looked up at her. "Hell no. I married you for the woman I met in the forest. The woman who fought to survive. The woman who danced the Shawnee corn dance in my arms. The fact that you were Mary Lambert was only an added bonus," he answered honestly.

Her lower lip trembled. She felt so stupid. Why had she never suspected? Why hadn't she demanded to know who he was before she married him?

Because it hadn't mattered.

Why hadn't it mattered?

Because she loved him anyway. Even now, even as angry as she was with him, she loved the way his auburn hair fell across his shoulders. She loved that gallant smile he had been so generous with downstairs in the front hallway. She loved his touch. She wanted his touch even now when she thought her heart would break with anger and pain.

"You should have told me," she murmured, as much to herself as to him. "You should have told me before we came here, Hunter . . . Geoffry."

He came to her, offering his arms. Reluctantly she allowed him to draw her into his embrace. "I should have. I'm sorry. What can I say? I was a coward. I can face a band of drunken Mohawks without a blink of an eye, but I was afraid to tell you who I was. I was afraid you would think I had somehow tricked you."

She sniffed. "You did."

He kissed the top of her head. "I didn't. Not really. I had already fallen in love with you by the time you told me your name."

"Jon should have told me. Wait until I see the cad."

He laughed and kissed her cheek. "Jon shouldn't have told you. I told him not to. That was my place."

"What were you going to do? Wait until we arrived in London and rode up to your father's house in a coach?"

"I don't know. I didn't think about it. I didn't want you to be angry with me. I didn't think it really mattered who I was. Either you loved me, or you didn't, sweeting. That was all that mattered."

"But I hadn't told you I loved you. I didn't even know it myself when we wed."

"Didn't matter. I knew you loved me. I knew I loved you."

She gave a laugh of disbelief. "But I didn't marry you voluntarily." She looked up into his hazel eyes. She wasn't going to let him off this easily, no matter how sweetly he spoke to her. "You forced me!"

He laughed, caressing her buttock through the soft leather of her tunic. "Not really."

"Yes, really."

"If you'd truly thrown a fit, I wouldn't have gone through with it," he told her. "I'd have married one of Jon's twins instead."

She punched him in the stomach and he laughed. "I'm not letting you off this easily. You'll not kiss your way out of this one. I don't even know what to call you now!"

He traced her lower lip with the tip of his tongue. "Call me lover."

"You're not being serious. We've not finished this discussion yet."

"What discussion?"

"The one about you not telling me who you were. About you forcing me to marry you, knowing who I was when I didn't know who you were. Don't you feel guilty for tricking me like that?"

"You *wanted* me to marry you," he murmured in her ear. "At least secretly, deep inside." He was kissing her neck now, his kisses making her hot and cold at the same time. "Admit it."

"I didn't." She tried to get away, but she didn't try too hard. Despite her anger she craved his touch. "I didn't want to marry you. It didn't make sense."

"You apparently wanted to marry me back in London when I was Geoffry Rordan, Viscount Ashton." He spoke the name as if he referred to someone else.

"That's not fair and you know it. I was young. My father made the arrangements just as your father did. Besides," she looked up at him coyly through a veil of dark lashes, "I thought you handsome."

He lifted his head from the open bodice of her tunic. "You knew me?"

She shrugged. "I'd seen you at a ball."

"Sly jade," he teased. "So tell me, if you were all so willing then, why not that night in the fort? I'm still the same man . . . more or less."

"I'm older. I make decisions for myself now. On the surface you and I don't seem to make a good match. You and I are nothing alike. You're crude, you're unconventional. You can be a wild man, Hunter."

"But that's what you like," he whispered, teasing the lobe of her ear with the tip of his tongue as he pressed his groin against hers. "Isn't it? The wild man in your bed." With one swift movement he swept her into his arms. She grabbed him by the shoulders to steady herself. "You like to be made love to by the savage, don't you?" he encouraged, his voice taking on a husky catch.

She was laughing with him now, returning his kisses. Her breasts were tingling, her body yearning to join with his, despite the fact that they'd made love only hours ago on the boat. "Hunter. You can't be serious. It's midday! We're no longer in the wilderness. This is my aunt's home. The servants!"

He tossed her onto the thick feather tick and leaped on top of her, pulling at the leather bindings of her tunic. "Servants be damned," he growled. "Let them find their own wenches."

Chapter Twenty-two

Alexandra squirmed in her chair. Her stays were so tight she could scarcely breathe and the lace at her cuffs was driving her mad. She nodded her head, trying to pretend she was listening to Mistress Haxton as she dug at her wrist where the Irish lace scratched.

Alexandra had been back in civilization such a short time, and already she was restless. Hunter had been so busy seeing old friends and looking into the possibility of a ship to take them back to London that she rarely saw him during the day. Those hours were spent visiting with the seemingly endless string of visitors Aunt Sally had invited to welcome Alexandra home. That was their excuse at least. Alexandra guessed they were coming around hoping to get some shocking gossip about her captivity and get a peek at the Viscount Ashton who had rescued her and then married her to save her name.

Aunt Sally cleared her throat for the second time

and Alexandra looked up. "Pardon?" She smiled hesitantly as she reached for her teacup.

Mistress Haxton repeated herself. "I said, only yesterday Emily Croften and I were discussing how you possibly could have survived the attack on the boat when dear Charles and Susan were not so fortunate." She crossed herself. "God rest their souls. How *did* you escape?"

Alexandra looked up at Mistress Haxton. She was a painfully thin woman with dyed red hair and an obvious moustache above her rouged lips. "I hid in the bushes," she lied for what seemed the one hundredth time in four days. "I didn't see anything. *I didn't see Uncle Charles and Cousin Susan die*, she thought. *I never heard them scream.* "I was too frightened. Soldiers found me and took me to a fort." *There was never a Mohawk called Two Crows. He didn't kidnap me. There was never a Captain Cain or even a beautiful Indian woman called Laughing Rain. Two Crows didn't save Hunter's life and lose his own in the sacrifice.* "Hun . . . Geoffry discovered me at the fort quite by mistake. I was ill. When I recovered, he brought me home."

"And that's where you married, child?" Mistress Haxton leaned forward. "At the fort?"

"I have the legal documents myself, Gerta," Aunt Sally chimed in, passing a plate of sugary sweets to her guest. "Quite legal and binding, I assure you."

Gerta Haxton took two pastries before passing back the plate. "Of course the marriage is binding." She lifted a heavy eyebrow in an insinuating manner. "But then, there's no way for you to know, Sally, what took place before the nuptials."

Aunt Sally smiled sweetly. "I would say it matters not, dear Gerta, whose first child was born so prematurely. You forget. Lord Ashton and my niece were betrothed. The agreement was never officially broken. You know full well a betrothal agreement is quite the same as the marriage itself."

Alexandra rolled her eyes heavenward as she pushed out of her chair and walked across the parlor in her too-tight leather shoes. She was amazed at how the entire town of Annapolis was interested in knowing the exact moment when Hunter had bedded her. With the Iroquois Indian uprisings, the fighting with the French up north and the constant raises in taxes and tariffs, Alexandra found it difficult to believe that her virginity was the most outstanding concern in all the American Colonies.

Her gaze drifted to the double windows. Outside, Aunt Sally's gardener was trimming back dead branches with a pair of shears. As he cut back the brown, shriveled foliage he dropped the sticks neatly into a basket at his feet. Alexandra wished she were outside in the garden right now. Trimming the shrubbery appeared to be far more entertaining than her conversation with Mistress Haxton.

Alexandra breathed on the cold glass to make it foggy and then wrote Hunter's name in the circle with her fingertip. Of course she would have to get used to calling him Geoffry now. She knew that.

He certainly couldn't remain Hunter of the Shawnee. But for some reason, every time she said Geoffry, the name sounded hollow in her ears. *It will just take time*, she told herself.

Hunter's name faded until she saw only the reflection of her own face in the glass. She closed her eyes. They had left the fort six days ago. She was beginning to grow concerned about Jon. Where was he? Hunter said he was supposed to wait with the old Shawnee man until help arrived and then return to the fort. Hunter had left directions at the fort for Jon to meet him here in Annapolis. Jon was to go to the Cock and Coddle Tavern down by the docks and Hunter would find him there. Hunter had gone every day but no one had seen a sign of Jon yet.

Alexandra sighed. Though at times in the last weeks Jon had certainly tried her patience, she missed him. Here in her aunt's home where everything seemed so foreign now, she craved the familiar. She wished she could put on her buckskin tunic and leggings and sit by the campfire and talk with Hunter and Jon while they smoked their pipes and teased each other about the women they'd tumbled and the horseraces they'd lost as young men.

Alexandra turned away from the window. Mistress Haxton was having yet another pastry. Alexandra wondered to herself how she could remain so slender and eat so much.

"Going somewhere, dear?" Aunt Sally asked.

Alexandra turned back and forced a smile. She was hoping to slip out of the room unnoticed. She touched her forehead. "Just a slight headache. I thought I'd go for a walk in the garden."

"Heavens no! You'll catch your death in the chilled air!"

Alexandra chuckled. "Aunt Sally. You forget, I—" She almost said she'd slept on the ground for more than two months, but she caught herself. She and Hunter had agreed that the less she said about the time she'd been gone, the fewer probing questions she'd have to answer. "You forget I'm an adult woman—married. I can walk out into the garden if I well please."

"Of course you can—when the day is warmer. When you're not feeling poorly." Aunt Sally rang a silver bell. "I'll just have Chastity bring up some sleeping powders to your room. You want to be fit for the ball this evening. You can't miss it. Everyone will be here to be formally introduced to Geoffry."

"Yes, everyone," Mistress Haxton echoed, sounding much to Alexandra like a magpie.

Alexandra fluttered her eyelids impatiently and continued out of the parlor and into the front hall. She didn't need any sleeping powders. What she needed was some peace and quiet. This household was so noisy compared to the silence of the forest that it was no wonder her head ached.

"Geoffry said for me to be certain you rested," Aunt Sally called after her. "He'll be so disappointed if you're too ill to dance this evening."

Aunt Sally was quite smitten with Hunter, or *Geoffry* as she called him. Smitten either with him and his handsome smile, or his title and fortune, she didn't know which.

"Alexandra! Alexandra! Do you hear me?"

Alexandra could hear Aunt Sally murmuring something to Mistress Haxton about her niece having still not recovered from her ordeal, and of course being newly married and the *pressures of that* . . .

Alexandra had turned in the hallway to head up the staircase to her bedchamber when the front door swung open. Her face lit up in a genuine smile. "Hunter! You're back early." She jumped off the bottom step into his arms. She kissed him on the mouth. "I missed you. I'm going to go mad with all this sitting about doing nothing. Do you think this afternoon you and I could—"

"Alex," he interrupted. "Look what I've picked up on the docks." Holding her in one arm, he hooked his thumb in the direction of the door.

There stood Jon, dressed in a pair of fringed buckskins, a deerhide cloak, and quilled moccasins. He wore a bow and quiver over one shoulder and a musket over the other. He looked tired, but strangely at peace with himself.

She laughed and threw herself into his arms, hugging him tightly and surprising them both. "God's teeth, Jon. I thought we'd have to go back after you!" She plucked at the hide cloak. "I've never seen you in Shawnee trappings! Where have you been?"

"Long story," Jon said.

She smiled up at him. "So give me the shortened version." The entire time they were on Cain's trail, she never once saw him in anything but Englishman's clothing. She was curious as to what would have made him want to don the clothes of his heritage. "Why the Indian costume?" she teased.

"My clothes are being pressed," he answered drolly. "I apologize for arriving late, but the old man I stayed with while Hunter went for his family died that same night. I returned to their village to see him buried." He grimaced. "Stop looking at me like that. They needed someone else to help carry the body. That's all."

She smiled. "I'm proud of you."

He rolled his eyes. "Christ, Hunter, I'm almost glad she didn't take me up on my offer. Now you're stuck with her the rest of your born days and I'm not."

Hunter offered her his hand. "I need to speak with you, sweeting. Upstairs." He sounded strangely solemn to her. Tired . . .

As Alexandra went to lift her arms from around Jon's shoulders she heard a horrendous screech from the direction of the parlor.

"Indians! We're under attack!" Gerta Haxton screeched from the doorway. "Help her, for Mother Mary's sake! They've come back for her!"

"Gerta!" Aunt Sally came hustling to the doorway. Her hands flew to her plump cheeks and she shrieked for all she was worth.

One of the manservants, Black Boe, came running down the hallway with a musket in his hands. "Stand back!" the Irishman called. "I'm comin'! I'm comin'!"

"Shoot him!" Aunt Sally ordered. "Save Alexandra, Black Boe!"

The servant took aim. "Let her go or I'll shoot you dead, redskin."

Alexandra, looked up at Jon who was still holding her in his arms. She knew this wasn't funny. It wasn't funny at all. Poor Mistress Haxton honestly believed they were under attack by wild Indians.

But Alexandra couldn't help herself. It had been days since she had a good laugh. She started to chuckle. Then Jon began to chuckle. Then Hunter.

Black Boe stood in the center of the hall beside the grand staircase, the musket poised to fire, a queer look on his face.

"It's all right, Black Boe," Alexandra said, still laughing. "Put down the weapon before you shoot me. He's a friend of Geoffry's, and a friend of mine."

"Sweet Mary, Mother of God," Mistress Haxton murmured from the doorway as she fluttered her handkerchief in her face. "I believe I may faint, Sally. Call for smelling salts."

"Indeed you'll not faint here, Gerta. Not in front of my guests." Aunt Sally grabbed Mistress Haxton by one bony arm and gave her a shake. "Get control of your vapors and take yourself home. We'll expect to see you this evening at the party."

With that matter settled, Aunt Sally, forever the proper hostess, rushed forward to greet Jon and Hunter. "My apologies, dear Geoffry." She looked to Jon, scrutinizing his face. "Excuse our behavior. I hadn't realized Geoffry would be bringing home a guest. Do you speak the King's English?" She peered into his face. "English?"

Jon released Alexandra and swept his hand, bending into a bow so deep that his forehead nearly touched the slate floor of the front hall. No court dandy being presented to King George himself could have looked better. "Pleased to make your acquaintance, madame." He took Aunt Sally's hand and pressed a kiss to the back of it, his lips lingering for a long improper moment. "Alexandra said she had an aunt, but she failed to tell me how utterly beautiful she was, and so young." He straightened, still holding onto her hand. "Had I realized what a paragon you were, madame, I'd have arrived sooner."

Alexandra cut her eyes at Hunter. Jon was like this with every woman he met. He was indiscriminate; tall, short, fat, thin, red or white. He seemed to like all women and he wanted them to like him.

Hunter shrugged at Alexandra with a sigh and then turned back to their hostess. "If you don't mind, Sally," he said, "I've invited Jon to remain here in your home for a few days."

Aunt Sally looked to Hunter, who was starting up the staircase. "Well, certainly, certainly he may. I . . . I don't know that I have any . . . any Indian food, but—" She looked to Alexandra for aid, but Alexandra was already starting up the stairs after Hunter.

"Brandy and a side of beef will be fine, Auntie. Now if you'll excuse us, we're in need of private conversation. Make yourself at home," Alexandra called down to Jon. "I'll be down directly."

Jon waved at her, flashing her a grin as he turned his attention back to Aunt Sally. "Sally, may I be so presumptuous as to call you Sally?" Alexandra heard Jon saying as he steered her aunt back toward the parlor. "Well, Sally dear, it seems I'm in a bit of a bind. I've no proper clothing but these ghastly hides and I understand there's to be a ball this evening in Geoffry's honor. Do you think—"

Alexandra turned the corner on the staircase and Jon's voice was lost to the sounds below. "Hunter, Hunter," she called. "Wait for me." Sensing something was wrong, she hurried after him, down the hallway and into his bedchamber. She closed the door behind them and leaned against it.

He looked pale to her.

"Hunter, what is it?" she asked softly. "Jon's all right, isn't he?"

He stood at the window. Alexandra couldn't resist a smile. What a striking sight he was, even with the lines of his face pulled taut with worry. Foregoing a wig, he wore his auburn hair pulled back sleekly with a black velvet ribbon into a neat queue. He was dressed in a pair of burgundy breeches that molded to his sinewy thighs and shaped calves drawing the eye downward to expensive black boots sewn of calfskin. He wore a linen shirt with a stock, a navy brocade shirtwaist, and a navy coat cut of the latest fashion. He was dressed simply, but elegantly.

"Jon's fine. Better than I've seen him in a long time. It was good for him to spend some time among his own people. I think he's come away with a better understanding of them."

"Then what is it? Hunter, tell me."

He pulled a folded piece of paper from inside his shirtwaist and offered it to her. He didn't make eye contact as it passed between them.

She took it. It was a brief letter. The ink was splotched with several illegible words, but the meaning was clear. She folded it carefully when she was done. "Your father, I'm so sorry."

He sighed, tugging at his lacy stock as he stared out onto the street below. "The letter is months old. He's probably already dead."

She linked her arm through his and slipped the paper back inside his waistcoat. "No. Maybe not. Maybe there's still time. With a little luck we can be there in eight weeks."

"A winter crossing?" He gave a derisive snort. "A friend once made record time crossing from London here only to sit off the coast six weeks trying to make it safely into the bay. A ship doesn't leave here for another ten days. It could easily be the first week of February before we make it back to England."

She rested her cheek on the soft brushed brocade of his waistcoat. "Was he ill when you left?"

"Healthy as a racehorse."

"You couldn't have known, Hunter." She looked up at him, wishing she could smooth away the obvious pain written across his face. "Regrets are useless now. You did what you did. I've forgiven you. Almost." She smiled up at him. "And I'm certain your father has too."

"I don't regret leaving, just having to hurt him the way I did. These last six years, even with the tragedies, have been the best years of my life." He took her hand. "If I'd not come I'd never have had you."

She laughed. "Of course you would have. Six years ago, remember? Our wedding."

He squeezed her hand, gazing out the window at a father and his son passing on the street. "It would never have been the same and you know it. It would have been merely another arranged marriage. I'd have cared for you as would have been my duty. I'd never have abused you. I'd even have given you children." He was silent for a moment. "But I doubt I'd have ever loved you."

"Hunter, how can you say such a thing? Of course we would have fallen in love."

He shook his head. "Listen to yourself. You call me Hunter in the privacy of our room. You call me Hunter when we make love."

"Only because I forget that's not your real name."

"No. You fell in love with the Hunter of the Shawnee, not Geoffry Rordan, the Viscount Ashton."

She didn't understand, but she was trying. "He's the same man."

His met her gaze, his hazel eyes studying her carefully. "Is he? I don't think so."

Alexandra didn't know what he was talking about. She hated it when he got melancholy like this. He didn't make any sense.

She stepped in front of him and lifted his hands,

bringing them around her waist so that she could lean against him and look out the window. "I guess this means we have to go to London, hmmm?"

"I thought you wanted to go back."

"Oh, I do." How could she tell him now that she was beginning to reconsider her own words. It was too late. They had to go. "I miss England," she lied. The truth was, she missed the forest. "There'll be so much to see and do again. We'll be busy. I know you'll have a great deal to do if your father—"

"—If he's already dead."

"Yes." She stroked his broad hands. "You'll be the Earl of Dunnon."

"And you the Countess of Dunnon."

She sighed. "I know so little about you, that I feel foolish sometimes. You mention your father, but never your mother. What of her?"

"My mother died when I was very young."

"And your father never remarried?"

"No." He smiled to himself. "I think he had a love affair with our housekeeper that ran for twenty-five years, but he would never admit it. If they were lovers, they were very discreet about it."

"No brothers or sisters?"

He smoothed her hair with his hand. "No, it was just father and me, and then Jon of course. He was my brother if not in blood, then in soul." He kissed the top of her head. "My father always said he regretted not leaving more heirs."

She turned in his arms, lifting her hands up to rest them on his broad shoulders. "So take me to your home and we'll make a line of heirs for your father, a line that will stretch on for centuries." She kissed him softly and then rested her cheek on his chest.

She knew this was the right thing to do. They would go home to London. Hunter would take up his duties as his father's heir and the two of them would make the life together she had dreamed of as a young woman. Everything was going to be fine. She had been brought up to be a nobleman's wife. He had been trained since childhood for the day he would take his father's title and lands. Their life would be as it was meant to be.

So why did she have this sinking feeling in the pit of her stomach?

Chapter Twenty-three

"Father." Hunter offered both hands to the man who lay in the center of the soft feather tester. He looked so small to Hunter, so old.

"Geoffry! My God, my Geoffry!" He squeezed Hunter's hands, but there was little strength left in him.

Hunter threw his arms around his father, hugging his frail body. His skin was paper thin, his fragile frame nearly weightless. There was nothing left of the strapping man he had known, but a bag of hollow birdlike bones. "I missed you, Father," Hunter murmured, squeezing his eyes shut. "So many times in the last years I turned to speak to you and you weren't there."

Tears shone in the Earl of Dunnon's pale grey eyes as he lay back on his pillow, winded. He shook his head. "God help you son, you look like I did thirty-odd years ago! Look at him, Mab, doesn't he look just like me?"

Mab, once the housekeeper, now the earl's nursemaid, smiled, her wrinkled face reflecting the happiness of another time. She nodded her head from where she sat discreetly in the corner of the room, far enough away not to intrude on the reunion of father and son, but close enough to aid the man she loved, if he needed her. "Aye, he looks just like ye, Horace. Just as if he was spit from your mouth all brawny and cock-certain of himself."

"And it's you, Father, I have to thank for all the taunting I've gotten over this red mane." Hunter grabbed a straight-backed wooden chair, turned it around, and straddled it so that he could lean forward on the back. "I have to admit, I've cleaned up many a tavern over my hair color."

The earl laughed heartily, touching his own sparse white hair. "I'll tell you the truth, Son, I was glad to see that orange fuzz the day your mama brought you into this world, God rest her soul."

"God rest her soul," Mab echoed.

"I knew it would make you tough," the earl went on. "I knew it would make you a man I could be proud of."

Hunter rose up off the chair and began to pace in the bedchamber. The heavy draperies were drawn shut, leaving the room in the semidarkness of tallow candlelight. Hunter felt hemmed in. The chamber smelled of stale air, herbal poultices . . . and lingering death. "Father, I've not always made you proud. What I did was wrong, or at least the way I went about it. I shouldn't have run off."

The old man waved his hand. "No need to speak of that. What's done is done, my son. What's important is you've come home to Dunnon Castle, home to take my title and monies, home to let me die in peace. I told Mab I wouldn't die until I saw you again." On the last word Hunter's father launched into a coughing fit. He choked and wheezed until Hunter thought his father would cease breathing. Mab rose off her chair and came to sit on the edge of the bed. She held the earl, bringing a handkerchief to his lips. When the fit passed, Mab rose and returned to her chair.

The earl spoke again. "How is Jon?" He cleared his throat. "Well?"

"Yes. He's downstairs in the kitchen trying to get cook to make him kidney pie for supper. He said to tell you he'd be up later if you're up to it." Hunter walked to the stone fireplace and drew his finger across the spotless mantel. "He hated it, you know. The colonies."

"Of course he did. I could have told you two boys that before you left," the earl grumbled. "That is if you'd only asked."

"I'm sorry, Father. I can't tell you how sorry I am."

The old man smiled and for an instant Hunter saw him as a young man again. He saw him as if he were a reflection of himself. Then his father was old once more.

"When you left, though you were nearly thirty years old, you were still a boy," his father said.

"Tell me what made you a man."

Hunter drew his hands into fists. "The American Colonies were all you said they were. Better." Visions of pine forests and sparkling clear streams flashed in Hunter's head. He smelled the salt spray of the Chesapeake Bay and heard the cry of an osprey. "I hunted wildcat, I fished for trout in the Chesapeake. I smoked the pipe of peace among the Shawnee and the Delaware; I danced the harvest dance." He looked into his father's fading eyes. "I married, Father. A Shawnee woman."

His father's face seemed to darken. "No, Son."

Hunter shook his head. He wouldn't bother his father with the long tale of Laughing Rain and Captain Cain. Maybe later. Maybe never. "She died, Father."

"Children?" the Earl of Dunnon asked, an odd tone in his voice.

Mab's chair scraped the wooden floor.

"No."

The earl lay back on his pillow and closed his eyes. "Not the same mistake," he mumbled. "Should have warned you. Not twice. Good."

Hunter came to the side of the bed. "What did you say, Father?"

His eyes opened again. "Nothing. Nothing. Mab says you brought a woman, a beautiful woman. She is your wife, I hope?"

Hunter couldn't resist a smile. "You'll not believe this. It's little Mary Lambert."

"Your betrothed?" The earl cackled. "Miracles never cease. I told Georgie you'd be back. Damned if he doesn't owe me a bottle of brandy and an expensive one at that. My choice." He looked up. "Tell me about your bride."

"I call her Alexandra. She's sassy, but she's a good woman. I want you to meet her later. You'll like her. I know you will."

The earl closed his eyes for a moment. "And tell me how it is that you married your betrothed across the ocean so far from here." It was obvious he was pleased. "How did you find her?"

"I just came upon her." He and Alexandra had decided that for reasons of English propriety, they'd reveal no more of their courtship than necessary. They were legally married and that was all that was important now.

"What's meant to be is meant to be, Horace. I always told ye that," Mab said from the corner of the room.

"True, true." The earl closed his eyes again. "Good to have you home, Son. Good to see your handsome face."

"Good to be home," Hunter answered quietly.

Mab rose and came to the bed. She began to smooth the covers. "Your father is tired, Master Geoffry. He don't take visitors much anymore. It wears on him. He's been so excited since he got the message from London that ye were on the way home. He hasn't slept in two days' time."

Hunter nodded. His father was dozing off now. "Thank you for taking care of him, Mab."

She looked up at Hunter. "It was my duty." She went back to fussing with the counterpane draped across the earl's bed. "And all of us come to our duties someday, don't we, Master Geoffry?"

Alexandra sat on a stone bench in a small garden behind the west walls of Dunnon Castle. She stared up at the third-floor windows with their closed draperies. Hunter had waved to her from there only a few moments before. She hoped his meeting with his father had gone well. She hoped the Earl of Dunnon had no hard feelings for his son.

Alexandra brushed back a lock of her hair and tucked it beneath the ermine hat she wore pulled snugly around her ears. The February wind was cold and sharp and it tugged at her heavy cloak, but it felt good. All those weeks below decks on the ship had worn on her. She swore to Hunter that once she set foot on British soil, she'd never travel by ship again.

She looked up at the cold grey stone walls of the home that had been in the Dunnon family for more than four hundred years. She'd been to Dunnon Castle once as a young girl. It had been Christmastide and she and other children had played tag beneath the trees in the earl's orangery. But a child of nine or ten never realizes the magnitude of a man's wealth, especially when the child herself grows up in prosperity.

The Earl of Dunnon was indeed a wealthy, influential man, and upon the death of the earl, Hunter would inherit his father's title, and he too would be an influential man. The earl owned Dunnon Castle and all the land around it as far as the eye could see. Just over the crest of the hill behind the family fortress was the village of Dunnon. The small community housed the men and women who worked for the earl and his family both in the fields and within his household.

The original grey stone and mortar castle was built shortly after the Normandy conquest, or so Hunter said. A sprawling E-shaped structure, it was built onto in prosperous years and became part of the Dunnon family estates in the thirteen hundreds. Once, the home had been self-contained for times of civil war—with stables, and even a small chapel built within the walls. But now, with the coming of relative peace to the country, outbuildings had been built around the main structure and some of the outer fortress walls had been torn down.

Stables and a dairy could be seen over Alexandra's left shoulder beyond the boxwood hedgerows of the private gardens. Behind her and to the right was a smokehouse, a muse, an icehouse, and several other buildings small and large that she couldn't identify from where she sat. She turned back to stare at the stone walls of the place she would call home the rest of her life. To her right was the glass-walled orangery she had played in as a child. The cold glass was frosted from the heat and humidity inside so that she could see only the outline of the tall potted orange and lemon trees she remembered lining the western wall.

"Alex? Alexandra?"

At the sound of Hunter's voice, she rose from the stone bench. "Here. I'm still in the garden."

He appeared around the side of the house, his

black cloak flapping in the wind. "God's teeth, it's colder than a witch's teat out here. Why don't you come in?"

She caught his hand. "I just needed to get outside for a few minutes." She started to walk with him back toward the house. "So how did it go? How was your father? Was he terribly angry with you?"

Hunter draped his arm over her shoulder. "One question at a time, woman," he teased. "He's not well at all. I don't know how he's lived this long. Sheer will, I think."

"I'm sorry."

"Our talk went better than I'd expected. He says he's so thankful I've come home that he doesn't care anymore about my leaving. He wants to see you later. He's resting now."

They stopped beside the glass wall of the orangery and she turned to him, smiling. "Everything's going to be all right, isn't it? I told you it would be."

He hugged her against him. "He seems so old, Alex. He's aged twenty years in the last six. He looks like my grandsire did."

She smoothed his cheek with the back of her hand. "Parents get old and they die, Geoffry." The name sounded so odd on the tip of her tongue.

"Speaking of parents, sweeting. What of yours?" He smiled artificially. "I know you're anxious see your father and mother."

Of course, she wasn't and he knew it. Now that she had Hunter, her parents and her brothers and sisters seemed to be from another lifetime. She had never gotten along with any of them and now, they just didn't seem to matter. "I sent a message to the London house and the country house. I told them I was here and that we were married. Once I find out where they are, I suppose I'll have to pay a visit."

"My father says your father owes him a bottle of brandy, his choice of year and cellar. He says he bet your father I'd be back. Apparently the Earl of Monthrop thought I was gone forever."

"Well, Father may owe it to him, but good luck to him in getting it. You know Lord Monthrop—tighter than a pitched rainbarrel. When I go to stay, no doubt I'll be expected to bring my own firewood for my bedchamber."

He caught the lock of her dark hair that had escaped her cap again and twisted it around his finger. "You don't have to go if you don't want to, Alex."

"Of course I do."

"Why?"

"It's part of that matter of responsibility we talked of on the ship. Now that we've returned to England, we can't live as carefree as a Shawnee. You have your duties and I mine. One of my duties is to see my parents and brothers and sisters. Besides, believe it or not, I did have friends. I'd like to see them."

"Who?"

"Roland."

He lifted an eyebrow. "Who's Roland?"

"I told you. The second man I almost married. But you needn't be jealous, he's just an old friend."

"Who said anything about jealous? Too much

seriousness in one day," he grumbled, grabbing her around the waist and pushing her against the glass panels of the orangery.

Her laughter blended with his as he nuzzled her neck. "Hunter!" Realizing her mistake, she groaned. "Geoffry. Someone will see us!"

"Someone already has," came Jon's voice out of nowhere. "And shocked he is."

Alexandra looked up to see Jon walking by, headed in the direction of the stables.

"I told you there's no privacy in a home like this," Hunter said mockingly. "The servants are always spying on us noblemen." He looked over his shoulder, refusing to move despite Alexandra's attempts to escape. Jon hadn't taken the bait. He kept walking. "Where you going, *neekah-nah?*" Hunter called.

"London." Jon answered back.

The wind howled so loudly as it came around the corner of the house that their voices were difficult to hear. "But we just came from London," Alexandra hollered after him.

"What? Cook wouldn't make the kidney pie?"

Jon waved his hand over his head. "Just going in for a hand of cards. Please don't worry, lover."

"Cards! In a pig's eye! A roll with a tart, no doubt," Alexandra bantered.

The men laughed.

"Be back tomorrow, Hunter—excuse me—Lord Ashton," Jon said as he went over the crest of a small hill that led down toward the stables. "Tell Father I'll be up to see him tomorrow when he's rested. Tell him to have the cards ready. I'll bring coin.''

Jon's last words were nearly lost in the wind as he disappeared from sight.

Alexandra turned her attention back to Hunter, who still held her trapped against the orangery glass. The biting wind stung her cheeks, but she didn't mind. She actually felt more comfortable outside the walls of Dunnon Castle than inside. "He calls your father, *Father?*"

"He refers to him as Father. Calls him Horace to his face. Sometimes Lord Father if he's being silly. Now where was I?" Hunter nipped at her earlobe peeking out from beneath her ermine cap. "Ah yes."

She pushed at his face. "You were about to take me into the orangery and show me the miniature orange trees. One of the gardeners was telling me your father just had them sent from Italy."

He grimaced. "I was going to show you *orange trees?* I don't remember saying anything about *orange trees!* Quite the seducer I am. *Madame, have you seen my orange trees?* Bloody wounds, what woman would turn her skirt for a line like that?''

Alexandra laughed as she ducked beneath his arm and ran for a door just to the left of the glass walls. He dove for her, but caught nothing but a corner of her cloak. "I'm serious! I want to see the trees. Just for a moment. It'll be time to dress for supper soon."

He followed her in the door and down a drafty hallway. "All right, all right," he surrendered.

"We see the blasted trees." He took her hand. "But then we go upstairs."

She lifted an eyebrow.

"To dress, of course," he told her innocently.

She passed him in a receiving chamber, headed for the glass doors that led into the orangery. "You're sexually perverted, Husband. Has anyone ever told you that?"

He ran to catch up again and pushed the door open for her. He tugged at the back of her skirt as she brushed by. "Just can't get enough of you, sweet wife. I want to store it up. Once I find my way to Father's office, I'm liable to be lost in bookkeeping until I'm too old and weary to get it up any longer."

She rolled her eyes at him. "You sound like Jon, now," she chided. "Certainly not the language appropriate for a man about to be an earl."

He closed the door behind them and dropped the latch.

"Why are you locking the door?"

He shrugged. "To keep out the gardeners. They enjoy eavesdropping and I despise it." He took her hand. "Now, let me show you those trees."

The orangery wasn't as large as Alexandra had remembered, but it was certainly as beautiful. Built against the castle wall, the three outer walls were constructed of lead frames that held the panes of glass. Overhead, more glass made the pitched roof. It was warm inside, overly warm, and the air was filled with the overwhelming scents of fruit-bearing citrus plants.

Hunter took her cloak from her shoulders and

tossed it over his arm. "Hot as hell in here," he mumbled.

She walked between two rows of potted lemon trees, her heels clapping on the slate floor. Overhead, caged songbirds fluttered on their perches. "It's even more beautiful than I remembered," she mused.

He followed her through the maze of potted plants and trees deeper into the orangery. "You've been here before?"

"Mmm hmmm." She took off her fur hat and shook her head to let her hair fall free across her shoulders.

"When?"

She stopped to touch a lemon that hung from a branch. "Christmastime. I was nine or ten. My parents came for a party, a ball, something. I came with my brothers and sisters. We played here for hours. It was one of the most magical places I had ever been."

"Did we meet?"

She shrugged. "I don't think so. All I remember is the orangery and your father giving us each an orange to take home." She smiled at the memory. "Now where are these miniature trees?"

"Oh, I know." He walked several feet and then pulled back a thick bush that grew from a large painted pot. "This way."

Alexandra turned her head to one side. "That doesn't look like a path to me. Aren't they that way?" She pointed to the far west corner that was obscured by palm trees over ten feet tall.

"A short cut."

Suspiciously, she stepped through the hole he had created. He followed her and then let the branches fall. They were in the center of a square of trees. There was no way in, nor any way out except the way they'd come.

"Hunter!"

He dropped their cloaks on the slate floor. "It's Geoffry. Can't you remember your own husband's name, jade?" He took her by the waist.

She squeezed her eyes shut. "Geoffry. Yes. I'm sorry."

"Pay the price, madame."

"H . . . Geoffry!"

"Pay the price."

She lifted up on her tiptoes and pursed her lips comically. He kissed her. Then again and again.

She opened her eyes, laughing. "What are you doing?"

He had found the tiny row of buttons at her back and begun to unbutton them while he kissed the swell of her breasts above her low-cut bodice. "Need I explain?" he asked, his voice already husky with desire. "I've wanted you since we left London this morning."

"Here?" she protested. But she was kissing him back, that curious hot excitement already rising in the pit of her stomach. "It's unseemly."

"My father's house, my house," he told her as he peeled away her bodice, letting the material fall in a curtain around her waist. "Your house." He unworked her stays. "We'll do as we please. Always, sweeting. Remember that."

His thumb caressed her nipple through her thin

shift and she shivered despite the heat of the orangery. *This is insane,* she thought as she tugged at the stock at his neck. *Stripping naked in broad daylight in a public place!*

But he was already kissing her the way he knew she liked to be kissed. She pulled his shirt over his head and let it float to the floor. Even through the material of her shift, she could feel the heat of his skin against her breasts.

He was down on his knees, pulling down her skirting, stroking her with his hands. She rested her hands on his shoulders and stepped out of the gown and hoops. She laughed as he pulled off her heeled slippers one at a time and tossed them into the shrubbery. Then came her stockings. He made each move to stimulate her, to tease, to tantalize, to make her cry out in desire for him.

Piece by piece he disrobed her and she him.

Finally, when they stood naked in each other's arms, Hunter shook out her ermine-lined cloak and laid it on the slate, lining side up. Taking her in his arms again, they went down on their knees together, locked in an embrace. She brushed her fingers across his broad, bare back.

"Love me?" he whispered.

"Yes," she answered as her mouth found his. "I love you. I love you Hunter."

"And I you," he whispered in her ear as he brought a hand up to caress the fullness of her breast. "I'll love you always, no matter what," he said, his voice sounding almost desperate.

Alexandra thought to question him, but not now, not when they were already swept up in the fires of passion. Later . . . there would be time later.

Teasing her with his fingertips, Hunter rolled onto his side. Alexandra lay with her eyes closed, revelling in the feel of his rough hands on her sensitive flesh.

When she heard tree branches rustle above them, she opened her eyes to see him pluck a ripe orange.

"What are you doing?" she asked, looking up at him through a veil of thick lashes. She wanted him. She could feel her heart pumping, her blood racing.

"Nothing," he answered, a silly smile on his face.

She watched him tear the piece of fruit in half. She giggled as some of the juice dribbled from between his finger onto her belly. "Hunter! You're dripping on me!"

"Mmmm," he murmured as his tongue flicked across her flesh.

His laughter turned to purrs of contentment as he licked the juice from her belly.

"You'll make me sticky," she complained.

He crawled up toward her, touching his mouth to hers. He tasted sweetly of orange. She sucked on his lower lip. "Mmmm," she echoed. "You taste good."

"But you taste better."

With a slow deliberateness Hunter began to squeeze the orange half and drip juice onto her. A little on her cheek, a little between her breasts . . . His hot tongue lapped up the cool juice, sending tremors of pleasure through her limbs.

His mouth found her nipples, the insides of her elbows, the hollow of her shoulder. His hands, the sweet sticky juice, his tongue, they were everywhere . . .

"Hunter, Hunter," she cried finally. "Enough."

"Enough. You want me to stop?" He lay over her, his hard male body pressing her into the soft fur of her cloak.

"Yes," she breathed. "No." She smiled, looking up at him. "I want you to finish me off. Kill me before I die of the pleasure. That or—"

"Or what?"

She smiled up at him coyly. "You know."

His laughter was husky in her ear as he rose up, brushing his swollen member against her thigh. "Greedy wench," he chided, tossing the orange half into one of the tree pots. "Greedy, greedy."

"Yes," she whispered, her breath coming in short gasps, as she lifted up to take him inside her. "Always. Now hush your mouth, and hurry."

Their mouths met in a hungry, demanding kiss and the couple locked in a lover's embrace. The sweet smell of oranges enveloped them as they rose and fell to an ancient rhythm until finally both were spent.

Chapter Twenty-four

"If he's not invited, I don't believe Geoffry and I can attend," Alexandra told her mother flatly.

The countess stood in the doorway, the lines of her face pulling her mouth down into a frown. The countess was a plump woman whose face, though it had never been pretty, had held up to the years. As always, she was overdressed this morning in a low-cut tangerine gown, her wrinkled breasts thrust high above her lace stomacher. "I don't know why you insist upon being so difficult, Daughter. Your father and I have gone to a great deal of trouble, not to mention spent a small fortune, to give this masquerade ball in your and your husband's honor."

Alexandra, seated at her mother's writing desk in an antechamber off her sleeping rooms, spoke slowly as if in a discussion with a young child. "And I appreciate that, truly I do, but Jon is my friend."

"Jon is a servant."

"He isn't."

"Then what is he? Who is he? He's no one. He has no title, no last name that I'm aware of. He's simply the Viscount Rordan's savage. He's a troublemaker, everyone says so. Just last week he nearly called Marci Madden's grandnephew out in a duel over a Fleet Street whore. The man causes disharmony wherever he goes."

"So are you saying you don't want him in your home because he might draw attention to himself and away from you and Father and your party? Oh—I thought it was because of the color of his skin—because he's Shawnee and not English."

Her mother gasped, clasping her waist where her stays were obviously so tight that she could barely breathe. "I don't know what's wrong with you, Mary Alexandra! I try to welcome you home properly. I try to be a good mother. I try to tell you what your duties are, who you need to see and where you need to be seen." She gripped the carved doorframe, sagging. "I—"

"Mother," Alexandra looked away, refusing to fall for her mother's act, "do you want me to call Patience to take you to bed?"

"No." She took a ragged, dramatic breath. "I'll be all right. Don't let yourself be concerned with my health."

"Your health is fine. As for the ball, Hunter and I will come if Jon is invited and welcomed into your home. If he is not, then we are not." She looked up from her mother's desk. "It is honestly that simple."

Her mother straightened. "You don't think you

ought to discuss this with your husband?"

"I know what he'd say. He'll not have Jon left out because of your prejudices. They've been friends since childhood."

The countess shook her head. "We were all shocked when Horace brought home that wild animal of a child. We never understood why Lady Dunnon allowed him to remain in her household!"

"Your decision, Mother?"

She heaved an exasperated sigh. "All right! All right! I'll have the invitation delivered today. But I warn you, your father will be displeased. If the man becomes intoxicated and causes a scene, I can't be responsible for your father's actions."

"He'll behave himself. I promise." She smiled compliantly at her mother. "If you can give me a few minutes, I'll look over the menu."

"I should hope so." Her mother hung in the doorway. "You *are* going to the queen's drawing room with us this afternoon, aren't you?"

Alexandra looked up. "No—I told you—I'm not. I'll not be paraded like the Christmas duck. Besides, I'm expecting Roland."

Her mother made a clicking sound between her tongue. "Accepting male guests while your husband isn't present. A poor idea I must tell you, Daughter. People will gossip."

"No one will gossip if you don't tell anyone he's been here."

"I'm surprised you would wish to see the man after he called off your betrothal so suddenly the way he did."

"Mother, I told you, I don't wish to speak on the matter." She turned back to the papers on the desk. "I'll send these down when I'm done. Have a good morning."

The countess stood in the doorway another moment. When her daughter said nothing more, she made her exit with a swish of her skirts.

Alexandra bent over her mother's writing desk and attempted once again to set her mind to the menu she held in her hand. For two days her mother had prodded her, insisting it was her place to approve the foods and beverages the cook and steward had laid out for the masked ball to be given at the end of the week. The truth was, Alexandra didn't want the blessed party to begin with.

With a sigh she glanced out the window, framed in heavy burgundy and blue draperies. It was raining for the third straight day. The streets of London below were flooded. The rotting garbage that usually remained in the sewer trenches was washing across the streets and up on doorsteps. The homeless who generally remained well hidden in the shadowed alleys and below the bridges and docks were now wandering the streets, wet and half frozen, without hope.

In her months in the American Colonies, Alexandra had forgotten the putrid smells and frightening sights of London. She had remembered the ostentatious ballrooms and galleries, but she had forgotten the slums. She remembered the sound of music drifting off garden balconies overlooking Hyde Park, but she had forgotten the cries of the hungry and the desperate. She remembered the taste of delicate sweetmeats and French wines, but she had forgotten the taste of fear she knew the men who rolled by in carts bound for the gallows must be experiencing.

Then she wondered, had she forgotten all these things or had she never really seen them before?

She and Hunter had been in England less than four weeks and yet it felt like four years. She kept trying to tell herself it would simply take time to adjust to her old life and then she would feel better, she would be happier. But deep inside she was afraid. She was the one who had insisted they return to London. She was the one who had told Hunter this was where they belonged and now that she was here, she hated it.

Her parents were absolutely ecstatic that she had managed not only to find her own husband, but the one originally intended for her. Her father had immediately sent Alexandra's dowry, which included monies and the title to some prime acreage. Hunter had been so insulted by the Earl and Countess of Monthrop's attitude toward their daughter, now that she had *married properly*, that he nearly refused the dowry. Alexandra, too, found her parents' behavior annoying. Her mother was filled with advice about what was now proper and improper for the Lady Rordan, and insisted upon passing each suggestion along to her daughter promptly. Alexandra had only been in her childhood home two days and already she feared she was going to go mad. To add to her discontent, she missed Hunter. He'd not be arriving in London until Saturday, the day of the masked ball.

But it wasn't just her mother and father that Alexandra was dissatisfied with. It was her entire life, the life at Dunnon Castle she knew she would have until her death. She was bored by the endless round of visiting, the long ride to and from London to never-ending teas, balls, and shopping. She had tried to take over some of the duties the lady of the house would oversee at Dunnon Castle, but they seemed overwhelming. Time and time again she tried to be enthusiastic over responsibilities she knew would come to be hers when Hunter became the Earl of Dunnon, but in the end she found herself letting the steward make the decisions while she wandered aimlessly through the cold rooms.

Lord Dunnon, Hunter's father, was a pleasant old man, and despite his illness, he had made her feel welcome. He had opened his home to her, insisting that she was already the lady of the castle. Why did that make her so unhappy? It was what she had dreamed of since her childhood.

Then there were the little things. At supper parties she was never seated with Hunter. Husbands and wives were not expected to like each other, or even get along for that matter. Her clothing always seemed too tight; she couldn't breathe. There was no privacy; there were servants to cook and clean, to dress her, even to bathe her if she didn't force them out of her bedchamber.

But the worst thing of all was her relationship with Hunter. Nothing was as it had been in Maryland. She saw him early in the morning and then late at night when he fell into bed, contrary, with the smell of brandy on his breath. He had warned her he would have many duties to see to; he had warned her that at times she would be lonely. But she hadn't listened. She hadn't realized how long a day could be when she didn't get to speak to him between dawn and midnight. And then even when they were together, he was preoccupied. At times, his sense of humor, which she had come to appreciate so much, seemed nonexistent. He argued with Jon over frivolous matters. He drank too much and then he and Alexandra fought over his drinking.

She sighed, glancing down at the menu on the oak desktop. These days Hunter reminded her of a caged wildcat her Uncle Charles had had as a pet when she'd first arrived in Annapolis. He had kept it out back in the gardens in a small shed as an oddity to show his friends. For weeks it had paced back and forth in the wooden pen snarling and reaching out to strike anyone who came too near. The animal had tried desperately to claw its way out of the box that kept it caged so far from its native hills farther west.

Alexandra looked down at the piece of paper in her hand, the writing blurred by the tears in her eyes. The wildcat had finally stopped eating the raw meat that was brought to it each day, and before her uncle could make the decision to set it free it had died in the corner of its cage.

A knock came at the door. Alexandra wiped at her tears with the back of her hand, feeling foolish for crying over a dead animal.

"Yes?"

"Lady Ashton, Lord Carlisle to see you."

Alexandra looked up at her mother's man-servant. "Roland?" She smiled. She had been looking forward to seeing dear Roland. He was the one person she had remembered as being a true friend to her in England. "Send him up, Walter. Then have refreshment sent up. The kitchen will know what Lord Carlisle prefers."

The manservant nodded his head and retreated. A minute later Roland came sauntering into the room. Alexandra ran to him, throwing her arms around his shoulders. He was a tall man, thinner than Hunter, but very athletically built. He had golden hair and a smile that could soften the heart of any man, woman, or child.

"Roland," she sighed, hugging him tightly. "It's been weeks since I sent you a message. I was beginning to wonder what had happened to you."

Still holding her in his arms, he took a step back so that he could look at her. "Been out of the country, dear." He shook his head. "By the king's cod, you look good! I take it, marriage agrees with you."

She laughed, stepping back, knowing her cheeks were coloring. "I love him, Roland."

"Do you now?" He was smiling back at her. "I knew you'd find someone. The right man, a man who could love you the way you deserve to be loved. But, I have to admit I was surprised when I heard who you'd married. All of London is gossiping about it, and everyone has a different tale to tell, each one more preposterous than the next. Yesterday at the Exchange, I heard your father had him captured and brought by ship back to London in chains." He sat down on a small upholstered settee and crossed his legs, making himself comfortable. "I'm dying to hear the truth."

She sat down in a chair beside him. "What if I say *I* brought him in chains." She lifted an eyebrow mischievously.

He tapped her on her knee. "I say good for you."

She laughed. "The truth is, and this is for your ear only so you'll have no gossip to take out of here with you, is that I was captured by Indians."

The pleasant smile fell from his face. He reached to take her hand. "God, Alex, I'm sorry. I shouldn't have pried. We needn't discuss it."

"It's all right, really." She broke into a smile. "When I forget the pain of the circumstances, my cousin and uncle's death, I can honestly say it was the best thing that could have happened to me."

"Why?" he prodded gently.

She squeezed his hand and then let it go, leaning back in her chair. It felt so good to sit and talk with someone she felt comfortable with, someone she could speak candidly with. "Because Hunter"— she looked up—"Geoffry was called Hunter in the Colonies—because Hunter found me. He bought me from an Indian called Two Crows. Hunter led me over half the Maryland Colony searching for Captain Cain who killed his first wife. I slept on the ground, in Shawnee wigwams, in forts, on the ground under the stars. I fell in love with him and we married. I didn't even know he was Geoffry

Rordan until we reached Annapolis."

Roland screwed up his face. "Christ, this tale sounds better than anything one could possibly have made up."

A knock came at the door and Alexandra was silent while a maid brought a plate of fruit and cheeses and a decanter of sweet wine and two glasses. Alexandra poured Roland a drink as the maid left, closing the door behind her.

"When I think back, it all seems ridiculously impossible. I can't believe all I went through, and now I'm back here in my father's house where nothing has changed."

He took the glass from her hand. "Nothing but you?"

Her gaze met his. "Do you see it? Is it me? Everything here seems so much the same and yet so different. I'm so confused. I was beginning to think I'd left part of my senses somewhere in the wilderness across the ocean."

"Then you're not happy?"

She twisted her hands in her lap. "No," she finally answered. "I thought this was what I wanted but . . ." She sighed, at a loss for words. "I don't know what to do to make things right."

"Your husband is not the devoted man you thought him to be?"

She shook her head. "No, it's not Hunter. It's me. It's us. It's this place." She looked up at him. "I haven't been able to tell anyone about the colonies, because we decided it was best if people didn't know the circumstances of our marriage, but Roland, it was the most magical place you could ever imagine. It's so beautiful, so vast and empty. The people, the Shawnee, are like no one you've ever met or even known existed."

He set down his glass. "And now Mother England can never be the same for you?"

She looked down into her lap at her hands twisted in the azure blue folds of her sack gown. "No."

"So what does Geoffry say of all this?"

She looked up at Roland. "I haven't told him. I can't."

"And why the hell not?"

"Because." She sighed. "Because I insisted we come back to England. I insisted he return to the responsibilities he left behind when he left me six years ago." She lifted her hand. "The Earl of Dunnon is dying. Hunter will inherit all that's his. This is where he belongs, where he must stay. I can't tell him I've changed my mind!"

"And why not?" Roland reached for a square of cheese and tossed it into his mouth. "You love the man. I assume he loves you. What can there be in a marriage if there's no honesty?"

She rose and walked to the window, but didn't allow herself to focus on the filthy street below. "This is where I belong. My duties as my husband's wife are here in England. The colonies were just a dream, a good dream, but one that had to end. I'll get used to England and our way of living again. I know I will. I just need time."

Roland rose and crossed the room to come stand beside her. "You're a fool, Mary Alexandra."

"What?"

"You're a damned fool. Ask a man who spent thirty-odd years denying who he was, pretending he was happy when he wasn't, all for the sake of confounded duty!"

Alexandra brushed her fingertips over Roland's ruby red coat. "Roland, you don't understand."

"The hell I don't!" He spoke quietly but his voice was filled with fervor. "I lived a lie and I know what it does to a person inside. It kills one, Alexandra. It took me a long time to realize that. But it was killing me one day at a time. What good was I to my father only half a man? What good will you be to Geoffry if you're slowly wasting away inside?"

She sighed. What Roland said made sense. Yet, she knew she couldn't take Hunter away from all he was entitled to. All that he had returned for. She would just have to make herself content here, that was all there was to it.

After a moment of silence, she rubbed Roland's arm. "Thank you for coming. I needed to talk to a friend."

He kissed her cheek. "Think about what I've said, Alex. Believe me, I know what I'm talking about."

She smiled. "Please come to see us at Dunnon Castle. Come and stay a few days. I'm lonely there."

"I will. I swear it."

She followed him to the door. "You're coming to the masquerade ball aren't you?"

"Of course. Wouldn't miss it, not to dine with the king."

"Who are you coming as?"

"Hah! I'll not give away my secret." He walked out the door and into the hallway. "I'll see myself out. I still know the way. Take care, Alex. Do what you know is right in your heart."

She waved halfheartedly to him, leaning on the doorframe until he disappeared down the stairs and then she went into the room and closed the door quietly behind her. If she was to see to the musicians in an hour, she would have to get the menu back to the cook. With a sigh, she went back to the desk, sat and bent her head over the papers, vowing to set her mind to the task at hand. Everything would work out for the best. She knew that. It would just take time.

Chapter Twenty-five

Alexandra stood at the door in her corset and shift with a silk powdering mantle thrown over her shoulders. "You're late."

Hunter crossed his arms over his chest and stood in the hallway. "No, *I missed you, dear husband. Good to see you*, dear? Perhaps a wifely kiss on the cheek?"

Alexandra sighed. She was glad to see him. But he was hours late, a fact her mother had been reminding her every hour on the hour since three o'clock. "Please come in before someone hears you. The guests are already beginning to arrive."

Hunter hesitated for a moment and then strode in. She closed the door behind him. "How's your week gone?" she asked, trying to smooth things over. She went to sit at her dressing table and finish applying her makeup before one of her mother's maids came in to help her put on her gown.

"Well enough."

"And your father?"

"Worse."

"I'm sorry."

"I don't think he'll live much longer, Alex." He touched his ear, an old habit from when he had worn the earring. "But he says he's ready to die. He says now that I'm home, he'll die in peace."

She glanced up at him through the reflection in her oval mirror. Hunter looked tired. He was dressed in plain, worn breeches and a shirt without a stock. He wore no shirtwaist, only an old coat. "Are you going to dress?" she asked softly.

He came to her and lifted the curls of hair off her back to kiss the nape of her neck. "I thought I'd go as Adam and walk stark naked through your father's ballroom," he murmured in her ear.

She chuckled. Of course it wasn't funny. If she encouraged him in any way, he might well do it. But it was so good to hear that voice that was so familiar to her, the voice she loved—Hunter's voice, not Geoffry's. How odd it was that she had begun to think of him as two different men. "Does that mean I should go as Eve?" She watched him in the mirror as he peeled back the silk powdering mantle and covered the creamy skin above her shift neckline with soft, fleeting kisses.

"I was getting to that."

She laughed, leaning against him and taking his hands to wrap them around her. She closed her eyes. It felt so good to feel his touch, so reassuring. "I did miss you," she whispered. "I'm sorry I was cross with you. I've had a horrible week. My mother is about to set me mad. I'm going home the first of the week with you."

"But your week wasn't worse than mine." He kissed the top of her head and then wandered to the window. "My father's financial affairs are a mess."

"Poor investments?" She powdered her face with rice powder, using a hare's foot for a brush.

"Hardly. Excellent investments. Staggering. He's bought one plantation in Maryland, buying a second. Tobacco is still extremely profitable."

She began to rouge her lips. "So what's the trouble?"

He pulled back the draperies and looked out at the dark street below. It was raining. "Little bookkeeping and what there is, is poor. The money is with too many banking houses. It'll take me a year to straighten it out into any semblance of order."

Adding a dab of color to her cheeks, she rose. "I'm sorry you've had to come home to such disarray. Can't you get anyone to help you?"

"Eventually, but at this point I'd rather not share the information with a hired man. There's so much damned money that I don't know where it all is. It would be too easy for someone to steal from us right now, and I can't let that happen. My father's worked too hard to make this fortune." He exhaled, obviously frustrated. "Damnation, Alex. I don't know where all of Father's land is or even the deeds. He's got priceless artwork I've never seen, lands in places I've never been. I'm just not cut of the right cloth to manage monies and lands as my father did." He shook a finger. "Now Jon, Jon's the one with the head for this."

"Then ask him to help you."

He let the draperies slip from his hand to cover the black window. "I can't. It's not fair. This is my responsibility." He rubbed his temples. "Damn it, I should never have left. If I hadn't gone—"

She touched his lips with the tip of her finger. "If you hadn't gone to the colonies, you'd never have had me. I'd never have loved you as I love you now, Hunter of the Shawnee." She rose up on her high-heeled scarlet slippers and kissed him.

He wrapped her in his arms, pulling her against him to rest his head on her shoulder. "God, I love you, Alex. I don't want to hurt you. Please don't let me be like this, act like this."

She looked up into his hazel eyes. "Like what?"

"Like an ass. Like all the men I despise in my father's world. Troubled, arrogant, self-centered, possessive."

"You're none of those things."

He dropped his head to her shoulder again. "I hope not, but I'm afraid . . ." He sighed, his warm breath tickling her ear. "I can see myself becoming all those things in a few years, all the things I ran to the colonies to avoid becoming."

"It doesn't have to be like that," she told him, stroking his soft, thick, auburn hair. "I won't let it happen."

He lifted his head and let go of her. "I suppose I need to go dress. Your mother had my clothes sent elsewhere. The next bedchamber over, I think." He looked up at her, grimacing. "Christ, doesn't anyone in England share sleeping rooms with their own wife?"

"We do." She shooed him with her hand. "Now

go dress. I'll have your bags moved in here tonight."

He went to the door and turned to face her. "What are you wearing tonight? Who are you going as?"

She smiled mischievously. "Mind your knitting. You'll have to find me among the other ladies."

He reached into his coat and took something out. He shook it in his palm as if considering whether or not to show her. "I have something, something for you. Now that I've had it made, I don't know that you'll like it. It won't go with any of your clothes, I'm sure."

She came to stand in front of him, one hand resting on her hip. "Show me."

"I won't be offended if you don't wear it."

She grasped his hand. "You're being silly. Let me see. I'll be the judge of what I like and don't like."

He opened his hand. Nestled in his palm was a black obsidian arrowhead surrounded by diamonds.

"For me?" She looked up at him as she took it from his hand. "Hunter, it's beautiful."

"Geoffry. You've got to get into the habit of calling me Geoffry."

She ran a finger over the triangular shaped broach. The arrowhead was warm to the touch from being inside his coat, next to his skin. "I'll call you what I want, in private," she told him. She looked up at him again. "Thank you." She could feel a lump rising in her throat. "It's the most precious gift I've ever received.''

"I made the arrowhead when I first went to the colonies. It took me all damned winter and then it wasn't good enough to go on the shaft of an arrow.''

"It's the most beautiful piece of jewelry I've ever owned,'' she marveled, still fascinated by the way the light played between the brilliantly clear diamonds and the shiny black stone. "Thank you.''

He winked at her and went out the door. "See you at the ball, my lady.''

"At the ball, my lord.''

"My lady, will you be needing help with your gown now?'' the maid in the doorway asked. "The mistress, your mother, sent me to tend to you.''

"Yes, come in,'' Alexandra nodded. "I'm ready to be dressed.'' She squeezed the brooch in her hand, thinking to herself, *the sooner this is over, the sooner I can get away from here and return to Dunnon Castle with Hunter.*

Not half an hour later Alexandra came down the grand staircase of her father's home. The Earl of Monthrop, wearing a leopard's mask, met her at the bottom. She was dressed in a scarlet red gown with an embroidered linen stomacher with gold cord lacing. Around her neck she wore a ribbon of red velvet with Hunter's brooch at the pulse of her throat. On her head she wore a red and white Shawnee headdress with feathers dangling down her back. Her papier-mâché mask was painted bronze in the face of a sleeping Shawnee maiden, the marking of Hunter's adopted family painted across one cheek.

"God's bowels, Daughter. Where did you get that contraption?" her father asked, staring at her headdress in disgust. "Where's the unicorn mask and headdress I had sent up last night?"

Alexandra was smiling beneath the mask she'd secretly had made. "You don't like it, Father?" She nodded to the Earl and Countess of something, old friends of her parents.

"It's not that I don't like it." He took her arm and led her toward the ballroom. "I just don't know that it's appropriate."

"Has Geoffry come down?"

"I haven't seen him. Your mother said he was late. She was concerned he wouldn't make it on time. The redman is here. He was one of the first guests to arrive."

"Jon? Where?"

"Gaming tables, I believe. Wearing an orange wig with the mask of a buffoon."

Alexandra laughed.

Her father led her into the bright white crystal chandelier light of the ballroom. The music of French horns and violins filled the large, opulent room. Laughter, voices, and the clink of glasses mingled. There were more than two hundred guests present, all dressed in their finest, and wearing masks.

An ancient Greek couple fluttered by, calling a greeting. The Earl of Monthrop spoke, Alexandra smiled behind her mask and nodded. As she walked beside her father, speaking pleasantly with guests, she looked for Hunter. He hadn't said what he would be wearing. She knew she'd recognize him immediately, but she was anxious to see who he would come as.

Alexandra's mother came bustling after Alexandra and her father. "Heavens to handmaidens, where did you get that apparatus on your head, Daughter? Where's the horned headdress?" She considered her daughter from head to toe. "Didn't you like the lavender and pink ribbons? I had it made to go with the lavender gown which you're not wearing either, I can see."

Alexandra glanced at her mother, a smile tugging at the corners of her mouth. Her mother was wearing hundreds of yellow false curls that covered her head in a halo. Her mask was that of a young girl's face with round rouged cheeks and a perfect little red mouth. The costume was not becoming.

"You don't like my feathers?" Alexandra tugged at the train of dyed red and white feathers that trailed down her back.

Her mother's eyes widened behind her mask. "And where did you get that hideous brooch, child?" She reached out to touch it, but Alexandra drew back. "It was a gift, Mother." She smiled to both of her parents, curtsying. "If you'll excuse me, I'll start greeting everyone. If you see Geoffry, tell him I'm looking for him."

Before her mother could speak again, Alexandra sailed off. She was already hot beneath her mask, but she liked it. She liked the feel of the feathers on her back.

"A Shawnee maiden! Is she in need of rescuing yet again?"

Alexandra turned to see a buffoon in an orange wig and matching coat and breeches, the breeches so tight she doubted he could bend if his life depended upon it. "Jon." She laughed, leaning to kiss the only part of his skin that remained bare, the line of his jawbone. "Don't you look the fool!"

"No more than I am. Have you seen my merry grig?"

"Hunter? No."

"God's teeth, Alex. Can't you remember the man's name. It's Geoffry—very soon to be the Earl of Dunnon, I fear."

Alexandra looked up at Jon. "Yes, he told me the earl is worse. I'm sorry."

She saw him smile sadly behind his mask. "He's lived a good life. He was a good man. He treated me like a son, better. If there's a God, and indeed a heaven, I'm certain that's where he'll go."

Alexandra looped her arm through Jon's. "Come with me and we'll make some introductions. Try not to cause a scene, will you? I promised my mother."

He patted her hand, his laughter mixing with hers. "No matter how intoxicated I get, I swear I won't strip naked, don Lady Warner's shift, and dance on top of the spinet. Fair enough?"

"Fair enough."

So arm and arm they made their way around the ballroom, speaking to old acquaintances and making introductions. Manservants in silver and green livery served goblets of French champagne and trays of sweetmeats. Alexandra had just finished her second glass of champagne when someone walked up behind her and laid a possessive hand on her shoulder.

"A dance, my lady?"

She turned around to see Hunter staring at her through a mask that looked much like her own. She smiled up at him, delighted that they had both had the same idea, that their hearts were both in the same place. "A Shawnee."

"Supposed to be a medicine man but the maskmaker had his own ideas." He tugged at the two black feathers that fell from the mask to dangle at one cheek.

She slipped her hand into his. "I've been introducing Jon to all my relatives. Everyone thinks he's you."

"I told her it's a sign from God." Jon grabbed two glasses of champagne as a servant walked by with a tray. "She should have come back with me, not you."

"Touch my wife, Jon, and I'll cut off the offending hand," Hunter said sweetly.

Jon sighed, pushing his mask up on his forehead so that he could drink. "Well, I'm off. The cards are calling me. I understand a game of basset is about to begin. Madame." He bowed to Alexandra, holding both glasses up so that neither spilled. He stuck his tongue out at Hunter and walked away.

Hunter took her by the hand and led her out

onto the dance floor, joining two lines that were just beginning a country dance. "Sometimes I don't know why I associate with that man."

She curtsied as he bowed and they began to dance the Roger de Coverley. "Because you love him," she answered.

"Yes, but beside that."

She laughed as he danced away, his form as fine as that of any gentleman on the floor. A few moments later, after several different partners, Hunter joined her again. "Admirable dancing, sir," she teased from behind her papier-mâché mask. "But I believe I prefer the moves of the corn dance. You were wearing far less, as I recall."

His laughter floated back to her as he danced away with yet another partner. When he returned to her, the Roger de Coverley ended, but they remained on the dance floor dancing minuets and reels and other country dances until neither could catch a breath.

"No more," she cried as she walked off the dance floor. "I've got to sit down and rest. I have to have something to drink."

Hunter grabbed two glasses of sweet red wine as a servant walked by with a full tray. He pushed one into her hand and led her to a corner. Alexandra sat and just as Hunter was about to sit beside her, the Earl of Monthrop waved to him.

"Son! My dear Viscount. Come and settle this matter at once! William here swears John Clouse had the fastest horse in the city, but I beg to differ."

Hunter looked down at Alexandra, lifting an eyebrow.

"Go," she urged. "You'll not escape him. You might as well get it over with. I'll just sit here and wait for you."

He drank down his wine and handed her the glass. He pushed his mask back farther on his head. "Be back as soon as possible. Don't move."

She watched him walk away as she sipped her wine. Maybe everything was going to be all right. *Maybe she was just worrying too much,* she thought to herself. *Because we do love each other. Isn't that all that matters?*

"Alexandra!"

She looked up to see a man standing before her in a wooden half mask, half painted white, half black. She narrowed her eyes speculatively. "Roland?"

He yanked the mask from his head. "Damnation, I don't know why I bother. Everyone always knows me. A dance, sweet Alex."

She groaned. "I was resting. Have a seat." She patted the gold damask seat cushion on the gilt chair beside her.

He sat down, crossing his legs at the calves.

"Enjoying yourself?" she asked.

"Your father always did know how to throw an event of any sort."

"How's Mark?"

He watched the crowd as he reached out to tap her knee. "Good of you to ask. Doing well."

"Have you met my Geoffry?"

"Not yet." He took a glass of wine a servant offered. "But I understand he's the best looking sot in London since Roger Matthews went into the country with the pox."

She smiled at him. "You are a dear friend."

"Are you telling me I should have married you when I had the chance?" he teased.

"I'm saying mayhap I should have married you, when *I* had the chance."

He looked at her over the rim of the glass. "Have you thought any more on what I said the other day about being true to yourself?"

"I'm fine, Roland. Truly. And Hunt—Geoffry is fine; he's simply preoccupied. His father's taken a turn for the worse. We don't think he'll live much longer."

"A good man, Dunnon. I'll be sorry to see him go."

For the next hour Roland and Alexandra sat watching the dancers as the two of them talked, sampled delicacies prepared by French cooks, and drank her father's wine. Twice she spotted Hunter, but each time he was drawn away by someone else wanting to meet or greet the long-lost Viscount Rordan.

"Enough refreshment!" Roland said after his second glass of wine. He grasped her hand and lifted her out of the gilt chair. "A dance."

She swayed one way and then the other, looking for Hunter. He had disappeared again. "I was waiting for Geoffry, but I guess he's still occupied."

Roland motioned toward the dance floor where a minuet was about to begin. "No excuse, savage woman. A dance or your life!"

She shrugged. "Then what can I say?" She

tossed her mask onto the chair behind her and walked with him to the dance floor.

They danced two minuets and then a reel, but Alexandra was restless. She'd had too much wine and rich food. Her stays were too tight, her shoes tighter, and she needed a breath of fresh air.

She grabbed Roland's hand as the musicians struck up another song. "Oh, Roland, I don't want to dance anymore. It's too hot in here. Can't we step out onto the balcony? The rain's stopped."

"With a married woman, not my own? Gads, what a scandal."

She rolled her eyes as she walked off the dance floor headed for the double French doors that had been flung open to let in cold air to the overheated guests. "I don't know where Geoffry is. At the gaming tables with Jon I would wager." She wrinkled her nose. "And since when did you care what anyone thought?"

Roland dropped a hand casually on her bare shoulder and whispered in her ear as he led her out onto the balcony.

Hunter lifted another glass of wine to his lips. This was his fourth or fifth glass in half an hour's time, but he didn't care. He needed the strength of the liquor. He needed that feeling it gave him that filled the void in his chest. The gentleman in the lime green hose with an alligator mask on the back of his head rambled on about the king's new mistress, but Hunter blocked out his voice. He was watching Alexandra.

The man she was with, the man she'd been with more than an hour, was Roland, he was told. He was the man she had been betrothed to after he'd left for the colonies. Alexandra had never said why the marriage hadn't taken place, but it was obvious to him that it wasn't because they didn't care for each other. They were laughing like old friends, comfortable with each other, at ease in their surroundings.

He gulped down the last of the wine and dropped the glass onto an empty tray on a small table behind him. It fell over hitting another. Glass shattered, but he didn't bother to turn around to survey the damage.

Now this Roland and Alexandra were walking out onto the balcony arm and arm. He tugged absently at his earlobe, thinking of the earring Alexandra still wore on her finger.

Who am I kidding to think she'd be happy married to me, he thought. *She should have married the fop when she had the chance. He's the kind of man she wanted, not a man like me. I'm as out of place at this ball as an opossum in Versailles. This isn't me. I can never be happy here. I'll just make her life miserable.*

Alexandra disappeared into the darkness out on the garden balcony, but Hunter could have sworn he could hear her laughing, them laughing. What was she doing, a married woman, being so familiar with an unmarried man?

Hunter gave a curt nod to the gentleman still babbling on, halting him in midsentence. "If you'll excuse me, my lord . . ."

The alligator gave a harrumph as he stepped out of Hunter's way.

Hunter strode across the ballroom floor oblivious to the dancers whose paths he crossed. Alexandra was his wife, damn it! She belonged at his side—not this dandy's!

He stepped out onto the dark balcony. The rain had ceased. The smell of the warm ground and upturned dirt of the gardens below mixed with the scent of the fallen rain and rose to fill his nostrils. There it was again. He could hear her laughing.

"Geoffry!" Alexandra spotted him and waved. She and the dashing Roland were leaning over the balcony. She touched his hand casually as they turned to greet him.

Roland stood erect. "Viscount, allow me to introduce myself. I'm—"

"I know who the hell you are, and I'd like to know what it is you're doing with my wife!"

Alexandra stepped away from the balcony, releasing Roland's arm. "Hunter!"

Several guests standing on the balcony turned to the threesome with interest.

Roland smiled, bowing slightly. "My apologies if I offended you, sir." He spoke softly. "Alex and I are good friends, but I can assure you she is safe enough with me. I'd not lay a hand on her."

"And you expect me to accept your word? Accept a gentleman's word when every man in London seems to be futtering another man's wife!"

Alexandra grasped Hunter's arm, speaking angrily under her breath. "Hunter, you've had too much to drink. That's enough. You don't know what you're saying."

"I repeat myself, sir," Hunter went on, pushing Alexandra's hand from his arm. "Why would I trust you? The two of you are obviously familiar with each other. I understand you even once considered marrying my wife."

"Hunter, you're making a scene. Others are watching. Let's go."

"No, I'll go, Alex," Roland said. "It's time I was on my way, anyway. I thank you for the—"

"I've not finished my conversation with you," Hunter said, grabbing the lawn collar of Roland's waistcoat.

"Hunter! Unhand him and take your leave," Alexandra shouted angrily.

Roland looked directly into Hunter's enraged eyes. "You can take my word that your wife's virtue is safe with me," he said, "because though your wife is charming, yonder is where my attentions lie." He pointed through the open doors, into the ballroom.

Hunter turned his head. A tall, pretty, young man in a yellow-blond powdered wig was standing just inside the doorway in conversation with another man, oblivious to what was occurring on the balcony. He held a black and white half mask identical to Roland's.

Hunter felt his throat constricting. He released Roland's coat. He'd made an ass of himself. He knew it now. The blond gentleman looked up at them, nodding his head and then turning his gaze to Roland. The look on the man's face was all-revealing. They were lovers, he and Roland. There was no mistaking it.

Hunter turned to Roland. He couldn't bring himself to look at Alexandra, not after he'd embarrassed her so. "My grave apologies, sir," he said, formally. Then, with a stiff bow, he pulled his mask off the top of his head, down over his face, and strode away.

Alexandra shouted after him, but he didn't turn back. He figured he'd already hurt her enough for one evening.

Chapter Twenty-six

"Son of pox-faced beggar," Alexandra raged, as she ripped her Indian maiden's mask off her face and hurled it across her bedchamber. It hit the mantel, sending an unlit candelabrum crashing to the floor.

The maid in the doorway cringed, unused to such displays of emotion. "Have . . . have you need of me tonight, my lady?"

Alexandra turned around. "No! I'll have no need of anyone tonight."

"You . . . you don't want help with the gown, mistress?"

"No." She stomped toward the door. "I'll rip it off, cut if off! I don't know! Just leave me!"

The girl backed up, closing the door behind her.

Alexandra thrust the key in the lock and turned it. How could he have embarrassed her like that? How could he have insulted Roland, the only true friend she had, other than Jon? How could he have made such a scene in her father's home? She yanked off her red-and-white feathered headdress and threw it on the bed. Next came her shoes and then her stockings.

The whole incident on the balcony was bad enough. He'd had too much to drink. He'd said things he shouldn't have said. But then the worthless, cowardly lout walked out on her! He couldn't even stand there and face her!

She yanked her modesty piece from her bodice and then began to unlace her stomacher, jerking at the gold silk cord. When a piece snapped off, she threw it to the floor and went on unlacing herself. Whose idea could it possibly have been to dress a woman in such a manner that she couldn't dress and undress herself? A man's . . . she was certain of it!

"I don't know where you've gone," she hollered at the empty room, because Hunter wasn't there to holler at. "But you'd better run, because when I find you, Geoffry Rordan, Viscount Ashton, I'm going to knock that thumping smirk off your face," she seethed.

She pulled the gown off her shoulders, not caring that she tore the delicately laced seams in the process. "I hate you! I hate you!" She pushed the scarlet red gown down around her waist, letting it fall in a puddle at her feet. "I should have married Jon!" She jerked her corset cover over her head. "He'd not have made a fool of himself in front of me and half of London!"

A knock came at the door. "Alex."

"Go away!" she shouted, struggling with the ties of her corset.

"Alex, it's Jon."

"Go away, Jon. I don't want to talk to you. I don't want to talk to anyone."

He rapped on the door again. "Alex, I'm not leaving, so you might as well let me in. I can shout and carry on if you like, but then everyone downstairs in the ballroom will hear me."

Finally getting the corset loose enough to slide down over her hips, she stepped out of it and threw it too to the floor.

"Alex."

She felt a sob rise in her throat. Why was Jon here? It was Hunter who should be at her door begging to come in. Where was he?

"Alex . . ."

"All right, all right!" she moaned. Her head was pounding. She wanted to just lie down and cry. She picked up her powdering mantle off a chair and covered her shift with it. She didn't bother to tie the powder blue ribbons. God's teeth, Jon had seen her in less on the trail.

She twisted the key in the door. The knob turned and Jon stepped in, closing the door behind him.

"Now there'll really be a scandal," he said. "Just how many men are you keeping company with?"

She didn't know how she could laugh at a time like this, but his words struck her funny. "God, Jon, why do these things keep happening to me? I just want a normal life."

"What's a normal life? I certainly can't tell you." He lifted her boned corset up off the floor with one finger and held it up in the air.

She snatched it from him and threw it against

the handpainted wallpaper. "Did you want something? Or have you just come to annoy me?"

"I just don't want you to be too hard on him. This has all been very difficult, Alex."

She gave a laugh, but she wasn't amused. "And what, you don't think it's been hard on me?"

"His father is dying. He's had all this responsibility dropped into his lap. He doesn't even really want the money and lands, nor the title. At least he doesn't think so."

"So why doesn't he just give it all up?"

He went on speaking quietly. "Give it up? How? He's an only son. The title, the homes, much of the property has been in the family for hundreds of years. He can't just walk away." He hesitated for a moment. "Besides, this was what you wanted."

"Says who?"

"Come now. When you married him, this was what you intended to come home to, wasn't it?"

"I didn't know who he was," she defended.

"You're not stupid. You had an idea, if not of his true identity, then at least of his circumstance."

She threw up her hands. "I don't know what all this has to do with anything. He was drunk."

"Not drunk. I've never seen him drunk. That's my forte. But he did have too much drink. He wasn't thinking clearly."

"He jumped to conclusions without speaking to me. He didn't trust me or my judgement."

"It's easy for men to become jealous over the women they love. Why didn't you tell him the truth of why you didn't marry Roland?"

"It wasn't any of Hunter's business. Roland was a friend. When I found out he was in love with Mark, I couldn't marry him. But I didn't want his reputation marred. That's why no one ever knew why the betrothal was broken." She turned her back on Jon, not wanting him to see the tears that gathered in the corners of her eyes. "But none of that matters. Hunter embarrassed me, he embarrassed himself, and he insulted Roland."

"Not on purpose."

"It's no excuse!"

He rested his hand on her shoulder. "No, it's not, but it's a good enough explanation to deserve a little understanding from you."

"So why did he walk off? He's not the first man to make a jackass of himself at a party. Every man in that room's done it once. I'd wager you have."

"More than once. But not Hunter. He's not used to being out of control. I imagine he was afraid he would hurt you more than he already had, if he stayed."

She turned to face Jon. "I love him." She wiped her eyes with the back of her hand. "No matter what he's done. I love him, Jon. I just want to be with him."

"So tell him, not me."

"I've tried." She walked to the windows and tugged absently at the closed draperies. "But all he does is go on about responsibility and how overwhelmed he is. He keeps putting words in my mouth and saying what I want, what I feel."

"It's just going to take time, Alex."

She sighed, wrapping her arms around her waist. "I want to go back to Dunnon Castle. I hate it here. Do you know where he is? Do you know where Hunter's gone?"

"No. But I've a good idea. We spent many a night in our younger days on the streets of London. I'll find him."

"Tell him to come get me. I'm angry, but that doesn't mean I don't want to see him. Tell him we'll go back together. If his father is as near to death as he thinks, we should all be there."

Jon went to the door. "You get some sleep. I'll find him and send him home when he's sober and got some sense about him."

She followed him into the hall. "Thanks, Jon, for everything." She kissed him on the cheek. "Good night."

"Night, love."

Alexandra went back into her bedchamber and closed the door behind her. She looked at her clothing strewn about the room. Her scarlet ball gown was in shreds. But instead of picking the clothes up, she threw off her mantle and walked around the chamber, blowing out the candles. She was so tired. A night's sleep was what she needed. Nothing ever seemed to look as hopeless by the light of the day. She pushed the clothing and accessories off her bed and onto the floor and climbed under the counterpane. She closed her eyes and fell asleep almost immediately.

Sometime in the night Alexandra woke to the sounds of a terrible ruckus. Servants were racing through the hallway shouting. She could hear her mother screeching. Her father's dogs woke and began to howl.

"God's teeth," she mumbled, climbing out of bed. What was going on? In the hallway she heard her grandmother's tall case clock strike four in the morning. All the ball guests should have gone home by now, or at least they should have been bedded down in the guest rooms. What was going on?

As she went to her door and peered out, she realized she was dressed in nothing but her shift. "What is it?" she called to a manservant racing down the hall in a nightshirt, carrying a candle-stand.

"A madman!" he called to her. "Better you get inside your room, my lady. Your father's sent for the sheriff."

"A madman? Where?" She rubbed at her sleepy eyes. "Who?"

"Help! Help us!" The countess moaned, coming down the hallway in the opposite direction of the manservant. She was wearing a yellow taffeta dressing gown, her sparse hair tied in rags. "Mary Alexandra! Get inside your chamber! Lock your door! There's a bedlamite about!"

"Where?"

"In the house! Your father's gone for his musket!"

"Where is this madman?" Alexandra asked suspiciously.

"Downstairs! God help us, Daughter! Noah says he rode straight up the front steps and into the front hallway, practically running the poor soul into the marble!"

"Oh, no . . ." Alexandra spun around and headed down the hall toward the grand staircase that led to the first floor.

"Mary Alexandra! Where are you going? Blessed Holy Jesus! You're in nothing but a shift! I can see your possibles!"

Alexandra ignored her mother. There were others in the long hallway now. The old Viscount of Cushion and his wife, both in nightcaps and gowns stood outside their bedchamber. Several frightened maids ran down the hallway headed for the servants' quarters. Alexandra ran past them. A spooked tabby cat passed her.

"Hunter!" she shouted. "Hunter, is that you!"

"Someone stop her!" her mother cried after her. "My daughter's taken leave of her senses. Someone please stop her!"

Alexandra turned the corner and reached the top of the circular staircase. She leaned over the railing, peering down to the first story below.

In the front hallway on her mother's Italian marble floor was a mounted horseman in a black cape.

"Hunter!" Alexandra shouted. "Is that you? Because if it is, you'd better identify yourself before my father shoots you!" It had to be him, of course. What other man would dare ride a horse into the Earl of Monthrop's home?

The man looked up. His face was concealed by a black frowning mask, his hair covered with the hood of his cloak. The man's eyes, peering out from slits in the wooden mask, were so dark and alarming that for a moment she thought she was mistaken. Perhaps this *was* a madman escaped from bedlam and not her husband.

"Alex?" He yanked off the mask and let it fall to the floor. "Jon said you wanted me. He said you wanted me to take you home to Dunnon. Well, it's for Dunnon I'm bound."

His baritone voice echoed in the hallway, sounding almost ghostly.

She came away from the railing and down the curve of the steps to the first landing. Now he was in full view of her. "What are you doing?" The truth was, she was glad he was here, even if it was on horseback in her mother's hall.

"Told you. Come to fetch my wife if she's willing to go with me." The spirited grey horse pawed restlessly.

It was a dare. She knew it was. He wanted her to turn him away. He wanted an excuse to walk away from her yet again. She could hear hushed voices behind her. A crowd of guests and servants were gathering in the hallway above. Faces peered over the railing.

"Now?" she asked her husband calmly.

"Dawn will be here shortly. I thought to get an early start. I've bookkeeping to attend to at Dunnon."

Her gaze met his. "I'm not dressed for travel," she stalled.

"You mean you won't go?"

She rested both hands on her hips, knowing that from here he could see every inch of her naked flesh beneath the thin shift she wore. "Is it cold out?"

He lifted a black gloved hand and pushed back his hood to reveal his thick mane of red hair that spilled down his back. "The rain's stopped. I've my cloak if you grow chilled."

His voice was haughty. He taunted her.

She shrugged. "All right."

The crowd of people above her gasped in unison.

He raised a dark eyebrow. "You go with me now, my lady?"

"Yes." She went to take a step, but he held up his hand. "No wait there, sweeting, and I'll come for you."

Before she could speak again, he sank his heels into the grey gelding's sides and rode straight up the marble staircase. Alexandra heard her mother shriek and then the thud of a falling body. Someone shouted for smelling salts. But Alexandra was oblivious to all but the red-haired horseman who rode up the steps to fetch her.

The gelding threw back its head prancing up the steps, but Hunter held a steady rein. He reached the landing and turned the steed around. "Your coach, my lady." He offered her his hand.

She placed her palm in his. "I can't believe you've done this," she whispered under her breath.

"I can't believe you're doing this," he retorted, his gaze boring down on her. He pulled one foot from his stirrup. "Up you go, my lady."

In the loose flowing shift it was easy enough for Alexandra to raise her foot high enough to slip it into the stirrup. With a tug of Hunter's hand she lifted up and he pulled her into the saddle in front of him.

"Alexandra," Alexandra heard her mother cry out.

Hunter lifted the reins and urged his mount forward. "Open the door!" he bellowed.

The frightened manservant standing in the center hallway raced for the front door.

Alexandra held tightly to the horse's mane as it barreled down the staircase at a precarious angle.

"I'll not let you fall," Hunter murmured in her ear, one hand wrapped tightly around her waist.

He rode the horse down the grand staircase, through the hall, outside, and down a small flight of steps into the drive.

"I'll be all right," Alexandra called over her shoulder to her mother and father and the guests who were running down the stairs after them.

Hunter urged the grey gelding into a full gallop down the center of the deserted London street. He lifted his cloak and pulled her inside it so that only her bare ankles were exposed.

"I'm not good at apologies," Hunter said softly. The thunder of the horse's hooves reverberated off the stone and frame buildings as they cut across the Strand onto Bow Street.

She leaned against him, savoring the warmth of his body. She could still smell the wine on his breath, but he was obviously sober. "It doesn't matter, none of this matters," she said, looking over her shoulder up at him. "All that matters is you and me. You do love me still, don't you, Hunter?"

He brushed his lips against the fringe of dark hair that fell across her forehead. "I love you, sweeting."

She turned back around, snuggling inside his wool cloak. "Then the rest we can deal with."

"I hope so," he whispered. "I sure as hell hope you're right."

Hunter scratched out a figure and went to replace it with another, but the quill was dry again and it marred the paper. Frustrated, he pushed the quill into the inkwell and tried again. "Ad's blood! Will I never get this right?" he mumbled to himself.

It was late, well after midnight. Everyone in Dunnon Castle had turned in, but the candles in the earl's private library still burned. Hunter was trying to make sense of his father's bookkeeping. Piles of ledgers were stacked on the heavy oak desk he sat at, and on the floor around his chair.

He scratched out another number, refigured it and then refigured it again.

The Earl of Dunnon was barely breathing when Hunter had left him after supper. Coughing spasms had racked his body until finally he'd slipped into the relative peace of unconsciousness. Mab said she doubted he'd live through another night. As Hunter sat at his father's desk, he kept half expecting to see Mab at the doorway announcing that his father had passed away.

"Still working?"

Hunter looked up to see Alexandra in the

doorway dressed in a filmy, pale green dressing gown tied with satin green bows. She was a picture of loveliness standing there in the doorway, her dark chestnut hair falling loose down her back, her face sleepy, her bare feet peeking from beneath the lace of her robe.

He looked back at the rows of figures on the paper in front of him. "Yes. I've got to start getting through these, Alex. I keep putting it off."

She lifted her hair off her shoulder and pushed it back. "Must you start at one in the morning?"

"I can't sleep." He sprinkled a little sand across the wet ink on the page. "Mab fears Father won't live through the night."

Alexandra came behind him and placed her hands on his shoulders. She kneaded his tired muscles. "Come to bed," she beckoned. "I'll help you sleep."

He dumped the sand off the page and reached for the quill again. She was trying so hard to make him happy. She said all the right things; she did all the right things. She truly loved him. So why wasn't he happy? Why wasn't her love enough for him? And why was *he* making *her* so unhappy?

Alexandra had forgiven him completely for his behavior at her father's home. Even Roland had forgiven him. He'd been to supper earlier in the week and he and Hunter had played cards well into the night. But Hunter couldn't forgive himself. He was making Alexandra miserable. He could see it in her eyes. These days he was beginning to think that maybe she'd be better off without him.

She rubbed his neck. "Won't you come to bed with me?" she repeated.

"Soon."

She lifted her hands and let them fall to her sides. She started to speak, but then didn't. "All right," she conceded. "But come soon, promise me?"

He began to add up the next column of figures. "Soon," he answered.

He heard her walk across the room. There was a pause. He knew she was looking at him, but he didn't look up. "Good night," she murmured.

As her footsteps died away Hunter rose and with one swift movement of his hand, he swept the desk clean, knocking ledgers, inkwell, and quill to the floor. The ink bottle shattered as it hit the hardwood planking. The ledger he had been working on fell face down, bending pages.

Cursing beneath his breath, Hunter went to the sideboard near the door and poured himself a healthy portion of brandy wine. As he lifted it to his lips, Jon came strolling in.

Jon took the glass from his hand before the warm brandy touched Hunter's lips. "A drink? Excellent. Just what I need before I turn in." Jon perched himself on the edge of the desk. He sipped Hunter's brandy as he surveyed the ledgers and loose papers that littered the floor.

"Strong winds pass through the library?"

Hunter ran his hand through his hair in frustration. "I go over and over the numbers. Nothing makes sense. It's so damned tedious!"

"You're trying too hard." Jon leaned back on

the Earl of Dunnon's carved oak desk that had been in the library for more than a hundred years. It was the desk Hunter and Jon had played under as boys. "Not just with this." He balanced the glass of brandy on his chest making a game of it. "With everything. You're trying to take over your father's duties that he's been long remiss in. You're trying to balance books that haven't been balanced in five years. You're trying to straighten out the household and the servants. You're trying to be the perfect host to every noddy who knocks on your door. And I'm telling you, it can't be done."

Hunter leaned against a bookcase that ran floor to ceiling and was crammed with precious leatherbound books. "And what am I supposed to do, He-Who-Is-All-Knowing?"

"Say to hell with it! Hell with it all! You've got the rest of your life to do the damned books."

Hunter frowned but said nothing.

"But you don't have the rest of your life to make things right with Alex . . ." Jon said gently. "She's slipping away from you, friend."

Hunter turned so that Jon couldn't see his face. "I made a mistake. I shouldn't have come home. This isn't where I belong."

"Don't say that."

"I shouldn't have married her."

Jon sat up. "Don't say it!"

"You should have married her. She'd have married you if you'd asked."

Jon drained the glass of brandy and set it down on the desk. "No. She wouldn't have. She fell in love with you the moment you nearly shot the balls off Two Crows at the trading post."

Hunter laughed, remembering the incident. He'd played it so calm, but he remembered how frightened he had been for the woman, for Alex. "I can't be what she wants me to be, Jon. I guess that's why I left England in the first place. I'm a man for adventure. There's no adventure here. There's nothing here for me."

Jon dropped his arm around Hunter's shoulder. "Listen to yourself. You're not making any sense, man. When was the last time you slept?"

Hunter rubbed at his eyes. It was true. He was tired, deathly tired. "I need to clean up here. I've got another hour's work at least. Besides, Mab thinks Father won't make it through the night. I should sit up and wait."

"That's what she said last night. Leave it." Jon went back to the desk and began to pick up the ledgers and papers strewn on the floor. "Let me have a look at the books. I always had a head for numbers."

Hunter stood in the doorway. All he wanted was to climb into bed with Alexandra and hold her in his arms. Only when she was in his arms did he feel like he was keeping the world at bay. "You certain you don't mind?"

Jon was stacking the ledgers back on the desk. "Go, sleep with your wife. Better yet, make love to her. If Father gets worse, I'll wake you."

Hunter nodded with a grim smile and left the library. Jon was a good friend. There was no better.

Chapter Twenty-seven

Two days later, in the middle of the night, a knock came at Hunter's and Alexandra's bedchamber. "Yes?" Hunter called sleepily.

Alexandra sat up in the bed. "What is it?"

The door swung open. "Master Geoffry." Mab held up a candlestand, the yellow light forming a halo around her grey head. She was dressed from head to toe in a flannel nightgown with a cap perched on the back of her head. "Come quickly, Master Geoffry."

Hunter leaped out of bed and grabbed his breeches off the floor. "I'm coming, Mab."

"I'm coming too." Alexandra slid her feet over the side of the bed and reached for her dressing gown.

"You stay," Hunter said. "Go back to sleep. You've not been getting enough rest."

She covered her naked body with the gown and slipped her feet into a pair of silk mules. "I'll go. I want to. I want to be there."

Hunter started across the bedchamber, barefoot, pulling a crumpled linen shirt over his head. "He's not dead yet?" he asked Mab, following Mab out of the chamber and down the hall. Alexandra trailed behind.

"Not yet, but he's on his last breath," Mab answered grimly, lighting their way down the dark hall. "I thought you'd want to be there."

Reaching his father's bedchamber, Hunter pushed open the door. "I do. Thank you, Mab. You'll be well rewarded for the care you've given my father."

"Want no reward." Mab stood back to let Alexandra pass. "His love was all I wanted, Master Geoffry, and he gave me that for thirty years."

Alexandra followed Hunter to his father's bedside. Candles lit the room in an eerie yellow light. He lay in the center of the soft tester bed, a light sheet pulled over his tiny shriveled body.

"Father?"

Hunter sat carefully on the edge of the bed and reached for the Earl of Dunnon's gnarled hand. "Father, it's Geoffry."

"Geoffry?" The old man squeezed Hunter's hand as he slowly turned his head toward him. "You're here, Son."

"Yes, Father."

"So glad you returned. Missed you. Wanted you to have what is yours."

Hunter rubbed his father's hand in a caress. His skin was so thin it was nearly translucent. "I'm here," he soothed. "Don't talk. There's no need."

"Wanted to tell you how proud I was of you."

He took a long, ragged breath. ". . . Wanted to tell you I was secretly envious. . . . Wanted to be in Maryland with you. . . . Wanted to see the forests one last time."

Tears filled Alexandra's eyes. She sat on the edge of the bed beside Hunter.

"I wanted you to be there with me, Father. I did."

The Earl of Dunnon closed his eyes, smiling, remembering the past, no doubt. After a moment, he spoke again. "You . . . you must care for my Mab for me, my sweet Mab."

Alexandra heard Mab stifle a sob. She hung in the doorway, wiping at her eyes with a handkerchief.

". . . Jon. You must care for him always."

"Of course Father. You know I'd never see him go without whatever he fancies."

". . . Spoiled the boy, I know I did," Dunnon went on. "But . . . but loved him like I loved you."

Hunter pressed his lips to his father's hand. "Don't worry about Jon. He'll always have a home here with Alexandra and me, I swear it."

"Jon . . ." Dunnon sighed. He opened his eyes, confused. "Where is he? Jon?"

Alexandra stood. "I'll get him."

"You stay," Mab said from the doorway. "You two stay with him. We said our good-byes. I'll fetch Master Jon."

Five minutes later Jon walked into the bedchamber. He wore nothing but a pair of wrinkled red breeches. His hair, usually pulled neatly into a queue, fell down his back like a sheet of ebony rain.

Hunter rose to let Jon have his seat on the bed. Alexandra rose with him, slipping her hand into his.

The Earl of Dunnon lay with his eyes closed. His chest still rose and fell, but irregularly. It was obvious he was struggling with each breath.

Jon looked to Hunter. Hunter nodded.

Jon covered the earl's hand with his. "You sent for me, sir?"

"Jon?"

"Yes. It's me."

The old man nodded. Then his eyes flickered open. "Wanted to see you one last time."

"I never beat you at loo," Jon said softly.

The old man, his eyes closing again, smiled smugly. "Because I cheated, Jon."

Jon smiled sadly. "You didn't cheat. I let you win."

"Liar."

Jon laughed, his hushed voice oddly comforting to them all. "So I am."

Hunter's father took Jon's hand and with his last bit of strength, brought it to his hollow chest. It rose and slowly fell and then didn't rise again.

Mab cried out.

Alexandra brushed Hunter's shoulder with her fingertips. "I'm sorry," she whispered, not knowing what else to say that could comfort him.

Jon sat on the edge of the bed for a long moment and then gently pulled his hand out from under the Earl of Dunnon's hand. Looking one last time on the old man's face he covered it with the sheet and rose. He walked past Hunter and Alexandra toward the door. "If you need me, I'll be in my chamber."

Hunter and Alexandra quietly stood there listening to the sound of Mab's soft crying. Outside a rooster crowed. Soon it would be dawn.

Hunter sat at the long mahogany dining table long after Jon, Alexandra and several overnight guests had taken their leave. A green glass decanter of brandy wine rested in front of him, but the glass was empty. Liquor wasn't going to solve his problems. Headaches lasting three days had convinced him of that.

Hunter wet his finger and ran it along the rim of the glass, listening to the hum. Earlier in the day, he had buried his father in the small churchyard beyond the south walls of the castle. He had laid him to rest in a grave among many graves. The funeral guests had called Hunter, Dunnon. Lord Dunnon. The Earl of Dunnon.

Hunter still couldn't believe his father was dead. And now the true weight of the earl's responsibilities were on his shoulders. Crossing his arms on the table, he lowered his head to rest his forehead on his forearms. He'd promised Alexandra he'd come up to bed and turn in early with her, but he couldn't bring himself to go upstairs.

"Master Geoffry?"

Hunter lifted his head to see Mab in the doorway. She was dressed in her cloak with a bag tucked under her arm. Now that the earl was dead—she had told Hunter—it was time for her to retire to her daughter's cottage in Dunnon village. Tonight she would sleep there.

"Mab?"

She stepped into the large dining hall and closed the door behind her. "I got something to say to you, Master Geoffry. Been thinking about it since your father died."

Hunter motioned for her to take the chair to his right but she shook her head. "He should have told you, but he didn't."

"Told me what, Mab?"

She hung her head. "I thought sure he would say. I never thought he'd go to the grave with it."

"What Mab, what are you talking about?"

She fussed at the cloth bag she held in her hand. "You take a look at it for yourself. You do what you think is best. I don't know that it's right to go against a dead man's wishes when he makes it obvious what they are, but . . ."

Hunter groaned, running his hand through his hair. "Mab, what are you babbling about? I don't have the patience or the energy tonight."

She lifted her head, her gaze meeting his. "I'm talking about a piece of paper you got to see."

He turned in the chair. "A paper?"

"Aye. In his desk. Pull out the center drawer. She sticks, so pull hard. Look on the bottom."

Hunter rose. "Some sort of document. You're not making any sense, Mab."

She turned away from him and shuffled back to the door. "Do what you will . . . what you think is right. I don't know. I just don't know."

Hunter followed her out. Mab, who had always been so sensible, was now making no sense at all. She was in shock no doubt. "I'll have someone take you down to the village in a coach."

She waved him away. "I need the walk, Master Geoffry. Now you see to the paper. Destroy it. That's what he told me to do, but I couldn't."

Hunter opened the door for her. It was the first of May. Already, the air smelled of turned soil and springtime. "Good night then," he said.

She shuffled out the door and he closed it behind her.

For a moment Hunter stood in the empty hallway. What document could Mab have possibly been speaking of? What could his father have wanted her to destroy?

What better way to know than to go see?

Hunter took a candle from a sconce on the wall and wandered down one hallway and then down the next, his footsteps echoing in his head. Dunnon Castle was so large, so empty.

Inside his father's library he lit the candlabrums on the mantel, then one on the desk. He sat in his father's chair and rolled out the center drawer. As Mab said, it wouldn't open all the way, but he yanked hard on it. A piece of wood cracked and the drawer came free.

Hunter dumped the contents of the drawer onto the desk, his curiosity piqued. How odd of his father to hide something from him. To his knowledge he had never done so before.

Sure enough, there was a flat square of leather

tacked to the underside of the wooden drawer. Hunter pulled it away and opened it. Inside was a slip of foolscap. He quickly unfolded it and scanned the slanted handwriting, faded by time.

A marriage certificate?

He reread it. Horace Geoffry Rordan, Earl of Dunnon married to a woman called Mary? It was dated May of 1683.

Mary? Who was Mary?

He read it a third time. The woman's last name was blurred, apparently on purpose. He pulled the candlestand closer to shed a stronger light on the faded document. "Mary She-Whispers?" he murmured aloud.

Then it came to him. It struck just as hard as if a man had hit him on the head with a warclub.

Mary. Mary She-Whispers. Mary, She-Who-Whispers-To-The-Wind.

"Jon!" Hunter leaped up out of his father's chair and ran for the door, the marriage certificate still in his hand. "Jon! Alexandra!"

He ran down the dark hallways to the grand staircase and shouted up. "Jon! Alexandra! Come here!"

A door opened upstairs.

"Geoffry?" Alexandra called.

"Alexandra, get Jon. Bring him down here. Immediately! Father's office!"

Alexandra frowned. What did Hunter want? He was driving her nearly to distraction with worry. Since his father's death he had been even more sullen and preoccupied. Nothing she had been able to say or do had seemed to help. Her life was falling apart around her and there seemed to be nothing she could do about it.

Alexandra lifted the skirts of her mourning gown and hurried down the hallway. She rapped on Jon's door. "Jon."

"Alex?" She heard footsteps and then he opened the door.

"Jon, Hunter wants us downstairs in his father's office."

Jon screwed up his face in a grimace. "Now? I'm dressing to go. I've a lady expecting a late-night visit. He knows that."

She shrugged. "He said *now*. There's something wrong, I just know it."

Jon rolled his eyes heavenward. He was only half dressed. He wore his stock loose around his neck and had not yet donned a shirtwaist and coat. "All right," he sighed. "All right. His father's just died. I suppose we can amuse him a little longer." He stepped back into his room. "Tell him I'll be there in a trice."

Alexandra turned back down the hall and went downstairs. She walked through the dark corridors to where the light shone from the Earl of Dunnon's study. She slipped inside. Hunter stood near the cold fireplace, a piece of paper in his hand. "What is it? What's wrong?"

He held up a finger. "Wait for Jon. He's coming?"

"Yes." She stared at him. He had such a peculiar look on his face, one she didn't recognize. What was wrong with Hunter? Was he losing his mind? "Jon said he'd be down in a minute," she said softly to the man who was her husband, but seemed like a stranger.

"Sit." He pointed to the chair behind the desk. She went to it and sat down, noticing quills and loose papers strewn across the desk.

The sound of heels hitting the floor echoed down the hallway and Jon appeared. "What the hell is it now, Hunter? You know I've plans."

Hunter waved the sheet of paper. He was grinning a grin that stretched from ear to ear. "Guess what I've found." He looked at Jon and then at Alexandra and then back at Jon again.

"What?" she asked.

He still fluttered the paper. "A marriage certificate."

"What? Whose? Make sense, Geoffry!"

"Our father's. Your mother's."

Jon looked at Alexandra. She rose out of the chair. "What?" she whispered.

Jon looked shocked, too shocked to speak.

"Tell us," Alexandra urged softly.

Hunter set the paper down on the desk and struck it with his hand. He gave a little laugh. "Our father, your mother, She-Who-Whispers-To-The-Wind. They were married."

"No," Jon managed. "It's not true."

"It is true. I have the legal document here in my hand."

Alexandra had never seen Jon so utterly caught off guard. He grasped the door frame, his knuckles turning white.

Alexandra lifted the document off the desk and scanned it quickly. It was indeed a marriage certificate. In 1683 the Earl of Dunnon had married a woman named Mary. She looked up at Jon. The earl had married his Shawnee mother before Jon was born.

It all came so quickly to her that she sat down. "Jon was your father's son."

"Yes." Hunter was still grinning like a madman.

"He didn't find me wandering in the woods. He kidnapped me," Jon said to himself, but loud enough for Alexandra to hear. "He took me from my mother. He was ashamed of me, but he couldn't leave me behind." He looked up at Hunter. "Then you and I, we're brothers."

"Half. He married your mother first. Then mine. Of course he didn't marry mine legally. You're father's only true son, his only legitimate son."

Alexandra covered her mouth with her hand in shock. Legally, Hunter was the bastard, not Jon.

After a moment of inability to speak, Jon seemed to gain control of himself. He stood in the doorway, an odd smile crossing his face. "My father didn't abandon me. He loved me enough to bring me here."

"He never told you who he was!" Hunter shouted. "He lied to you, to me, to my mother. For Christ's sake, he married my mother when he was married to your mother! He was ashamed of the color of your skin, Jon, of the Shawnee woman he'd loved. He brought you here to be a servant!"

Jon shook his head. "But I wasn't his servant. He never treated me like one. He treated me like his son and now we know why."

"And that's it?"

"I've lived a blessed life. I have him to thank for that."

Hunter shook his head. "You're a forgiving man, Jon."

He shrugged. "Why not be? He's dead. Anger will do us no good now. We all have our failings." He turned and started out the door.

"Wait. Where are you going?" Hunter asked, walking after him.

"I told you." Jon adjusted his Irish lace stock. "I've an appointment with a lady. Now tear up the paper."

"Tear it up?" Hunter grabbed Jon's arm. "You don't understand." He looked at Alexandra. "Neither of you understands what this means."

Alexandra came across the room and reached out to touch Hunter's shoulder. She didn't like the tone of his voice. He was scaring her. "What does it mean?" she made herself ask him.

"It means I'm free. We're all free."

Chapter Twenty-eight

"Free?" Jon wiped his mouth with the back of his hand. "What the hell are you talking about? We've all had a long damned day, Geoffry, we're not in the mood for your word games."

"Don't you see?" Hunter slapped him in the chest with the palm of his hand. "You're the Earl of Dunnon, not me. Father was legally married to your mother, never to mine." He was grinning. "It's not my title, not my lands, not my money that I can't even find where the hell it is!" He laughed, hitting his thigh with his fist. "None of it's mine, Jon! It's all yours! Every thumping bit of it!"

"You can't do this . . ." Jon insisted. "It's not what Father wanted." He tried to grab the marriage certificate from Hunter's hand, but Hunter pulled back. "He wanted you to be his heir, not me."

"So he should have thought about that before he married She-Who-Whispers-To-The-Wind. He should have thought about that before he conceived a child, before he decided to return to England without his wife."

Jon leaned against the door frame, tipping his head back, closing his eyes. "You know what you're saying here?" he asked gravely.

"I know exactly what I'm saying." He gripped Jon's arm. "I'm saying you're my brother, my elder brother, and now this estate is your problem."

Alexandra watched the two brothers' gazes meet and lock.

"You don't have to do this, Hunter," Jon said, his voice barely audible. "I'm happy with my life as it is. I'll take nothing away from you. I love you too much." He grabbed a handful of Hunter's lined shirt. "Destroy the document. I'll never say a word. Alex will never say a word."

"You're missing the point, Jon. I don't want it. I don't want any of it, I never wanted any of it, and now I don't have to take it. You're the man Father always wanted me to be. But because of some silly prejudices he carried hidden, he tried to alter his past. He tried to pretend you weren't his legal heir. Damned if the man didn't take his secret to his grave."

Jon shook his head again and again. "I don't know about this. I just don't know."

Hunter took his hand and squeezed it. "Help me, Brother. Help me out of this mess," he begged. "I'll die here. I'll die inside. Be the man our father wanted. For him. For me." Hunter turned to Alexandra. "And you know what this means to you, don't you, sweeting?''

Alexandra could do nothing but stand there, her arms limp at her sides. ''What?'' she asked.

''Our marriage can be annulled. I deceived you. You were betrothed and then married to the Viscount Ashton. That's him.'' He pointed to Jon. ''Not me.''

Alexandra felt her jaw drop. He was serious. He was utterly serious. She looked to Jon. ''Will you excuse us a moment, Jon?''

''Alex . . . Geoffry.''

Alexandra walked to the door, giving Jon a push. ''Excuse us,'' she repeated more loudly. She could feel her heart pounding beneath her breast. She was short of breath. Hunter didn't love her anymore. He didn't want her!

Jon took one look at Hunter and strode out of the room. Alexandra slid the door closed behind him and then turned around and leaned against it. ''You no longer wish to be married to me?'' she said, her voice sharp and cold. She was so angry, so hurt, that it was hard to speak.

''It's for the best. I'll submit the necessary documents before I go. Then you'll be free to remarry.'' He shrugged. ''Marry Jon if you like. That makes the most sense.''

She couldn't believe what he was saying. Her first instinct was to reach out and strike him across the face. How dare he turn the love they shared into a simple matter of whose name was on a marriage document!

''Go?'' She could hear the hysteria rising in her voice. ''Where are you going?''

"I'm going back to the colonies. I don't belong here, not anymore. Perhaps I never belonged here. I'm talking about freeing you, Alex. This wasn't working. It would never work."

She touched her hand to her cheek. "What are you talking about, Hunter?"

"I'm talking about setting you free. I'm sorry I've hurt you. I'm sorry I've made you unhappy these last weeks, but it needn't continue."

She stepped away from the door, staring at the face she loved, the man she thought she knew. "You could just leave me like that?" Her hand slid over her middle. Her flux was late. She might be carrying his child. She hadn't told him because she wanted to be sure. She stared at him. "You could just walk away from me?"

He turned his face away so that she couldn't see his expression. "It's what's best," he said coolly.

She watched him walk to the paneled door and slide it open. She was in such shock that she suddenly felt faint. *Hunter's leaving me*, she thought dully. *He doesn't love me. He must never have loved me.*

She laid her hand on the desk for support. She'd been strong enough to survive an Indian attack and all those weeks in the forest, she could certainly survive this. She had to. She had to be strong, if not for herself, then for the child whose father was about to abandon him.

"Hunter—"

He held up a finger, but he still didn't turn to face her. "Let's talk about the particulars later, shall we?"

He was being so stubborn. He seemed so sure of what he wanted . . . and what he didn't want. What he didn't want was her.

Alexandra felt a sob rise in her throat. Where had she gone wrong? Where had they gone wrong? They had seemed so sure of each other that night in the fort after Cain had died.

She looked up to see him walking through the door. He was leaving . . . he was leaving her . . . he was leaving England. She wanted to run after him, to shout to him, to make him turn around and tell her to her face that he didn't love her anymore. But she hurt too much. She had too much pride. She'd not beg. If he didn't love her, then she'd let him go.

His footsteps echoed in the hallway and Alexandra turned away and buried her face in her hands as the tears fell down her cheeks.

Alexandra paced back and forth across the Turkish carpet of her mother's antechamber off her sleeping quarters. Unable to spend another night in Dunnon Castle, Alexandra had fled to London, but not to her parents' house. She knew she would get no sympathy there, nor an ounce of understanding. It was Roland who had taken her in, that morning. It was Roland who had held her as she cried for all she was certain she had lost. It was Roland who had been insisting for days that it was time she ceased hiding and faced whatever her future would be.

For two weeks Alexandra had remained sequestered in Roland's town house. She had seen no one but him and Mark, and Jon who had come to visit twice. Jon said Hunter was absolutely serious about giving up his rights as the Earl of Dunnon. The marriage document of the late Earl of Dunnon and his wife, Jon's mother, Mary, had been filed with the proper authorities. Jon would be the new Earl of Dunnon.

Hunter had not come to see her. He'd not even sent a note, though Jon had told him where she was. Jon seemed to be as mystified by Hunter's behavior as Alexandra was, but he insisted she needed to go and see him, to talk some sense into him. He seemed to think that Hunter honestly thought she didn't want him, but rather the life she would have led as the Countess of Dunnon. When Alexandra said he obviously didn't love her, Jon had said she was a fool to think that. He said she and Hunter loved each other too much to let miscommunication and stubbornness ruin both their lives.

Alexandra heard the rapid footsteps of her mother as she came down the corridor. Alexandra had put off speaking with her parents long enough. As she turned to face the countess, Alexandra held her gloved hands clasped. The door swung open. She nodded cordially. "Mother."

The Countess of Monthrop threw up a heavily perfumed lace handkerchief. "Oh, thank heavens you're safe, my dear daughter. Thank heavens that beast hasn't harmed you!" She wrapped her arms around her daughter and brushed her lips near her cheek, taking care not to muss her own freshly painted lips.

"Where's Father?" Alexandra asked as her mother released her.

"Oh, he wanted to be here, but he had business to attend to. He asked me to make his apologies for him."

"Of course he did," Alexandra murmured. "His business has always been more important than us, hasn't it?"

"Now I'm just going to ignore that remark, Daughter. I know how difficult this has all been for you." She fluttered toward a brocade-upholstered red settee. "Oh, goodness, I see Mary Jane has brought refreshment." She sat down. "Will you sit with me, Mary Alexandra? We've your future to discuss."

Alexandra turned to face her mother. "I'd prefer to stand."

Her mother reached for a flaky fruit pastry. "Your father said he would see you this evening at supper. He said he'd send someone for your things."

"Mother, I'm not moving back in."

The countess bit into her pastry, leaving white sugar at the corners of her rouged mouth. "Not moving in. Well, of course you are—"

"Mother, I'm staying with Roland, at least for the present."

"An unmarried woman, staying unchaperoned in a man's house!"

"I'm still married. There's been no annulment . . . at least not yet," she added sadly.

"So the rumors are true. Word is all over London. Geoffry is not the legal heir to Dunnon?"

Alexandra turned away so that she wouldn't have to look her mother directly in the eye. She could feel that lump rising in her throat that came each time she thought of Hunter. "He is not."

"Pity. I should have known it was all too good to be true, you returning home with husband in tow. But this is not something we can't get you out of. Your father is already looking into it." She wiped her mouth with the corner of a linen napkin. "I'm shocked, of course. We're all shocked."

"Mother, just because Geoffry's no longer the Earl of Dunnon doesn't mean he's no longer my husband. We've been married months. I've slept with him!"

"Unfortunate, as I said, but nothing that cannot be righted with a few pounds and a few planted rumors." She lifted her hands heavenward. "Just thank holy Jesus you didn't find yourself with child." She made a clicking sound between her teeth. "That would have been unfortunate."

Alexandra walked to the wall where a large oil portrait of her paternal grandmother hung. She ran a finger across the bottom of the frame. She was pregnant. She was certain of it now. But she hadn't told anyone, not even Roland.

"Well . . ." Her mother clapped her hands together. "Now what of Jon? Do you think he'd be willing to marry you?"

Alexandra turned around, almost too shocked to speak. "Jon?"

"He was the Viscount Ashton we betrothed our daughter to. He is the Earl of Dunnon now that his father has passed away, God rest his soul. Who better to marry you? Surely he must feel some remorse at your having been deceived by his half brother."

"Hunter—oh blast it! *Geoffry* deceived no one! It was Dunnon!"

"Who deceived whom is irrelevant now. What matters is that the trouble be settled. Let me ask you again, will Jon marry you?"

"You ask me to throw myself at the feet of a man you didn't even want in your house a month's time ago?"

The countess fluttered her eyelashes. "I don't recall—"

"Mother!" Alexandra could feel the numbness she'd felt for the last two weeks beginning to wear off. Suddenly she was angry, angrier than she had ever been in her life. *"You don't recall standing in this room and telling me Jon was not welcome at the masquerade ball?"*

"I believe I've had quite enough of your insolence, Daughter. Are you telling me he wouldn't marry you? What if we gave a second dowry? This wouldn't be the first time a Lambert bought a title and Countess is well worth purchasing, I can tell you that."

Alexandra just stood there, staring at her mother. What kind of world was this she was living in that a mother could be more concerned about the title her daughter would marry into than the character of the man she would marry? How is that a mother who thought as she did of Jon a few weeks ago could now see him as a suitable bridegroom?

Alexandra turned away. Her mother started to speak again, but Alexandra didn't hear what she was saying.

This isn't where Hunter wants to be, she thought to herself. *Well this isn't where I want to be either. England is no longer my homeland, these people are no longer my family. I want to go home, home to Maryland, home with Hunter if only he'll have me.*

"Mary Alexandra! Where are you going? Mary Alexandra?"

Alexandra walked out of her mother's chamber and down the hall. She had to find Hunter. She had to tell him how she felt. If he didn't want her, then they would part. But she had to know. Once she knew where she stood, she would make a decision as to how she would raise their child. If she had to, she'd go to the colonies alone. She'd take her child and she'd make a life for him there where he would be free of this, of all this.

"Alexandra?"

Alexandra walked out of her mother's house, lifted her skirts, and stepped into Roland's waiting coach. "Dunnon Castle," she told the footman. "As quickly as you can get me there."

The coach rolled down the street. Alexandra never even bothered to look back at her mother.

A few hours later Alexandra arrived at Dunnon

Castle. The ride out of London and into the country had seemed to stretch for days, but finally she was there.

She jumped out of the vehicle, not even taking the time to wait for the footman's aid. She took the front steps two at a time, her azure cloak flapping behind her. She marched straight into the house. "Where's the master?" she demanded of the first servant she came to. It was a woman polishing silver wall sconces in the hallway.

"Master Jon?"

"Geoffry. Where's Geoffry?"

"We haven't seen much of him, my lady. Not since Master Jon—"

"Jon. Where is he, then? Do you know where he is?" she stated impatiently.

The young woman pointed down the hallway. "The earl's library, ma'am. Said he wasn't to be disturbed," she called after Alexandra who had already walked away.

Alexandra marched into the library without even bothering to knock. Jon looked up from behind a pile of ledgers. He smiled. "Alex!"

"Where's Hunter?" she demanded.

He got a sly smile on his face. "I was wondering how long it would take you to come to your senses. Hunter, he's too damned wooden-headed, but you, I knew you'd come around."

"Where is he?" She pushed her dark hair back off her face. It had come loose from its pins to fall down her back in waves. "Just tell me."

"The gamekeeper's cottage. Apparently the man accidentally killed himself early this morning while hunting. Got drunk and fell on his musket, the sorry whoreson. Hunter went to his cottage to clean out the man's belongings. Said he'd go mad if he didn't get some physical exercise."

Alexandra turned and ran.

"Take a horse. You know where the cottage is?" Jon called after her.

"I'll find it!" she hollered back.

Ten minutes later she was riding through the woods on a grey gelding. At a gallop she rode down the path in the direction the stable boy had given her.

"Not far," he'd said. "Just down the road a piece. A shame what happened to poor Kells. Blew his face off, we hear. You'll find the cottage easy enough."

Sure enough, less than a mile into the woods, the path broke into a clearing. Nestled among the gigantic oak trees was a tiny cottage. A lone horse stood tied to a tree—Hunter's horse.

"Hunter?" Alexandra leaped off the gelding. Her cloak caught on the saddle as she came down. She untied the ribbon to the basque of her silk cloak and left it hanging. "Hunter!" she shouted again. "Are you here? Come out, coward! Come out and face me!"

"Alex?" He appeared from around the back of the cottage. He was wearing leather breeches, a lawn shirt open to the waist and knee-high moccasins.

"Son of a stinking whore's cur!" she shouted as she hurled herself at him. "How dare you!

How dare you!"

"Ouch! Damn! Stop!" He lifted his hands to fend off her blows. "Have you taken leave of your senses, woman?"

She shoved him so hard that he nearly toppled backward. "Just say it. Say you don't love me and I'll go!"

He ran one hand through his hair. He looked terrible. His cheeks were gaunt, his eyes bloodshot. "This is best. You'll see," he tried to tell her.

"Best for who? You never asked me what I wanted!"

"I—"

"Shut up! I'm the one doing the talking!" She pointed a finger at him. "You never asked me what I wanted—not once since we arrived in London. I know I told you this was where we belonged, but I was wrong."

"Alex—"

She pushed her hand into his chest. "I'm not done," she hollered. "Let me say it! You never asked me what I wanted, not in all these months. Why not? You knew I was unhappy but you never asked why."

"I thought—"

"I was unhappy because I hated it here and I didn't know how to tell you. I was unhappy because I was the one who insisted this was where we belonged, only I was wrong. I was unhappy because I wanted to go back to Maryland only I couldn't admit it, not to myself, not to you. I didn't want to ruin your life, Hunter. I wanted to be your wife, the woman you would need here at Dunnon, only I knew I couldn't be her. Maybe once, but not now. But I loved you too much. I didn't tell you because I knew you were having such a hard time with your father's affairs. I didn't want to add to your troubles." She took a deep breath. "There. I said it." She touched the copper wedding band she still wore on her finger. "Now just tell me you don't love me and I'll go. Just tell me."

"Alex . . ."

She hung her head. She couldn't bring herself to look up at him. She loved him so much. Why did it have to be like this?

"Alex, did anyone ever tell you that you talk too much?"

She looked up at him. He was smiling. He was holding his arms out to her.

"Oh Hunter," she cried as she flung herself into his arms. "Hunter, I'm so sorry. I'm so sorry for everything."

"Hush, hush," he murmured in her ear as he covered her tear-stained face with kisses. "I've been an ass. I'm the one who should be saying I'm sorry. Just tell me you'll go with me. Tell me we'll go home to Maryland together."

She was laughing; she was crying. "Yes, yes. Home, home where we can raise our child."

Hunter grabbed her arms and then lifted her chin with the tip of his finger. "What are you telling me, sweeting?"

She smiled, wiping her tears away with the back of her hand. "What does it sound like I'm saying? You didn't think you could tumble with me all these months and not plant your seed, did you?"

It was Hunter's turn to laugh as he pulled her against him, kissing her soundly on the lips. "You certain you can travel?" he asked, his voice choked with emotion.

"If we go soon, yes."

"There's a ship leaving the end of the week."

She was smiling up at him. "Not soon enough."

"Ah, Alex, Alex, how could I have been so stupid? Will you forgive me? I wanted so badly to give you the life I took away from you when I left you that night at our betrothal party so many years ago. I wanted it so badly that I lost track of the reason."

"The reason?"

"To make you happy. To make up for what I did."

"Hunter." She lifted up on her toes, wrapped her arms around his neck, and kissed him. It was a hard, demanding kiss. She had missed him so much. She had needed him for so long.

He slid his hand up to cup her breast as his tongue delved deep to taste her. "Alex," he crooned.

"Hunter." She ran her hand over his corded shoulders, remembering every curve of his muscular body. She pressed her hips to his. "Hunter, make love to me," she whispered between his kisses. "Please. I need you."

"Here?"

She brought her hand up to boldly caress the bulge in his tight breeches. "Yes, here," she whispered, her voice throaty with desire. "Now. I've had enough of Geoffry. I want Hunter. I want my wildman back."

He groaned as she caressed him. "You'll be the death of me," he muttered as he swept her into his arms.

"You can hope," she teased.

"Inside?" he asked, pressing his lips to the valley between her breasts.

"No. Here." She slipped her hand inside his shirt to caress his bare chest. "Here outside beneath the trees. Here where we can smell the wind."

He knelt, still holding her in his arms. She kissed him again and again, driven by a passion she'd never experienced before. She wanted no soft sweet lovemaking, not now. She wanted to possess and be possessed.

Hunter yanked at the laces of her stomacher, freeing her breasts from the confines of her bodice. He took her nipple into his mouth and nipped at it with his teeth.

She moaned, arching her back, running her hands through his sleek auburn hair. "Yes," she whispered. "That feels so good."

He lowered her to the ground—her urgency was contagious. She pulled at the leather laces that bound his breeches. Releasing his member, she stroked it, unabashed.

He lifted her skirts. Later would be time for wooing. Now the two wanted nothing but fulfillment. Their hunger had to be satiated after so many weeks of yearning.

Alexandra pulled up her skirts and raised her hips up to meet his groin. She could feel the heat of her lust for him pulsing through her veins. Her heart was pounding, her nostrils filled with the secret scent of desire.

"Now, Hunter," she begged.

"I don't want to hurt you."

She laughed, rolling her head in the dry leaves left behind by winter winds. "Give me release and I'll pain no longer."

Kissing her softly on the lips, he lifted his body over hers and took her with one stroke. She raised herself up, crying out in pleasure.

"Hunter," she whispered in his ear as her body rose and fell with his. "Hunter I love you. I'll love you always."

"Always," he managed as he moved faster. "Always we'll have each other."

Alexandra dug her nails into the flesh of his shoulders. Her entire being was alive with the sensation of pleasure, her heart filled to bursting with the confidence of their love.

One final stroke and both cried out in unison, finally fulfilled, finally satisfied. Panting, Hunter rolled off her into the new sweet-smelling grass of springtime. They were both laughing.

"You think we'd never done it before," he teased.

"You'd think. And us a married couple. Shocking!"

Suddenly both heard the sound of hoofbeats approaching. Alexandra sat up and began to pull at the ties of her bodice. Hunter leaped to his feet and yanked up his breeches. "You stay here," he said as he started around the corner of the cottage that shielded them from the main road. "I'll see who it is."

He disappeared around the corner and just as Alexandra was standing to brush the leaves off the back of her gown she heard Hunter call to her.

"Make yourself decent," he hollered. "But it's just Jon."

Jon was swinging out of the saddle as she came around the corner of the cottage and looped her arm through Hunter's. Her clothing and hair were such a mess that she knew Jon had to know what they'd been about. But she didn't care. All that mattered was that she and Hunter were going home to Maryland, together.

She looked to Jon, but then the smile fell from her face. There was something wrong. She could tell by the look on his face.

"What is it?" Hunter asked.

Jon was panting from the hard ride.

"You're not going to believe this," he exclaimed. "The high sheriff's come for you."

Hunter frowned. "Come for me, for what pray tell? She's still my wife." He laughed. "I've still the right to lay her."

Jon wiped his lips with the back of his hand as if he had a bad taste in his mouth. "This is no jest, Hunter. I tell you they've come for you, the sheriff and soldiers. You're to be arrested."

Alexandra gripped Hunter's arm suddenly more afraid than she'd ever been in her life. "For what? Tell us!"

"The murder of Captain John Cain."

Chapter Twenty-nine

Alexandra could feel the weight of the world suddenly crashing down on her shoulders. Her hand went instinctively to her flat stomach where her child, their child, grew. "There must be a mistake," she said shakily. "The man was an animal. He raped and murdered women, he sold them to savages!"

"Yes, but John Cain was the lord chancellor's nephew, great-nephew, something."

"What difference does that make?" Alexandra was struggling to understand. *Hunter arrested? Thrown into Newgate. They wouldn't!*

"It makes a great deal of difference, my innocent one." Hunter brushed his lips across her forehead. He looked back to Jon. "So they wait for me?"

"Yes. I told them you'd be back shortly and that they were free to wait outside. I left through the servants' quarters and came as quickly as I could."

Alexandra hung to Hunter's arm. "You'll have to go and explain yourself. You'll have to tell why you did it. There'll be a trial. No one would convict you!" She was trying to convince herself as much as she was trying to convince them.

Jon glanced at Alexandra. "You're missing the point here, Alex. It's doubtful there'll be a fair trial, if there's any trial at all."

Hunter pushed a lock of red hair back behind his ear. "Christ's bones, most likely I'll just be left in Newgate to rot. It would be nothing personal— politics."

Alexandra could feel the tears stinging her eyes, but she fought them. How could Hunter remain so calm? Moments ago they were talking about sailing to the colonies to begin a new life together and now he was contemplating a lifetime prison sentence or hanging. "What do we do?" She looked from Jon to Hunter. "We can't let them take you. I almost lost you once, Hunter." She set her jaw with determination. "I'll not lose you again."

Hunter looked to Jon.

Both men were silent. As Alexandra watched their faces, she could almost see the wheels of their minds turning.

"Angry I took your title, Hunter?" Jon asked slyly.

"Um-hmmm."

"Angrier I could well take your wife?"

"Most certainly." Now Hunter was smiling.

"How's your acting, brother?"

"Fair to middlin'. Yours?"

Jon's eyes narrowed daringly. "Better than yours, I'd vow."

"What are you two talking about?" Alexandra demanded. "You have to tell me!"

Jon grabbed Alexandra's arm and started for the gamekeeper's cottage. "Inside. Hurry. We've only got a few minutes to make plans and then I'll have to get back to the house to set things up."

"You got a musket, Hunter?"

"On my horse." Hunter sprinted for his mount. Jon ushered Alexandra inside the cottage.

"What's going on? Tell me!"

"Get inside," Jon ordered, pushing her ahead of him. "We can save his hide, but we're going to need your help . . ."

Ten minutes later Jon walked out of the gamekeeper's cottage, mounted his horse, and rode off through the woods toward Dunnon Castle. Hunter and Alexandra stood arm and arm in the shadows of the oak trees that stretched high above their heads and sheltered the cottage.

"You ready?" Hunter asked calmly.

"I'm scared."

"But are you ready?"

She turned to face him so that she could look deep into his hazel eyes. "I can do this."

He squeezed her hands. "I know you can."

"I just don't want you hurt. If anything goes wrong . . ." She sighed. They had no choice. She knew that this was the best plan they could have come up with considering the circumstances.

"You want to see pain?" he said gently. "See a man trapped in a fetid cell in Newgate prison with no one but the rats and the vermin for company. I'll not go, Alex. I'll die before they take the sun away from me, before they take you and our child."

They kissed one last time, his lips lingering over hers. "I love you," he whispered. "Always."

She smiled up at him, taking his strength and making it her own. "I'll love you always."

"Something goes wrong, you do what you think's best. Jon will always see you cared for. Stay here and let him love our child. It's doubtful he'll ever have any of his own. Hell, marry him if you like. He'd be my second choice for you right after me."

"I couldn't do that. This isn't my home, not any longer."

"Then go back to Shawnee country and raise our son or daughter. You'll always be welcome among Creeping Turtle's people."

She pressed her fingertip to his lips, silencing him. "Don't speak of it. It's ill luck. Nothing's going to happen. We're going to be together."

He took one last look at her, touching her cheek with the back of his hand, brushing a stray lock of dark hair off her shoulder. "It's time."

Hand in hand they walked to the horses. Hunter boosted her up into the saddle. Somewhere she had lost her straw bonnet—on the ground where they'd made love, no doubt.

Hunter pushed the reins into her hands. He gave her a wink and flashed that charming smile she had fallen in love with. Then he slapped her gelding's hind quarters and the horse bolted. Alexandra leaned forward in the saddle, hell-bent on Dunnon Castle.

She rode straight up the woods road through the barnyard toward the front door of the castle. Sure enough, soldiers on horses and a high sheriff waited. She pushed her horse through theirs. "Jon! Jon!" she cried.

On cue, Jon appeared in the front doorway. "Alex." He came running down the stone steps. "Alex, are you all right, what's happened, love?"

She pushed back her hair, loosened and tangled from making love on the ground with Hunter. "He attacked me," she cried. "Geoffry! I went to say good-bye, to tell him I was in love with you and that we were to wed." She grasped Jon's hands, leaning against him for support.

"But what?" Jon stared into her face, utterly serious. "Tell me, Alex. Tell me what the whoreson cur has done."

She hung her head; miraculously tears began to slip down her cheeks. She could hear the soldiers talking in hushed tones among themselves. They were obviously catching every word. "He . . . Geoffry wouldn't listen. I told him no. I told him our marriage was to be annulled, but he said I was still his! He said—" She dropped her head to his shoulder. "Oh, Jon."

Hoofbeats thundered as a rider approached Dunnon Castle at a full gallop. Alexandra looked up to see Hunter riding straight for them, his hair blowing off his shoulders, a musket cradled in his arms. The only thing that appeared different about him now was the coat he wore pulled high to his neck. From the ground, his eyes wide and wild, he truly looked like a madman.

"Alexandra!" Hunter shouted as he came into voice range. "Come back here. You're my wife! Mine to do as I please with! He'll not have you! I swear by God I'll kill you both first!"

The high sheriff wheeled his horse around, but before he could ride toward Hunter, Jon darted forward, dragging Alexandra with him and cutting off the sheriff's path. "She's mine," he cried venomously. "It's all mine now, bastard! Bastard son! My title, my lands, my monies—" He grabbed Alexandra and kissed her hard on the mouth. "My woman!"

Hunter pulled back hard on the reins, and his horse reared to a halt. "No. You can take everything else, but not the jade. She's mine. I'll not give her up!"

"Don't do this!" Alexandra screamed, pulling away from Jon, attempting to add to the confusion. "Please don't do this!"

She heard the sheriff behind her give his soldiers orders to take Hunter. Another moment and all would be lost.

"Give her to me, or I take her," Hunter challenged. He swung his musket with one hand, directly toward Jon.

Jon moved so quickly that Alexandra saw nothing but a flash of flesh and steel. He drew his pistol from the waistband of his violet-colored breeches and fired, his shot echoing Hunter's.

Hunter flew backwards off the horse.

Alexandra screamed, not for the sake of the scene they had orchestrated but out of true fear. Blood, she had seen blood . . .

The horse reared as the rider flew off his back. Alexandra ran for Hunter. "Oh my God! Oh my God!" she cried.

The horse thundered past her.

"Alexandra!" Jon hollered after her.

She ran for Hunter and fell to her knees beside his still body. He was lying face down in the dirt. There was blood, blood everywhere!

Jon knelt beside her, brushing his mouth against her ear as he reached out to touch Hunter. "A game," he whispered. "Just a game, sweetheart."

"Oh God," Jon groaned loudly. "I'm so sorry, Alex. I've killed him. I've killed my brother!" He threw himself across Hunter's back, pulling at his dark coat.

The soldiers rode up and formed a circle around them. The high sheriff dismounted, coming to stand directly behind Jon and Alexandra.

"Is this him? Is this Geoffry Rordan?" he asked.

Jon lifted his head from Hunter's body. Alexandra could have sworn she saw real tears. "Yes. It's him. I didn't mean to kill him. You have to believe me. He fired first. I had to protect myself. I had to protect the lady."

"He fired first," one of the soldiers echoed. "I saw him. The horseman raised his musket first."

Alexandra could do nothing but keep her face buried in her hands. Her heart was racing. She was petrified Hunter was truly hurt. She was petrified the sheriff would not believe what he had seen.

The sheriff shuffled his feet uncomfortably. "Is

he dead, my Lord Dunnon?"

Jon showed his bare hands now covered in blood. "Dead. My brother's dead," he muttered as if in shock. "It's not my fault my father lied. It's not my fault I was the heir and not him."

The sheriff looked to his men. "We'll need to take the body."

"No!" Alexandra screamed, throwing herself across Hunter dramatically. "He's dead! His body must be prepared for a decent burial. You can't take him! I won't let you." She lifted her face staring at Jon. "And you!" She smacked him hard across the face. "You killed him! You killed my Geoffry."

Jon stood. "You said you loved me. You said you never cared for him."

"Go away," she cried. "Go, all of you!" She laid her cheek on Hunter's warm back. "Leave me be! Leave me to my grief."

Jon turned to the sheriff. "It was self-defense, you saw it yourself," he said.

The sheriff nodded, glancing down at Hunter's still body one last time. "Self-defense. Aye. There'll be no need to waste taxes hanging the poor bastard." He turned toward his horse, grasping the reins in his gloved hands. "Men!" He mounted. "There'll be a report filed, Lord Dunnon, but no charges." He lifted his reins. "I'm sorry for your loss."

Alexandra looked up at the sheriff through teary eyes. He was actually leaving!

"Mistress." The sheriff touched his large brimmed wool hat and then turned his horse around and rode away, the soldiers following behind him.

"Hunter," Alexandra whispered. She shook him gently. "Hunter, are you all right?"

"Shhht," he answered.

She felt his body move ever so slightly as he spoke.

"We have to carry it out," he whispered. "Remember, I must be dead to all. The servants mustn't know."

Servants were beginning to spill out of the house and barns now. One of the maids wept.

Jon stood by the front steps. "Malcolm," he called. "You help me carry him inside." Malcolm was the manservant Hunter and Jon had grown up with. He could be trusted. "Caleb, run for Mab in the village. She'll prepare his body for burial. I want no man, woman, or child to touch the body," he ordered harshly. "That is a direct order from me, from Dunnon. You might as well get used to your new master now."

Another wave of whispers rose among the servants.

Jon and Malcolm walked to Hunter's body. Jon took his arms, Malcolm, his feet. Alexandra followed them up the steps through the front hall and into the antechamber off the orangery.

"That will be all," Jon told Malcolm as they entered the dimly lit room. They laid him gently on the floor, still face down.

The manservant just stood there as if in shock staring at Hunter's body.

"I said that will be all, Malcolm," Jon repeated.

Still, Malcolm didn't move.

Hunter lifted his head off the floor. "Did you hear your master, Malcolm, get the hell out of here!"

The man stumbled backward in surprise. "I knew you couldn't have done it, Master Jon. Knew you two wouldn't fight like that, not even over the mistress!"

Hunter pushed up on one elbow. His face and chest were covered with pulpy blood but it was obvious to Alexandra that it wasn't his. He was looking too pleased with himself to be in any pain.

"You must keep this to yourself to the grave, Malcolm," he whispered. "You heard the sheriff had come for me. I did indeed kill Cain back in the colonies, but he well deserved it. Now, Jon will tell you what you must do to get the lady and me out of this in one piece." Hunter smiled up at him. "Go. Do as you're told."

"Be back." Jon winked at Alexandra and followed Malcolm out of the room, taking care to close the door behind him.

"Hunter . . ." It was all Alexandra could say. She was still so frightened. She couldn't believe they had pulled it off.

Hunter sat up on the floor, wiping the blood from his face. The floorboards where he'd lain were bloody as well. "Think I went a little heavy on the stag entrails?" he asked.

She covered her mouth with her hand. "You did it," she whispered.

Jon came back into the room. "We all did it." He came to Hunter and Alexandra, grinning.

Then he frowned. "Superior acting Alex, but what the hell was the slap for?" He touched his cheek. "Ad's blood, I'll have a welt come morning for certain."

She dropped her hands to her hips. She was beginning to relax now. Everything really was going to be all right. "What was the kiss for?"

Hunter leaped up, slapping Jon hard on the shoulder with one bloody hand. "Yes, brother, what was the kiss for?"

Jon tugged on his inky black queue, still grinning smugly. "Figured it would be the only chance I ever got at a real kiss from Alexandra without having to worry about you taking my scalp for it."

Their laughter mingled as they gathered to make their final plans in their charade.

Chapter Thirty

"You ready?" Jon whispered, slipping her hand into his. "Last leg of the journey."

She pulled down the dark blue veil that would shield her face from prying eyes. Her hand trembled in Jon's. She knew Hunter wasn't dead. She'd made love with him only a few hours ago in the gamekeeper's cottage where he'd been hiding the last two days. Still, it was upsetting to attend his funeral.

"I'm ready," she finally whispered.

"Good girl," Jon intoned. "It'll soon be over. Tonight you and my brother set sail on the evening tide for paradise."

He was teasing her, of course, but his words steadied her hands. Once she got through the funeral, they would stage her fight with Jon and then she would ride off in Roland's carriage, never to be seen again.

They had decided Roland must be let in on the farce because they had to have a way to disguise her disappearance. Hunter, of course, was already taken care of. To all who attended the funeral today, to all of England, he would soon be buried six feet under, beside his father's fresh grave.

Jon gave a nod to the doorman. The front door of Dunnon Castle swung open and together they stepped into the morning sunshine.

The yard was filled with coaches. Everyone who was anyone in London had turned out for the funeral, perhaps not so much because they cared for Geoffry Rordan but because they were eager to see what was passing between his widow and the new Earl of Dunnon, Jon.

Jon led her on his arm past the coaches down the road toward the family cemetery, to the east of the castle. There on the hillside the Rordan family had been burying their loved ones for four centuries.

Alexandra walked at Jon's side, her head held high, a blue handkerchief knotted in her gloved hand. Funeral guests parted to allow them to pass. Everyone spoke in hushed tones, but they were all staring.

Jon, like a true Lord of the manor, strutted through the crowd already gathered at the grave site. Once he and Alexandra stood before the mahogany coffin, he nodded regally to the reverend who stood to the side, a leather-bound Bible in his hands.

The holy man began his eulogy, and latecomers hurried to the circle around the coffin. Alexandra looked up through her veil to study the crowd cautiously. She had no doubt there were more jewels and fine clothing present here than in the queen's drawing room this morning.

Alexandra's gaze wandered back to the coffin. She had to keep her mind on the game they played. It was imperative that all who were present believe Hunter was truly dead. She sniffed loudly.

Several guests' attention fell upon her.

The priest went on speaking of the unfortunate circumstance of Geoffry Rordan's death and reminded the crowd to think of the man they had known in the past.

Alexandra drew her handkerchief beneath her veil and dabbed at her eyes as she attempted a sob.

A smile tugged at the corners of Jon's mouth, but he went on staring sternly. He was dressed this morning like a barnyard cock in a hideous red-and-yellow shirtwaist and coat with matching red-and-yellow silk stockings and a feather hat.

Alexandra managed another sob, getting the hang of it, almost enjoying the attention she was drawing. She purposefully pulled her hand from Jon's. He took it back. She removed it again.

A murmur rippled through the aristocratic crowd. Alexandra spotted her mother sagging against her father. Roland stood to the side, his face completely passive.

Alexandra smiled behind her veil and let out a little moan.

The minister was bringing his eulogy to a close. Heads bowed and he began to pray. Then it was over and Jon gave a nod. Two gravediggers began to lower the coffin into the ground with wide cloth strips.

"One moment," a voice called from behind.

Alexandra looked up at Jon, panic rising.

"A moment," the voice repeated. The crowd of ladies and gentlemen parted to allow the high sheriff to approach Jon. "My apologies, my lord," he murmured. "But the lord chancellor has insisted that the body be viewed before burial."

Alexandra gave a strangled cry of fear.

Jon grabbed her arm. "I beg your pardon," he addressed the high sheriff haughtily.

The sheriff refused to make eye contact. "I said I must see the body before burial," he repeated. "Merely a technicality."

"How dare you come to us in our time of grief and make such demands," Jon shouted.

Alexandra lowered her head, too frightened to move. *Play the part,* she heard Hunter say in her mind. *Play the part of the grieving widow and you'll be fine.*

"You'll have to bring the coffin back up," the sheriff told the scraggly dressed men.

The gravediggers began to raise the coffin up and out of the hole.

Jon leaned over and rested his hand on the polished mahogany. "How dare you. I won't permit it."

"I'm afraid you must, Lord Dunnon."

The funeral guests were speaking louder now, all talking at once. They had come for a show and it seemed a show they'd indeed get.

"You must allow me to view the body now, or else I'll be forced to come back with a writ to have him dug up." The sheriff lowered his voice. "You don't want that, do you, my lord. Just let me have a look and be done."

"No," Alexandra wailed. "Leave him in peace. Leave him be." She fell to her knees, throwing her arms over the coffin. All she could think of was that if the sheriff opened this empty casket, she and Hunter would lose all they had fought so hard to gain.

"I'm sorry," the sheriff said quietly. "But it has to be done. I must know that Cain's murderer is dead. I must report back to my lord chancellor."

"No, no," Alexandra cried laying her cheek on the coffin.

Jon grabbed her forearm. "Enough, Alex," he said harshly. "You've shamed this family enough! Get up!"

Alexandra's eyes widened behind her veil. What was he doing? He would give them all away.

Jon pulled Alexandra to her feet and away from the coffin. He gave a nod to the gravediggers. They slowly lifted the lid.

Alexandra didn't want to look. She didn't want to see the high sheriff's face when he saw the empty casket, but she couldn't help herself.

The sheriff brought his hand to his mouth in sudden revulsion.

Alexandra swung her head around to look into the mahogany coffin. She saw the flash of a human form in Hunter's new burgundy waistcoat as the gravediggers lowered the lid on Jon's order.

Several women in the crowd cried out in horror. Someone fainted and there was a flurry of activity as someone ran for cool water.

Alexandra felt herself sway against Jon. What

was going on here? There was a body in Hunter's clothing in that casket!

"Steady," Jon whispered. "The game, love."

His words calmed her. She had to trust that Jon knew what he was doing.

She pulled away from him, swatting at him with one hand. "Whoreson cur!" she cried. "You killed him! You killed my Geoffry!"

He reached out to her. "Alex, come inside," he said loud enough for everyone to hear. "You'll make a scene!"

"I don't care!" she screamed. "I hate you! You killed him! You didn't have to kill him."

"Alexandra," he barked, feigning angry embarrassment. "I said that will be quite enough. Now step inside and go to your bedchamber until you can control yourself."

"You can't tell me what to do!" she shouted. "You don't own me, you stinking half-breed! I'm not married to you! My husband is dead, dead at your hands."

"If you don't shut your stupid mouth now, I'll not take you back," he insisted, shaking a finger.

She was backing up now. The ladies and gentlemen stepped back, giving her room. "I don't care! I never wanted you anyway! I only wanted Dunnon Castle, but not this way! Not in bloodshed!" She turned and ran for Roland's carriage waiting along the roadside just beyond the gravesites.

"Man!" Roland shouted, pushing through the crowd. "Help her!"

One of Roland's footmen in red and gold livery

and white periwig and large hat hurried for the Lady Alexandra. He put out his arms to steady her. "Easy, easy my lady," he muttered.

It was all Alexandra could do to keep from snapping up her head to stare at the footman. Hunter? He wouldn't have dared come? Would he?

"This way, my lady," the footman soothed, taking her by the hands and leading her. "My master's coach waits for you."

"Leave and you'll never be welcome on Dunnon soil again!" Jon threatened. "I warn you, I'll not take you back. I'll not marry you, chit!"

Alexandra kept walking, only now her knees truly were weak. She truly feared she wouldn't make it to the coach.

The footman . . . Hunter in footman's livery . . . swung open the carriage door and lifted her up into the coach. Roland stepped in behind her.

The footman slammed the door and the coach rolled off.

Alexandra fell into the leather seat and yanked the veil off her face. "Roland! There was a body in that coffin. A body!" she cried. "And, and Hunter! He was dressed as your footman!"

The coach went around the back of the castle and halted. The door swung open and the footman leaped in. The coach jerked forward again and rolled down the main road into London.

The footman pulled off his hat and periwig. He was laughing. Beneath the white wig was a shock of red hair.

Hunter ran his fingers through his hair, sliding

onto the leather seat beside Alexandra. He was laughing, for God's sake.

Alexandra shook her head in disbelief. "I can't believe you stood there and listened to your own eulogy!" She pushed him in the shoulder. "You could have been caught!"

Roland was laughing too. Both men seemed to think it had been a grand joke.

But Alexandra wasn't laughing.

"The body," she said. "What poor soul was in that coffin?"

Hunter slapped his hat on his knee, obviously pleased with the outcome of their charade. "Kells, of course!"

"Kells?" She shook her head. "I know no Kells. What are you talking about?"

"The gamekeeper, sweeting. The one who blew his face off in the forest. Poor bloke, he'd never have gotten such a fine funeral if he'd been buried down in the village plot!"

The coach rolled to a sudden halt and Roland stood to get out. "My man will take you to the docks. He can be trusted. Jon said to tell you he'd be along to make his good-byes as soon as it was safe."

Alexandra reached for Roland's hand. She knew she would have to say good-bye to both Roland and Jon, but she hadn't realized how difficult it would be. "You're going?"

"Yes." He took her hand and brushed his lips against it. "Have a good life Alex, and be happy, will you? You deserve it."

"Thank you," she whispered, too choked with

emotion to say more. "I'll never forget what you did for me, Roland."

He blew her a kiss and then stepped out of the coach. Alexandra lifted the leather curtain to see him get into another. The vehicle rolled off, taking a fork in the road.

Hunter banged on the ceiling of their coach with his fist and it lurched forward again, continuing on to London. He lifted his arm and draped it over her shoulder. "Damnation, we were good, weren't we?"

"I can't believe you did that," she said, staring at him. "Dressing like Roland's footman in that stupid wig! You could have been caught! You really are mad!"

He brought his hand behind her head and pulled her to him, kissing her mouth soundly. "Mad, yes, but only for you."

"Wait." She reached into a slit in her gown and took a small object from her pocket. "You can't have my wedding ring back, but if we're headed for Shawnee country, I thought you might want this." She opened her palm to reveal a gold hoop earring.

He chuckled as she leaned against him and slipped it through his earlobe.

"Thank you."

She was smiling at him as she touched the earring with her fingertip. "You're welcome."

He drew her into his arms again and brushed his fingertips against the swell of her breasts above her bodice. "'Tis a long ride into the docks," he said, a familiar husky catch in his voice. "A long, boring ride. What say we enjoy a little pleasure . . ."

"Here?" He was already kissing his way down the length of her neck to the low-cut lace of her bodice. Her body was already growing warm and pliant beneath his fingertips. "Make love with you now?"

He raised his head to look into her eyes, his own hazel eyes sparkling with mischief. "Well certainly not with anyone else, sweeting! I told you. I'll not share you. Not with anyone. Not after I've been to hell and back for you."

"Hunter—"

He covered her mouth with his, pushing her back and pressing her into the soft leather seat of the coach. "Hush," he murmured against her lips. "Kiss me now, Wife. You've a lifetime to prattle . . ."